COBRA GAMBLE

BAEN BOOKS by TIMOTHY ZAHN

Blackcollar: The Judas Solution

Blackcollar
(contains *The Blackcollar* and
Blackcollar: The Backlash Mission)

The Cobra Trilogy
(contains *Cobra, Cobra Strike,* and *Cobra Bargain*)

COBRA WAR
Cobra Alliance
Cobra Guardian
Cobra Gamble

COBRA GAMBLE

COBRA WAR, BOOK THREE

TIMOTHY ZAHN

COBRA GAMBLE

This is a work of fiction. All the characters and events portrayed in this book are fictional, and any resemblance to real people or incidents is purely coincidental.

A Baen Books Original

Baen Publishing Enterprises
P.O. Box 1403
Riverdale, NY 10471
www.baen.com

ISBN: 978-1-4516-3769-4

Cover art by David Mattingly

First printing, January 2012

Distributed by Simon & Schuster
1230 Avenue of the Americas
New York, NY 10020

Library of Congress Cataloging-in-Publication Data

Zahn, Timothy.
Cobra gamble / Timothy Zahn.
p. cm. — (Cobra war ; bk. 3)
ISBN 978-1-4516-3769-4 (hc : alk. paper)
1. Human-alien encounters—Fiction. I. Title.
PS3576.A33C5677 2012
813'.54—dc23

2011040763

10 9 8 7 6 5 4 3 2 1

Pages by Joy Freeman (www.pagesbyjoy.com)
Printed in the United States of America

COBRA GAMBLE

CHAPTER ONE

The Troft demesne-ship was dark and mostly silent, only the soft rumble of the engines playing about the background, when Jin Moreau Broom suddenly awoke.

For a minute she lay unmoving in her bunk, wondering what had awakened her. She could hear the steady breathing of her husband Paul on the other side of the tiny cabin, the terrible injury that had torn away most of the flesh on his left leg apparently not interfering with his own slumber. Or maybe it was the massive load of painkillers flowing through his bloodstream that was the source of his untroubled sleep. Jin keyed in her optical enhancers, confirmed that she and Paul were the only two people in the room, then raised the level on her audios.

Paul's breathing and the rumble of the engines grew louder. Trying to shut them out of her consciousness, Jin listened.

There it was: footsteps coming from somewhere below her. Irregular footsteps, continually changing in both rhythm and intensity.

Frowning, she keyed her audios back down and checked her nanocomputer's clock circuit. It was three-ten in the morning, an unlikely time for a shift change. Not really the time for any other serious activity, either.

So who was running around at this hour?

She keyed in her infrareds again, studying her husband's face.

He was deeply asleep, with little chance he would wake up soon and need her. Slipping out of bed, she dressed and left the cabin.

They'd lifted from Caelian less than twenty-four hours ago, but Jin had made a point of memorizing the ship's deck plans as soon as she and Paul were settled into their cabin. From the direction of the sounds, she tentatively concluded they were coming from the engine core area. Working from her memory of the plans, she found the nearest stairway and headed down.

The engine core was a long cylinder at the lowest part of the ship, bracketed by a pair of narrow, four-meter-high access corridors that doubled as heat-flow mixers. Jin arrived at the catwalk grid running above the starboard corridor and looked down.

In the narrow passageway below her were two of the Qasaman Djinn warriors, Carsh Zoshak and his commander Siraj Akim. Both men were dressed in their powered combat suits, complete with gloves and soft helmets. As Jin watched, Siraj leaped upward, twisting sideways and firing a short burst from the laser that ran along his left forearm to his glove's little finger, targeting a bundle of empty ration cans that had been placed against the far wall. At the same time, Zoshak dived to the floor beneath him, sliding for a meter on his stomach and firing a burst of his own into a similar package at the opposite end of the passageway. As he slid to a halt he rolled over onto his back, kicked his legs up over his head in a somersault, and ended up facing the opposite direction just as Siraj landed back on the floor in front of him. Over the engine hum Jin heard a triple tongue cluck, and Siraj dropped flat onto the floor in time to get clear as Zoshak fired another shot over his back.

"One of these days," a soft voice murmured from Jin's left, "*one* of them is going to miss."

Jin turned. Her younger son Lorne was sitting on a thick heat-exchange return pipe, gazing at the activity below them. "I would hope they've cranked their lasers down to some kind of practice mode," she said.

"I'd hope that, too," Lorne agreed. "But from the damage they're doing to those cans, I'd say they're still set high enough to hurt. A lot."

Jin grimaced. Knowing the Qasamans, Lorne was probably right. "How long have they been here?"

"I don't know," Lorne said. "They were already hard at it ten minutes ago when I arrived." He gestured. "They also haven't started repeating themselves yet."

"*We* certainly have more than ten minutes' worth of drills," Jin pointed out. "I can't see Djinni training being any less rigorous than ours was."

"Probably not," Lorne murmured. "I wonder what they're going to do when they get to combine the two regimens."

Jin looked sideways at her son. "You having second thoughts about this?"

Lorne sighed. "I don't know, Mom. Nissa Gendreves was right, you know. Technically, what we're doing *is* treason."

"No *technically* about it," Jin agreed soberly. If there was any single secret the Dome politicians back on Aventine would fight to the death for, it was the Cobra technology.

And now she, her son, and her husband were on their way to Qasama to hand over that technology to people they barely knew.

People, moreover, who'd once sworn to destroy the Cobra Worlds.

And not just any Cobra technology, either. Dr. Glas Croi's fancy Integrated Structural Implantation System represented a giant leap forward in the hundred-year-old Cobra program. With the help of the Troft who called himself *Warrior*—more properly Ingidi-inhiliziyo—Croi had developed Isis to be a fully automated, fully computerized system for implanting bone laminae, servos, and weapons.

In more basic terms, a self-contained Cobra factory.

Governor General Chintawa had intended to announce the Isis project with all due pomp and ceremony and then set up the prototype in Aventine's expansion regions, where the need for Cobras was the greatest. Instead, he'd ended up scrambling desperately to get the equipment off Aventine before the Troft invaders could discover it. Croi's mission had been to get it to Caelian, where it could be hidden away from prying Troft eyes and hands.

Instead, Jin and Paul had talked them into giving the whole thing to the Qasamans.

"Maybe it won't be as bad as we're thinking," Lorne said hesitantly into her thoughts. "Dr. Croi said that when Warrior was collaborating on Isis he wasn't allowed to study the Cobra equipment itself. Maybe the gear's sealed somehow."

"Warrior was working with Isis under strictly controlled conditions," Jin reminded him. "He was also kept at a distance while the tests were being done. So were the rest of the Tlossies. But the Qasamans will be right there in the middle of it."

"I meant that maybe the nanocomputers and laminae depositors will be fail-safed so that the Qasamans observing the operation won't be able to get hold of them," Lorne said.

Jin shook her head. "If Moffren Omnathi and the Shahni want to get hold of the raw components, they will."

"I suppose," Lorne conceded. "From what I've heard of the Shahni, they'll haul one of their own people right off the assembly line and dissect him if they have to."

Jin felt her throat tighten. Barely two weeks ago, the Shahni had in fact been planning to do essentially that very thing to Jin herself. For all their ingenuity in mimicking Cobra capabilities with their Djinni combat suits, the Qasamans had hit a roadblock when they tried to duplicate the nanocomputer and preprogrammed reflexes that were the core of the whole Cobra project.

They'd wanted Jin's nanocomputer. She'd made a counter-offer: she and her elder son Merrick would instead go back to Aventine and bring them more Cobras.

But that was before Merrick had been seriously wounded in the Qasamans' final and successful bid to reclaim their capital city of Sollas and drive the invaders at least temporarily from their world. So badly wounded that it had been impossible for him to accompany Jin back to the Cobra Worlds.

Omnathi had promised that the Qasamans would work to heal her son. He'd further pledged that they would leave Merrick's implanted Cobra equipment strictly alone.

But while Omnathi was a highly-regarded senior advisor to the Shahni, he wasn't an actual member of that elite group. Some of those leaders appreciated the work Jin and Merrick had done to help defend their world. But others bitterly resented the fact that the Troft invasion had forced them to work with representatives from the hated Cobra Worlds.

And Jin had no idea which side of that argument was the stronger. Would she arrive at Qasama to find that Merrick had been stripped of his equipment?

Would she arrive to find him dead?

A flicker of pain shot through her head. She fought it back, trying not to let it show in her face. *The great, legendary Moreau family*, she thought with a touch of bitterness. Merrick's fate was unknown, Jin's husband Paul was lying in their cabin with his leg mostly blown away, and Jin herself stood here with a brain tumor that was inoperable by all Cobra Worlds standards.

Not only was the future of a half dozen worlds hanging by a thread, so were the lives of nearly everyone she loved.

"You okay?" Lorne asked.

"I'm fine," Jin assured him, trying to sound nonchalant.

It was a waste of effort. As a boy, Lorne had had an uncanny ability to sense pain or sickness in his family and close friends, and that skill had only improved with age. "Right," he said darkly. "Your head again?"

"It's all right—it's passed."

"Right," Lorne said again, hopping off his seat on the pipe. "Come on—I'm taking you back to your cabin."

He was reaching for her arm when, with a suddenness that nearly triggered Jin's programmed evasion reflexes, Zoshak leaped upward and caught the section of catwalk grid beside Jin. He steadied himself, then let go with one hand and fired his glove laser in four carefully aimed bursts at the corner screws that connected his section of mesh to the support rails. Shifting his grip, he pushed up the now released section of catwalk, deftly swung his legs up and through the opening, and landed on top of the next section over. "If you'll permit me, Lorne Moreau," he said as he straightened up, "I would be honored to escort Jin Moreau back to her quarters."

"I appreciate the offer, Carsh Zoshak," Lorne said, inclining his head. "But I wouldn't want to take you away from your practice."

"For the moment, my part of the practice is over," Zoshak said. "Ifrit Siraj Akim humbly requests that your part begin."

Lorne frowned. "*My* part?"

"We seek your advice on narrow-space maneuvering and combat," Siraj called up from the deck below. "We have several techniques of our own, and would like to show them to you and hear your thoughts. After that, perhaps we could see some of *your* techniques."

Lorne looked at Jin. "Mom?"

"It's fine with me," Jin said. "Actually, all three of you could get busy with that. I can make it back to my quarters on my own."

Lorne shook his head. "No," he said firmly.

"Agreed," Zoshak said, just as firmly. "And I would request the honor of escorting our ally back to her place of rest."

Jin felt her stomach tighten. Allies. The Shahni, at least by proxy, had indeed made promises of alliance and cooperation. Harli Uy, temporarily sitting in for his wounded father as governor of Caelian, had accepted those promises and given some reciprocal promises of his own, going so far as to back up his side of the deal by sending two of his own precious Cobras and an equally rare linguist to travel to Qasama with them.

But Harli had no authorization whatsoever to make such a deal. On the contrary, the single genuinely official voice who'd spoken on the matter had vehemently disavowed the entire transaction.

If her family lived through this, Jin thought morosely, they would very likely spend the rest of their lives in an Aventine prison. Or be executed.

But she already had way too many things to worry about to add that one to her list. "Very well," she said, nodding to Zoshak. "I accept with thanks. Lorne, I'll see you later. And don't hurt each other, all right? It's going to take a while to get Isis up and running, and we're going to need all of you in good fighting trim until then."

"Don't worry, we'll play nice," Lorne said. He looked at Zoshak, still standing on the catwalk, and made a small gesture downward.

For a moment Zoshak frowned. Then his face cleared, and he gave Lorne a short nod. Lorne nodded back.

Without warning, Lorne leaned forward like he was going to fall on his face and shoved himself off into a low dive straight toward Zoshak.

But even as his feet pushed off the floor Zoshak was also in motion, dropping into a crouch and snatching up the section of grid that he'd cut free. Lorne reached the opening, caught the supporting side rails with both hands, and turned his flat leap into a roll-and-drop through toward the deck below. As he fell he spun a hundred-eighty degrees and landed on his feet a meter away from Siraj.

"Impressive," Zoshak called down as he returned the section of catwalk to its proper place. "We look forward to seeing what you can teach us."

"As I'm looking forward to learning your tricks," Lorne called back up. "Hurry back."

"I shall." Zoshak straightened up and offered his arm to Jin. "Shall we go?"

"Thank you," Jin said, nodding at the catwalk and curling her hands into fingertip-laser firing position. "But first we need to tack that down. Warrior won't be happy if one of his crewers bumps it loose and falls through. I'll do these two corners—you take the other two."

CHAPTER TWO

It was an hour after sundown, and the stars were blazing down through the canopy of trees above them, when the fourteen men from the Qasaman village of Milika arrived at their chosen hunting spot.

"There," Gama Yithtra murmured, pointing toward the north. "Do you hear them?"

"Yes," Merrick Moreau Broom murmured back as he keyed in his optical enhancers. The trees were thick in that direction, but he was able to catch glimpses of the grav lifts' glow through the branches. From the high infrared output, he guessed the Trofts had been at this for at least three hours. "Sounds like four of them, all spotters. I don't hear a transport."

"Don't worry, it's here," Yithtra said. "Marslo Charak saw it late in the afternoon, about two kilometers west." He turned to Merrick, his lips twisting in a smirk. "It would seem that your worlds are about to receive yet another dose of your own chosen medicine."

Merrick didn't answer. The second Troft invasion of Qasama was well underway, with all the alien ships that had fled two weeks ago already returned, with probably more on the way. The scattered reports that had come in from the rest of the Great Arc indicated that the invaders were unhurriedly and systematically blasting the capital city of Sollas to rubble, and had put the

Qasamans' other four main cities and three smaller ones under siege. So far the Trofts seemed to be mostly ignoring the villages, but Merrick knew it was only a matter of time before the sky out here would also fill up with alien warships.

Yet in the midst of all that, Yithtra somehow always managed to find time to get in a dig about what the Trofts were probably doing to Aventine and the other Cobra Worlds with the razorarms they were harvesting from Qasama's forests.

Earlier that day, Merrick had tried explaining to Yithtra why the Cobra Worlds had seeded Qasama with the predators two generations ago, that it had been an attempt to free the Qasamans from the subtle grip of the semi-sentient native birds called mojos. But Yithtra hadn't seemed interested in hearing the Cobra Worlds' side of the story, and Merrick had given up the effort.

Fortunately, not everyone in Milika was so antagonistic toward their offworld visitor. Most were at least neutral toward him, while a few had apparently heard reports from friends or relatives about the battles in Sollas that Merrick and his mother had taken part in. Those few treated Merrick with a degree of actual respect.

And even some of the neutral ones were starting to get tired of Yithtra's verbal barbs. "Seems to me there's plenty of medicine to go around," an older Qasaman named Balis Kinstra growled. "Can we perhaps keep our minds on the job, Gama Yithtra?"

"My mind *is* on the job," Yithtra said calmly. "Teams of two: spread out and find the freighter. You, Balis Kinstra, since you're such a friend of demon warriors, will pair with Merrick Moreau. Runners meet back here in thirty minutes with reports."

There were murmurs of acknowledgement, and the Qasamans paired up and slipped away into the woods.

"I must apologize for Gama Yithtra," Kinstra said as the others' footsteps faded into the forest. "He doesn't speak for all of us."

"I know that," Merrick assured him. "And to be honest, he has a point."

"Point or not, this is not the place for such debates." Kinstra gestured around them. "You're the one most experienced with these invaders. What are your thoughts?"

Merrick looked around them. During the Trofts' first incursion onto Qasama, the aliens had simply sent out spotter aircraft equipped with infrareds and motion sensors to locate their target razorarms, which were then neutralized with small tranquilizer gas bombs. When the spotters decided they had enough for a pick-up, a freighter would put down in a convenient clearing and armed parties would go out to collect the sleeping predators.

The parties had been careful to steer clear of the villages scattered through the forest. But they'd quickly learned that avoiding the villages didn't necessarily mean avoiding the villagers. The rural Qasamans were just as outraged by the invasion as their city counterparts, and while there were few actual soldiers among them there were plenty of expert hunters.

It wasn't long before the Trofts discovered the flaw in their harvesting technique: there simply weren't all that many clearings large enough for even a small freighter to put down in. That meant the harvesting parties had to locate a suitable landing spot before they sent out their spotter ships. All the Qasamans had to do was study the search pattern and figure out which clearing the Trofts were planning to use, then be waiting in force when the freighter put down.

The Trofts had lost a couple of harvesting parties before they caught on. Their next approach had been to create their own clearings, blasting the trees with lasers and occasionally with missiles from above so that the villagers wouldn't know in advance where they would be landing.

The Qasaman response had been to track the razorarms, concentrating on the larger family groups that the Trofts preferred, and scatter their own hunters around the most likely target zones. Often they guessed wrong, but there were enough times when they guessed right. And of course, once the trees started falling, any team within earshot knew exactly where the evening's entertainment was going to be held.

The harvesting had stopped, along with all other Troft activity, when the Sollas forces drove the invaders off the planet. But with this second incursion the razorarm raids had resumed. The aliens' latest tactic was to not land the freighters at all, but to simply hover over their latest prize and rappel a team of soldiers down to roll the sleeping animal onto a lift pad and winch it up.

Unfortunately for them, hovering freighters made wonderful targets, and the five days of calm between invasions had given the Qasaman military enough time to get a few heavy weapons into the villagers' hands. Two of the village teams south of Milika had succeeded in severely damaging Troft freighters with mortar fire a couple of days ago, and there were rumors that a team still farther south had destroyed one completely.

The Troft response had been to again halt the hunts, and for the past two nights the spotters and freighters had stayed close to the forces besieging the cities. But tonight they were back.

Merrick was looking forward to seeing what new wrinkle they'd come up with.

"For starters, I'm guessing they're finished with the hover-and-rappel approach," he told Kinstra. "That one cost them way too much."

"Agreed," Kinstra said. He paused, and with his enhanced vision Merrick saw the man's nose wrinkle. "You smell that?"

Merrick took a cautious sniff. The air was brimming with the usual mix of Qasaman woodland aromas. "Is there something different?" he asked.

"I don't know," Kinstra said, sniffing harder. "It just smells odd. Like . . . springtime."

Merrick frowned. "Come again?"

"I know that sounds strange," Kinstra said. "But it just smells somehow like it's springtime."

"Okay," Merrick said, sniffing the air again. Like that would help. He'd been on Qasama barely three weeks, and was just now starting to figure out which aromas came from cooking or perfumes and which were from the local flora and fauna. Even the spine leopards the Cobra Worlds had seeded here, the predators the Qasamans called razorarms, smelled slightly different than they did on Aventine. Probably a result of their altered diet.

There was a sudden quiet rustle from the trees behind them. Merrick spun around, his arms snapping up and his hands curling into fingertip-laser firing positions. Sure enough, there was a razorarm back there, striding through the undergrowth.

But it wasn't heading toward Merrick and Kinstra. In fact, it didn't seem to even notice the two humans. It was angling somewhere off to Merrick's right, its ears twitching, the mojo clinging onto its back fluttering its wings for balance. The predator and its avian symbiont passed by and disappeared again into the forest.

"That's odd," Kinstra murmured. "I've never seen a razorarm do *that*. They always at least *look* at a hunter. So does the mojo."

"Assessing the threat versus snack benefits," Merrick agreed, frowning after the departed razorarm. It had been a long time since he'd been on duty out in Aventine's frontier region, but there was something about the way the razorarm had moved that had seemed vaguely familiar.

And then, abruptly, he got it. The razorarm's disinterest, the spring-like smell, the predator heading directly into the gentle wind—"It's pheromones," he told Kinstra. "The Trofts are using razorarm mating pheromones. In the spring, when it's mating season—"

"Yes, yes, I understand," Kinstra interrupted hastily. The Qasamans had a long list of topics that were taboo for casual, non-family conversation, and reproductive issues were near the top of that file. "Clever. They send up spotter aircraft to distract our attention while luring the razorarms to an entirely different location."

"Clever and elegant both," Merrick agreed. "Certainly compared to some of the other stuff they've been pulling lately." He gestured after the animal. "I'll go after it, see if I can find the pickup spot. You wait here until the runners get back and follow me."

"No time," Kinstra said. "It's thirty minutes until the runners return, and then they'll have to go back and collect their huntmates. If the invaders are smart, they'll have gathered their quota and left by then."

Unfortunately, he was probably right. The Trofts had certainly had enough experience with the Qasaman attack teams to have figured out their typical response profile. "You'd better stay here anyway," he said. "Gama Yithtra may return early, and he'll be highly annoyed if he misses the party."

"Gama Yithtra's wounded feelings aren't our concern," Kinstra said tartly. "We go together." He gestured in the direction the razorarm had gone. "And this talk wastes time."

Merrick hesitated, then nodded. "All right," he said. "Quickly, and quietly."

Kinstra slung his rifle over his shoulder. "Lead the way."

Quickly was easy. The forest floor was deeply dark at night, but Merrick's optical enhancements were more than able to compensate. He circled the various trees and bushes with ease, dodging the more subtle obstacles nearly as effortlessly. Kinstra, running two meters behind him, would be making sure he precisely hit each of the Cobra's footprints.

Quietly was more problematic. If there was a way to move silently through knee-high branches and a bed of dead leaves, Merrick had never learned it.

But that was all right. The Trofts would be expecting to hear the sound of large creatures traveling through the undergrowth.

And then, suddenly, they had arrived. Through the trees, Merrick spotted a curved wall of dark metal in the middle of a clearing, with silent figures moving restlessly back and forth in front of it.

He slowed to a halt, signaling for Kinstra do the same. "There," he whispered, pointing.

"I see them," Kinstra whispered back as he unslung his rifle from his shoulder. "We need to get closer."

Merrick considered suggesting the other stay back while he scouted, decided it would be a waste of breath, and nodded. "Quietly."

A minute later, they had reached the last line of big trees at the edge of the clearing. They took up position behind two of the largest and Merrick cautiously peered out.

The freighter was a bit smaller than some he'd seen the Trofts use. But it looked more than capable of the task of hauling predators across the forty-five light-years separating Qasama and Aventine. There were four Trofts on guard duty, their laser rifles held ready, a compact missile launcher squatting on the ground in front of them like a short cylindrical guard dog. Four more of the aliens were off to the side, maneuvering a sleeping razorarm onto a cart for transport through the open hatchway behind them.

Kinstra leaned close. "Launcher."

Merrick nodded. The Trofts' tiny antipersonnel missiles had proved to be one of the invaders' most devastating weapons. Their primary targets were always Qasamans radio transmitters, after which they were designed to home in on the sounds of gunfire and the heat signatures of large lasers. Daulo Sammon, Merrick's mother's old friend from her first covert visit to this world some three decades ago, had been severely wounded by one of those missiles during the Qasamans' first counterattack back in Sollas.

Throughout the twelve days of Merrick's own recovery the Qasaman doctors had pumped him full of their exotic rapid-healing drugs, one side effect of which had been to leave his memories of his convalescence extremely hazy. Still, he could distinctly remember several occasions where he'd asked about Daulo. What he couldn't remember was whether he'd ever gotten a straight answer back.

With an effort, he shook away the thought. His recovery was

still incomplete, and while his current regimen of drugs didn't make him go all loopy the way the last batch had, they did have a tendency to encourage mental wandering.

He focused again on the enemy encampment. The missile launcher was definitely the first thing on their to-do list. Merrick keyed a target-lock onto the launcher's base, where the weapon's sensor/guidance array was located, then turned to the roving soldier patrol. They were wearing full armor, but at this range a shot from the antiarmor laser running down Merrick's left leg should cut through the aliens' neck protection with ease and rack up a couple of quick kills.

Four guards, plus the launcher. Five shots in all. With the task of aiming and firing controlled by Merrick's nanocomputer, he could probably get off that many blasts before the Trofts even had time to react. He targeted the nearest soldier, moved on to the second.

And paused. For no particular reason, a story about his great-grandfather Jonny Moreau floated up from his memory. How the legendary First Cobra and revered Cobra Worlds statesman, when faced by a ship full of Trofts, had chosen to merely neutralize instead of kill.

Of course, that situation had been entirely different. Jonny had been alone and hoping to make a deal with his captors. Merrick was in the midst of an invasion, facing attackers who were currently running a grinding machine across Qasama's capital city and probably killing untold numbers of citizens in the process.

Merrick had already killed in this war. He'd taken more lives than he'd ever dreamed would fall by his hand. But all of those enemies had been already shooting at him or other humans, or had been in the process of taking civilian hostages whom Merrick was committed to rescuing. These particular Trofts weren't doing any such thing.

But they *were* collecting predators to use against Merrick's own people. Wasn't that just as bad?

He grimaced, his sudden indecision both unexpected and disconcerting. Was he rethinking the whole concept of this war and his place in it?

Or was this simply a reaction to his own near-death on the battlefield? Was he shying away from killing in the hope that by doing so he might himself survive?

"Merrick Moreau?" Kinstra prompted.

Abruptly, Merrick came to a decision. Releasing the target locks on the Troft guards, he instead locked onto their weapons. The ultimate purpose of these counterattacks was to discourage the razorarm hunts and drive the Trofts from the forests. He could do that just as well by chasing them back to the cities, where they would be the Qasaman military's problem.

"Merrick Moreau?" Kinstra repeated, more urgently this time.

"Ready," Merrick said. "Keep your head down." Moving out of the relative safety of the tree, he rolled onto his right side, giving his left leg the freedom of movement the nanocomputer would need to handle the fire pattern Merrick had set for it. He took a deep breath, and triggered his laser.

The brilliant beam slashed through the darkness of the night, a multiple stuttering of light cutting through leaves and undergrowth and flash-vaporizing the metal, ceramic, and plastic of the launcher and the Trofts' lasers. The last of the five shots blazed out and Merrick pushed himself up off the ground for a quick assessment.

And dropped instantly back down as the launcher erupted in a blistering staccato fire of its own, its antipersonnel missiles screaming through the forest and blasting huge chunks of wood from the trees above Merrick's head.

Reflexively, he reached out a hand to grab Kinstra and pull him down. But the Qasaman was already there, pressed against the matted covering of dead leaves, his mouth moving as he shouted something. Merrick adjusted his auditory enhancers, trying to filter out the cracks of the explosives. "—posed to kill them!" he caught Kinstra's last words.

"We're supposed to *stop* them," Merrick called back. A new crunching sound penetrated his hearing, and he looked up to see the tree he'd been hiding behind starting to lean sideways as the Troft missiles tore apart its trunk half a meter above Merrick's eyes. "Come on," Merrick called, getting a grip on Kinstra's arm. The tree above them leaned farther and farther, then ponderously toppled over, crashing through the other trees and bushes beside it.

And as it slammed into the forest floor, its impact raising a blinding cloud of leaves and dust, Merrick pulled Kinstra up onto his elbows and knees and headed away as fast as they could crawl.

They'd made about twenty meters when the missile launcher

finally fell silent. Even as both men turned carefully around, they spotted the glow of the repulsorlifts flickering through the trees as the freighter headed hastily into the night sky.

A thin layer of clouds had covered up the stars by the time the team once again passed through the gate into the village of Milika.

It was, for Merrick, an odd homecoming. When he'd first been brought back here eight days ago to complete his recovery, the village's lights had glowed cheerfully long into the night. But not anymore. Since the second wave of Trofts had arrived, Milika and the other forest villages had returned to the rhythms of humanity's past, to the time when activity was governed by the sun. Now, the town began to close down when the sun reached the treetops, the vendors bidding farewell to their final customers of the day and hurriedly closing up their shops. By the time the first stars appeared, the open areas of Milika were all but deserted, the people busy with their evening meals and quiet indoor activities as the village was slowly swallowed by the darkening forest.

It was a little silly, in Merrick's opinion, given that the Trofts' infrared detectors were perfectly capable of picking out the heat signatures of several hundred humans from the relative coolness of the forest around them. If they came looking for villages, they could certainly find them.

The Qasamans had to know that, too. Perhaps the darkness and silence were a matter of token defiance, something to help the villagers keep their focus, to keep their animosity toward the invaders fresh in their minds.

The team began to split up as they trudged through the village, each of the men and teens heading to their individual homes where anxious family members awaited them. Kinstra was the last to leave, murmuring a final farewell as he walked up the steps to his home.

And Merrick was alone.

He'd never had trouble with solitude before. Solitude was time to observe the world around him, and to think in the quietness.

But the world now wrapped around him was hardly conducive toward peaceful contemplation. And all of his thoughts were edged with fear and darkness.

What was happening in the cities? More importantly, what was happening to the people he'd left behind there? Daulo Sammon, badly injured, whose fate he still didn't know. The Djinni warrior Carsh Zoshak, who in a few short days of combat had grown from a suspicious and reluctant fellow soldier to a trusted comrade and true friend.

But worst of all were the haunting questions of what was happening to Merrick's family.

He looked up at the clouds drifting by overhead. Had his mother made it safely back to Aventine? Or had she been intercepted by the Trofts and captured or killed?

Merrick's younger brother Lorne was also on Aventine, most likely smack in the middle of whatever the Trofts were doing there. Merrick's father and sister were probably in even worse shape, stuck on the hell-world Caelian.

Were any of them looking up at their own stars right now? Were they thinking about Merrick, and wondering if he was dead?

"So you return."

Merrick lowered his eyes from the sky and his contemplation. Davi Krites, the doctor who Senior Advisor Moffren Omnathi had sent from Sollas to monitor Merrick's recovery, was standing at the entrance to the courtyard of the Sammon family home. His arms were folded across his chest, and Merrick didn't need his Cobra opticals to see the annoyance in the other's face and stance. "Did you think I wouldn't?" he asked as he walked up to the doctor.

"We could hear the sound of the missile attack from here, you know," Krites said grimly. "I fully expected the others to bring you back in pieces."

"It wasn't that bad," Merrick assured him. "Probably sounded worse than it was."

"I'm sure you know best," Krites said, running a critical eye over Merrick's body. "At least you're not bleeding. Not externally, at any rate."

"I really am fine," Merrick said. "If you're concerned, you can haul me in for an exam right now. I promise I won't argue."

"Tempting," Krites said. "But you'd just fall asleep on my table. Morning will be soon enough. Besides, Master Sammon wants to see you."

Merrick felt his stomach tighten. Fadil Sammon, Daulo's son, had been wide awake earlier this afternoon, and for longer than usual. Merrick had hoped the young Qasaman would be asleep by now. "I'll go at once," he said.

He started past Krites, stopped as the doctor caught his arm. "He'll want to know about his father," the other warned.

"I know," Merrick said. "I'll just have to tell him again that there's no news."

"I don't like to see him agitated," Krites said, still gripping Merrick's arm. "Can't you give him some hope?"

"You mean lie to him?"

"You're not Qasaman," Krites reminded him. "You grew up in a different culture. Your reactions and facial nuances are different from ours. You might be able to get away with it."

"I'll take it under advisement." Merrick gestured to Krites's hand on his arm. "May I?"

Reluctantly, Krites let go. Nodding a farewell, Merrick crossed the courtyard and went into the house.

Fadil's suite was at one end of the north wing, with the size and lavish decoration that befit the son of an important village leader. The furniture in the gathering area was made of carved wood and tanned krissjaw hide, dyed with subtle and shimmering stains. There were layered paintings on the walls and sculptured plant holders with flowing greenery scattered around the room. Embedded gemstones in the ceiling gave the illusion of the night sky, and night breezes flowed in through wide, open windows.

All of which made the stark metal medical bed resting in the center of the darkened room a disconcerting visual shock.

"Merrick Moreau?"

"Yes," Merrick confirmed, keying in his opticals as he started across the room. Fadil had turned his head to look toward his visitor, and even in Merrick's artificially enhanced view the young Qasaman's eyes looked unpleasantly bright. "How may I serve you?"

It took Merrick eight steps to get to the bed. Fadil watched him the whole way in silence, then turned away. "No news," he said quietly.

"No," Merrick said. So much for lying to the other. The powerful mind-enhancing drugs that Fadil had taken back in Sollas still saturated his brain, giving him powers of observation and analysis well beyond those of normal human beings. The effect was usually temporary, Krites had told Merrick, but sometimes could be permanent.

There was no such uncertainty about the drugs' side effects. The paralysis that had engulfed Fadil's body below his neck barely an hour after the mind-enhancement procedure *was* permanent.

Fadil's contribution to the war effort had made him a quadriplegic. Forever.

"What's happening in Sollas?" Fadil asked.

Merrick wasn't even tempted to lie. "According to the last report, the Troft ships spent most of the day blowing up more of the western and northeastern parts of the city," he said. "They've probably stopped now—so far their pattern's been to break off the demolition work at nightfall."

"They want to see what it is they're destroying," Fadil murmured. "They don't want to risk missing something when they have only infrared and light-amplification to see by."

"Probably," Merrick said. "It still seems like they're taking an awfully long time to destroy a single city."

"Because they're not really interested in Sollas itself," Fadil told him. "Their goal is to destroy the subcity—all of its levels, all of its chambers. The part that's aboveground is merely in the way."

Merrick nodded. That last part was sadly obvious. What *wasn't* obvious was whether or not the Shahni and the Djinn would be able to mount any sort of defense or counterattack before Sollas and all the rest of the cities had been turned to rubble and dead bodies.

"And you've heard nothing about my father?" Fadil asked into Merrick's thoughts.

"No," Merrick said. Fadil had already concluded that, of course, from his reading of Merrick's face and body language. But even so, he asked the question.

As he always did, every time he saw Merrick. Always at least twice. Sometimes three or four times.

For a moment Fadil was silent. "Perhaps tomorrow there'll be news," he said at last. "I'm told the invaders launched a missile attack on you tonight. Were there casualties?"

"None," Merrick said. "And it wasn't exactly an attack. I blew up the guidance section of one of their antipersonnel launchers, and the thing went berserk. Probably programmed to shift to a random, rapid-fire spread within a defined arc to try to drive away whoever's attacking them."

"Thus giving themselves time to regroup for counterattack or escape."

"In this case the latter," Merrick said. "They were in the air before the rest of the team even caught up with us."

"Did they leave with razorarms?"

"I don't know," Merrick said. "But if they did get any, I'm guessing they didn't get the number they were hoping for. I think we can claim at least half a victory on this one."

"Indeed," Fadil said. "Now tell me: why are you still alive?"

Merrick felt an unpleasant tingle run up his back. Gama Yithtra, after the rest of the team had belatedly arrived, had been furious that Merrick and Kinstra had taken on the Trofts all by themselves. Was Fadil suggesting that Yithtra might actually have ordered some kind of lethal action against them for that? "I don't understand," he said carefully.

"You said the launcher fired a random pattern," Fadil said. "How is it none of the missiles struck you?"

Merrick frowned, thinking back. "Because we were flat on the ground," he said slowly, "and all the shots were over our heads."

"Does that seem odd to you?"

"Yes, now that you mention it," Merrick agreed. "I didn't even notice at the time."

"Of course not." In the darkness, Merrick saw Fadil's bitter-edged smile. "You still have your arms and legs."

Merrick felt a fresh ache in his heart. "Fadil Sammon—"

"No, Merrick Moreau, don't speak," Fadil interrupted quietly. "That was unfair and cruel. My apologies. The decision that put me in this situation was mine and mine alone. And many others have suffered far worse."

He gave a small nod toward the window. "And through it all, I did my part for the people of Qasama. My gamble and sacrifice were not for nothing."

"I know," Merrick said, wishing he knew what that meant. Whatever Fadil had taken the mind-enhancing drugs for, it had apparently been secret enough that neither Merrick nor anyone else in Milika had heard anything about it.

"No you don't," Fadil said, a touch of wry humor peeking through the depression. "But that's all right. Someday, if we win, all Qasama will know. And if we lose, no one will be left to care."

"We're going to win," Merrick said firmly. "I know my mother. One way or another, she'll get Aventine to send the Cobras we need. The next time we throw the Trofts off Qasama, it'll be for good."

"Perhaps." Fadil nodded again, this time toward Merrick. "You'd best get to bed. Though the invaders' missiles may not have harmed you, I doubt you made it through the mission unscathed."

Merrick shrugged. "I'm mostly unscathed."

But once again, Fadil was right. Merrick could feel fresh aches and pains in a couple of places where his not-entirely healed muscles and skin had taken fresh damage. Dr. Krites would undoubtedly find more small injuries in the morning when he did a complete exam, and Dr. Krites would be very unhappy about it.

But that was tomorrow's trouble. Merrick had already had enough for today.

"You'd better get some sleep yourself," he told Fadil, backing toward the door. "Maybe there'll be news in the morning."

"Perhaps," Fadil said. "Good-night, Merrick Moreau. May God watch over you."

"And you, Fadil Sammon."

And with that, Merrick escaped from the room. And from the pitiful creature that Fadil Sammon had become.

After all the stress of the night's attack Merrick had looked forward to sleeping at least a little later than usual into the morning.

He didn't. The sun was barely up when he was jolted awake by the sound of heavy grav lifts. Rolling out of his bed, wincing at the fresh strains in his muscles, he slipped over to the window and eased aside the curtain.

To find a Troft warship like the ones he and the Djinn had fought in Sollas settling onto the road that led to the main Milika gate.

CHAPTER THREE

They were ten minutes from Qasama when Dr. Glas Croi, who'd hardly showed his face since the departure from Caelian, finally appeared in the dining area where Paul, his wife and son, and Carsh Zoshak were finishing up their lunch.

Paul's leg had been feeling better that morning, enough so that he'd taken only half of his prescribed painkiller dosage. He felt well enough, in fact, that Croi actually looked worse than Paul felt.

Jin noticed it, too. "Dr. Croi," she said, gesturing him toward the empty seat beside Lorne. "Are you all right?"

"What?" Croi asked, blinking like someone still trying to pry sleep-goo out of his eyes. "Oh. Hello, Cobra Broom." He frowned. "I guess that's Cobra Brooms all around, isn't it?"

"Except for me," Zoshak said, lifting his hand a few centimeters. "Though perhaps someday soon I shall be Cobra Zoshak."

It seemed to Paul that Croi's jaw tightened slightly. "Yes. Perhaps."

Lorne had picked up on it, too. "Something wrong?" he asked.

Furtively, Croi's eyes flicked to Zoshak, flicked away again. "I don't know yet," he said. "I hope not."

Lorne glanced at his father. "Meaning?"

Croi's jaw tightened again. "It's just that Isis was never meant to be taken off Aventine," he said reluctantly. "It was certainly never meant to be a secret installation."

"We could throw a blanket over it," Lorne suggested.

"This isn't a joke," Croi bit out, glaring at him. "It turns out there's a substantial and highly distinctive radio leakage signal that comes from the assembly coordination computer."

Paul felt Jin stir in the chair beside him. "Distinctive how?" she asked.

"Distinctive enough to show it's coming from a manufacturing computer," Croi said.

"Surely there are other manufacturing computers on Qasama," Paul said, frowning. His wife's reaction had been small, but still stronger than it should have been.

"You're missing the point," Jin said. "The Trofts monitor all radio usage here. Their antipersonnel missiles automatically target any transmissions within range."

"We believe they also had some of their shipboard missiles programmed for larger-scale attacks," Zoshak said. "Jin Moreau is right, Dr. Croi. Any radio signal on Qasama, distinctive or otherwise, will be an invitation to death."

"So we'll just have to make sure it's well shielded," Paul said, a lump forming in his throat. No wonder Jin had reacted to Croi's news. Lugging Isis all the way here just to have it blown up would pretty much end it for all of them. "How do we do that?"

"Well, that's the question, isn't it?" Croi said heavily. "And the answer is, I don't know." He waved a hand vaguely aft. "Ingidi-inhiliziyo and I have spent the past five days working on it. The problem we keep coming up with is that even if we shield the main computer, there's still leakage around the cable connections and from the intersect planes. I have a bad feeling that if the invaders return before we've finished equipping the new Cobras we're going to have serious trouble on our hands."

"I see," Jin said. She turned to Zoshak. "Djinni Zoshak? May I?"

Paul looked at the young Qasaman warrior. His expression was tight, but he nodded. "Under the circumstances," he said, "I think it acceptable that you tell them."

"Perhaps we should consult Ifrit Akim first," Jin suggested.

"No need," Zoshak said, more firmly. "We're allies now." He gestured. "Go ahead."

Jin nodded and looked back at Croi. "There shouldn't be any problem with leakage," she said. "The Qasamans have underground chambers deep beneath their cities. Between the steel, ceramic, and native rock, there should be enough material to block any signals from getting out."

"Really," Croi said, his voice a mixture of relief and chagrin. "You couldn't have told me all this five days ago?"

"I didn't know what you were working on," Jin reminded him. "Besides, the subcities are as much a military secret as Isis."

Croi took a deep breath. "Yes, of course. My apologies."

There was a ping from the intercom system. [Jasmine Jin Moreau Broom, she will come immediately to the bridge,] a tight Troft voice called.

Jin and Paul exchanged looks. "That doesn't sound good," Paul said as Jin got to her feet.

"No, it didn't," Jin agreed. "I'll be back as soon as I can."

"If you think you're going anywhere without us, you're nuts," Lorne said, tapping Zoshak's arm and standing up. He looked at Croi and crooked a finger. "You, too, Doc—come on."

"But they only asked for her," Croi objected.

"I must have heard it wrong." Lorne looked at Paul. "You staying here?"

"Not a chance," Paul said firmly, getting a grip on the arms of his chair and using his arm servos to lever himself upright. "Go—I'm right behind you."

Jin had already disappeared through the forward door, with Zoshak close behind her. Lorne looked in that direction, then turned and rounded the table to his father's side. "I said you should go ahead," Paul repeated, trying to fend him off.

"I must have heard that wrong, too," Lorne said. He evaded his father's brushing movements with ease and moved up beside him, wrapping his arm around the older man's waist. Paul tried to push the arm away, but Lorne had locked the servos and the arm wasn't going anywhere. "Just relax and let me take the weight."

"I thought we taught you to respect your elders' wishes," Paul grumbled as they headed toward the door. Still, he had to admit this was a lot easier than trying to limp around on his own.

"Stop having silly wishes and I will," Lorne said. "Easy now, and watch the door jamb."

Jin and Zoshak were standing behind the helm console when Paul and Lorne reached the bridge. Between them, Paul could see the Troft at the helm, and the fluttering arch currently being formed by his upper-arm radiator membranes. Something was wrong, all right. "What have we got?" he asked, glancing around at the other Trofts at their stations. All of them were showing the same degree of stress as the helmsman.

[The Drim'hco'plai invaders, they have returned,] a Troft voice came from the side of the room.

Paul looked toward the voice. The ship's master, Ingidi-inhiliziyo—*Warrior* to all the humans aboard except Croi, who could actually pronounce the alien's name—was standing by the communications board, resplendent in the red heir-sash that identified him as the second in line to the Tlos'khin'fahi demesne-lord. Unlike the other Trofts on the bridge, his radiator membranes weren't fluttering, but were barely extended from his arms.

But then, a Troft of his rank and position was supposed to stay calmer than his crew. "How seriously have they returned?" Paul asked.

[A siege, they have mounted one at all Qasaman cities.] Warrior said. [Our presence, they demand an explanation of it.]

A hollow feeling formed at the pit of Paul's stomach. He'd assumed the invaders would run home with their tails tucked, where they would regroup, restrategize, and collect fresh ships and soldiers before taking another crack at the Qasamans.

Yet here they were, already well into a fresh campaign. Clearly, they were more determined than he'd realized.

And with that, everything he and Jin and the others had discussed and thought about and planned over the past five days was gone. With the invaders already back and settled into siege mode, there was no way Ingidi-inhiliziyo could get his ship close enough to Sollas to offload the Isis equipment and hide it in the depths of the hidden subcity.

That was bad enough. But for Paul and Jin personally, it was even worse.

Because the Qasamans' best medical facilities were in the cities. A siege of those cities meant that Paul's ravaged leg would not, in fact, be healed. Not any time soon.

Nor would the tumor that was slowly killing his beloved wife be removed.

"Maybe there's still a way," Lorne murmured hesitantly from his side. "It's possible Warrior can play the demesne-heir card and get us permission to land at least somewhere near Sollas. If the subcity extends outside the city wall, maybe we can get some of Isis into it without the invaders noticing."

[The cities, permission to land there we may not have,] Warrior said. [Such instruction, it has already been achieved.]

"But you're a demesne heir," Lorne pressed. "Can't you do *something*?"

"It would serve no purpose for us to land there, Lorne Moreau," Zoshak said quietly, his eyes on one of the helm displays. "Sollas is gone."

Jin caught her breath. "*What*?"

[The truth, show it to them,] Warrior ordered.

[The order, I obey it.] The helm officer touched a switch, and a section of the wraparound display changed from a view of the stars around the ship to a close-up of the planet ahead.

Paul felt his lips curl back from his teeth. Zoshak was exaggerating, but not by much. Probably a third of the city was still there, mostly the southern and eastern sections, snugged up inside their outer wall.

But the northern third was completely gone. The buildings there had been turned to rubble, the ground beneath them gouged out at least three or four stories deep. The third of the city in the middle was in transition, many of the buildings already down and the excavation below them just starting.

"They're trying to destroy the subcity," Jin murmured. "That's where their defeat came from the last time. They want to make sure that doesn't happen again."

"Terrific," Croi said grimly. "What do we do now?"

"We figure out something else," Lorne told him. "That's a big planet down there. There has to be some other place you can set up shop."

Croi snorted. "Where? We need power, Cobra Broom, power and buildings and people. We can't just drop Isis in the middle of nowhere."

Paul looked at Jin, a sudden thought stirring inside him. A bit of family history his wife and son seemed to have forgotten... "How many buildings would you need?" he asked.

"I don't know," Croi said, turning puzzled eyes on him. "Someplace to set up the Isis machinery, plus a prep area, plus a post-operative recovery area. Three at least, or I suppose one really big building might do."

"You have an idea?" Lorne asked.

"I think so," Paul told him. "Remember, Jin, on your first visit to Qasama you saw a mine that Daulo Sammon's family was operating inside Milika. Do you know if it's still there?"

"No, I don't." She looked at Zoshak. "Carsh Zoshak?"

"Yes, it's there," the Qasaman said, his tone oddly hesitant. "It may work."

"Except . . . ?" Lorne prompted.

Zoshak's lip twitched. "The people there are villagers," he said reluctantly. "Not . . ."

"Not city dwellers?" Jin asked.

Zoshak's lip twitched again. "Not soldiers," he said. "It may be difficult to find the proper subjects for the Isis transformation."

Paul looked at Jin. Over the years she'd talked about the political and philosophical divide between the Qasaman cities and villages, those conversations usually in the context of some policy the government geniuses at Dome were trying to inflict on Aventine's own rural and expansion regions.

She'd always hoped the antagonism would fade with time. Apparently, it hadn't.

"Don't worry, we'll find the right people," he told Zoshak. "I doubt the villagers are any less patriotic than the city dwellers. There'll be plenty of volunteers."

"Perhaps we should call Siraj Akim," Jin suggested. "He's the senior here. He might have other ideas."

[A response, the invaders await it,] Warrior spoke up. [Instruction, I await it.]

Zoshak took a deep breath. "Ifrit Akim's presence is not required," he said. "The idea is sound. We'll use it."

He turned to Warrior. "We go southwest of Sollas approximately twelve hundred kilometers," he said. "Follow the Great Arc to Azras. Milika is in the forest approximately thirty kilometers northwest of Azras."

"You could tell them you're here looking for plants with possible pharmaceutical value," Jin suggested.

"Isn't that the story you spun the Trofts at Caelian?" Lorne asked. "I seem to remember it not working out so great."

[A reason, it is still a logical one,] Warrior assured him, gesturing to one of the other Trofts. [The response, you will give it.]

[The order, I obey it.]

The Troft murmured the story into his microphone, and for a moment the bridge was silent. Paul gazed at the image of the ruined city far below, feeling his leg throbbing with fatigue and sympathetic pain. How many Qasamans, he wondered, had been killed in the invaders' demolition? Was the destruction a genuine and reasoned reaction to the Qasamans' hidden subcity arsenal, and a military desire to eliminate that threat? Or was it driven by a desire for revenge over the invaders' earlier defeat?

The Troft at the radio had made his request, and the conversation had now switched over to some kind of oddly poetic give-and-take bargaining or posturing that Paul had never heard before between Trofts. He continued to study the image of the devastated Qasaman capital, his mind drifting away from the conversation.

Three months. That was what the Qasaman doctors had told Jin. Three months to get that tumor out of her brain before it killed her.

She'd accepted that diagnosis calmly, reminding Paul whenever he brought up the subject that if they couldn't beat back the invaders within that timeframe that they weren't likely to ever do so. Plenty of time, she continually reassured him, for her to go under the knife and be healed.

Only what if the doctors had been wrong? What if it was only two months, or one and a half? She'd already used up two weeks of that time flying from Qasama to Aventine to Caelian and now back to Qasama. What if there was only a single month left?

Even worse, what if the doctors were right about three months before the tumor killed her, but that there was only a month or two before the point of no return on an operation? Jin had always had a bad tendency to run medical things right up to the last minute. What if she pushed this one to the edge, only to discover that the edge had already been crossed?

[Warrior, an infrared scan of the ships, may I have it?] Lorne asked suddenly.

[The purpose of a scan, what is it?] Warrior asked.

[The invaders' ships, I wish to know if they have been recently moved,] Lorne said. [Future movement, I wish to estimate its likelihood.]

With an effort, Paul dragged his attention back from a bleak future to the equally bleak present. "What for?" he asked.

Lorne pointed to the display. "You see that warship on the far left? It can't be more than fifty meters from the edge of the forest.

Once we have a few more Cobras, I'm thinking we could sneak up or even rush it, take over, then use its lasers and missiles to blast all the others. But that only works if it's likely to stay put for the next few weeks."

"Hence, the IR scan," Paul said, nodding. "You want to see how cold the grav lifts and drive are."

Lorne nodded back. "Exactly."

[The floatators and drives, they are inactive and cold,] Warrior said. [But the plan, it will not succeed.]

"Sure it will," Lorne said. "All we have to do is—"

[The plan, why will it not work?] Paul asked.

[Encrypted ally-identification systems, all Trof'te warships have them,] Warrior explained.

"Yeah, of course they do," Lorne said sourly. "Damn."

"What's an ally-identification system?" Croi asked.

"Probably like an IFF," Paul told him. "That's short for *Identify Friend or Foe*. It's a set of transponders designed to keep an army's warships from accidentally firing on each other."

"You sure they actually have something like that?" Lorne asked. "You saw how easily we got the armored trucks to fire on their ships on Caelian."

[The ally-identification system, ground vehicles do not have it,] Warrior said. [The risk of enemy capture and deciphering, it is too great. But the ally-identification system, all air combat vehicles and sensor drones will carry it.]

[Certainty, you have it?] Lorne persisted.

[Certainty, I have it,] Warrior said, starting to sound annoyed. [The ally-identification system, I saw it when Harli Uy and I toured the Drim'hco'plai warship.]

"Give it a rest, Lorne," Paul advised. "I'm sure he knows what he's talking about."

"Fine," Lorne growled. "It still might be worth taking that ship."

"Let's get safely down first," Paul said. "Then we can discuss strategy."

There was a ping from one of the consoles, and cattertalk script appeared on the display. [Official clearance, we have been given it,] Warrior announced.

"We're going to Milika?" Paul asked him.

"We're going *close* to Milika," Lorne said, giving his father an odd look. "He already said that."

"Oh," Paul said with a flush of embarrassment. That must have happened while he was contemplating his and his wife's medical situations. "Yes. Right."

"You okay?" Lorne asked, still giving him that look.

"Of course," Paul told him. "I got distracted, that's all. How close—?"

"Is your leg hurting?" Jin put in. "Maybe you should go lie down."

"I said I just got distracted," Paul said, more firmly this time. "Is there a problem with Milika?"

[A problem, it has not been specified,] Warrior said. [The village, we must not approach it.]

"Which I just said sounds a little ominous," Lorne said, "and asked if there was any way to get a look at the place."

[The attempt, we will make it.] Warrior gestured to one of the other Trofts, and the image of Sollas suddenly disappeared into a dizzying flurry of forest. Hastily, Paul averted his eyes as a surge of vertigo threatened to overwhelm him. [The added distance, it may make seeing difficult,] Warrior added. Out of the corner of his eye Paul saw the image steady...

"No," Jin breathed.

Paul snapped his eyes back to the display. For that first second all he saw was a hazy image of tangled Qasaman forest with an equally hazy walled village in the center.

And then, belatedly, he spotted what had sparked his wife's reaction. There was a Troft warship squatting in the middle of the road outside the main gate, its stubby weapon-laden wings poised like hawk talons over the village.

For a long moment no one spoke. Then, Croi stirred. "So that's it," he said, an edge of bitterness in his voice. "We have a traitor aboard."

Warrior's radiator membranes fluttered. [Your words, explain them.]

"Isn't it obvious?" Croi snarled. "Someone leaked the news that we were going to Milika." He turned and looked pointedly at Zoshak. "Someone who knew how to privately contact the invaders."

"You mean one of the people who helped us wreck one Troft warship on Caelian and capture the other one?" Lorne asked scornfully.

"If we hadn't won on Caelian we wouldn't have brought Isis to Qasama, would we?" Croi countered.

"They didn't know about Isis until after we won the battle," Lorne said.

"So they say." Croi's eyes narrowed. "So *you* say. You whose family is awfully cozy with the Qasamans."

"Enough," Paul put in. "With all due respect, Dr. Croi, you're being an idiot. Look at the infrared display—that ship's gravs are stone-cold. It's been sitting there for hours."

Still glowering, Croi looked at the sensor control board. Warrior pointed silently to the proper display, and there was another moment of silence. "Fine," Croi growled, turning away again. "Whatever. In that case, what in hell *are* they doing there?"

"It's Merrick," Jin said, her voice so quiet Paul barely heard her. "He's there."

"You sure?" Lorne asked, frowning up at the display. "How do you know?"

"I just do," Jin said, her voice filling with dread. "It's the logical place for Moffren Omnathi to send him for his convalescence. Somehow, the Trofts found out he was there." She exhaled in a painful-sounding huff. "And to get him... they're going to destroy Milika."

"No," Paul said as firmly as he could with his own heart suddenly racing. She was probably right about Merrick being there. With Jin having left, he was the only Cobra on Qasama, and the invaders would be seriously motivated to find and neutralize him.

But there was still a ray of hope that Jin apparently hadn't yet grasped. "I just said they've been there for hours," he reminded her. "If they were going to destroy the village, they would surely already have started."

"He's right," Zoshak said. "We still have time."

"Time for what?" Croi asked glumly. "Milika was our last chance. Now it's gone."

"Not for long," Zoshak said evenly. "First, we unload and secure Isis. Then we—"

"*Secure* it?" Croi cut him off. "Secure it where? In the middle of the *forest*?"

"Yes." Zoshak turned to Warrior. "Thirty kilometers west and south of the village is a clearing. It should be large enough for you to land. Can you take us there?"

Warrior's arm membranes fluttered. [The clearing, we are familiar with it.]

"Wait a second," Croi objected. "I was *joking*."

"This isn't a joke," Zoshak assured him. "Thirty years ago, after Jin Moreau's first visit to Qasama, the Shahni calculated that that clearing was where her team had intended to land."

"Except that we were shot down," Jin murmured. "But you're right, that *was* our planned drop zone."

"And so the Shahni prepared for the next expected incursion," Zoshak said. "There's a military watch station buried beneath the forest floor in sight of the clearing."

"It's *buried*?" Croi said, a fresh hope stirring in his voice. "How deep?"

"Not deeply enough, I'm afraid," Zoshak told him. "Besides which, it's almost certainly too small, and the generators are unlikely to still be functional. The station was abandoned over ten years ago."

"But it should be a good place to stash the gear while we find out what's going on in Milika," Paul said. "Warrior?"

[Your analysis, I agree with it.] Warrior gestured to the helm. [The clearing, we will go there.]

[The order, I obey it,] the other Troft said.

Lorne took a step closer to his father. "Okay, we stash the gear," he said quietly. "But then what? If they've really got Merrick pinned down in there—and if they know they've got him pinned—they aren't going to be inclined to just give up and go away."

"Do not fear, Lorne Moreau," Zoshak said, a dark edge to his voice. "We've taken down Troft warships before. If necessary, we can do it again."

Paul felt a fresh throbbing in his injured leg. They'd taken down Troft warships on Caelian, all right. Two of them, in fact.

But it had taken nearly the planet's entire contingent of Cobras to do it. And even then, victory had come at a terrible cost.

But Zoshak was right. That was Paul's son down there in danger. Whatever it took, they would get him out.

CHAPTER FOUR

The evacuation warning was so subtle that at first Daulo Sammon didn't even notice it. He was still lying in his recovery room bed, wondering what the gentle warbling meant, when a doctor hurried in, his mouth moving but no sound coming out. "What is it?" Daulo asked. His own voice sounded odd, deep and strangely distant. "Speak up. Speak *up*."

The doctor came to a halt beside the bed, his hand reaching up to touch something in Daulo's right ear.

And suddenly the warbling exploded into a howling roar.

"Ahh!" Daulo gasped, grabbing for his ears.

The doctor was faster, doing something else with his ear that brought the howl down to something much more manageable. "Apologies," the man said, his voice carrying easily over the din. "Your hearing hasn't fully recovered. That's an evacuation order. We need to leave here at once."

Daulo frowned. Then, suddenly, it all flooded back in on him. That first, failed counterattack against the invading Troft forces—his own severe wounding—doctors and drugs and foggy images of faces and noise and fury—

"*Come*," the doctor snapped.

With another jolt, Daulo realized that the tubes connecting him to the feeders and other devices by his bedside had been removed from his arm. "Where are we going?" he asked as the doctor swung his legs off the bed and slid wraparound shoes over his feet.

"To a departure area," the other said, steadying Daulo with one hand as he pulled over a wheelchair with the other. "We're leaving the city."

"Now?" Daulo looked at the dangling tubes as he settled into the chair. "But I'm not healed yet." A sudden, horrible thought blew away some of the cobwebs still filling his brain. If this was as good as he was ever going to get— "*Am* I?"

"I don't know," the doctor said, and Daulo had to grab for the armrests as the chair suddenly took off toward the door. "It all depends."

"On what?"

"On how long the Trofts let us live," the doctor said grimly. "Hang on."

Daulo had expected the corridor outside to be buzzing with activity as doctors and attendants wheeled out the sick and injured. But to his surprise, the two of them were the only ones in sight. Thankfully, the alarm that had been rattling his room was also barely audible out here. "Where is everyone?" he asked, grabbing for the armrests again as the doctor took a corner way too fast.

"All those who remain should already be gathering at the staging area," the doctor panted. "But there was someone who wished first to say farewell to you."

Whether from the fresher air, the lack of medicine being pumped into his body, or the sheer adrenaline-driven fear caused by the doctor's reckless driving, Daulo's head had mostly cleared by the time they reached their destination. It turned out to be a medium-sized conference room equipped with a table, a dozen chairs, and a line of blank monitor screens. Seated at the table were three older men, while six younger men dressed in the gray Djinni combat suits stood silently at the ready around the room's edges.

The three older men looked up, and with a jolt Daulo realized he knew two of them. One was Moffren Omnathi, special advisor to the Shahni and a legend among the Qasamans. The other was Miron Akim, who with the rank of Marid was overall commander of the planet's entire Djinni combat force.

"Daulo Sammon," Omnathi said gravely as the doctor wheeled Daulo's chair up to the table. "My apologies for bringing you here instead of letting you go directly to your departure area."

"No apologies needed, Your Excellency," Daulo said, making the gesture of respect and throwing a furtive glance at the unknown man. From the look on his face, it was clear he wasn't happy with this interruption to their meeting. "But what is this departure area business? Why is everyone leaving in such a hurry?"

"The invaders are destroying Sollas," Omnathi said, "and that destruction is nearing this area."

Daulo winced. No wonder the doctor had been in such a hurry. "Then you're right, we'd best get moving," he said, glancing down at his robe and recovery jumpsuit. "It would be very embarrassing to die looking like this."

"No fears of that," Omnathi assured him. "Some of the earlier refugees were met with violence, but the later groups have been allowed to leave unharmed." He gestured at Daulo's clothing. "And more suitable travel clothing is waiting at the departure area. The doctor will help you change before you go."

"Thank you, Your Excellency, that will be very helpful," Daulo said, a small relief trickling into the simmering darkness of fear and uncertainty. At least they weren't going to be shot the moment they reached the outside air. "My apologies for the impertinence, but may I ask why exactly I'm here?"

"Marid Miron Akim and I wished to say a final farewell," Omnathi said. "You and your family have served Qasama well, and we wanted you to know how grateful we were for that service. May God watch over you, and may you win through to see your village again."

"Thank you, Your Excellency," Daulo said, again making the sign of respect. "To both Your Excellencies," he added, this time including Miron Akim in the gesture. "But if we're all leaving the city together, it would seem to me that your farewells are premature." He frowned as a thought occurred to him. "Or *won't* we be traveling together?"

"Our paths will lead—" Omnathi's lip twitched "—along different roads. When you and the remaining civilians from this sector depart from the subcity, the invaders will learn the location of one more hidden passageway. With that knowledge, they'll undoubtedly enter to explore for data or useful items that may have been left behind. We will remain behind to make one final assault upon them."

Daulo looked at the six gray-suited men standing silently against the walls. "What, *six* of you against the entire force of invaders?"

"Seven," Akim corrected calmly. "Though I'm a civilian, as Marid-commander I also count myself among the Djinn."

"My apologies, Marid Akim," Daulo said. "But I fail to see how one extra Djinni will tip the military balance. In fact, I can't see how you can accomplish anything but a waste of all your lives."

"Your impertinence is not welcome, villager," the third man said brusquely. "These men are warriors of Qasama. They'll attack the invaders because it's their duty to do so."

"Their duty is to die uselessly?" Daulo countered.

The man's eyes narrowed. "You've said your farewells, villager. Now leave."

There was something in his tone and manner that told Daulo the smart thing to do would be to close his mouth and obey. But just as he had thirty years earlier, when Jin Moreau came to Milika and asked for his help, he ignored the quiet warning. "Not until I understand why you're doing this," he said firmly. "I've faced the invaders' weapons. You may be able to kill a few of them, but you can't prevent them from ultimately winning through. Is there something in here of military value that can't be removed or destroyed?"

"No, nothing," Akim said.

"Then why not just leave with us?" Daulo pressed. "Out in the forest, you can regroup and choose a better time to resume the fight."

"You will be silent, and you *will* leave," the third man repeated, and this time there was no mistaking the authoritative anger in his tone. "Or I will order you to stay and fight alongside them."

Daulo snorted. "And who are you who presumes to order me *and* the Djinn?"

The man drew himself up. "I am Shahni Dariuz Haafiz."

Daulo felt his tongue freeze against the roof of his mouth, a sudden swell of horrified panic washing over him. Dressed in civilian clothing, bereft of the elaborate robes of office, he hadn't been as instantly recognizable as he would normally have been. "My most sincere apologies, Your Excellency," Daulo managed, bowing over in his wheelchair and hastily making the sign of respect.

"Your apologies are tardy and not accepted," Haafiz growled. "Now leave us as you were ordered."

Daulo straightened up. The doctor was starting to pull the

wheelchair back from the table, and once again the smart thing to do would be to simply go.

But there was something in Omnathi's expression . . . "Forgive the further impertinence, Your Excellency," Daulo said, grabbing the wheels and bringing the chair to an abrupt halt. "But I still fail to see why these men are to be needlessly sacrificed."

"Your impertinence is not forgiven," Haafiz bit out. "Nor is your understanding required or sought. Your only task is to obey the orders you've been given."

"The Djinn cannot simply leave with you and the others, Daulo Sammon," Omnathi said. "Their combat suits will instantly identify them to the invaders. If they try to leave, they'll be cut down instantly." He looked at Haafiz. "And their lives will be even more uselessly sacrificed."

Daulo stared at Omnathi, then at Akim and Haafiz. Were all three of them blind? "Then why not have them simply remove the combat suits?" he asked.

"Impossible," Haafiz said. "Without their combat suits, they are nothing."

Akim and Omnathi, Daulo noticed suddenly, were watching him closely. "Your forgiveness, Your Excellency, but that's simply not true," he said firmly. "Without their combat suits—without any weapons at all—they're still warriors of Qasama. As you yourself said only moments ago." He looked into the eyes of the young man standing behind Akim. "And as such they're too valuable to our world to be needlessly thrown away."

Haafiz sniffed contemptuously. "Are you of the Shahni now, Daulo Sammon?" he demanded. "Do you now make the law for Qasama?"

Daulo grimaced, looking around the room. The six Djinn stood stiff and proud, their expressions those of men ready and willing to die for their world and their people.

But as he looked deeper into their eyes, he could also see that they, too, saw no honor in dying in a useless ambush that would serve no genuine purpose.

And they were young. So young. No older than Daulo's own son Fadil.

What had happened to Fadil? With a flush of surprise and shame, Daulo realized he hadn't even thought to ask.

But this wasn't the time for that. There were other young lives balanced on the edge here. Somehow, he had to find a way to save them from this madness.

He looked at Akim as a sudden flash of inspiration struck him. "Of course I'm not of the Shahni," he said. "I'm a citizen of Qasama, wounded while defending this city, who desperately needs help escaping."

One of the Djinn stirred but said nothing. Akim's expression remained unreadable. "Are you asking for our help?" he asked.

"This is ridiculous," Haafiz snapped before Daulo could answer. "Doctor, remove Daulo Sammon and take him to the departure area. You, Marid Akim, will deploy your Djinn as ordered."

"That may not be possible, Your Excellency," Akim said, his eyes still on Daulo. "Daulo Sammon is one of the leaders of his village. The provisions of the war act clearly state that warriors must assist such leaders wherever possible."

"When it does not interfere with other duties," Haafiz said. "Don't quote the law to me, Marid Akim. I *wrote* the law."

Daulo had a second flicker of inspiration— "And if I come under that provision," he said, "it would seem to me that a Shahni of Qasama would be even more firmly under Djinni protection."

"I don't need their protection," Haafiz spat. "I've given them their orders, and they *will* obey them."

Abruptly, he stood up and leveled a finger at the young Djinni behind Akim. "You—Djinni Ghushtre—by order of the Shahni you're hereby promoted to Ifrit and given command of this unit. Escort Marid Miron Akim and Senior Advisor Moffren Omnathi to the staging area and prepare them and your Djinn for combat."

"Wait a moment," Daulo said, frowning as he focused on the deep age lines crisscrossing Omnathi's face. "Advisor *Omnathi* is to be part of the attack? Why?"

"Djinni, you've been given an order by a Shahni of Qasama," Haafiz said, ignoring Daulo's question. "You will carry it out."

Ghushtre hesitated, his eyes flicking uncertainly to the back of Akim's head— "What about me?" Daulo put in, trying one last time. "I'm a village leader. What about you, Shahni Haafiz?" He waved a hand behind him. "For that matter, what about the rest of the civilians at the departure area? They're city dwellers—once outside the wall they'll be helpless. Where will they go? How will they find food and shelter? They need an escort of trained warriors."

"We need no such escort," Haafiz scoffed, his eyes still on Ghushtre. "Travel supplies are available at the departure area, and there are straight and clear roads to Purma and the towns and villages around it."

"There are still the dangers of the forest," Daulo pressed. "*And* those of the invaders."

"Ifrit Ghushtre, I give you one final chance," Haafiz said, again ignoring Daulo. "Obey my order, or be executed where you stand for treason."

"There will be no executions," Akim said firmly. "Nor will there be any such charges against my Djinn. I am the Marid, and decisions of discipline are mine. All honor or shame is ultimately gathered to me."

Haafiz glared down at him. "And your decision, Marid of the Djinn?" he demanded.

Akim's eyes flicked down to Daulo's wheelchair. "Daulo Sammon, are you able to walk?"

"For short distances, yes," Daulo said. "But my strength and stamina aren't yet fully returned. I don't know how far I can go before they give way."

Akim grunted. "For now, stay in the wheelchair—you should be able to cross most of the city in it. Djinn, your first priority is to escort Shahni Haafiz and Village Leader Daulo Sammon to safety. Accordingly, you are ordered to remove your combat suits—"

"Miron Akim, I warn you—" Haafiz began.

"—and report to the departure area," Akim said, his voice deathly calm. "Collect what food and water is available and assure that the civilians and medical personnel are prepared for travel. Moffren Omnathi and I will follow in a moment with Shahni Haafiz."

"Marid Akim—"

"You have your orders, Djinn," Akim said. "Carry them out."

There were twenty civilians, including five women and three children, waiting in a tense atmosphere when Daulo, the doctor, and the six Djinn arrived at the departure point. Accompanying the group were two other doctors and three medical attendants. As Omnathi had said, there were plenty of changes of clothing available, and within two minutes the Djinn had stripped off their combat suits and transformed themselves into six more civilians.

Daulo had also changed into more appropriate travel clothing, and was helping one of the Djinni load water bottles into the small carrier bag beneath his wheelchair, when Akim, Omnathi, and Haafiz arrived. Akim looked tense, Omnathi seemed oddly calm, and Haafiz looked like an afternoon thunderstorm looming on the horizon waiting to explode in all its fury.

But at least he wasn't threatening anyone. At least not at the moment. In fact, he didn't seem inclined to say anything at all.

Ten minutes later, with two of the civilian-clothed Djinn in the lead and Haafiz glowering right behind them, the group filed up a long ramp and through a door out into the open sunshine.

Into a ruined city.

Daulo looked around, his heart sinking, as the doctor wheeled him along the silent streets. Omnathi had said the invaders were destroying Sollas, but Daulo had had no idea how deep and thorough that destruction had been.

The southern part of the city, the part their group was traveling through, was still relatively intact, though there were numerous cracks and ridges in the pavement. But as they passed the wide avenues leading northwest, Daulo could see mounds of rubble to the north where buildings had once stood. Further north, beyond the rubble, were places where there was nothing but gaping holes, the devastation half concealed by a haze of dust or smoke.

Occasionally, he heard one of the others in their group murmur something to a companion, most of the comments edged with sadness or shaking with anger. But mostly the only sounds were the shuffling of feet through gravel, the creaking of the wheelchair as it moved across the uneven terrain, and the crackle and thud of the distant and ongoing destruction.

Aside from themselves, the only living beings in view were the invaders.

From the way Omnathi had talked, Daulo had expected the Trofts to be standing right at the exit as the refugees emerged onto the street, stopping each in turn and checking them for weapons, contraband of whatever sort, and Djinni combat suits. To his mild surprise, the aliens instead kept a cautious distance, watching warily but never approaching closer than fifty meters as the little clump of humans made their way along the deserted streets.

From a tactical point of view it seemed dangerously careless. It also made Daulo wonder what the whole fuss back in the conference room had been about.

The refugees had covered about half the distance to the city's southwest gate when he found out. As the group rounded a corner, they abruptly found themselves surrounded by a double ring of Trofts. The aliens in the inner circle gave a single order.

"Humans: halt."

The Trofts then proceeded to do a quick search of everyone, including taking brief but thorough looks beneath the men's robes and tunics. The outer ring stayed well back, their lasers trained on the humans, until the search was over. Then, as silently as they'd descended on the refugees, the aliens withdrew, returning to doorways, alleys, and the other places where they'd apparently been standing their unobtrusive watch.

The group had made it another two blocks before an odd thought suddenly struck Daulo.

Why was Haafiz still with them?

He stared at the back of the Shahni's head, frowning as his chair bumped its way down the street. One of the Trofts' first objectives in their invasion had been the Palace, with the clear intent of capturing or neutralizing Qasaman's leaders.

Yet now, with one of those Shahni standing a meter away, they'd failed to take him. Could the aliens really be so careless or gullible that a simple change of clothing could deceive them?

"Clever, wouldn't you say?" Omnathi murmured from beside the bouncing wheelchair.

Daulo looked up, startled. "Excuse me?"

"The invaders' tactic of waiting until we were well away from the exit passage before searching us," Omnathi said, nodding behind them. "By letting us first get out of sight of the subcity exit, they were able to avoid the risk of a coordinated attack from that exit or others nearby."

Daulo thought about that. "Unless they happened to pick a spot for their search that was in view of another exit, one they knew nothing about."

"At which point such an attack would have given them the location of another exit," Omnathi said. "All warfare involves risks. The goal is to balance potential losses with potential gains."

"I see," Daulo said. Jin Moreau, he remembered from all those years ago, had also been able to think that way. So had he, once, at least to a limited degree.

Right now, though, that gift seemed to have deserted him. Probably it was the medication still flowing though his not-yet-healed body.

Maybe that was why he couldn't figure out why the Trofts hadn't plucked Haafiz from the midst of the group.

"Tell me, Daulo Sammon," Omnathi said into his thoughts. "When we leave the city, where would you recommend we go?"

Daulo felt his eyes widen with surprise. "You're asking *me*, Your Excellency?"

"I am," Omnathi said, and Daulo was startled by the sudden dark edge to his voice. "Our friend up there, he whom we will not name in public, may think nothing of a brisk walk to the next town down the road. He might even make it all the way to Purma before the supplies ran out. Unfortunately, for some of us that isn't a practical solution."

Belatedly, Daulo noticed the slight limp in Omnathi's step. How old *was* the man, anyway? Somewhere in his eighties, certainly, possibly even in his early nineties. A long, wearying trek to the next major town or minor city along the Great Arc was out of the question.

There were, of course, a number of smaller towns along the road that would be much easier to reach. But given the quiet and apparent lifelessness of the Sollas neighborhoods around them, Daulo suspected that all of those towns were already filled to capacity with earlier refugees.

"The problem is that all the towns along the main road will probably have all the newcomers they can handle," Omnathi continued, echoing Daulo's own unspoken musings. "In addition, the invaders will most likely maintain a presence there, certainly in the larger towns. I'd prefer to avoid any additional scrutiny."

"Understood," Daulo said. "I suppose that leaves only the outlying villages. But travel through the forest carries its own set of risks."

"True," Omnathi said. "Though the forests are safer than they were even ten years ago. So you think one of the forest villages would be our best hope?"

Daulo frowned. Had he said that? "They'll certainly be less crowded," he said cautiously. "Though I'm not sure how many of us a single village could take. Even this close to Sollas, most of them are pretty small."

Omnathi was silent for a few more steps. "Do you know anything about a village called Windloom?"

"Yes, I think so," Daulo said, searching his memory. "It's about thirty kilometers northwest of Sollas. Decent-sized place—maybe nine hundred residents—on the bank of the Westfork River."

"That sounds correct," Omnathi confirmed. "I gather you've visited the place?"

"A few times, but the most recent was several years ago," Daulo told him. "They support a small artists' community which makes metal and carved wood jewelry and trinkets, mostly for sale to the citizens of Sollas. At one time they bought some of the more exotic metals from our mines."

"Do you think they'd accept strangers into their midst?" Omnathi asked. "Especially city dwellers?"

"No," the doctor pushing Daulo's wheelchair said.

Daulo twisted his head around to look up at the other. "Your pardon?" Omnathi asked.

"If you're thinking of dragging us all into the forest, the answer is no," the doctor said firmly. "We have women and injured men who need the kind of medical facilities that can only be found in a town. A *real* town, not some dirtback village." He looked down at Daulo. "So does this one, for that matter."

"The nearest sizeable town is Tazreel," Omnathi said. "Nearly forty kilometers away. Windloom's closer."

"Tazreel has proper medical facilities," the doctor countered. "*And* it lies along a wide, well-maintained road that predators have learned to avoid. There's also a way station about halfway from Sollas where we can rest for the night."

"And the invaders?" Omnathi asked. "They'll be certain to be watching all such towns and way stations."

"I seriously doubt the invaders will have the resources to examine each individual refugee," the doctor said. "Besides," he continued, lowering his voice, "you wouldn't need to stay in Tazreel for long. You could commandeer a vehicle there and go to Purma or anywhere else you wished."

"*If* there are still any vehicles left, and *if* there's still fuel to run them," Omnathi said.

The doctor sniffed. "It's still better than a village."

"Perhaps," Omnathi said. "At any rate, you must do whatever you feel is best for your charges."

The doctor's mouth dropped open. "*My* charges? But you're—"

"Your charges," Omnathi said firmly. "I hereby place you in command of this group of refugees. As for my companions and me, we shall attempt to join up with Daulo Sammon's friends in Windloom."

The doctor looked down at Daulo, then back up at Omnathi. "If that's your decision, I will obey," he said. "But I strongly advise against it." He gestured a hand up and down Omnathi's body. "Especially for a man of your years. One never knows when immediate medical care will be required."

"Perhaps it would be more proper for a man of my years to graciously step aside and allow what medical care still exists to be given to the young," Omnathi said. "But I appreciate your concern." He gestured ahead. "For now, though, I suggest we concentrate on getting safely through the city."

From somewhere to the north came a muffled *crack* and the stuttering rumble of yet another building coming down. "A point well taken," the doctor said grimly. "Watch your step there."

Fifteen minutes later, they reached the southwest gate.

There were more Trofts standing guard there, and Daulo felt himself tensing as the little clump of refugees approached. But to his relief, the aliens merely stood by watchfully as the humans filed between the vehicle barriers that had been set up.

Daulo half turned in his chair as they passed through the gate, moved by some obscure impulse to have one final look at the once-proud capital of his world.

One way or another, he doubted he would ever come here again.

The sun was low in the sky by the time the group reached Bay Grove Road, with no more than two hours before dusk and perhaps two and a half before full dark. There, Daulo's doctor made one last effort to persuade Omnathi to continue on with them to Tazreel. Once again, Omnathi quietly but firmly declined.

"Now what?" Haafiz demanded in a low voice as they watched the rest of the refugees disappear around a bend in the road.

"Daulo Sammon?" Omnathi invited.

"What?" Haafiz cut in before Daulo could answer. "You're putting *him* in charge?"

"I am," Omnathi said calmly. "Daulo Sammon has been to this village. More than that, he's the only one among us with extensive forest experience." He turned to Daulo and raised his eyebrows. "Daulo Sammon?"

Daulo grimaced, running his eyes over the group. Six young Djinn, warrior-trained but unarmed. Two old men, plus one more—Akim—who had prematurely aged after years of dosing himself with enhancement drugs. And Daulo himself, still recovering from near-fatal injuries. With the daylight rapidly diminishing, the plan looked a lot less feasible than it had in the bright sunlight inside the Sollas wall.

But it was the forest or the Trofts. Under the circumstances, razorarms and baelcras were still the better bet. "It's still almost twenty kilometers to Windloom," he said. "There's no way we're going to make it that far before dark."

"I don't suppose there are any way stations as there are on the *real* road," Haafiz growled.

Daulo shook his head. "There weren't the last time I was there."

"But there's a large flood-control culvert under the road about five kilometers ahead," Akim said. "It's large enough to accommodate all of us, and we should be able to get there while we still have enough light to put together some sort of barriers at the ends to discourage predators."

"A *culvert*?" Haafiz echoed, sounding outraged. "You expect me to spend the night in a *culvert*?"

"Not at all, Your Excellency," Akim said courteously. "You're welcome to remain outside in the forest instead."

Haafiz glared at him. "There will be payment for this day, Miron Akim," he said, his tone dark. "And for you as well, Moffren Omnathi." With an effort, he straightened up. "If this is our path, let us get on with it."

"Very well, Your Excellency." Akim half turned and gestured to one of the Djinn. "Kavad, you'll be first on wheelchair duty. The rest of you, screen formation."

"And watch for danger," Omnathi added as they all set off together. "In every and all directions."

They headed off, Akim and Omnathi in the lead, a glowering Haafiz a few steps behind them, Daulo and Kavad bringing up the rear. The rest of the Djinn formed a sort of moving circle around them, their eyes continually sweeping the landscape.

And as they reached the edge of the forest and continued on beneath the canopy of branches and leaves, Daulo found himself wondering if this really had been his suggestion, the way Omnathi had said.

And wondered, too, how exactly Akim knew about a culvert five kilometers up a lonely forest road.

CHAPTER FIVE

Jin had wanted Warrior to fly the demesne ship over Milika as they headed out into the forest, arguing that they needed to get a better look at what the Trofts were doing in and around the village.

But Siraj had argued that such a move might be seen as provocative or at least suspicious, and that the last thing they could afford was to spark a reaction from one of the invaders' warships. Warrior had agreed, and had ordered his pilot to give Milika a casual but wide berth as they headed to the drop point.

From Zoshak's description of the clearing, and Warrior's response to that description, Jin had already concluded that it was the same place where she and Merrick had been dropped on their clandestine arrival two and a half weeks ago. That conclusion turned out to be correct. The demesne ship was considerably larger than the freighter she and Merrick had traveled in, but Warrior's pilot managed to squeeze it into the available space with only a single stand of crushed bushes at one end.

Having seen firsthand the extensive subcity the Qasamans had created beneath Sollas, Jin had expected Zoshak's watch station to be a similarly extensive system of rooms and corridors and defenses, though of course on a much smaller scale. It was a slight disappointment to find that the station consisted of a single large room with living facilities at one end, an empty weapons rack at the other, and a set of blank monitors in the center.

But of course, the station *was* thirty years old. The Qasamans had probably been new at this whole rabbit burrow thing back then.

The watch station entrance was a simple trapdoor leading to a narrow fold-down stairway, the station itself wasn't exactly spacious, and the Isis gear consisted of a hundred good-sized crates. But Jennifer McCollom, the amateur linguist that Harli Uy had sent along with the expedition, turned out to be a master of packing. With her diminutive frame darting around everywhere, directing the Cobras and Djinn as she just barely managed not to get trampled underfoot, they were able to fit everything inside.

And then, to Jin's surprise and dismay, Warrior announced it was time for him to leave.

[Two hours on Qasama, the Tua'lanek'zia demesne has limited our stay,] he explained as his crew resealed the ship's cargo compartments. [Our departure, we must take it immediately.]

"I don't remember hearing anything about a time limit," Lorne said. His tone was respectful enough, but Jin could hear the suspicion lurking behind the words.

[The limit, it was not imposed by the Balin'ckha'spmi demesne upon our arrival,] Warrior explained. [The limit, it was given later. The unloading, you were performing it at the time.]

"Wait a second," Lorne said, frowning. "You just said it was the Balin demesne who we talked to, and that the Tua demesne is kicking you out. But on our way in you said it was *Drim* invaders who'd returned. Just how many demesnes have we got on Qasama, anyway?"

[Three demesnes at the least, they are represented here,] Warrior said. [The demesne that rules, its identity I cannot say.]

"But you must have *some* idea who's—" Lorne began.

"However the order came, you'd better obey it before your time limit runs out," Paul interrupted, shifting the arm he had resting for support on Jin's shoulder. "Thank you for getting us here."

[Your future, it lies now in your own hands.] Warrior's arm membranes fluttered. [That future, do not allow it to slip and fall to destruction.]

"We won't," Paul promised. "And you'll speak to your demesnelord about sending ships back to Caelian and taking off the Drim prisoners?"

[The request, I will make it,] Warrior said. [Good fortune, I wish it for you.]

Ten minutes later, with the Cobras and Djinn gathered together at the clearing's edge, the demesne ship lifted on its gravs and rose swiftly into the darkening sky. "And with that," Paul murmured, "we're back where we started: humanity standing alone against the Trofts."

"Large bunches of Trofts, from the sound of it," Lorne said sourly. "Why did you cut me off back there? There have to be some interesting politics going on between the different groups of invaders. We might have gotten Warrior to tell us more about it."

"If he knew more of the situation, would he not have spoken of it in more detail during the voyage?" Siraj asked.

"Not necessarily," Lorne said. "We already know Warrior has at least one agenda of his own going, namely for us to kick the invaders hard enough that the Tlossies and some of the other demesnes can come in and hopefully stare them down. Warrior may have other cards he's not showing."

"In which case, more questioning wouldn't have gotten us anywhere anyway," Paul said. "More importantly, Warrior's new two-hour limit was about up. He had to get moving before the invaders—*any* of them—decided to come out here and shoo him off Qasama."

"I suppose," Lorne conceded reluctantly. "So what now? We head to Milika and find out what's going on?"

"Two of us will, anyway," Everette Beach, one of the two Caelian Cobras, put in. "Either Wendell or me to drive the spooker and Siraj, Zoshak, or Khatir along as native guide."

Jin looked up at the sky. No more than another hour until nightfall, she estimated. Predator-wise, nighttime travel on Qasama was more dangerous than doing so in the daytime, though it wasn't nearly as bad as it once was. "Not much time left before dark," she warned.

"Which will be perfect," Siraj said. "By the time we reach Milika the larger nocturnal predators will be out and about, which will help diffuse the attention of the invaders' infrared scans."

"So let's make it a party of four," Lorne suggested. "We've got two spookers, and two of you to drive them. That way I can go, too."

"No," Paul said before Beach could answer. "Let's keep it at two."

"But—" Lorne began.

"That leaves one spooker here in case there's an emergency," his father continued calmly. "Besides, it's only an assumption that the invaders won't wonder what Warrior and the Tlossies wanted out here. We need to keep as much of a force here as possible in case someone decides to come out and take a look."

"Agreed," Beach said before Lorne could say anything else. "You care which of us goes?"

"Not really," Paul said. "Jin? You have a preference?"

Jin eyed the two Caelians. Everette Beach was a big man, a couple of years younger than her own fifty-two, with a lot of gray sprinkling his brown hair and a seemingly permanent half-grin on his face. Wendell McCollom, who also happened to be Jennifer's husband, was even bigger, though he usually maintained a more serious air than his colleague. Possibly something that had rubbed off from his wife, who was apparently the closest thing Caelian had to an expert on matters Qasaman and Troft. Both men, Jin suspected, had probably been formidable fighters in their youthful days, even before they became Cobras. "Everette will go," she decided. "I'm also thinking Carsh Zoshak should be the one to accompany him. He's been inside Milika, and therefore knows both the area and the village layout."

"Your reasoning is sound," Siraj said, nodding. "Djinni Zoshak? Retrieve your outer clothing and two survival bags and meet Cobra Beach at the spookers."

Fifteen minutes later, dressed in Qasaman clothing and equipped with survival bags, the two men zoomed out of the clearing on their battered grav-lift cycle and disappeared into the forest.

"I'll take the first watch," Wendell volunteered. "The rest of you can head downstairs and get something to eat."

"I should probably stay with you," Jin offered. "I know the local predators. You don't."

"Don't worry about it," Wendell assured her. "Anything with teeth or claws gets too close, I'll just kill it. Once I've got a collection, you can come and tell me which is which."

Jin grimaced. Still, the razorarms were the most dangerous predators out here, and with mojos riding herd on them they should steer clear of human scent. "Just don't let them get too close," she warned. "And use your sonic whenever possible. Laser shots will start being more and more visible as the sun goes down."

"Thank you; I *had* figured that one out," Wendell said dryly. "One of you can relieve me in a couple of hours. Oh, and make sure Jennifer eats too, will you? She sometimes gets so busy she forgets."

"We'll force-feed her if we have to," Paul promised. "See you in two hours."

Jin, Lorne, and Wendell had unanimously decided that Paul and his damaged leg weren't fit to stand guard. They had thus taken it with varying degrees of consternation when he calmly pulled rank as senior Cobra present and added himself to the sentry rotation anyway.

He was midway through the third watch shift, shivering with the unexpected nighttime chill and wondering whether perhaps he should have just let the others give him a night off, when he heard the sound of an approaching vehicle.

He had levered himself into an upright position and had his thumbs resting lightly on the triggers of his fingertip lasers when the spooker floated into view between the trees and coasted to a halt.

"Over here," Paul called softly as Zoshak and Beach started to dismount. Beach nodded and kicked the spooker forward, crossing the clearing and bringing the grav-lift cycle to a second halt beside Paul. "I wasn't expecting you back until morning," Paul said, notching up his light-amps. There was a hard set to both men's faces. "Do they have Milika blocked off?"

"No, we reached the village just fine," Beach said grimly. "We also heard the Trofts' demands, which they seem to be blasting over a loudspeaker once an hour."

"They want your son, Paul Broom," Zoshak said quietly. "He's to surrender himself to them by dawn or they'll begin destroying the village."

"I see," Paul said, dimly surprised at how calm he sounded. Jin had called it, all right. The Trofts had come to Milika for the express purpose of smoking Merrick out.

And now his earnest, conscientious son was being forced into the most horrible choice any human being could ever face: whether or not to offer himself in exchange for the lives of innocent people.

"The villagers are Qasamans, Cobra Broom, and they're at war," Zoshak said. "They know the risks and the sacrifices required. They won't give him up."

"Are you sure about that?" Paul countered, trying hard to think. What was Merrick going to do? What *could* he do? "Remember,

Merrick's a demon warrior. Everyone in Milika probably grew up hating them."

"Perhaps," Zoshak said. The ghost of a smile touched his lips. "But by now they surely hate the invaders far more."

"Don't forget that ship's been sitting there for hours," Beach reminded him. "I think Zoshak's right—if they were going to turn him over to the Trofts, they'd have done it by now."

Except that so far all the Trofts were doing was threatening, and threats by themselves were pretty easy to stand up to. Would that shoulder-to-shoulder human solidarity survive mass death and destruction when the deadline passed and the threats turned into violent action?

And even if the village didn't hand him over, what then? Would they all fight to the death as Milika was leveled around them?

And if *that* happened, what would happen to the mine where Dr. Croi was hoping to set up his Cobra factory?

Merrick was Paul's son, and dearer to him than his own life. But there were bigger things at stake here. If it cost Merrick's life to get the Trofts to leave Milika, that might very well be what he would have to do.

Unless . . .

"I need to talk to him," Paul said. "Can you get me there?"

"It won't be comfortable," Beach warned, eying Paul's bandaged leg. "And I doubt we can get you inside. The ship's sitting in front of the gate, and the entire top of the wall is within their view."

"I just need to get close enough to see and be seen," Paul said. "If I can get his attention we can use Dida code to communicate."

"Okay," Beach said, sounding doubtful. "Is Wendell in the bunker?"

"Why?"

Beach frowned slightly. "Because we're going to need the second spooker and someone to drive it," he said.

"I'll go get him," Zoshak volunteered, hopping off the spooker.

"That's all right," Paul said quickly. "Don't wake him. We can manage with one."

"How you figure that?" Beach asked, his frown deepening. "You and Zoshak going to ride double?"

"We leave Djinni Zoshak here and you take me," Paul said. "I assume your stabilization computer's got an inertial track memory, so we should be able to find Milika again without him."

"Or you and I could go alone," Zoshak offered. Like Beach, there was something in the Qasaman's voice that indicated he'd figured out something was going on, even if he didn't yet know what that something was. "I'm sure I could do an adequate job of driving the vehicle."

"And if he can't, I can," Paul said. "I've driven regular grav-lift cycles before. Whatever extra juice spookers have, I can handle it."

"Uh-huh." Deliberately, Beach folded his arms across his chest. "Okay, let's have it."

"Have what?" Paul asked.

"Whatever it is you're cooking up," Beach said flatly. "Come on, give."

"I agree," Zoshak seconded.

Paul sighed. "We need to get Isis into Milika," he said. "We can't do that while the Trofts are there. They aren't leaving without a Cobra." He braced himself. "So we'll give them one."

Beach's eyes narrowed. "You?"

"Me," Paul confirmed.

Beach looked at Zoshak, back at Paul. "And how exactly do you plan to explain to the Trofts how a young, fit Cobra inside the Milika wall managed to transmogrify himself into an older, half-crippled Cobra *outside* the wall?"

"I don't know yet," Paul said. "And I won't until I talk to Merrick and find out what exactly the Trofts know." He gestured. "So am I getting on that spooker with you? Or to I have to knock you off it and head out on my own?"

"I'd like to see you try," Beach said absently, gazing hard into Paul's face. "Okay, I'll go this far. I'll take you to Milika, but I want a decent plan on the table before you do anything. There's no point in losing both you *and* Merrick to the Trofts. And I still think I should wake Wendell and make this a foursome."

"There's no time," Paul said. "Besides, if we wake him, we'll probably also wake Jin and Lorne."

"Which we probably should," Beach pointed out. "They deserve to know what's going on."

"They'll find out soon enough," Paul said. "And if they find out now, they'll want to argue about it. As I said, we haven't got time."

"You should at least say good-bye," Beach persisted.

"You don't understand," Zoshak asked quietly. "The choice we would set before Jin Moreau would be that of giving the life of her husband or the life of her son. Do you really wish to force that decision upon her?"

Beach's lip twitched. "Yeah, I see your point," he conceded. "Fine. Go ahead and hop on." He shook his head. "Though it occurs to me that if I'm going to have to face her with this after it's over, maybe *I* should be the one the Trofts take."

"Don't worry about it," Paul said as he maneuvered himself carefully onto the spooker. "With two of us against a Troft warship, there's a good chance we'll both be killed anyway."

"Yeah, that's looking on the bright side," Beach said dryly. "Zoshak, mind the store. Broom, you just focus on hanging on."

From the southern edge of Milika the booming translator voice drifted over the village with the same message it had been delivering since the warship first appeared outside the gate.

"To the *koubrah*-soldier of Milika: you will surrender to this vessel by sunrise. If you do not surrender, the village will be destroyed and the people within the wall will be killed."

Merrick listened as the message repeated the usual three times. Then, the loudspeaker fell silent, and the normal forest noises once again began to drift across Milika.

"Only two and a half more hours before sunrise," Dr. Krites commented from Fadil's bedside.

"Yes, I know," Merrick said. Either Krites or Fadil, before the latter had fallen asleep, had made sure to remind him of the approaching deadline roughly every hour since he'd sought refuge and counsel here a little after midnight.

"Knowledge is silver," Krites said tartly. "Wisdom is gold. What do you plan to do?"

Merrick stared at the darkened buildings and homes stretched out beneath the window. It was a question he'd been struggling with ever since the ship had first appeared outside Milika at yesterday's dawn.

On one hand, the answer was simple. He couldn't just sit here while the Trofts destroyed the village, or even started that process. With the first actual laser blast or missile he would have no choice but to leave the Sammon house and march toward the warship with his hands held high in surrender. Certainly that was the reaction the Trofts were counting on.

But the more he dug below the surface of that supposedly simple answer, the more he realized things weren't nearly that straightforward. If the Trofts wanted to kill him, then they would kill him, and there was little Merrick could do except hope that his death would buy Milika a release from this siege.

But what if the Trofts wanted to take him alive? As the hours shrank toward the deadline, that possibility seemed more and more likely. Especially after Fadil had pointed out that the aliens could have forced Merrick's death long ago by simply opening fire on the village and forcing him into a suicidal counterattack.

So what *did* the Trofts want him for? There was only one reason Merrick had been able to come up with, and the very thought of it made his skin crawl.

The invaders had been defeated once by a coalition consisting of hundreds of Qasaman Djinn and two Aventinian Cobras. They'd presumably captured enough Djinn combat suits along the way to know how they operated, and to counter future attacks.

But that was the Djinn. So far, the Trofts hadn't been able to crack the full range of Cobra weapons and capabilities. Remedying that deficiency was very likely the goal of this current operation.

They were hoping to take Merrick so that they could dissect him. Possibly while he was still alive.

Merrick couldn't let them to that, of course. Personal dread aside, he had no intention of giving the invaders a head start in fighting whatever troops his mother succeeded in bringing back.

Fortunately—or as fortunately as it got—he had ultimate veto over that particular scenario. Once the warship opened fire on Milika he could ensure that he ended up in the midst of their attack. With his speed, strength, and reflexes, he should be able to arrange a quick and mostly painless death for himself.

And yet . . .

He raised his eyes from the darkened village to the stars twinkling against the cloudless sky. Merrick's great-grandfather Jonny Moreau had also been taken alive during his war against the Trofts a century ago. He, too, had realized that the enemy planned to use him to glean information about Cobra abilities and equipment.

But instead of simply sacrificing himself to keep that from happening, Jonny had found a way to turn his captors' plan against them.

Shouldn't Merrick at least try to find a similar solution before he gave up?

There was an urgent knock on the door. "Enter," Krites called softly.

The door swung open to reveal one of the Sammon family servants. "Your pardon," the man panted, glancing at Fadil's closed eyes and then turning to Merrick. "I have an urgent message for Merrick Moreau. One of the wall guards has sighted a small light in the kundur trees to the east."

Merrick frowned. And this had had to do with him how? "Okay," he said cautiously. "And?"

"He speaks of the kundur grove to the east," Fadil said. Merrick jumped—he'd thought Fadil was still asleep. "A light shining into Milika from there would be invisible to the invaders' warship."

"The light gives five short flashes, then a pause," the servant added. "Then five more flashes, then another pause."

Merrick caught his breath. That was Dida code. Five flashes—*dit dit dit dit dit*—was the signal for *calling—anyone there?*

His mother had returned. And she had indeed brought more Cobras with her.

"I need a spot where I can see the light," he told the servant as he scrambled to his feet, a sudden surge of hope blasting away the fatigue hovering at the edges of his brain. "Someplace where I also won't be seen from the ship."

"The meditation dome above the library should work," Fadil said. "Sharmal will take you there."

"Yes, Master Sammon," the servant said. "If you'll follow me, Merrick Moreau?"

Three minutes later, Merrick was in the dome, a small flashlight in hand, his light-amps at full power as he quickly but methodically scanned the area the servant had identified as the kundur tree grove.

There it was, back against one of the tree trunks, between two leafy branches where not even a glint of reflection would be visible to the warship's cameras and sensors. *Dit dit dit dit dit. Dit dit dit dit dit.*

Merrick keyed his flashlight to touch mode and pointed it at the tree. *Dit dit dah dit dit dah*, he sent. *Ready—proceed.*

There was a short pause, and then the other light changed to a new pattern of flashes. *Identify.*

Merrick smiled tightly. Like there was anyone else on Qasama who knew Dida code. *Merrick Moreau Broom*, he tapped out. *Identify.*

Paul Broom.

Merrick's smile vanished. His *father*? *Here*?

But that was impossible. Jin Moreau Broom had gone to Aventine, not Caelian. This had to be some kind of trick by the Trofts, perhaps something designed to flush him out of hiding and then keep him in one place long enough for them to sneak an assault team into the village to nail him.

But how could the invaders have learned Dida code?

Merrick cranked up his opticals to full power, trying to pierce the gloom and rustling leaves. But whoever was back there was too well concealed. All he could see was a shadowy, indistinct form that could be anyone.

Muttering a curse under his breath, he keyed his light again. Whatever was going on, he was not going to let his father's name spook him. *Prove it*, he challenged.

You're an excellent cook, the reply came. *Especially when mixing drogfowl cacciatore with conversations of treason. Situation?*

Merrick felt some of the tension in his chest ease. Not only were his culinary skills his most closely guarded secret, but the figure behind the light out there had even described the meal the family had had the night this whole thing had first started. Impossible or not, that was definitely his father out there. *Trofts demanding surrender by sunrise*, he sent back. *No clean exit available. Suggestions*?

One hour; north wall, his father signaled. *Use Sammon family mine explosives to create exit hole in base. Grav-lift cycle will be waiting beside wall; evasive ride into forest. When pursuit has been lost, go to Shaga.*

Merrick nodded to himself. Shaga was the next village south along the road, about ten kilometers away. *What about you*?

I'll leave the cycle by the wall and retreat to safety. Once the Trofts have left, I'll travel to Shaga and rendezvous with you there.

Merrick pursed his lips. The plan was definitely on the dicey side, especially the dual questions of whether Fadil's people could come up with enough explosives fast enough to make the required exit and what the villagers were going to say about having a section of their wall blown to gravel.

But it was probably the best plan they were going to come up with, given the time and resources they had available. *Acknowledged*, he sent reluctantly. *One hour*?

One hour, his father confirmed. There was just the slightest hesitation. *Good luck, Merrick. I love you.*

I love you too, Dad.

The other light flicked the close-off signal. Merrick sent the proper countersign, then headed down the meditation dome's spiral stairway.

Time to see how fast Fadil could get his people moving.

Fadil's eyes were closed as Merrick related the conversation and described what he and his father needed. The eyes remained closed after Merrick had finished, and Fadil himself remained silent long enough that Merrick wondered if he'd fallen asleep again.

He was just about to check when Fadil's lips puckered. "No," he said, finally opening his eyes.

Merrick stared at him, his heart sinking. After everything else they'd gone through, a flat refusal to help was the last response he'd expected. "Is it about the wall?" he asked. "Because if it is, I make a vow right now that I'll come back to Milika personally and repair it."

"It's not the wall," Fadil said, his voice thoughtful. "It's the plan. There's something wrong with the plan."

Merrick looked at Krites, back again at Fadil. "I agree that it could be tricky to get the grav-lift cycle to the wall without the invaders seeing it," he said. "But—"

"No, that shouldn't be a problem," Fadil said. "Not at the northern wall. There are several wooded approaches that would provide sufficient cover. Tell me, did your father explain why he wanted you to break through the wall?"

"I assume so that I can get out of Milika without getting vaporized," Merrick said.

"Yet there are guards even now walking the top of the wall," Fadil pointed out. "If you joined the patrol as one of them, you could simply drop through one of the many gaps in the wall's upper extension. You'd be beyond easy reach of the invaders' lasers before anyone aboard the warship could react to your action."

Merrick felt a chill run up his back. Fadil was right. With razorarm attacks no longer a problem in the Qasaman forest, the metal mesh extension that had been long ago erected atop Milika's wall had fallen into neglect and disrepair. Merrick had seen the gaps Fadil was talking about, including a couple in the vicinity where his father had called for the blast. "But if the explosion isn't to get me out, what's it for? A diversion?"

"Are you certain it was your father behind the signal light?" Krites asked.

"I am," Merrick said firmly. "He knew things that only he would know. Including the code he used to speak to me."

"Then the answer is clear," Fadil said. "The explosion isn't a diversion, nor is it intended to let you escape. Its purpose is to *prevent* your escape."

Merrick blinked. "*What*?"

"Consider," Fadil continued. "Where will you be when the explosion takes place? Somewhere under protection several meters away at the least. How long after the explosion will it take the debris to cease falling and for you to make your way across the rubble and out into the forest?"

Merrick felt his stomach tighten. Now, of course, it was obvious. Painfully obvious. "He has no intention of letting me hop on any grav-lift cycle and get out of here, does he?" he said, hearing the dark edge in his voice. "He just wants me to draw the Trofts' attention to that part of the wall so that *he* can tear out of here like a bat out of hell and try to draw them away."

"So I would read the plan," Fadil said. "Your father, Merrick Moreau, honors himself and you."

"He is indeed an honorable man," Merrick said, taking a step back toward the door. "Thank you, Fadil Sammon, for your insights. I'll take my leave of you now."

"What will you do?" Fadil asked.

"What I have to," Merrick told him. "If I don't return, please accept my gratitude for all that you, the Sammon family, and the village of Milika have done for me."

"I trust you remember that your body is still not at full capability and function," Krites warned. "Especially considering the internal injuries you reopened in the forest two days ago. If you start bleeding internally again, you could die."

"I'll remember," Merrick assured him. "Thank you, too, Doctor Krites, for your assistance and care." He took a deep breath. "Farewell, Fadil Sammon."

"Farewell, Merrick Moreau," Fadil replied gravely. "May God go with you."

Paul had said he would be waiting by the wall with the grav-lift cycle in an hour. Merrick's nanocomputer clock circuit showed ten minutes to that deadline as he joined the other guards walking the Milika wall and headed casually toward his chosen gap in the metal mesh.

He tried to watch everywhere at once as he walked, his heart thudding painfully in his chest. There had been no way to physically rehearse what was about to happen, but he'd run the whole operation over and over in his mind as best he could, throwing in all the variants, possible problems, and potential obstacles that he could come up with.

Time now to find out how closely his imagination and planning matched reality.

The clock showed two minutes left as he approached his planned drop zone. A casual glance over the side of the wall showed that his father was already in position, seated on an unexpectedly large and intimidating grav-lift cycle about ten meters from where the explosion was supposed to happen, and about three from the gap Merrick was heading for.

The clock had just passed one minute to zero when Merrick reached the gap. Without breaking stride, he half turned and dropped himself through it.

He landed with a crunch of broken bushes, a controlled bending of knees to absorb the impact, and a look of startled consternation on his father's face. "*Merrick*?" Paul breathed. "You were supposed to—"

"Hi, Dad," Merrick said. "Nice try."

And with a flick of a target lock and a pair of bursts from his fingertip lasers, he neatly cut the wires leading to both of the cycle's left-hand stabilizer sensors. "Merrick—no!" Paul snapped.

But he was too late. The big machine lurched beneath him, its left side canting twenty degrees downward as the grav lifts on that side lost the sensors' feedback.

And as Paul scrambled for a grip on his now badly angled mount, Merrick heard the sounds of the warship's gravs as they revved to full power. "It's okay, Dad—I've got it covered," he said. He took a step toward the forest, then hesitated. "If this doesn't work, say good-bye to Mom and Lorne and Jody for me, will you?"

"I will," Paul said. There was a deep sadness in his voice, and Merrick could hear the almost-echo of words still unformed, words that were still only thoughts and emotions deep within his father's soul.

Words that would never be anything more than those feelings.

From the other side of the village came the sibilant hissing of displaced tree branches as the warship lifted from the ground. "Stay safe, Dad," Merrick said quickly, and sprinted away from the wall. The reflected glint of the warship's grav lifts was just hitting the outer ring of trees as he slipped between them and headed into the forest.

And the race was on.

Merrick never knew afterward just how far from Milika he got during the chase. He wove back and forth between the trees and bushes, his light-amps at full power as he looked for the fastest route, his programmed reflexes working hard to maintain his balance on the treacherous footing. Swarms of insects and small groups of birds burst from concealment at various places along his path, and small animals scurried madly to get out of his way. Even the larger predators seemed to realize this was a phenomenon that should be steered clear of and crouched motionless as they watched him sprint past.

All the while, the Troft warship stayed right on top of him, or just behind him, the hum of its gravs audible over the crash of his feet through the dead leaves, the gravs themselves occasionally glowing briefly through the canopy of leafy branches above him. It never opened fire, and none of Merrick's tricks ever lost it for more than a few seconds. The Trofts simply stayed up there, pacing his mad run, waiting for their quarry to finally exhaust his strength.

On that count, at least, they were going to be in for a surprise. New Cobra recruits invariably tried to do this kind of long-range running on their own power, which inevitably led to muscle fatigue and exhaustion. Experienced Cobras like Merrick knew how to let their leg servos do all the work. He could probably run halfway to Sollas without serious problem.

The other possibility, that the ship wasn't trying to run him to ground but was instead subtly herding him toward in a particular spot, never even occurred to him. Not until it was too late.

Not until he hit the trap.

It was a simple trap, really: a wall of thick, sturdy netting, laid flat against the ground beneath the leaves and spring-loaded to snap up in front of him at his approach. Almost before his eyes even registered the obstacle, certainly before his programmed reflexes could stop his forward momentum, he hit the wall, yanking the netting out of its frame and wrapping it securely around him.

All three of his lasers flashed, but the bits of netting vaporized were small and insignificant. He tried pressing outward with his arms, but the mesh was highly elastic and merely stretched without tearing. His legs could also stretch out the mesh, and for a few seconds he managed to keep going. But the netting was self-adhering, and his scissoring legs merely tangled it against itself, and a few steps later he found himself sprawled face-first onto the ground.

He was firing his lasers again, trying to maneuver his hands enough to cut an actual tear in the material, when the world faded away into blackness.

The sky to the east was still dark with pre-dawn gloom as Jin walked tiredly through the gate into Milika.

The first news was good. Paul was standing near a few silent villagers, clearly alive and no worse off than he'd been when he slipped away from their encampment a few hours ago.

But Merrick wasn't with him. And the expression of guilt and grief and pain on his face was all she needed to know that the worst had indeed happened.

But something deep inside her still needed to make sure. "He's gone," she said as she came up to him.

Paul nodded heavily. "I'm sorry, Jin," he said. "I tried to stop him."

Jin took a deep breath. He had indeed tried. She knew him well enough to know that he'd done his very best to protect their son.

And yet, if he'd succeeded, she would have gained her son and lost her husband. Or she might have lost them both.

She'd been furious when Zoshak told her about Paul's unilateral decision on what to do about Merrick's situation. But the anger had long since evaporated. All that was left now was weariness and sorrow.

And, to her own private shame, a small nugget of guilty gratitude that he'd taken the decision on his own shoulders instead of giving half of it to her.

A woman should never be forced to choose between the lives of her son and her husband.

"It's all right," she said, reaching up to rest her hand on his cheek. "Merrick's smart and clever, and he has his great-grandfather's genes. He'll get through this."

"I know," Paul said.

He didn't, of course, Jin knew. But then, neither did she.

Many of the families on Qasama and Caelian had lost loved ones to the Troft invasion. It was probably inevitable, she knew, that sooner or later her family would be one of them.

All she could do now was try her damnedest to make sure that Merrick's sacrifice—that *all* of their sacrifices—weren't wasted.

"Did you talk to Fadil Sammon?" she asked, giving Paul's cheek one final caress and then lowering her hand back to her side.

"Yes, and it's all set," he said. "The foreman has three crews below ground right now, clearing out the mining equipment and checking the ventilation, safety, and power systems. By the time we get Isis here, it should be ready for us to move right in."

"Good." Jin took a deep breath, pushing the pain as far back as she could. It wasn't far, but it would hopefully be enough to allow her to function. "Let's see what progress the Djinn have made in organizing a vehicle caravan." She glanced around, spotted Siraj and Zoshak talking to the gate guards while a circle of villagers stood quietly around them. Ghofl Khatir, the third Djinni, was nowhere to be seen. "Do you know what happened to Djinn Khatir?" she asked.

"He's talking to Fadil Sammon," Paul said. "Some high-level conference, I gather, from the way both of them looked when I left."

Jin nodded. She'd wondered why Fadil hadn't been down here to meet her and the others as they arrived. "Is Fadil doing all right?" she asked.

"Actually, no," Paul said, a fresh edge of grimness to his voice. "But we can talk about that later. Right now, we have to get Isis here and get Dr. Croi started putting the pieces together."

"While we meanwhile dig up some recruits," Jin said. "I just hope we can find enough of them."

"I don't think that's going to be a problem," Paul assured her. "From what little I've seen of Milika, I think Siraj Akim and the others should have plenty of volunteers to choose from."

"Assuming he can find whatever qualities the Shahni consider necessary for good Qasaman warriors." Jin looked toward the east, where the sun would soon be coming up, and where the Troft invaders had long since settled in across the Qasaman landscape. "He'd just better find them fast," she added. "Even starting right now, it's ten days minimum before we can get any new Cobras into the field. That's ten more days the invaders will have to work on consolidating their positions and wrecking Qasama's infrastructure."

"We'll make it," Paul said firmly. "Whatever we have to do, we'll make it."

CHAPTER SIX

The sound of hammering and power tools from the northern edge of the Caelian capital of Stronghold had begun right at sunup, jarring Jody Broom out of an already troubled sleep. By the time she finished her morning routine, including the tedious but vital job of scraping the spores and other floating organics off her silliweave clothing, the hammer-and-tongs were going full force.

The door to the rented house's other bedroom was closed, which meant at least one of her two business partners, Geoff Boulton and Freylan Sanderby, was still trying to sleep through the racket. Probably Geoff, she made a private bet with herself. For all of his outgoing energy and easy social enthusiasm, he'd never been much of a morning person. Freylan, the shy introspective one of their research team, was much more likely to have risen at dawn, quietly eager to get back to work on the two combat suits the Qasaman Djinn had given them.

Besides which, Freylan was a light sleeper. There was no way he was still zonked out in there.

Jody had expected to find him outside on the house's small veranda, surrounded by the equipment Geoff had begged or borrowed, working on the puzzle of how exactly the electronics in the Djinni outfits were able to resist the floating organics that attached themselves to all non-living surfaces. But he was nowhere to be seen.

Unfortunately, with the planetary communications system still down, there was no way for her to call him, or even to call someone else to ask about him. At this hour, she decided, her best bet would be to check in with the men at the wrecked wall and see if any of them had seen him. Readjusting the stiff silicon-based fabric across her shoulders, she headed toward the noise.

Caelian's original settlers had quickly learned that the trouble with the floating organics wasn't the tiny spores per se. It was, rather, the tiny insects that eagerly descended on any and all bits of such entrenched vegetation, eating both the spores and bits of whatever carbon-based clothing or building material the spores happened to be attached to at the time. Tiny insects attracted larger insects, which attracted small birds and reptiles, all the way up the food chain to the larger predators that could take on human beings with impunity.

There was nothing anyone had ever been able to do about the spores except try to keep them from finding something edible to attach to. The big predators, though, were another story. They could be shot and killed by projectile weapons and laser fire, which explained Caelian's relatively large contingent of Cobras and its heavily armed non-Cobra populace. Alternatively, the predators could be kept out of the settlements entirely, which explained the tall stainless-steel wall that had been erected around Stronghold.

Only the wall wasn't very stainless anymore. In fact, for about seventy meters of its length along the northern part of the city, it wasn't even a wall. The Troft warship that had fallen sideways squarely on top of it had seen to that.

Since it was the Troft invasion that had brought that warship into proximity to the wall in the first place, it was only fair that it should be the Troft prisoners who'd been tasked with the job of cleaning up the mess.

They were doing a good job of it, Jody saw as she arrived at the downed warship. Or if not a good job, at least a busy and noisy one. The aliens were moving in and out of the wreckage, all two hundred of them, hammering at the ship's lower hull, lugging sections of grav-lift panels, or using pry bars and cutting torches on the weapons pods on the stubby wings. Standing watchful vigilance over the operation were twenty Cobras, some standing above the crowd on the intact sections of wall, others forming a barrier between the prisoners and the rest of the city.

"You're up early."

Jody turned. Harli Uy, Cobra commander and son of Caelian's governor, was walking briskly up behind her. "So are you," she said, eyeing the fatigue lines and blotches in his face. "Only *I* got a decent night's sleep."

He grunted as he came to a halt beside her. "So did I," he said. "As decent a night's sleep as any of us gets these days, anyway."

"That bad, huh?"

"We're doing okay," Harli assured her. "We're just spread a little thin, that's all."

"We knew that was going to happen," Jody reminded him. Now that he was closer, she could see the extra tension that was simmering beneath the tiredness. "How's your father?"

Harli gave a microscopic hunch of his shoulders. "Recovering."

"And?" Jody prompted.

"And what?"

"And what does he think about our agreement with the Qasamans?"

"He's dealing with it." Harli waved at the working Trofts. "So you here for the circus, or the Biblical epic?"

Jody frowned. "The *what*?"

"The Biblical epic," Harli said. "Someone was saying yesterday the whole thing reminded him of Israelite slaves building pyramids back on Earth in some big screen epic."

"Yes, I guess I can see that," Jody agreed, looking closely at Harli's face. "He doesn't like the agreement, does he?"

Harli huffed out a sigh. "No, he's not very happy with it," he conceded. "*Or* with me." His lip twitched. "And to be honest, I'm starting to agree with him."

"He's worried about the Qasamans having Isis?"

"He's more annoyed that we *don't* have it." Harli gestured at two of the Cobras standing on the wall. "I mean, look at them. They're just standing there, doing absolutely nothing except ride herd on a bunch of prisoners. Meanwhile, Stronghold is running low on food, and the other towns are having to stay inside their own walls because they haven't got enough Cobras to escort anyone heading outside."

And without the ability to send out hunting parties, Jody knew, those other towns would also soon be running short of food. "Maybe we should lock them up in the ships," she suggested. "Or maybe just that one," she added, pointing to the second Troft warship, the one still standing upright beside the sideways one. "At least that would eliminate a lot of the guard duty."

"Then who would do all the work to get the other ship out of there and start repairing the wall?" Harli countered. "Besides, there's no way to know what's still aboard that ship. They could have a hundred of those big hand lasers hidden behind the walls for all we know. Worse, they might find a way to wire around the power and control cables we cut and reactivate what's left of their wing-based weapons."

Weapons that had devastated sections of Stronghold and killed or injured three hundred Cobras, including Jody's own father. Not to mention nearly getting her mother killed outright. "You're right," she acknowledged. "Sorry—I didn't think it through."

"Don't worry about it," Harli said. "We've been working through all the options longer than you have, that's all. The idea actually surfaced almost a week ago, right after your parents and the rest of the crowd headed off for Qasama." He hesitated. "We also considered the idea of just dumping them out in the forest somewhere and letting Wonderland deal with them."

Jody felt a shiver run through her. *Wonderland*—Caelian slang for everything on the planet not under direct human control. Out in the forest, without weapons or defenses, the aliens would be dead within days. Probably within hours. "You might as well just shoot them."

"Which would be completely unethical," Harli agreed grimly. "I know. But ethics don't feed the bulldog, as my grandfather used to say. Doesn't get us any more Cobras, either."

"If sending Isis to Qasama wins us the war, it'll be worth it," Jody reminded him.

"*If*," Harli said. "And if it doesn't kill all of us first."

For a minute they stood together in silence, watching the Trofts work. Most of the aliens she could see had their upper-arm membranes fully extended, the equivalent of heavy sweating for humans. Their overseers were working them hard, all right. Occasionally, Jody caught a flicker of light as one of the Cobras on guard duty fired his antiarmor laser, probably at some predator nosing around the work zone. "What did you mean, the circus?" she asked.

Harli turned a frown onto her. "What?"

"You asked me if I was here for the circus or the Biblical epic," she said. "What circus?"

"Oh. Right." He gestured to her and started walking again toward the gap in the wall. "I just got the word—I was heading to see it myself. This way."

They passed the line of sentries, maneuvered carefully over the crushed wall with its torn and twisted edges and past the equally hazardous wreckage of the downed warship. Some of the Trofts gave them baleful looks as they threaded their way through the work parties, but most of the prisoners ignored them entirely.

And as they approached the last two parties, Jody finally saw what Harli had been referring to.

Standing fifty meters off to the side, his gray combat suit in sharp contrast with the Cobras' muted white silliweave outfits, was Freylan.

Jody rolled her eyes. Freylan knew better than this. Even with all those Cobras on hand to watch for trouble, he really should have known better than this.

He was fighting with a section of support beam twice his size, trying to get it up onto his shoulder, when Jody and Harli reached him. "Freylan, what in the Worlds do you think you're doing?" Jody demanded.

"Oh—hi, Jody," Freylan said, puffing with exertion as he got the beam up high enough to rest on his shoulder. "Hi, Harli. You two are up early."

"All the best shows start early here," Harli said, craning his neck as he looked up at the end of the beam towering over them. "The lady asked you a question."

"What?" Freylan frowned, then his face cleared. "Oh. You mean what am I doing?" He gestured to the beam. "I'm trying out the suit. Wanted to see how much strength the servos have, how the power curve plays out—you know. Try it out."

"You couldn't have done this back at the house?" Jody asked.

"Yeah, I suppose," Freylan said with a shrug. "But I figured as long as I was going to be lifting stuff, why not lift stuff that needed lifting anyway?"

"Except that out here we have to protect you," Harli reminded him. "I don't suppose that occurred to you."

"No, you don't," Freylan said brightly. "Organics don't stick to the suit, remember? And the giggers and screech tigers seem to be avoiding the area—"

"I was thinking about them," Harli said patiently, nodding back toward the toiling Trofts.

Freylan's eyes flicked over Harli's shoulder. "Oh," he said, sounding a little deflated. "You don't think they'd—? But there are Cobras all around them. They wouldn't try anything."

"Who knows what they might try?" Jody said, trying to keep her tone gentle. It wasn't Freylan's fault that the universe and its inhabitants didn't always behave according to his idea of logic and rationality. "Harli's right. You need to move your experiments indoors."

"Okay." Making a face, Freylan carefully eased the beam off his shoulder and lowered it back to the ground. "But you can see how strong these suits—"

"Quiet," Harli snapped, twisting his head around toward the broken wall.

Jody froze in place, her eyes darting back and forth as she searched for signs of trouble. But the Trofts were still working, the Cobra guards were still at their posts. There was nothing she could see that might have caught Harli's attention.

And then, even as Harli hissed out a curse, she spotted one of the Cobras on the distant wall with his hands cupped around his mouth. Clearly, he was calling something that only Cobra enhanced hearing could pick up. She opened her mouth to ask Harli what the problem was—

"*Damn.*" Harli spun halfway around, his head jerking back and forth as he looked around them. "Where's that woman gotten to? The Qasaman woman—Rashida Vil. Either of you see her? Quick!"

Jody felt her breath catch in her throat. Rashida Vil had been the main pilot on the Qasaman team's trip to ask for the Cobra Worlds' help in fighting off the Troft invaders. Siraj Akim had decided that she should stay behind on Caelian, where her Troft language skills would be useful in helping the Caelians work with their prisoners.

"I think she's in there," Freylan offered, pointing to the more intact of the two warships. "I saw her a few minutes ago with a couple of techs—"

He was still in mid-sentence when Harli took off at a dead run toward the ship.

"What is it?" Jody called after him. But there was no answer. "What were they doing?" she asked, grabbing Freylan's arm. "Could you tell? Who was she with?"

"Just a couple of the city's techs," Freylan said, confusion and apprehension stuttering his words. "You don't think—because she's a pilot—?"

"Stay here," Jody ordered him, and took off after Harli.

Harli was long gone by the time Jody reached the ship. But one of the other Cobras, a man named Kemp, was on guard in the troop guard room just inside the door. "What's going on?" Jody panted as she charged in. "Where's Harli?"

"Communications room," Kemp told her, his voice grim. "Deck one—top of the ship. Traffic Control's spotted a Troft ship on its way in."

Jody felt her pounding heart try to seize up inside her. "One of *these*?" she asked, gesturing at the mass of the warship around them.

"Harli doesn't think it's a warship," Kemp said. "Too small. More likely a courier here to check on the situation."

Jody winced. A courier wouldn't be as bad as a full-fledged warship. But it would be bad enough. "We can't let it see what happened here."

"No kidding," Kemp growled. "He's up there trying to see if that Vil woman can wave them off."

Jody nodded. "I'll see if I can help."

The warship had nine decks, which meant eight flights of narrow stairs between her and the comm room. Coming on top of that hundred-meter sprint, Jody's legs felt like rubber by the time she finally emerged from the stairway onto Deck One. Following the sound of voices, she stumbled her way down the corridor to the comm room.

There were three people already there. Rashida was seated at the main console, with Harli and another man standing stiffly behind her. Harli looked back as Jody came in, a warning finger at his lips.

Jody nodded. Like she had extra breath to spare for questions right now anyway.

[The proposed landing area, it is not on our schedule,] a Troft voice was coming from the speaker. [The primary attack site, it is elsewhere on the planet.]

[The primary attack site, it is secure,] Rashida replied in fluent, flawless cattertalk. [The site, you may visit it afterward. But the scouting party, it is in danger. The soldiers, they must be first retrieved.]

Frowning, Jody beckoned to Harli. He hesitated, then silently crossed to her. "What?" he whispered.

"Kemp said you were going to try to wave them away," Jody whispered back. "But she's inviting them down?"

Harli's eyes narrowed. "Is *that* what she's saying?"

"You don't understand cattertalk?"

"Not a word. What's she saying?"

Jody focused on the conversation again. "It sounds like she's telling them there's a scouting party somewhere else on Caelian that needs to be picked up," she said. "She's insisting they do that before they swing by here."

Some of the tension smoothed out of Harli's face. "No, okay, that's good," he said. "She convinced me there was no way they were just going to go home without a look, so I told her to try to stall them. A little side trip into Wonderland ought to do the trick."

At the console, Rashida looked back at Jody, her face tense, her eyes desperate. "I hope you've got a Plan B," Jody warned. "Because it doesn't look like they're going for it."

"Hell," Harli muttered, turning back to Rashida. She shifted her eyes to him and gave a small shake of her head.

"Plan B?" Jody prompted.

"Yeah, yeah, hold on a second," Harli said, his eyes darting around the room as if searching for inspiration. "Okay. If they insist on coming down, tell them fine, come ahead. Then shut down the comm."

Rashida nodded and turned back to her board. [The primary attack site, you may come to it,] she said.

[The instruction, I obey it.]

Rashida touched a switch, and a row of lights went out. "I'm sorry," she said, turning to Harli again. "He insisted."

"That's all right," Harli said, pulling out his field radio. "No—wait a second," he said, stepping back to Rashida's side and running his eyes over the board. "I remember there being some kind of external loudspeaker system that keys in here somewhere. Find it for me, will you?—it'll be a lot faster than using the radios."

Rashida peered at the board, pointed to a set of controls. "There."

"Turn it on," Harli ordered. "How long before they get within eyeshot?"

"Not long," she said, keying the controls and handing him a slender mike. "Five or ten minutes."

"Terrific." Pursing his lips, Harli lifted the mike. "This is Harli," he announced. "We're about to get some company. All Cobras, find yourselves some spots where you'll be out of sight but still able to control the prisoners. Renny, Bill—make it clear to Captain Eubujak that if his people step out of line we *will* shoot to kill."

He covered the mike and gestured at Rashida. "Where did you tell them to land?"

"On the rectangle to the south of the village," she said. "I told them we were doing repairs on a downed ship, and that there was no room for them to land anywhere nearby."

"Good." Harli raised the mike again. "They should be putting down in the landing area," he continued. "Smitty, grab a team from town and get into attack position down there. If and when we get them to open the hatch, you take them out. There's no time for questions—they'll be here in five minutes. Play it by ear and do the best you can. And keep in mind that once they're down we do *not* want them leaving again."

He keyed off the mike and tossed it back to Rashida, his eyes again darting around the room. "Is there any way to see what's happening down there?" he asked.

"There's the drone control room," Jody offered. "Deck Four. That's where—"

"Yes, I know," Harli interrupted. "Except that all the wing cameras on that side of the ship are gone. Plus half the controls got slagged when your brother and Carsh Zoshak ran amok through the place."

"Right," Jody said, wincing with embarrassment. She should have remembered that.

"I was hoping there were some extra cameras somewhere tied in up here," he continued. "But I don't see anything." He snapped his fingers. "But the drone hatchways should still be open. Get down there and see if everyone's doing what I told them to."

"What do I do if they aren't?" Jody asked, backing toward the door.

"Pretend you're their mother and yell at them," Harli growled. "Just get them out of sight."

Jody grimaced. "Right."

The Stronghold techs had finished their checks of Deck Four a couple of days earlier, and the entire area was quiet, dark, and deserted. Fortunately, there was enough light coming in through the open drone hatches for Jody to pick her way across the battle debris and through the damaged barrier to the portside drone hatch. The rectangular opening was a little above her head; getting a grip on the lower edge, she pulled herself up and looked out.

Wherever the Cobras had found to disappear to, they'd done a terrific job of it. The Trofts were still laboring away, but she couldn't see a single white silliweave tunic anywhere among or around them.

No white tunics, but there was still one gray one. Freylan had obeyed the general order to hide, but he'd done it by crouching behind a clump of pankling bushes between Jody and the Troft work groups.

Which left him nicely hidden from the latter, but completely visible from overhead.

Jody ground her teeth. But then, Harli hadn't actually said where the company was coming from. She raised her eyes from Freylan and gave the sky a quick look, wondering if she still had time to shoo Freylan to a better hiding place.

But no. She could see the incoming ship now, a small silvery dot glinting in the sunlight as it approached across the western sky. It was still too far away for Jody to make out any details, but it surely had telescopic cameras already trained on Stronghold and the damaged warships.

Which meant that any movement on Freylan's part would be instantly visible. Awkward and risky thought it might be, at this point Freylan would probably do better to just stay put and hope the drab color of his combat suit would keep him from being noticed. Suppressing a curse, Jody looked back down at the ground.

And blinked in surprise. The Troft prisoners had obviously spotted the incoming ship as well. But instead of continuing their work, they'd dropped their tools and were waving.

Not just normal waving, either. They were putting their whole arms into it, swinging them over their heads like parade float-masters trying to be seen from the back row.

Jody chewed at her lip, indecision tearing at her. Should she stop them? Or, rather, should she order them to stop, which might or might not be the same thing?

Or was it perfectly natural for Drim'hco'plai soldiers on the ground to salute a group of fellow soldiers flying over their heads? Worse, was it *required* that they do so? Without knowing more about the demesne's cultural rules, there was no way to know. If it was a form of military etiquette, ordering them to stop would be a dead giveaway to the courier that something was wrong.

But if it *wasn't* something they were supposed to do, wouldn't that be equally likely to arouse suspicion? Feeling sweat popping out on her forehead, Jody stared down at the gesticulating Trofts, trying to figure out what she could do.

And then, abruptly, she caught her breath. The waving arms...

She took a deep breath and stuck her head as far out of the hatch as she could. "Cobras!" she shouted. "Stop them! They're signaling the ship. *They're signaling the ship*!"

For a long, horrible moment nothing happened. The Trofts continued their waving and the Cobras remained out of sight. Could they not have heard her? Or had they simply decided that Harli's orders superseded hers? A movement from beneath her caught her eye, and she looked down to see Freylan rise from his inadequate concealment, take a couple of quick steps forward with his right arm cocked over his shoulder, and then throw something as hard as he could toward the prisoners. The object arced across the group and disappeared somewhere into the mass of upstretched arms.

Jody frowned. What in the Worlds had he thrown? A rock?

And then, abruptly, the Trofts at the point of impact collapsed to the ground, their falling bodies jostling against those nearest to them. Before their off-balance neighbors could recover, they too staggered and disappeared beneath the sea of waving hands. For a few seconds the effect rippled outward, dropping the aliens as if a silent grenade had been tossed into their midst. Below Jody, Freylan was again in motion, throwing a second object into a different part of the group. Again, the Trofts at the impact point began to stagger and fall.

An instant later, all hell broke loose.

Ten of the Trofts on the edge of the group closest to Freylan abruptly turned and charged away from the latest rippling mass collapse, forming themselves into a close-packed sweeping wedge as they ran. They were maybe ten meters from the rest of the prisoners when the Troft in the lead gave a hand signal, and the whole wedge shifted direction.

Heading directly toward Freylan.

Jody gasped. "Freylan!" she shouted out the drone hatch. "Get inside! Quick!"

But it was too late. Freylan was midway through his third throw, his body twisted and off balance, his feet out of position for any sort of movement, let alone a mad dash anywhere. Jody saw him twitch violently as he spotted the wedge of Trofts charging toward him, and he tried desperately to get himself back into balance. There was some sort of guttural shout from down there, but she couldn't tell whether it came from Freylan or from the Trofts. Freylan's knees gave a sudden, hopeless twitch, which the powered Djinni suit transformed into a two-meter leap.

Only it was his final mistake . . . because instead of taking him sideways or back toward the warship or anywhere else useful, the reflexive leap had instead sent him soaring straight upward. He would hit the ground again, Jody estimated, just in time to land right in front of the charging Trofts.

At which point they would have the choice of simply knocking him over and continuing on toward the forest, or of pausing long enough to beat him to death.

Clenching her hands around the edge of the drone hatchway, Jody watched helplessly as Freylan hit the top of his arc and started back down.

And jerked in surprise as a multiple burst of laser fire flashed across the landscape beneath him.

She'd completely forgotten about Kemp, standing his quiet guard down at the warship's entrance. Apparently, so had the Trofts. The bolts slashed across the line of charging aliens, dropping them into sprawling, smoking heaps on the ground. The fire cut off as Freylan hit the ground, once again blocking Kemp's line of fire.

He was starting to straighten up when the last two surviving Trofts slammed full-tilt into him, hurling him three meters backward to slam onto the ground.

Jody gasped with sympathetic pain. But even before the aliens had recovered their balance two final laser blasts dropped them to the ground with the others.

Jody took a deep, painful breath . . . and only then did it occur to her to look back up into the sky.

The Troft ship was considerably closer, close enough now that she could see it was definitely the size of a freighter or courier. But it was no longer coming toward Stronghold. It had instead veered ninety degrees toward the south and was hauling its gravs for all they were worth. They'd gotten the look they'd come for, all right.

And Caelian was suddenly in very big trouble.

"They were forming letters," Jody told the small group that had gathered around Governor Romulo Uy's hospital bed. "Tracing them out, actually, like a child might trace out an up-down-across to make a capital A." She demonstrated. "Each Troft had one letter, repeating it over and over, the whole mass of them tracing out the complete message."

"Only the letters were being traced out horizontally instead of vertically," Harli added. "Visible and obvious from above, but not from ground level." He looked at Jody. "Semi-obvious from above, anyway," he amended. "That was a good call."

Governor Uy gave a sound that was half groan and half grunt. "Don't know as I necessarily agree," he said. "That little battle has now put us in serious jeopardy. The enemy knows beyond a doubt that their invasion failed."

"They would have known that anyway," Harli pointed out. "If Jody and Freylan hadn't garbled the message, it would have given them that and probably a lot more."

"Or they might not even have noticed it was a message," Uy countered. "Or even if they had, they might have thought it was a joke."

"That seems unlikely," Harli said, his tone respectful but giving no ground. "Captain Eubujak certainly thought it would get through."

"Could you tell what it was, Jody?" Kemp asked.

"I didn't get very much," Jody admitted. "The first word was definitely *danger*, and I think the next four were *defeated Cobra numbers diminished.* Two of the ones in the middle, near where Freylan threw the first of his gas canisters, looked like *drone hatch*. But that's all I got."

"He was probably warning them how we got into their ship during the battle," Kemp suggested. "Good thing that little tidbit got erased. We might need to use that back door on the next ship."

Uy grunted again. "It would have been nice if the Qasamans had told us they'd left sleep-gas canisters with their combat suits." His eyes locked on Jody. "Or was that supposed to be a surprise?"

"The canisters are part of the suits," Jody said. "It probably never even occurred to them to mention them."

"And *your* excuse?"

"No excuse, Governor," Jody said, fighting against a surge of annoyance at the injured man. Despite what he obviously thought, none of any of this was her fault. "That wasn't the thrust of our work on the suits, so it also never occurred to us to mention them."

"And we *did* know about them," Harli put in firmly. "I'm mildly surprised that Freylan remembered the things and was able to use them. But I'm glad he did."

For a moment he and his father locked eyes, and Jody had the uncomfortable sense of the silent argument going on between them.

Uy blinked first. "I suppose," he acknowledged, shifting his eyes to one of the other Cobras standing around the hospital room. "Gaber, I assume you've had a talk with Captain Eubujak about this little stunt?"

"For all the good it did," Gaber said ruefully. "All he'll say is that escape is the right and privilege of every prisoner of war, and more or less dared us to punish him for it."

"You ask him what the message was?" Kemp asked.

"I did, and he wouldn't tell me." A hint of a smile touched Gaber's lips. "I did get the impression that he's rather astonished we figured out there *was* a message, let alone figured it out fast enough to do something about it. He did admit that the frontal assault on Freylan was mainly to force us to show the courier that we still had Cobras at our disposal."

"They would have guessed that anyway," Harli said. "This way, at least it cost Eubujak another ten of his troops."

"For whatever that's worth," Uy said. "So to summarize: they know we defeated their initial attack, that we wrecked one of their ships in the process, that we took nearly half of the Troft forces prisoner and killed the rest, and that we still have Cobras. That about cover it?"

"I think so," Harli said. "The next question is what we do now."

"Starting with how long we're going to have to come up with a plan," Gaber said. "It's, what, about five days to Qasama from here?"

"Qasama?" Harli growled. "They can get all the ships they want from Aventine."

"Oh, hell," Gaber muttered. "I hadn't thought about that. They could have a new force here in two days."

"I don't think so," Jody said. "Lorne and Rashida both said that the demesne markings on the warships at Aventine were different from the ones here."

"So?" Gaber asked. "They're allies, aren't they?"

"They may be allies, but they're still Trofts," Jody said. "The ones I've worked with have been extremely competitive, to the point where they'll waste ridiculous amounts of time and money rather than let even a business partner know about a weakness that they can exploit. A Drim courier ship isn't about to tell even an ally that the invasion team muffed it. They're going to go to the nearest Drim force, and according to Rashida that force is on Qasama."

"Unless the Drim have ships on Palatine or Esquiline," Gaber pointed out grimly.

"It doesn't matter," Harli cut in. "If they get help from any of the Cobra Worlds we're dead, period—there's no way we can be ready for them in two or three days. So let's assume Jody is right, and they have to go to Qasama. In that case, what's our timing look like?"

Jody curled her hands into fists. She was hardly an expert on Trofts, especially not on Troft military matters. But with Jennifer McCollom gone to Qasama, and given the rest of the Caelians' self-absorbed isolation, she was probably the best they had. "Let's assume the courier takes five days to get to Qasama," she said slowly, thinking it through. "That's about top speed for our freighters, so it's probably a fair guess. Warships, with all their extra mass and cross-section, will almost certainly be slower—six or seven at least. It may also take a day or two for the Drim commander on the scene to digest the report and decide what he wants to do."

"Or maybe not," Uy said. "Let's go with your eleven-day estimate. In fact, let's err on the safe side and say ten."

"Terrific," Kemp murmured. "Ten days to prepare for another invasion."

"We'll find a way to do it," Uy said. "Because we really don't have a choice." He looked over at his clock. "I want everyone back here in two hours, along with the city council and anybody from Essbend or Aerie who are still here. At that time, you're each to have at least two ideas to bring to the table. Understood?"

An affirmative murmur swept the room. "Good." Uy looked at Jody. "That goes for you, too, Ms. Broom. You *and* your two friends. Two ideas each, and they'd better be good."

"Yes, sir," Jody murmured.

"So get to it," Uy said, looking around the room. "I want answers, gentlemen, and I want them today."

CHAPTER SEVEN

The under-road culvert was exactly where Miron Akim had said it would be, five kilometers up the road to Windloom. It was also as roomy as he'd said, and as easily rigged to be defensible against nocturnal predators.

He hadn't, however, said anything about its comfort, or lack of same. It wasn't long after they'd settled in for the night that Daulo realized why that part had been left out of the discussion.

Even Akim was apparently not all that impressed with the accommodations. During one of Daulo's frequent awakenings, this particular one a little after midnight, he saw Akim slip through the makeshift barrier at one end of the culvert and head out into the night, in the opposite direction from the clump of trees that Omnathi had earlier designated as the group's latrine. For a few minutes Daulo kept his eyes pried open, wondering whether Akim was searching for better padding for his sleeping blanket or whether he was giving up entirely on the culvert and had decided to take his chances with the predators.

But idle curiosity was no match for fatigue. Even with his aching muscles and back, the rigors of the day's events soon forced Daulo's eyelids closed again. The next time he awoke, the culvert and its occupants were once again silent and still.

He was still exhausted when the diffuse sunlight of morning awakened him for the final time. The rest of the group was already up, he saw as he carefully levered himself into a seating position, wincing at each movement and muscle twinge. Akim was passing out ration bars and water bottles, the six Djinn were busily repacking the equipment for travel, and Shahni Haafiz was scowling as he bit pieces off his breakfast.

Daulo had made it to his feet and was working himself into his wheelchair when Akim came over. "Good morning, Daulo Sammon," he said as he offered Daulo a ration bar and water bottle. "Did you sleep well?"

"Not especially, Marid Akim," Daulo confessed. "I'm afraid Sollas's hospital beds have spoiled me. Culverts just don't seem all that comfortable anymore."

Akim chuckled. "Yes; the soft decadence of a convalescent's life. Don't worry—I'm sure you'll readapt to real life soon enough."

"We can make a contest of it, you and I," Daulo offered. "I noticed you also needed to get up once or twice during the night to stretch your muscles."

Akim's eyes narrowed slightly. "You saw me leave?" he asked, an odd tone to his voice. "When?"

"It was a little after midnight," Daulo said, wondering if he should have lied, or perhaps said that it might have been just a dream. Too late now. "You said something to the Djinni standing guard at the western opening, then slipped out."

"And the second time?"

Daulo frowned. "The second time?"

"You said I left once or twice," Akim reminded him. "When was the second time?"

Daulo frowned. *Had* he said Akim had left twice? He must have. So what exactly had he meant by that? "I think I woke up again a little before dawn and saw you come in," he said slowly, trying to sort through the images, dreams, and half-dreams from the long night. "I just assumed you were coming back from another walk, that you hadn't been gone that whole time. Should I have not said anything?"

For a moment Akim gazed into his eyes, perhaps trying to discern whether or not Daulo was leaving anything out. Then, his lip twitched. "No, that's all right," he said. "But keep this between us, and don't tell any of the others." He looked significantly over at the glowering Haafiz. "*Any* of the others."

"I won't," Daulo promised.

"Good." Akim gestured at the food and water in Daulo's hands. "Then eat up, and prepare yourself for travel. We still have a good fifteen kilometers to go before we reach safety."

The road to Windloom and the villages beyond had been reasonably well maintained. But it was hardly up to the standards of the Great Arc's major roads, and Daulo's wheelchair bounced and bucked on the uneven surface as the group made their way along it. Occasionally they hit a patch that was rougher than usual, or else pockmarked with pits and potholes, which the wheelchair simply couldn't navigate. At those spots Daulo was obliged to get up and hobble across with the assistance of one of the Djinn while a second carried the chair.

But at least the forest predators seemed to be leaving them alone. That was something to be grateful for.

They'd been traveling for three hours, and Daulo was wondering if he should just give up on the chair for a while and see how far he could get on foot when he spotted the shadowy figures silently pacing them through the forest on both sides.

His first panicked thought was that they'd hit a pack of razorarms or some other predators. But the figures seemed to be maintaining their distance, making no effort to either leave or move closer. He kept watching, and a minute later one of them crossed a better-lit section of the woods, and Daulo saw to his relief that it was just a man. A group of villagers, then.

But if they had come out to escort the newcomers into Windloom, why were they skulking out in the woods instead of joining the refugees on the road? And if they were out here for logging or hunting, why were they bothering to pace the visitors at all?

Daulo was still turning the question over in his mind when Akim cleared his throat. "The village should be just around the next bend in the road," he told the rest of the travelers. "You can expect us to be challenged at the gate and our belongings searched."

"*Searched*?" Haafiz demanded, his eyes widening with outrage. "On whose authority do villagers search a Shahni of Qasama?"

"It's not because you're a Shahni," Akim said hastily. "It's merely the fact that we're city dwellers."

"City dwellers whom they dislike?" Haafiz growled, turning his glare onto Daulo. "Is that it, villager? They hate us?"

Wincing, Daulo searched frantically for a diplomatic response. Fortunately, Akim was already on it. "It's not hatred, Your Excellency, but distrust," he said. "With the fall of Sollas they fear a flood of refugees who will severely overtax their resources. More than that, they fear those refugees may bring in weapons or illegal substances that will pose a threat to their people."

Haafiz snorted. "More likely they hope to find medicines or food they can steal."

"That could also be the case," Akim conceded. "In addition, there are rumors that some city dwellers have made devil's bargains with the invaders. They thus also fear the infiltration of spies and saboteurs."

"Ridiculous," Haafiz bit out. "No Qasaman would make such a bargain." His eyes narrowed as he turned his glare onto Omnathi. "Unless you speak of the bargain made with the demon warriors Jin Moreau and her son. *That* pact may prove even more of a disaster for the Qasaman people than the alien invasion itself."

"Yet the Shahni *did* approve the sending of Jin Moreau back to her people for aid," Omnathi pointed out calmly.

"At *your* instigation," Haafiz retorted. "Even then, you had authorization from only three. The rest of us weren't even consulted."

"I had the approval of all who were present," Omnathi said. "That's the law."

"No, that's an excuse." Haafiz flicked his hand in an ancient gesture of challenge that Daulo had never seen anyone use in real life. "And rest assured that I shall deal with those Shahni once the invaders have been pushed forever off Qasama."

"There was no time for further consultation, Your Excellency," Omnathi said. "You in particular were in another part of the subcity, and all efforts to find you failed."

"So you say," Haafiz said. "We shall see. If those three Shahni survive this war, I'll gladly take the judgment seat at their trial for treason." He raised his eyebrows. "As I'll also gladly sit in judgment at *your* trial on those same charges."

Daulo stared at them, a fresh wave of disbelief washing over him. Moffren Omnathi, venerated hero of Qasama, under suspicion of *treason*? How could anyone, especially one of the Shahni, even think such a thing?

"The future is in its own hands," Akim said. "And if I may say so, Shahni Haafiz, this is neither the time nor the place for such discussions. Windloom and sanctuary lie directly ahead of us. We should continue on."

"*You* may continue on," Haafiz said. "But my part of this journey is at an end."

For the first time since they'd left the Sollas subcity Akim actually seemed taken aback. "What?" he asked.

"I'm leaving." Haafiz gestured around him at the silent Djinn. "The Djinn will accompany me back to the main road. We go to Tazreel and from there to Purma."

"You can't be serious, Your Excellency," Akim said. "We've been over this."

"And I've reconsidered," Haafiz said. "Whatever this haven is that you spoke of, it's now abundantly clear that it's too far out of the main stream of activity to be of any use to me."

"But the cities aren't safe for you," Akim persisted.

"Nowhere on Qasama is safe," Haafiz said. "At least in Purma I'll be able to lead my people."

"You can't," Akim insisted.

Haafiz's eyes narrowed. "Are you now of the Shahni, that you presume to dictate another Shahni's choice of path? Or do you merely presume to circumvent Shahni rule as does Moffren Omnathi?"

Akim flashed Omnathi a look. "But you agreed to come here, Your Excellency."

"I agreed to allow you to offer the protection of the Djinn to an injured village leader," Haafiz countered. "Daulo Sammon is now as safe as it's possible for him to be on Qasama. I now choose to move on."

"But you also must be protected," Akim insisted. "Back in the Great Arc is where the invaders are the strongest."

"Back in the Great Arc is also where any Shahni still alive and free will have gathered," Haafiz countered. "There are rendezvous and communication points in Purma that have been established for this situation. With no ground communications and no radio, I must physically travel there to learn whether others have survived or whether I alone now lead the Qasaman people."

"Let me instead send my Djinn," Akim offered. "They can assess the situation and return with that news."

"While I meanwhile sit uselessly in the middle of the forest?" Haafiz shook his head. "No."

"At least come to Windloom long enough for some proper food and rest," Omnathi said. "I'm certain that Daulo Sammon, as a fellow villager, will use his full influence to make sure you aren't searched or otherwise mistreated."

"Of course," Daulo said, wondering if Omnathi realized how little influence he was likely to have here. Unless some of the metalwork artists he'd dealt with all those years ago had managed to become Windloom's leaders, he would be lucky if anyone here even remembered him.

"Then it's settled," Akim said. "We'll go to Windloom, rest, and take some refreshment. Then, if you still want to go to Purma, you and the Djinn can go with proper equipment and provisions."

Haafiz studied Akim's face. "Very well," he said at last. "An hour, no more, and I leave. Agreed?"

"Agreed," Akim said.

With a loud sniff, Haafiz strode away, passing Akim and Omnathi as he continued down the road. Akim flicked an unreadable look at Daulo, then turned and hurried to catch up.

Daulo's memories of Windloom were several years old. But like Milika, the village hadn't changed appreciably in that time. The outer wall looked just the way he remembered it, though he was pretty sure the gate's hinges had been replaced recently. Most of the buildings clustered together inside the wall had the look of comfortable permanence about them, the same look he'd seen in many of these older Qasaman settlements.

But while the village itself had remained largely unchanged, the villagers had not. The last time Daulo had been here the people had been cautiously welcoming, the typical attitude of people living not far from a major city whose inhabitants looked down on them even while they were buying their goods. Now, though, there was no friendliness in the men at the gate. They were cold and aloof, their questions brusque and suspicious. And all of them carried rifles or sidearms.

As Daulo had privately predicted, he had no influence whatsoever with the guards. But Omnathi's name seemed to carry some weight, and he was able to convince them that Shahni Haafiz should be exempt from any search. The others of the group weren't so lucky, or perhaps weren't so intimidating, and went through the full procedure. Even Daulo's wheelchair was taken away for closer examination, leaving him once again hobbling with Djinni assistance.

Fortunately, he didn't have to hobble very far. Two of the guards escorted them to a house near the gate, where one of them set out food and water while the other headed off with Akim through the narrow streets to meet with the village's leaders.

Daulo was working his way through a second dried meat ring, watching Omnathi and Haafiz studiously not speaking to each other and feeling extremely uncomfortable about it, when Akim and one of the village leaders returned.

And they weren't alone. Flanking them were four more armed men.

"Finally," Haafiz growled, glowering briefly at Akim and then turning his attention to the villagers. "Have you prepared the provisions for my journey to Purma?"

"I regret, Your Excellency, that there will be no such journey," Akim said, his voice tight. "Not for you or anyone else."

"What?" Haafiz demanded. "Marid Akim—"

"Because this was found beneath Daulo Sammon's wheelchair, attached to the front of the carrier bag." Akim held out a slender cylinder about thirteen centimeters long and three in diameter. "It's a radio."

Daulo felt his stomach tighten, peripherally aware that all eyes had turned toward him. Everyone in the room, probably everyone in Windloom, knew that the invaders' weapons were keyed to home in on Qasaman radio transmissions. Even through the hazy memories of his recovery in the subcity he had a vivid image of men coming through the hospital collecting all radio transmitters and other wireless equipment and emphasizing that the use of such instruments could bring death and destruction down on them all. "That isn't mine," he said, striving to keep his voice calm. "It's not even my wheelchair—it was assigned to me in Sollas."

"It doesn't look like any radio I've ever seen," Haafiz said, his eyes flicking between the cylinder and Daulo.

"It's a Djinni field radio," Akim told him. "One of those that were being experimented on in hopes of making them undetectable to the invaders."

"Were the experiments successful?" Haafiz asked.

Akim snorted. "Would we be talking about letting you walk all the way to Purma if they'd been successful?" he countered. "More significant even than the radio, though, is the name of one of the men who worked on that project." He raised his eyebrows slightly. "Fadil Sammon, son of Daulo Sammon."

Daulo felt his mouth drop open. *Fadil*, on a secret high-tech project?

But that was impossible. Fadil was intelligent enough, and dealing with the radios they used in the family mine had given him a working knowledge of the theory and hardware involved. But he didn't have nearly the expertise that Akim would have needed for such work.

Omnathi wasn't buying it, either. "Your logic is tenuous," he rumbled. "Daulo Sammon has been in the Sollas subcity since the first attack, while Fadil Sammon is . . . elsewhere. How could the son have delivered a radio to the father?"

"I don't know," Akim said. "The more intriguing question for me is *why* he would send it to him."

And suddenly, with a rush of fear and horror, the answer slapped Daulo hard across the face. The only way Fadil could have become smart enough to join such a high-level project— "You son of a venomous snake," he snarled, his eyes boring into Akim's face. "What poisons did you pump into his blood?"

"I gave him precisely what he asked for," Akim said, his voice and expression carved from midwinter ice. "And it was at *his* request. *He* volunteered himself to be part of the project."

"You lie," Daulo bit out, an agony of fire filling his lungs. He'd heard whispers about these secret drugs, chemicals that could temporarily enhance creativity and intelligence to an astonishing degree. But their aftereffects were the stuff of fever nightmares. "What did you do to him? Where is he?"

"Your son's condition and location are not the point, Daulo Sammon," Akim said. "The point is whether—"

"God damn you all to hell!" Daulo exploded, leaping to his feet and sending his chair crashing to the floor behind him. "*Where is my son?*"

"He's at your home in Milika," Akim said. He hadn't even twitched at Daulo's outburst. "I'm afraid he's been paralyzed. I'm sorry."

For a long moment Daulo just stared at him, feeling the blood drain from his face and the strength fade from his legs and body as his mind tried to wrap itself around Akim's words. His son, *paralyzed*? "No," he whispered. "Please, God. No."

"I'm sorry," Akim said again.

"We mourn your loss," Omnathi said in a voice that reeked of suspicion and impatience and had not a drop of genuine mourning that Daulo could detect. "Now sit down."

One of the Djinn stepped behind Daulo and set his chair up again. Slowly, Daulo sank back into it. "Because the point, Daulo Sammon," Omnathi continued, "is not what the drugs have done to your son, but what your son may have done to Qasama."

Daulo shook his head tiredly. "I have no idea what you're talking about."

"He's talking about the radio," Akim said. "Why it's here, and whether you've used it to communicate with the invaders.

"And whether you or your son has committed treason."

The word took several heartbeats to register through the frozen turmoil in Daulo's brain. Then, like the flash of a cutting torch, it abruptly sliced though the swirling emotions. "What did you say?" he demanded. "*Treason*? You can't possibly believe that."

"My beliefs are irrelevant," Akim said. "It will be the facts that ultimately define reality."

Daulo stared at him, then looked at Omnathi. They were serious. God above, they were actually serious. "This is insane," he said, hearing the quaver in his voice but unable to suppress it. "I was nearly killed defending my world and my people. My son is now trapped in a living death for doing likewise. How can you possibly think such things about us?"

"How can this radio have come into your possession?" Omnathi countered. "There are facts here which must be brought into the light."

Daulo raised his head a little higher. "Then assemble your facts, Advisor Omnathi," he said. "I don't fear the truth. Bring your facts into the light, and allow me to face them."

"*After* you've set me on my way to Purma," Haafiz said, standing up. "If there's treason here, there's even more reason for me to quickly make my way elsewhere."

"Elsewhere, certainly," Akim said. "But not to Purma. Without knowing what Daulo Sammon may or may not have told the invaders, we cannot risk you traveling to any place we've spoken of during our journey. The invaders may be even now setting a trap for you there."

"Did you mention Windloom in his hearing?" the village leader put in. "If so, you can't stay here, either."

"Agreed," Akim said. "But we shouldn't need to go far. I'm

told there's a quarantine cabin half a kilometer into the forest to the west."

"That's correct," the villager said doubtfully. "But it hasn't been used in years. I can't make any promises for its comfort or even its structural soundness."

"Whatever its condition, we'll make it do," Akim assured him. "Can you provide us with two weeks' worth of food and water?"

"Two *weeks*?" Haafiz echoed. "We're speaking of a summary trial, Marid Akim, not something long and involved. I can't be away from Qasama that long."

"This *is* Qasama," the villager said, an edge to his voice.

"I mean the *real* Qasama," Haafiz retorted, not even wasting a glare on the man. "The Qasama the invaders are conquering and destroying. The Qasama that's *worth* conquering and destroying."

"I understand your wish to return to the main theater of war, Your Excellency," Akim said hastily. "But I'm afraid the delay can't be avoided. We need to bring Fadil Sammon here to testify as to his part in this, and even for Djinn a journey to Milika through forested lands will take at least a week in each direction."

"And thus you rob me even of knowledge," Haafiz growled.

Akim frowned. "I don't understand."

"If you send the Djinn to fetch Fadil Sammon, they can't also go to Purma to learn what the invaders are doing," Haafiz reminded him.

"Ah," Akim said, looking sideways at Omnathi. "Yes, I see. But again, I'm afraid it can't be helped. Before we can make any moves against the invaders we need to learn the extent of the Sammon family's actions against us."

Haafiz hissed between his teeth. "Very well. For the moment, we'll go to this quarantine cabin." He leveled a finger at Akim. "But only for the moment. *I* will decide later just how long my exile will last."

"Of course," Akim said.

"And while we await the son's arrival," Haafiz added, turning to Daulo, "you'll begin your examination of the father. The sooner we determine the extent of his treason, the sooner I'll be able to get back to Purma and locate the remaining Shahni."

He waved a hand at the villager. "Go," he ordered. "Prepare our provisions."

A hint of a scowl touched the other's lips. But he merely nodded, made the sign of respect, and left.

✧ ✧ ✧

There was an old, overgrown, barely visible path leading away from the clearing around Windloom westward toward the quarantine cabin. It looked way too narrow and plant-choked for the wheelchair, and as the group approached it Daulo found himself wincing at the prospect of trying to drag himself the entire half kilometer on foot.

Fortunately, Akim had already thought it through and come up with a solution. As they reached the path he gave a murmured order, and four of the Djinn took hold of the corners of Daulo's wheelchair, lifting both him and the chair off the ground. With the other two Djinn in the lead, they headed into the forest.

The path was bumpy, with hidden obstacles that threatened to trip up the wheelchair carriers with every step. Daulo was nearly pitched out at least a dozen times along the way, and it was with a sense of relief that he finally spotted the roof of the cabin ahead between the trees.

He'd relaxed too soon. Two steps later, the two Djinn in the lead abruptly turned left, leaving the path and turning southward. Daulo's carriers, and of course Daulo himself, did likewise.

Daulo tensed, a hundred horrible and ominous scenarios flashing through his mind. But whatever was happening, it was quickly clear that he wasn't the only one who hadn't been told of this additional change of plans. "What's this?" Haafiz demanded, stopping in confusion as Akim and Omnathi veered off alongside the Djinn. "Marid Akim? What's going on? Where are you taking us?"

"To the secret haven I told you about back in Sollas," Akim said. "It's a place that was long prepared for just such a situation."

"A place the details of which you were extremely vague about," Haafiz said.

"Be patient, Your Excellency," Akim said. "Your questions will all be answered soon."

They'd been walking for fifteen minutes, and the Djinn carrying Daulo's wheelchair were starting to stagger with their burden, when they reached their destination.

Though for a minute Daulo didn't realize that. The small clearing that had been created by a pair of toppled trees wasn't at all remarkable. It was only as the Djinn set Daulo and his wheelchair down that the ground between the trees magically opened up to reveal the top of a three-meter-diameter shaft leading downward.

"Its designation is Reserve Command Post Sollas Three," Akim said as a pair of young men in gray Djinni combat suits stepped out of the shaft, their hands in laser-firing positions as they eyed the newcomers. "There are thirty such bases scattered around the rural and forested areas of Qasama, designed to serve as regrouping points in case of an overwhelming attack."

"I was never told of these places," Haafiz said, his voice dark with suspicion. "Why were the Shahni not told?"

"As you pointed out earlier, the Shahni have their own emergency gathering places," Akim reminded him. "As we of the military haven't been told where those are, so you of the Shahni haven't been told of these."

"We are the rulers," Haafiz retorted. "We're to know *everything* that happens on our world."

"The high command evidently thought otherwise." Akim gestured to the two Djinn still waiting at the shaft. "Ifrit Narayan? Come near and report."

One of the Djinn lowered his hands, jumped easily over the fallen trees, and strode forward. "We are twenty-eight strong, Marid Akim," he said, making the sign of respect first to Akim and then, almost as an afterthought, to Haafiz. "Two other Ifrits, twenty-five Djinn."

Akim expelled his breath in a huffing sigh. "I'd hoped for more."

"As had we," Narayan conceded heavily. "The invasion has cost many lives."

"Indeed," Akim said. "We can hope that the other posts have had better fortune. Equipment status?"

"Thirteen of us were forced to leave our combat suits behind," Narayan said. "They've been replaced from the stores, with thirty-seven suits remaining." He ran his eyes briefly over the six Djinn in the group. "I'll need to check the available sizes, but I believe we'll be able to refit your escort. As to other equipment, we have full stores."

"Good," Akim said. "Once everyone is below, and Shahni Haafiz and Daulo Sammon are settled, I'll want to meet with you and the other Ifrits. An urgent mission has come up that we need to discuss."

"Yes, Marid." Narayan raised his arm and whistled.

From the woods around them a dozen combat-suited Djinn slipped into view. "Escort Shahni Haafiz and the others below," Narayan ordered. "Daulo Sammon is injured, and will need to be carried in his wheelchair."

Three minutes later, after a slightly nerve-wracking descent down a way-too-steep stairway, they were inside the post.

Daulo had expected to find a place built along the same lines as the Sollas subcity, and he was mostly correct. It was smaller than that vast labyrinth, of course, and cramped to the point of being claustrophobic in places. But it had been constructed of the same steel and concrete, with a similar layout of sleeping, meeting, eating, storage, and medical rooms.

His handlers took him directly to the latter facility, where one of the other Djinni launched into what turned out to be a very thorough examination.

An hour later, as the doctor was finally finishing up his tests, Narayan arrived. “Leave us,” he ordered the doctor.

“Yes, Ifrit,” the other said. Setting his instruments aside, he slipped past Narayan and disappeared out the door.

For a moment Narayan eyed Daulo in silence. “I understand from Marid Akim,” he said at last, “that you may be a traitor.”

Daulo sighed, suddenly unbearably tired of this whole thing. “Marid Akim may believe that,” he said. “But he’s wrong.”

“More importantly—and more interestingly—Shahni Haafiz believes it, too,” Narayan continued. “Tell me, what have you done to make an enemy of the Shahni?”

“I don’t know,” Daulo said. “Maybe because I’m a villager, and he doesn’t like villagers. Maybe because I helped defend Sollas, and he thinks that somehow makes the city dwellers look bad. Though I can’t imagine why he would think that.”

“Or maybe because you’re a friend and ally of the Cobra warrior Jasmine Moreau and her son Merrick Moreau.” Narayan’s lip twisted. “Whom Shahni Haafiz tried his best to kill.”

Daulo felt his eyes widen. “He *what*? I hadn’t heard that.”

“We took great pains to keep it quiet,” Narayan said grimly. “But it’s true. Shahni Haafiz stabbed Merrick Moreau while he was attempting to rescue him and Shahni Melcha from the Palace. Apparently, he believed the Cobras were in collusion with the invaders. He probably still does.”

“That’s completely untrue,” Daulo said firmly.

“I know,” Narayan said. “So do all of us who fought alongside them. But Shahni Haafiz has a reputation for stubbornness, as well as a reputation for never admitting an error if he can avoid it. He prefers to cover over his mistakes, either with words or with diversions.”

Daulo sighed. And here he was, Daulo Sammon, a living reminder of the service Jin Moreau had done for Qasama. Not just in this war, but also thirty years ago when she and Daulo helped destroy a quieter but no less insidious threat to their world. "He plans to destroy me, doesn't he?" he murmured. "And my son." Tears abruptly blurred his vision. "What's left of my son."

"It does look that way," Narayan admitted. "For whatever it's worth, I think Advisor Omnathi's willing to hold off judgment until all the facts have been assembled and presented. Still, he's only an advisor, not one of the Shahni. His opinions may or may not carry much weight."

"Against Shahni Haafiz," Daulo murmured, "I suspect they won't."

"No," Narayan said. "But whatever the final outcome, it won't happen for a while. The law states that a trial for the charge of treason must be overseen by one of the Shahni. And since Marid Akim believes your son is a vital part of the charges against you, he's insisted that he be brought here before that trial can begin."

"Insanity," Daulo ground out. "A poor, sick, paralyzed man, and he's going to drag him halfway across Qasama? He can't be serious."

"He's very serious," Narayan said, his voice turning dark. "Eighteen of my Djinn and two of the group Marid Akim brought from Sollas have already set off through the forest toward Milika."

Daulo stared at him. "He sent *twenty* Djinn? How dangerous does he think my son is?"

"I have no idea," Narayan said. "All I know is that he told us he needed as many Djinn as possible for a special mission, then interviewed each of us in private before selecting the twenty." He snorted gently. "Which, considering the questions he was asking, he might as well have done by random calling of names."

"What kind of questions were they?" Daulo asked, intrigued despite his fear and frustration.

"Strange ones," Narayan told him. "More psychological than operational. How we felt about villagers, what we thought of Jasmine and Merrick Moreau and the Cobra Worlds. That sort of thing."

"Finding out which Djinn already share his preconceptions about my guilt."

"Possibly," Narayan conceded. "I myself have no problem with either villagers or the Moreaus, and I was chosen to remain behind." He pursed his lips thoughtfully. "Yet several of those who were sent also fought alongside Merrick Moreau and have the highest respect for him and his mother. One of them, in fact, Domo Paneka, has even suggested that a new Qasaman award of honor be established in their name when the war is over."

"So what qualities *was* Marid Akim looking for?" Daulo asked.

Narayan shook his head. "To be honest, I have no idea."

"No," Daulo murmured. "I just hope . . ." He trailed off, not wanting to even think the thought, let alone state it.

Narayan picked up on it anyway. "He'll be all right," he assured Daulo. "A man is not condemned without cause and proof. Not even in the midst of a war, not even if the charge is treason, not even if the Shahni who sits in judgment has already made up his mind. My Djinn know that. If it's within their power to bring your son here safely, they will."

And as Daulo looked into Narayan's eyes, he knew the other meant it. "Thank you," he said. "I suppose I can accept that Shahni Haafiz wants to execute me, for whatever real or fancied reason he believes. But I wish he'd do it without disturbing my son."

"The ways of the Shahni are often unclear to ordinary men," Narayan said philosophically. "In the meantime, I have work to do, and you need to rest and heal. I'll send the doctor back in to finish his tests, then have you moved to the recovery room."

"Again, thank you," Daulo said.

"No thanks needed," Narayan said. "It's my honor to assist a friend of Merrick Moreau. And don't give up hope. Events will unfold as they will, in their own way and with their own timing."

His considered. "And never forget that the universe always has a few surprises of its own to deliver. Surprises that are always worth the wait."

CHAPTER EIGHT

Merrick's first impression as he came slowly out of the gray fog filling his brain was that he was uncomfortable.

Really uncomfortable. The air around him was cold and dry, his body ached in at least a dozen places, and a half-reflexive attempt to shift position showed his arms, hands, and legs inexplicably incapable of movement.

And then, abruptly, he remembered.

Carefully, keeping his eyes closed, he activated his opticals. He was in a small room, about three meters square, with a single metal door to his right and no windows that he could see from his current angle. The ceiling light was something of a surprise: soft and diffuse instead of the white-hot blaze that Merrick would have expected in an interrogation cell. The ceiling behind the light was also a surprise: textured, reinforced concrete instead of metal. Did that mean he was on the ground instead of inside one of the invaders' warships? Possibly in what was left of the Sollas subcity—what he could see of the room he was in looked very much like the holding cell the Qasamans had had him locked in for a few hours.

Unless he wasn't on Qasama at all. There was no reason why the invaders couldn't have taken him to one of their own worlds instead.

And if they had, not only would he probably never escape, but his remains would probably never even be found.

It was a somber and embarrassing demonstration of his still

shaky thought process that it took him another few seconds of swirling panic to recognize the obvious way to answer that question. And with his nanocomputer's clock circuit showing only a little over three days since his capture, it was almost certain that he was still somewhere on Qasama.

He was listening to his thudding heart as it started to slow down when there was a soft click from the door.

He froze, his brain finally kicking into full gear. Now, when his captors thought he was still unconscious, would be his best chance to make his move.

Only an instant later he realized to his chagrin that he couldn't. The immobility of his arms, hands, and legs wasn't because of fatigue, but because they were encased in heavy cast-like wraps bolted to the frame of the bed on which he was lying. Even if he'd had better leverage, it was unlikely he could break the bolts free. He still had his sonic weapons, but there was no advantage in stunning his visitors if all he could do afterward was lie here while other Trofts strolled over and locked the door on him again.

No, all he could realistically hope for right now was to gain some information. Opening his eyes, he turned his face toward the door as the lock clicked again and the heavy metal panel swung open.

A Troft stepped into the room, his clothing a civilian-type leotard instead of the armored ones the invaders' soldiers typically wore. He had a small case in his hand, similar to the sort that Merrick had seen doctors from the Tlossie demesne carrying. Behind the alien he caught a glimpse of a long corridor, its ceiling bowed and battered in places. As the door closed behind the Troft, there was movement behind him and a second figure stepped into view.

Merrick caught his breath. The second person wasn't another Troft. It was a human female.

She was young, he noted in that first glance, probably a few years younger than he was, with a slim but muscular build and the slightly darkened skin of a lifetime spent out in the sun. Her expression was as odd as the rest of her, blank for the most part, yet edged by a hint of wariness.

And framing that unfamiliar face and strange expression was a swirling halo of the brightest blond hair Merrick had ever seen.

The Troft stepped to the bed, set his case down and opened it, and as he reached inside he jabbered out a stream of cattertalk.

Not a single word of which Merrick understood.

Merrick felt his heart picking up its pace again. Like everyone else in the Cobra Worlds, he'd slogged his way through four years of cattertalk lessons in school. While he'd never really cared for those classes—he'd found Qasaman much easier to learn—he'd nevertheless gotten through them, and had even placed in the top half of his class.

Now, it was as if that whole section of his memory had been wiped clean. Was his brain still not functioning at full capacity yet?

Or had the Trofts done something to him in the seventy-five hours he'd been their prisoner? [Your words, I do not understand them,] he said. At least he still remembered how to speak cattertalk. Assuming he *was* actually speaking it right now. [Your comment, will you repeat it?]

The Troft's radiator membranes fluttered as he held a small sensor over Merrick's chest, his eyes flicking sideways to the young woman. "He said that he is your doctor," the woman said in Anglic. "He asks how you feel."

It took another few seconds for Merrick to find his voice. Her faint accent was like nothing he'd ever heard before. "I'm a little groggy," he told her. "Otherwise, I think I'm all right."

The woman looked at the doctor and rattled off some cattertalk of her own. The words were just as incomprehensible as the Troft's had been. The alien made a sort of clucking noise deep in his throat, pointed a finger at Merrick's torso, and said something back to her. "The doctor says you are wrong," she translated. "You have injuries to your spleen, your right kidney, and your stomach which as yet are only partially healed. You also have several areas of torn muscle and strained tendons."

Which were the same injuries Dr. Krites had listed back in Milika. At least the Troft doctor knew what he was doing.

Or at least he could read a medical scanner. "You only asked how I *felt*," Merrick reminded the woman. "You didn't ask what my actual condition was." He started to gesture, but with his arms pinioned all he could manage was a little wiggling of his fingertips. "So what's the prognosis?"

The woman again spoke to the Troft, and there was another brief exchange between them. "A few days more of treatment and you will be sufficiently healed," she said.

Merrick frowned. "Sufficiently healed for what?"

"For the Games." She waved a hand in a way that reminded him of a stage magician preparing to make his assistant disappear. "Rest now, and heal."

"I'd heal more comfortably if you'd get all these restraints off me," Merrick said, again wiggling his fingers. "Would you ask the doctor if he could please do that?"

The woman's forehead wrinkled slightly, but she launched into more cattertalk. The doctor replied, and the woman shook her head. "The doctor says that you would kill us if he did that. It is not his wish to die that way."

"What if I promise not to kill him?" Merrick offered.

The woman looked him straight in the eye. "*Do* you so promise?"

Merrick held her gaze without flinching. "Yes," he said firmly, and meant it. He wasn't here to kill non-combat personnel.

Besides, between his sonics and his stunner he already had plenty of non-lethal weapons in his arsenal.

But either the doctor already knew that or simply didn't believe him. "No," the woman said. "You will heal as you are, until the Games."

"I'll do my best," Merrick said. It had still been worth a try. "What kind of games are we talking about, exactly?"

"*The* Games," the woman said, as if the word itself was definition enough.

The doctor put his scanner back in the bag and pulled out a hypo. "The doctor will now give you something to help you sleep," the woman continued. "It will also stimulate healing."

"How about if we just stimulate the healing and let me stay awake?" Merrick suggested. "I'm getting really tired of sleeping."

"Without the sleeping there cannot be the healing." Some of the severity seemed to slip from the woman's face. "Have no fear, Merrick Moreau Broom," she added in a marginally kinder tone. "We have all felt this medicine. It will not harm you."

"Thank you," Merrick said. His words struck him as slightly stupid sounding, but on the spur of the moment he couldn't come up with anything better. "I see you know my name," he said, wincing as the doctor slipped the hypo into his arm above the shackle and injected the contents. "May I ask yours?"

"My name is not for strangers to know," the woman said. "But among the common I am known as Anya Winghunter."

"Anya Winghunter," Merrick repeated, nodding his head. It sure sounded like a name to him. There must be some subtlety here that he was missing. "Will I see you again?"

"If the doctor so chooses," she said as the Troft returned the hypo to its place and closed the bag. "I come and go at his pleasure."

"Ah," Merrick said. Was the room starting to go foggy again? "You're his assistant?"

She shook her head. "I am his slave."

Merrick's last view before the room faded into darkness was that of Anya's face framed by her impossibly blond hair.

His last thought before that darkness was *what the hell*?

When he again awoke, his nanocomputer indicated that he'd slept for another seven hours. His head was aching, possibly with dehydration, and his stomach was rumbling with the reminder that that he hadn't eaten since Milika, over three days ago.

It was another handful of seconds before he noticed that the shackles that had been on his arms and legs were gone.

He sat up carefully, mindful of his low blood sugar, wondering where the hook was for this particular gambit. But no lasers blazed at him, no antipersonnel explosives shattered the silence, and there were no hungry predators waiting on the floor beneath his table in hopes of a quick snack.

Maybe that would come later. For now, he could focus on his hunger, his imprisonment, and this new mystery of why his captors apparently no longer feared him enough to nail him to the bed.

And, swirling through all of it, the puzzle that was Anya Winghunter.

She wasn't Qasaman, not with that hair. He'd seen Qasamans with hair as light as a dark reddish brown, but the vast majority of the people he'd met here had black or very dark brown hair. The official records of the Cobra Worlds' other incursions onto Qasama backed up that assessment. She wasn't from the Worlds, either, not with that accent.

Had someone hauled her all the way across the Troft Assemblage from the Dominion of Man? Or had the Trofts found another lost human colony somewhere closer, another colony like Qasama itself?

And what the *hell* was this slave thing?

The Assemblage, he knew, was in fact little more than a loose confederation of three- to five-system demesnes, most of which were in continual low-level and mostly polite conflict with each other, whether for influence, real estate, or trade advantage. The various demesnes had different customs, different goals and viewpoints and, as the Troft doctor had shown a few hours ago, occasionally some interesting and nearly incomprehensible dialects.

But never had he heard any hint that some Troft demesne kept slaves. Especially *human* slaves.

Could it all be a lie? Had they taken some woman, from wherever, tricked her up to look exotic and vulnerable, and dropped her in front of him to try to mess with his emotions? The Trofts a hundred years ago had tried that gambit with Jonny Moreau, he remembered, sending a woman into his cell in hopes that her presence and helplessness would induce him to help her escape and thereby reveal his abilities under controlled conditions and close observation.

If that was the plan, they were going to be sorely disappointed. Now that Merrick was on to them, he knew better than to fall for the trick.

He had just about concluded that the only way he was going to get food was to pound on the door and demand it when the lock again gave its distinctive double click. Getting a grip on the edge of the bed, ready to move in any direction he might need to go, Merrick braced himself. The door swung open.

To reveal Anya standing in the doorway, a covered tray in her hands. "I was told to bring you food," she said.

"Finally," Merrick said, glancing at the slot in the bottom of the door. There was no reason why she couldn't just have taken off the tray's cover and slid it in to him. Unless there was some reason she thought she should deliver it personally. "Thank you."

But instead of coming in, the woman just stood there. Just waiting.

Merrick frowned. Was he supposed to go over there and take the tray from her? Were the Trofts hoping that luring him that close to an open door would tempt him into an escape attempt that they could watch?

And then, belatedly, he got it. *Slave*... "Come in," he invited. "Just put the tray down here on the bed."

Silently, she crossed the cell and set the tray down where he'd indicated. Merrick watched her face closely, but he could see no hint of resentment at having just been ordered around like a child. In fact, she seemed almost relieved that he hadn't left her standing there without telling her what to do.

Maybe she really *was* a slave.

Was that what this invasion of Qasama and the Cobra Worlds was all about? Could all this death and destruction be because some group of Troft demesnes had developed a taste for human slaves and was looking to expand their stock?

If so, they'd badly miscalculated. Merrick had seen how hard the Qasamans fought to keep from being subjugated. They would fight even harder to keep from becoming slaves. Needless to say, so would the Cobra Worlds.

"Will there be anything more?" Anya asked, straightening up and looking emotionlessly at him.

"No, I think that will do it," Merrick said, forcing back a sudden flush of anger at whoever had done this to her. "Thank you."

A brief hint of something flickered across her face. Maybe she wasn't used to being thanked for her service. But she merely nodded, turned, and strode out of the room. "You want to stay and eat with me?" Merrick called impulsively after her.

She turned back, the same odd look briefly crossing her face. "I cannot," she said. "I must return to my master."

She was still facing him when some unseen warden swung the door shut in front of her.

For a few seconds Merrick frowned in puzzlement at the closed door. First a doctor's assistant, then a waitress. On the surface, it looked like whoever was pulling her strings was trying to create opportunities for the slave and the prisoner to interact.

But in that case, shouldn't the hidden puppet master have had her jump at Merrick's invitation to join him for a snack, thereby giving them even more time together? Either the Trofts were slow on the draw, or else Merrick was reading this whole thing completely wrong.

Which was, admittedly, the more likely scenario. Who really knew how Troft minds worked, anyway?

His stomach gave a long growl. "Right," Merrick muttered. "First things first." Turning to the tray, he lifted the cover and set it aside.

He wasn't really sure what he'd been expecting for his first meal as a Troft prisoner. But whatever that unformed anticipation was, this definitely wasn't it. There were three items on the oval plate: an angled piece of bone-in meat that might have been part of some creature's leg or wing, a greenish-yellow vegetable paste with red and off-white specks floating in it, and a small, lumpy loaf of bread shaped rather like a seashell.

Most of Merrick's brief time on Qasama had been spent in Sollas, eating ration bars or light and quickly prepared wartime meals. But he'd also had a slightly more leisurely meal at the Sammon residence in Milika, which had given him a general idea of what Qasaman cuisine was like. More importantly, he'd passed among the mix of cooking aromas in both Milika and Sollas, which had offered his self-trained cook's nose a range of the locals' cooking spices and condiments.

The aromas rising from his tray smelled nothing like any of those spices. And it was for certain that he'd never seen or smelled anything remotely like this with even the most exotic Cobra Worlds fare.

Either the Trofts were putting way more effort into this operation than anyone had any business doing, or else Merrick had been right the first time about Anya being from some distant and unknown world.

And if the meal sitting in front of him was from that same world, and if it contained spices or bacteria that didn't work and play well with his digestive system, this could be a very unpleasant evening.

The survival unit at the Cobra Academy had included a step-by-step procedure for finding non-poisonous plants in unfamiliar territory. But given that the Trofts obviously thought he would be able to handle this meal—and since they could poison him any time they wanted—it didn't seem worth the effort to run the checklist.

The Trofts hadn't provided any flatware with the meal, perhaps forgetting that keeping potential weapons away from a Cobra was wasted effort. The first challenge, therefore, was figuring out how to eat the meal while still maintaining a modicum of etiquette. After some trial and error he settled on the technique of tearing off chunks of the meat, picnic style, and using pieces of bread to scoop up the vegetable paste.

The blend of tastes was good and definitely exotic, reminiscent of various dishes Merrick had tried elsewhere but with enough of a twist to underscore the meal's alien origin. The effect on his digestive system was somewhat less positive, and he spent the next couple of hours lying on his bed listening to rumbles from his stomach and wondering if perhaps he should have gone through the food-testing procedure after all.

But nothing came back up, and his system eventually settled down. Merrick stayed awake for another two hours, just to be sure, before finally and wearily settling down for the night.

He'd been asleep for three and a half hours when he woke to stealthy sounds and the touch of surreptitious fingers on his forearms and shins. Before he could activate his opticals, he felt something close around his left forearm and heard the *snick* of a locking mechanism. The Trofts had apparently decided to put his restraints back on.

Merrick felt a snarl rising in his throat. Like hell they were.

With a jerk, he sat upright, simultaneously snapping open his eyes. The Troft who had been gently working his right arm toward its restraint made a desperate grab for the limb, missed, and gave an agonized grunt as Merrick hit him with a hard backhand punch across the helmet. The two Trofts at Merrick's feet likewise made desperate attempts to grab his legs. One of them flew backward as Merrick kicked him, the other jumped back before he could be hit. The latter grabbed for a belted laser—

And collapsed to the floor as a burst from Merrick's sonic slammed into him. The backwash bounced off the wall and echoed across Merrick, and he had a brief battle of his own for equilibrium as he turned to the two guards flanking the open door. Both were in motion, grabbing at their weapons as they sidled away from each other in an attempt to avoid a quick one-two attack.

Merrick tried to twist the sonic in his torso toward them, but with his left arm pinioned he couldn't turn far enough in that direction. Instead, he activated the capacitor connected to his right fingertip laser, firing a quick laser burst to ionize the air between him and the first guard and then sending a low-level jolt of current along the pathway. The Troft toppled unconscious to the floor just as his weapon cleared its holster, and Merrick's second stun blast took down the second Troft before he could bring his laser up into firing position. As the second guard hit the floor Merrick turned back to the restraint on his left forearm and fired a full-power fingertip laser burst at the clamps, blasting them into sprays of half-molten metal. He twisted his arm free, swung his legs around, and leaped off the bed onto the floor.

And as he finally paused from his reflexive attack in order to take stock of his situation, the possibilities of the open door and the deserted corridor beyond it abruptly flooded in on him.

This was probably the best chance he would ever have to escape.

But even as he lunged toward the door he discovered that he'd already missed his window of opportunity. From three different doorways down the corridor a Troft soldier leaned out into view, his helmet turned toward Merrick, his laser coming up to aim.

Cursing under his breath, Merrick ducked to the side of the door, using his last half-second of view to flick a target lock onto each of the weapons trained at him. So much for an easy exit. Now, he'd have to do it the hard way. He leaned out, keying his fingertip lasers.

Only to discover that all three Trofts had disappeared.

He had just enough time to frown in confusion when three more aliens poked their heads and weapons through an entirely different set of doorways. Quickly, Merrick cancelled his original lock and targeted this new group of weapons.

Only to have the Trofts again duck back through their doorways before he could fire. As they vanished, they were replaced by another trio, this group including one of the original three soldiers.

And Merrick finally got it. The target-lock system enabled his nanocomputer to aim and fire sequentially with a speed and accuracy no human gunner could ever hope to achieve. But it presupposed that all the targets in the sequence were still within firing range. If any one of them was no longer visible or accessible, the lock would simply pause and wait for it to reappear.

Which meant that by popping new targets in and out at random, the Trofts had effectively eliminated that particular tool from Merrick's arsenal. If he wanted to take out those soldiers or their weapons, he was going to have to do it without his nanocomputer's help.

Only it was already too late for that, he realized with a sinking heart. Whatever momentum and initiative his surprise attack had gained for him was now gone, and his captors' countermove was already up and running. Trying to escape now would do nothing but get him and a whole bunch of Trofts killed.

[Merrick Moreau Broom, I would have words with him,] an amplified Troft voice called from somewhere down the corridor.

Merrick sighed. It was over, all right. [Merrick Moreau Broom, he hears you,] he called back.

[Your captivity, you cannot end it this way,] the disembodied voice said. [Your cell, you will remain in it. Punishment for your actions, it will be not be given to you.]

Merrick pursed his lips. He already knew that his attempt had failed. But maybe the Trofts didn't. In that case, maybe he could still wangle a concession or two out of them. [The restraints, I do not want them,] he called. [Your pledge to not impose them on me, I seek it.]

There was a short silence. [Your pledge to not attempt escape, I seek it in return.]

Merrick felt his stomach tighten around his alien meal. His life literally depended on him finding a way to eventually get out of here. There was no way he could give the Troft that kind of promise.

Unless he did so knowing full well that he was lying.

Only he couldn't. Not just because it was unethical, but because a lie like that could come back to haunt him in a big and devastating way. Unless he could guarantee that his next escape attempt was successful, breaking his word would not only bring harsh reprisals but would forever eliminate any chance of making future deals with his captors.

He hunched his shoulders, feeling a brief ache from one of his still tender muscle groups. On the other hand, if he was clever, maybe he could have this both ways. [My pledge not to attempt escape until the Games, I give it,] he offered.

There was another pause. [Your pledge, I accept it,] the Troft said. [The restraints, until then they will not be used. Soldiers: the restraints, you will remove them from the prisoner's cell.]

Merrick eased an eye around the door jamb. Down the corridor, at least twenty armored Trofts had emerged from doorways, their lasers at the ready, while another smaller group of unarmed aliens marched in single file down the center of the hallway toward Merrick's cell. Merrick stepped away from the door, moving to the side of the room and placing his back against the wall. He kept his hands at his sides, but made sure his thumbs were resting on the fingertip laser triggers.

The caution proved unnecessary. In complete silence the Trofts unfastened the restraints from the bed and tucked them under their arms. Then they collected their injured and unconscious comrades, and the whole bunch retreated through the doorway.

And as the last Troft left the cell, Anya walked in. "What are *you* doing here?" Merrick asked, frowning.

"I brought you this," she said, holding out a small vial containing a light brown liquid. "It will aid in your healing process."

"Thanks, but the doctor already gave me stuff for that," Merrick reminded her.

"This will help more," she said. "Also, I have been sent to stay with you."

"Oh, no," Merrick said firmly, belatedly noticing the small bag slung over her shoulder and the bedroll bandoleered across her back. "No, no. This place is barely big enough—" He raised his voice. "This place is barely big enough for me," he shouted out into the corridor as he returned to the doorway. [This woman, she cannot—]

He broke off as the door slammed shut in his face.

For a moment he glared at the dull metal, wondering briefly how long it would take to slag the lock with his antiarmor laser.

Unfortunately, there was no point in trying. If he wrecked this cell, they'd just find somewhere else to move him.

Or to move *them*.

Slowly, he turned around. Anya was standing quietly by the bed, apparently waiting for orders. "So what now?" Merrick asked, for lack of anything better to say.

"You should take a few drops of the medicine," she said, again holding up the vial. "It will aid in—"

"In the healing process," Merrick cut her off. "Yes, I remember. I meant after that."

"I have been sent to stay here," Anya repeated. "I have been given to you, to serve you however you choose."

The obvious method by which a young woman could serve a young man flashed into Merrick's mind. Ruthlessly, he forced it back, feeling an unpleasant rush of heat in his cheeks. Getting involved in the middle of a war with someone—*anyone*—would be bad enough. But the absolute worst thing he could do would be to let himself get entangled with someone who was under Troft control. The minute he let that happen, they would have a lever they could use against him however they chose.

"Not much call for servants in a prison cell," he told her, trying to keep his voice light. "I could use a snack, though. Any chance they'll let you out to go get me something?"

"I will ask." Lowering her bag to the floor, she walked toward him. He stepped to the side out of her way and watched as she rapped lightly on the door. She called out, again using the strange cattertalk dialect she'd used earlier. This time, though, Merrick was able to pick out the words *master* and *food*. Maybe a little practice was all he needed to learn how to understand it.

There was no response to her question. She knocked twice more, repeating the message each time, and then turned to Merrick. "They do not seem willing to grant your request," she said.

"I'm not surprised," Merrick said. Bracing himself, he stepped up to her and held out his hand. "Your bedroll, please."

Silently, she slid it off her shoulder and handed it to him. "You can have the bed," he told her, moving to the narrow space at the foot of the bed and fumbling with the bedroll's fasteners. Like Anya herself, the clasps weren't quite like anything he'd ever seen before. "I'll sleep over here."

"Please," she said, crossing to him and taking the bedroll back. With three casually deft flicks of her fingers she undid the fasteners and spread the bedroll on the floor. A small hand pump was fastened to one side, and he watched in fascination as she gave it a few quick squeezes, inflating the roll into something that looked at least marginally comfortable.

And then, before he could do or say anything, she lowered herself onto the roll, stretching out across it. "Is there anything more you wish before I sleep?" she asked, looking up at him.

"No, no," Merrick said, pointing to the bed. "You sleep *there*. *I* sleep here."

Anya didn't move. "Is there anything more you wish from me?"

"Anya—"

"That is a master's bed," she said quietly. "This is a slave's bed. I will sleep here."

Merrick took a deep breath. He could argue with her, he knew. Better yet, he could simply order her to the more comfortable bed. He was the master, after all. He could do that.

But even if she obeyed, she would undoubtedly feel guilty about it the rest of the night. That would probably keep her awake, which would pretty well negate the whole point of giving her the more comfortable bed in the first place.

Worse, making any kind of self-sacrifice for her, even one this small, might be exactly what his captors were banking on. Even so mild an emotional interaction would start him on the road he'd already decided he couldn't take.

"Fine," he said shortly. Turning his back on her, he crossed over to the bed. "Maybe by morning they'll let you get me some food."

"I will ask when I awaken," she promised. "Will you take the medicine now?"

"Maybe tomorrow," he said. "I've had about enough Troft generosity for one day."

"As you wish." If she was annoyed at his refusal or his sarcastic tone, she gave no indication of it. "Sleep well, and call if you need anything."

Suppressing a sigh, Merrick lay down on the bed, wishing he could turn off the overhead light. Wishing even more that he could shut out the sound of her breathing.

It was, he suspected, going to be a very long night.

CHAPTER NINE

According to the tentative schedule Jody had seen the night before, the downed Troft warship had been due to be raised that morning. But as she and Geoff headed across Stronghold, she could see that the damaged ship was still lying across the broken wall.

"Uh-oh," Geoff muttered. "That doesn't look good."

"They're probably just behind schedule," Jody said. "I can't imagine that using Troft slave labor is the most efficient way to run a business."

"I was talking about that," Geoff said, pointing toward the wall ten meters away from the bow of the downed ship. "Isn't that Nissa Gendreves talking to Harli?"

Jody made a face. Two weeks ago, back on Aventine, Nissa Gendreves had been a lowly secondary assistant to Governor-General Chintawa, a career bureaucrat moving her slow but steady way up the Cobra Worlds' political ladder.

But all that had changed with the Troft invasion. Jody's brother Lorne had been tasked with the job of getting Senior Governor Tomo Treakness and his two companions clear of the Trofts, out of Capitalia, and off Aventine. At the height of their mad scramble to take refuge aboard the Tloss demesne heir ship where their more-or-less ally Warrior was waiting for them, a badly injured Treakness had given Nissa full authority of negotiation and treaty for the beleaguered Cobra Worlds.

Unfortunately, the woman was nowhere near ready to handle that kind of power. She'd quickly shown herself to be just another pre-machined and pre-formed cog from Capitalia's political machinery, unable to grasp the desperate new reality the Cobra Worlds faced and incapable of thinking or functioning outside the lines.

So Jody's father had been forced to do that offline thinking for her. His reward for that initiative had been Nissa's furious promise that he would one day stand trial for treason, along with his entire family and probably most of the Caelian government.

Nissa had kept mostly to herself for the past thirteen days, ever since Jody's parents and brother had headed for Qasama with Dr. Croi and the Isis equipment. She'd stayed holed up in the apartment Uy had assigned her—plotting or sulking, Jody didn't know which—coming out only for food and the occasional glowering walking tour of the war-torn city. Whatever it was that had lured her out into the fresh air today and over to the wrecked Troft ship, Jody was pretty sure she wasn't going to like it.

"Maybe we should take a little walk around the block," Geoff suggested. "Let the air clear out a little."

Jody squared her shoulders. If Nissa was hoping that Jody and the others would avoid her out of fear or anything else, the girl was sadly mistaken.

Besides, if there was one thing Jody's parents had taught her it was to hold loosely to any preconceptions, particularly preconceptions backed up by limited numbers of data points. Maybe instead of brooding, Nissa had spent some of her self-imposed exile thinking. "People can change," she reminded Geoff. "Maybe Nissa's thought it through and is ready to see things our way."

"Right," Geoff growled. "That exactly what *I'd* expect from a mindless government lock-stepper."

"She deserves the benefit of the doubt," Jody said firmly. "Anyway, what have you got to worry about? You've charmed the socks off dozens of reluctant investors. You can certainly stand around and smile nicely enough to keep yourself off Nissa's hit list."

"It's not her hit list I'm worried about," Geoff said sourly. "I'm more worried about Harli. If whatever they're arguing about escalates past words, I don't want to be in the line of fire when he offers to send her into orbit."

"Now you're just being silly," Jody chided. Though now that they were closer and Harli's expression was easier to read, she saw that Geoff's fears might not be all that exaggerated. "Anyway, Harli's way more accurate than that. Just stay behind me and you'll be fine."

Geoff grunted. "Yeah."

The argument had clearly been going back and forth, but it was Nissa who was the one speaking when Jody and Geoff came into earshot. "—can't wait any longer," she said, her tone the exact mixture of bombastic and whiny that always drove Jody crazy. "What if that courier ship didn't have to go all the way to Qasama to get help? What if they have reserves sitting somewhere out in space where they can jump anywhere quickly? In that case, they could be here any time."

"Why would they waste the resources to plant a force out in the middle of nowhere?" Harli asked, his expression stiff but his voice still well back from the breaking point. Maybe his parents had taught him about offering the benefit of the doubt, too. "It makes no sense."

"It's called a flying squad," Nissa said. "That's a unit that can move quickly to—"

"Yes, I know what it is," Harli interrupted. "My question is why the Trofts would bother setting up a flying squad that might need to come to Caelian."

"Because—" Nissa broke off, glowering at Jody and Geoff as they came up. "Aren't you two supposed to be working on something?"

"We are," Jody said coolly. "What seems to be the trouble?"

"It's a policy issue," Nissa said. "Not really any of your business."

"Ms. Gendreves is trying to convince me to move all the Troft prisoners out of Stronghold," Harli said. "What she apparently fails to grasp is that I already agree with her. The problem is where to put them where they won't be a threat to us *and* won't just end up as gigger snacks."

"I've given you three alternatives," Nissa said stiffly.

"Right—Essbend, Aerie, or the downed ship," Harli countered. "And if any of those was actually viable, I'd be happy to consider it."

"They're *all* viable," Nissa insisted. "You can put restraints on the prisoners or else drug them while you fly them to one of the two villages—that lets you transport at least four per aircar. Pull in all twenty aircars you have on Caelian, and you can do it in two and a half trips."

"And then we just clear out whatever town you want to put

them in?" Harli countered. "Move all the rightful residents out and let the Trofts do whatever they want with people's homes and property? Not a chance."

"Then put them in there," Nissa said, jabbing a finger toward the downed warship. "I've already told you how you can eliminate any possibility that they'll find something to use against us."

"Really?" Jody asked, intrigued in spite of herself. There'd been endless discussions and arguments across Stronghold over the past few days on how they could assure that any prisoners locked inside the warships couldn't access hidden weapons or equipment. "How?"

"Basically, by blowing it up," Harli growled. "No, seriously. She wants us to take one of the remaining missiles off the wing, set up the warhead on the command deck, and let it blow. Then we move the prisoners into an essentially empty shell."

"And again I ask, what's wrong with that?" Nissa challenged. "That much hullmetal should be strong enough to contain the blast."

"The key word being *should*," Harli said. "We don't know that even a completely intact hull will contain that kind of blast. We also don't know if this particular hull is, in fact, intact. There could be all kinds of damage to the plates, seams, or supports that we don't have the equipment to detect."

"Which is why you first move the ship away from Stronghold," Nissa said.

"Which we may not be able to do," Harli snapped, his voice starting to teeter on the edge.

"Wait a minute," Jody said, frowning. "You can't move the ship? I thought you had all the grav lifts in place and calibrated last night."

"The problem isn't the grav lifts," Harli said. "It's the question of what we do once the downed ship isn't filling in most of the gap where the wall used to be."

"I thought the plan was to raise it up off its side and then just move it back into the gap," Geoff said.

"It was," Harli said heavily. "Problem is, we've taken another look at how we've attached the grav lifts, and we're not sure anymore that we'll be able to move the ship once it's upright. There's apparently a whole raft of angle and lift-vector calculations no one bothered to do."

Jody winced. The broken wall already had an open three-meter gap at either end of the downed ship, which had to be guarded around the clock against gigger and screech tiger incursions. If those smaller gaps suddenly became a single, huge, seventy-meter opening, there would be no way to keep the predators out.

"What about the other ship?" Geoff asked, gesturing to the warship looming over the downed one. "Could that one be moved into the gap once the damaged one's out of the way?"

"That's currently our Plan B," Harli said. "Whether we can move it or not will depend on whether there'll be room to lower it into place once the other one is standing upright again. We're doing some calculations on that one, too."

"Can't we just try it?" Jody suggested. "If it doesn't work, you can always lower the wrecked ship back into place, can't you?"

"In theory, yes," Harli said. "But again, it boils down to the angles we've set the grav lifts at. They can lift it all right, but they may or may not be able to lower it again, at least not in a controlled fashion."

"How about this?" Nissa said, her forehead wrinkled in thought. "We take the grav lifts off the standing ship and put them in the correct lower-hull positions on the wrecked one. We use the first set to raise it up off the ground, then use the second set to move it back into the gap in the wall."

"That's not bad," Jody said, her opinion of Nissa going up a notch. Maybe she *had* spent some of her self-imposed isolation thinking. "That might be the answer."

"It might," Harli agreed, a bit grudgingly. "Problem is, I don't think we've got the time and resources to pull it off. Especially since that would leave the upright ship sitting there with no way to move it."

"Can't we put the grav lifts back after we've lifted and moved the first ship?" Jody asked.

"Again, not in the time we've got," Harli said. "The reinforcements could be here in as little as eight days." He grimaced. "And our available labor force isn't exactly enthusiastic about working fast."

"So let's try thinking outside the lines," Geoff suggested, a sudden, cautious excitement in his voice. "What exactly do we need the wall for, anyway?"

Harli snorted. "I don't have time for this," he growled, starting to turn around.

"No, no, I mean it," Geoff said, grabbing his arm. "Walk with me here. We need the wall mainly to keep out the organics and all the rest of the unpleasant ecology that comes rushing in after them. Right?"

Jody snapped her fingers as she finally figured out where he was going. "The Qasamans' combat suits," she said. "We already know that current flowing through the stiffeners and servos repels the organics, or at least prevents them from attaching. If we can build a curtain across the gap that can do that, it should keep out everything but the larger predators."

"Not much comfort to the citizens who end up being eaten," Nissa muttered.

"Actually, if the smaller animals stay away, most of the predators should, too," Harli said thoughtfully. "The few who get curious enough to come in should be easy enough to deal with. Problem is, unless those suits are a hell of a lot stretchier than they look, they're not going to begin to fill the gap."

"Right, but we don't need the combat suits per se," Geoff said. "We just need the electric fields they generate. If we can duplicate those in or around some other material, we should be able to pull it off. It's at least worth a try."

Harli turned toward the crushed wall, and for a moment gazed at it in silence. Then, abruptly, he turned back and nodded. "What do you need?" he asked.

"Freylan's running the final readings on the electric field right now," Geoff said. "Once he's done—"

"*Freylan's* doing the readings?" Harli said, frowning. "I thought he was still in the hospital."

"He was," Jody said. "He checked himself out early this morning."

"Said there was no way he was going to just sit around and listen to his ribs mend when there was work to be done," Geoff told him. "Anyway, once he's got the final specs, it should be easy to program a generator to duplicate the field."

"So you'll need a generator," Harli said, nodding. "What else?"

"Access to everything Stronghold's got in the way of electronics supplies," Geoff said. "Depending on what we end up needing, we might have to disassemble some of your entertainment or computer systems."

"We'll also need samples of cloth to try out," Jody said. "Drapes, extra clothing—anything we can attach the electronics to that won't block the electric fields."

"And once we figure out which material works best, we'll need probably every bit of it you've got," Geoff said. "In Stronghold, and possibly everywhere else on the planet."

"Plus you'll need a lot of hands to put it all together," Harli concluded.

Jody winced. Between the work on the warship, the general cleanup, and keeping everyone fed and safe, Stronghold's resources and personnel were already stretched dangerously thin. "Unfortunately, yes," she admitted. "I'm sorry."

"Don't worry about it," Harli assured her. "There are plenty of people out there sitting around loafing. A little real work will do them good. I'll have the orders cut by the time you know what you need." Abruptly, he held up his hand. "Quiet a minute." He turned around toward the downed warship.

Jody frowned, trying to figure out what he was looking at. A movement above the crowd of Trofts caught her eye: one of the other Cobras—Popescu, she tentatively identified him—was standing beside the ship's upper stern weapons wing, gesturing toward Harli, his mouth moving. Jody strained her ears, but without Cobra audio enhancements she couldn't tell what he was saying.

But Harli could. And it was clear he didn't like what he was hearing. "You two get back to work," he told Jody and Geoff. His eyes flicked to Nissa. "If you really want to make yourself useful, you can go with them."

Nissa's eyes narrowed— "We could certainly use your help," Geoff seconded quickly. "Freylan's basically glued to his chair right now, with his ribs and all. He could use someone to get equipment and lift things for him."

Nissa's eyes flicked to Jody. "Seems to me you've got plenty of help already."

"We will later," Geoff assured her. "Right now, Jody needs to go talk to Rashida Vil."

Nissa frowned. "The Qasaman woman?"

"Yes, that's what I came out here to ask you," Jody improvised, turning to Harli. She hadn't actually planned on talking to Rashida until later today after they'd finished their work on the combat suits. But Geoff was clearly angling to keep her and Nissa apart for a while, and she could easily readjust that part of her tentative schedule. "Any idea where she is?"

"She's over in the other warship," Harli said, eyeing Jody thoughtfully. "Come on—I need to head over there anyway. I'll walk you through the crowd." He flicked a finger at Geoff. "And *you* go get busy."

He took Jody's arm and led the way toward the broken wall and the Trofts swarming around it. "Well, *that* was interesting," he murmured as they walked. "I wouldn't have thought Gendreves was his type."

"I'm sure it's nothing like that," Jody assured him. "Geoff's always been good at politics and basic old-fashioned charm—it's how we got the funding to come to Caelian in the first place. I think he's decided she's a challenge he can't pass up."

"Maybe." Harli looked sideways at her. "Next question: how did you know I was going to ask you to talk to Ms. Vil?"

"I didn't," Jody said, frowning at him. "I just wanted to check in with her and see how she's doing. What did you want me to talk to her about?"

Harli made a face. "I wish I knew. There's just something . . . she's polite and all, and she takes orders just fine. But there's something going on behind those eyes I can't figure out. I figure since you're the closest thing she's got to a friend here, maybe you could get it out of her."

"Not sure I qualify as a friend, exactly," Jody warned. "But I'll be happy to give it a try."

"Thanks." Harli gestured ahead. "I need to talk to Popescu for a second. If you want, I can get one of the others to walk you the rest of the way."

"That's all right," Jody said. "I'd like to hear what he has to say, too."

Harli grunted. "Fine," he said. "But you aren't going to like it."

He was right.

"I found it wedged behind the number eight grav lift," Popescu said, showing Harli a small, gleaming wrench. "Right where we ran the connections to the ship's power system."

"Exactly where you'd put something metal if you wanted to short the whole thing out," Harli said.

"Yeah, pretty much," Popescu growled. "Sorry, Harli. Someone really dropped the ball on this one."

"Not your fault," Harli said, peering up at the ship. "You never had nearly enough men to ride herd on a work gang this big."

"Yeah, excuses always look so good on your gravestone," Popescu said sourly. "Anyway, I've got Brady pulling together a team to start rechecking everything."

"Good," Harli said. "Any guess as to how soon they'll be done?"

"Depends on how many men he can pull away from other duties," Popescu said. "No earlier than this afternoon, though. Maybe not until tomorrow."

"Damn," Harli said. "Well, if it's tomorrow, it's tomorrow. Just make sure to remind Brady that speed is good, but accuracy is better."

"Be nice if we could have both, though," Popescu reminded him. "What would you think about pulling the Cobras off outrim guard duty to help out? If the Trofts are going to play games, there's no reason we should knock ourselves out protecting them from giggers and screech tigers."

"Good point," Harli said. "You can take a few, but you need to leave at least half the current number of guards out there." He gestured to Jody. "You know the Tlossies better than I do. Does it make sense to keep the prisoners safe—you know, holding onto the moral high ground, and all that—if we want to get them in as allies?"

"Absolutely," Jody assured him. "The Tlossies put a high premium on playing by the rules."

"Yeah, fine," Popescu said. "But high moral ground isn't much use if all it does is open you to more enemy fire."

"Don't worry, I'm also going to have a little chat with Captain Eubujak," Harli assured him grimly. "I'm going to tell him that if we find any more sabotage from his troops I might just take Ms. Gendreves up on her suggestion to set off a warhead inside the downed ship." He glowered at the Trofts working at the edges of the wall. "And I might not wait until after the explosion to move him and his troops inside."

Jody felt her eyes widen. "You wouldn't."

"No, but Eubujak doesn't know that," Harli said. "Popescu, go help Brady form his crew and get to work. As soon as I've get Jody to the other ship, I'll come back and give you a hand."

They reached the second Troft warship without further incident. The Cobra guard passed them through, and Harli led Jody to the top deck. Rashida was right where Jody had expected to find her: seated at the helm and studying the angled control board.

"Ms. Vil," Harli greeted her as he and Jody walked past two small groups of techs testing the circuits in some of the other boards. "How are things going?"

"They go well," Rashida said, looking up at them.

Only they weren't going well, Jody realized as she studied the other woman's face. There was a tension behind Rashida's eyes, a tautness at odds with her confident words.

Harli was right. Something was wrong.

"Good," Harli said, and Jody could hear the false cheerfulness in his voice, as well. "I'll leave you two alone, then." He glanced at the techs, as if only then realizing how relative solitude was right now. "Just let the guard downstairs know when you want to leave, Jody, and he'll arrange an escort."

"Thank you," Jody said. "Good hunting."

Harli nodded to her, then to Rashida, then turned and strode out of the room.

"What is he hunting?" Rashida asked.

"Sabotage," Jody said, pulling up a chair and sitting down. "One of the Trofts working on the downed ship jammed a wrench where it would short out the power conduits. So now they have to check over everything before they can try to move it."

"Yes, I see," Rashida said, lowering her eyes back to the control panel in front of her. "How much will that put them behind schedule?"

"Don't know for sure," Jody said. "Several hours at least. Maybe a day or more if they find more sabotage."

"Which will then delay the moving of this ship?" Rashida asked.

"I'd say so, yes," Jody said, studying the woman's profile. "Is that a good thing, or a bad thing?"

A muscle in Rashida's cheek twitched. "Does it need to be either?" she countered evasively.

"No, but it usually is," Jody said, lowering her voice. "What's wrong, Rashida?"

Rashida's throat worked. "I . . ." Her eyes flicked to the side. "I can't tell you. Not here. Not now."

Jody felt a sudden stirring of anger. "Is someone bothering you?" she asked softly. "One of these men?"

"No, not at all," Rashida said quickly. "It's . . . there's trouble. I should have spoken of it sooner, but . . ." She trailed off.

Jody chewed at her lip. The techs working on the other side

of the room were theoretically out of earshot, especially if Jody and Rashida kept their voices low.

But there was at least one Cobra in the group, and maybe more who Jody didn't know, and distance didn't mean much where Cobra audios were involved.

Still, there was distance, and then there was *distance*. "Come on," Jody said, standing up and offering the other woman her hand. "Let's take a walk."

Rashida shook her head. "I was told to stay here."

"That's okay," Jody said, still holding out her hand. "I'll take responsibility."

Rashida seemed to draw back. "You can do that?"

Jody felt her lip twitch. For a moment she'd almost forgotten how male-dominated the Qasaman culture was.

And it suddenly occurred to her that the Caelian society Rashida was experiencing probably looked a lot like the one she'd left at home. Of course, that was really only because Governor Uy had declared the planet to be on a war footing, which meant that the Cobras—all of whom were men—were basically running everything.

But Rashida wouldn't know that. And whatever her world's rules were about women speaking out or approaching superiors with questions or problems, that system was what she was working under right now. "Of course," she said, trying to keep her voice light. "Come on. A little fresh air will do you good."

Rashida hesitated another moment. Then, almost gingerly, she got to her feet. "All right," she said, still sounding uncertain.

"Wait a second," the Cobra spoke up, frowning at them. "Maybe you missed it, but the fresh air down there is contaminated with Trofts."

"That's okay," Jody assured him. "That's not the direction we're going."

Two minutes later, she pushed open the ship's rear dorsal hatch and climbed up the narrow stairway onto the hull crest. "Here we are," she said cheerfully, offering Rashida a hand up. "Fresh air, no predators, and no Trofts. And a pretty nice view."

"Yes," Rashida said coming gingerly up onto the hull crest. "It's . . . a little high, though."

"You're afraid of heights?" Jody asked, frowning. "But you're a pilot."

"I don't mind heights when I'm encased in a flying vehicle,"

Rashida said. "Here, there's a chance I might fall." She craned her neck gingerly. "And it's a *very* long way down."

"That it is," Jody agreed, peering at the Trofts, the humans, and the town thirty meters below them. "So tell me what the problem is."

Rashida hesitated. "Can I trust you?" she asked. "I need to trust you. I need you to not tell them."

"Okay," Jody agreed cautiously. "Tell them what?"

"Tell them..." Rashida closed her eyes. "I was left here as a hostage, Jody Broom."

Jody felt her eyes narrow. "A *hostage*?"

"You weren't supposed to know," Rashida said. "None of you were. Djinni Ghofl Khatir wanted to show our determination to abide by the terms of our agreement. I'm that guarantee of our honor."

"There wasn't any need for that," Jody assured her. "We know you're honorable. Besides, we don't do the whole hostage thing."

"It was nevertheless Ghofl Khatir's wish that I remain," Rashida said. "From his discussions with Cobra Harli Uy, I believe your leaders accepted my presence because they thought my Troft language skills might prove useful."

"Which they have," Jody said, suppressing the urge to tell her to get to the point. Clearly, she had to do this her way.

"But I believe Cobra Harli Uy also thought my piloting abilities might prove useful." Rashida swallowed hard. "He still believes that."

Jody felt her stomach knot up as she finally saw where Rashida was going. "He wants you to fly the warships away from here," she said. "Only you can't, can you?"

"No," Rashida said, almost too quietly to hear.

Jody looked down at the town again. "But I thought Djinni Khatir said you were a better pilot than he was. Was he lying?"

"No, not a lie," Rashida hastened to assure her. "But certainly a mischaracterization. I can fly most Qasaman aircraft, most likely better than he. I was also the more capable pilot on the freighter we used to travel here from our home. But *this*—" she waved a hand helplessly downward at the ship they were standing on "—this is far beyond my capabilities."

Jody hissed gently between her teeth. Practically every plan she'd heard Harli or the others discuss over the past few days had included the unspoken assumption that they could move the two

Troft warships wherever they needed to go. If Rashida couldn't do that, there was certainly no one else on Caelian who could. "But you can learn, right?" she asked. "I know the warship's bigger, and probably has a gazillion times as many controls as the freighter. But the principles are still the same. In theory, all you have to do is apply what you were taught and ratchet it up a bit."

"You don't understand," Rashida said with a tired sigh. "Djinni Khatir and I weren't actually *taught* how to fly the freighter. The invader pilot was drugged and made to believe he was performing various maneuvers under various circumstances. Djinni Khatir and I merely watched and memorized his movements."

Under the influence of memory-enhancement drugs of their own, no doubt. "So you watched him working the controls—"

"There were no controls," Rashida interrupted. "There was no freighter. We memorized his movements as he sat at a long dining table in a Qasaman village and imagined himself aboard his ship. We watched where his fingers and hands worked the controls that he believed he was seeing."

Jody felt a shiver run through her. She'd had no idea Qasaman drugs could do anything like *that*. "I see," she said, trying to keep her voice calm. "So you're saying you never actually *looked* at the controls when you were flying the freighter?"

Rashida shrugged slightly. "I saw them," she said. "I could read their labels, and understand a little of what they said. But the control boards here are an entirely different layout. I can't translate my sequences and control movements to them."

"Got it," Jody said, wincing. Harli was *not* going to be happy about this. "Okay. We'd better go down and find Harli."

"No," Rashida gasped, grabbing Jody's arm. "You can't. If he learns that we lied to him, all will be lost."

"It was a mischaracterization, not a lie," Jody reminded her. "Regardless, he has to know, and he has to know now. His whole strategy's going to need revision, and he's only got eight days to revise it."

"I beg of you," Rashida said, her voice desperate, her fingers digging into Jody's skin. "You must not tell him. I cannot fail him, and you, and my own people. The dishonor would be too much to bear."

"Well, then, you'd better figure out how to fly this thing," Jody said bluntly. "Because those are your only two options."

Rashida stared into Jody's eyes... and then, to Jody's surprise, the tension seemed to melt out of her face. "No," she said quietly as she let go and let her hand fall to her side. "There is one other choice."

Jody frowned. "What do you—?"

And then, suddenly, she understood. "Whoa!" she said, taking a quick step forward and grabbing Rashida's wrist. "Don't do anything stupid. We need you."

"No, you don't," Rashida said, twisting her arm and freeing it from Jody's grip. "You understand the invaders' language better than I do. You can do whatever translation is necessary. That ability and my presence as a symbol of Qasaman honor are my only value."

"That's not true," Jody insisted, wondering if she should try again to grab the other woman's arm. But their footing was precarious enough up here, and if they ended up in a struggle there was a good chance both of them would fall to their deaths. "Neither of them is true. You speak cattertalk way better than I do."

"My speaking did not prevent the invaders' courier ship from obtaining information of our situation and escaping with it." Rashida gestured again at the ship stretching out beneath them. "No, their writing is what's important now. And you read far better than I do."

"We need you," Jody repeated desperately. "Look, at least you've *flown* a Troft ship. That's more than any of the rest of us have done. Let's put our heads together and figure out—"

She broke off as the hint of an idea suddenly came to her. "Wait a second. You say you flew the freighter on pure touch and kinesthetic positioning, right? What if we go to the freighter, *you* show me what you did, *I* translate the control labels, and we work out together how to adapt everything to the warships' control boards?"

Rashida stared at her, a cautious flicker of hope in her eyes. "But the warship controls are far more complex."

"Sure, because this thing can do a lot more than a freighter can," Jody said. "For starters, the helm probably has a weapons section so that the pilot or copilot can fire the lasers and missiles if the regular gunners are incapacitated. That's how Dominion of Man warships work. Or at least, that's how they worked the last time we saw one a century ago."

"What if you're wrong?" Rashida persisted. "What if we can't learn to fly the warship that way?"

"Then we won't be any worse off than we are already," Jody pointed out. "Are you at least willing to give it a try?"

Rashida's gaze dipped once to the ground far below and she took a deep breath. Then, she looked back up at Jody and nodded. "Yes," she said firmly. "How do we proceed?"

Jody took a deep breath of her own. The thought of having to watch while Rashida satisfied her Qasaman view of honor had terrified her more than she'd realized. "We go to Harli," she said. "We tell him—"

"No!" Rashida interrupted. "We can't tell him about this. My honor—"

"No, no, no," Jody said hastily. "What we're going to tell him is that we want to go back to the freighter. To, I don't know, check its control systems or something. Maybe say we have to double-check how the navigation system and history readout work—that's something we could only do back there. Once he gives the okay, we can check out an aircar and be at the wreck by mid-afternoon."

"I don't think Cobra Uy will let us use an aircar," Rashida said. "I overheard the other Cobras talking. Most are out on search or transport duty, and he's keeping the rest in reserve."

"Then we'll borrow a spooker," Jody said.

"You can drive one of those vehicles?" Rashida asked, sounding doubtful.

"Sure," Jody said. "I mean, how hard can it be?"

"I'll *tell* you how hard it can be," Harli growled. "Picture a typical grav-lift cycle and multiply it by about ten. Add in unfamiliar terrain, multiply *that* by ten. Then add in nasty, hungry predators and multiply *that* by fifty."

"You don't have to be so dramatic," Jody said stiffly. "I *do* know something about the forest, you know. I spent a full day tromping through it."

"And damn near got yourself killed in the process," Harli retorted. "What am I wasting time arguing about this for? No. The answer is no."

Jody braced herself. "Harli—"

"If you think you need to study the wreck, fine," Harli continued, "I'll have Kemp and Smitty drive you out there."

"Oh," Jody said, feeling the argumentative wind snapped straight out of her sails. She should have realized that was where Harli was going.

Only now, instead of pulling just herself and Rashida out of the already critically short labor pool, they were going to rob Harli of the use of a pair of Cobras, too. That hadn't been part of her original calculation. "Or we could make it simpler and just take an aircar," she suggested.

"The aircars stay put," he said tartly. "They're the only things we've got that can pull any altitude, and you never know when you might need that." He gestured to an older man, one of the non-Cobras, busily digging vegetables from one of the gardens by the broken wall. "Yamara, Kemp should be somewhere around the circle over there. Go get him, will you?"

"Sure," Yamara said. Laying down his shovel, he hurried away.

"He should be here in a minute," Harli said, taking Jody's arm and casually walking her a few steps farther away from Rashida. "You sure this trip is necessary?" he asked quietly. "It's not exactly safe out there."

"I'm sure," Jody told him. "I hadn't thought about taking two of your Cobras away, though. Maybe they could just drop us off, make sure we get inside the freighter, and then come back here. We could set a time for them to come get us tomorrow or the next day."

Harli shook his head. "That ship went through the wringer, and from what Kemp said the hull has a whole bunch of cracks and broken seams. Any number of nasties could already be inside, and if they aren't now they will be once they smell fresh meat." He cocked his head. "But come to think of it, there's no reason why *you* have to go. Kemp and Smitty could take Rashida, and you could stay here and help with this fancy curtain you and Geoff sold me on this morning."

"Thanks, but I'd better go with her," Jody said. "As far as I know, I'm the only other person left on Qasama who reads cattertalk script. She might need me."

Harli grunted. "Fine," he said. "But you've got *one day* to find whatever you think you need. After that, you're back here, even if Kemp has to nail you to the back of his spooker for the ride. Got it?"

"Yes," Jody said. After all, it shouldn't take long for Rashida to run through her flight simulations and for Jody to record it all. After that, whatever analysis they needed to do could be handled here in Stronghold.

"Okay," Harli said. "And the two of you should probably wear the combat suits, too, assuming your friends are through testing them by then. In fact, once they're done you might as well just hang on to them. They'll give you an edge if you need to get near the prisoners, and they fit you better than anyone else around anyway."

"All right," Jody said. The suits were a little uncomfortable, but the built-in strength enhancements would certainly be nice to have. Not having to scrape spores and other organics off them every morning would be a nice bonus, too. "I'll check with Geoff and Freylan and find out when they'll be finished."

"There's no hurry—it's too late for you to head out today anyway," Harli said. "We'll set it up for first light tomorrow morning. You think that'll give Rashida enough time?"

Jody grimaced. "I hope so. Yes, I'll make sure it is."

"Good," Harli said. "And watch her. That whatever-it-is is still bothering her—I can see it in her face." He looked over Jody's shoulder at Rashida. "And don't forget that whatever crazy relationship your family has with the Qasamans, it may not be nearly as solid and secure as you think. Be sure you watch your back."

"Don't worry," Jody said, a shiver running through her. "I will."

CHAPTER TEN

"All right," Lorne called, looking over the twenty men standing at quiet attention in front of him, the sleek gray wraparound computers snugged around their necks making an odd contrast to their simple villager clothing. "This is where it begins. This is where we decide whether you have what it takes to be called Cobras."

The word seemed to echo through the forest. Or maybe it was just echoing through Lorne's own mind.

Because there was certainly good reason for him to pause and consider both the word and the men. This was the most unprecedented group of human beings Lorne had never in his wildest dreams expected to see. Men who only a week ago had been standing restlessly in line waiting for their psychological interviews were now Cobra trainees.

They weren't just any men, either. They were *Qasaman* men.

He looked across the group again, a shiver running through him. Their backs were straight and firm, with no hint of pain or even discomfort despite having had forty hours of surgery over the past five days. Their eyes were shiny with the effects of the learning-enhancement drugs they'd been dosed with this morning, drugs that Fadil Sammon had assured Lorne would cut the usual training period from weeks down to mere days.

And behind the studied calmness of their expressions, Lorne could see the burning fire of men with a mission. Men who'd had their home invaded, and were ready and eager to shove the war back down the invaders' throats.

Back in Stronghold, in the heat and excitement of their victory over the Caelian invaders, Lorne had brushed aside Nissa Gendreves's objections to bringing Isis to Qasama. He'd seen her concerns as merely more of the same unimaginative and inflexible bureaucratic thinking that he and the other Cobras on Aventine had been putting up with for too many years.

Now, as he gazed into the Qasamans' faces, he wondered uneasily if maybe she'd had a legitimate point.

"Cobra Broom?"

Lorne shook away his thoughts. There was work to be done, and it was way too late to indulge in second-guessing. "Yes, Trainee Yithtra?"

"I once again question these," Yithtra said, reaching up to tap the computer around his neck. "It may be both necessary and prudent for those of your worlds to learn their new abilities in slow and controlled stages. But we're Qasamans. We're faster than that."

"That's good to hear," Lorne said. "Because you're absolutely not going to get the slow, controlled course. You're going to get the full-bore, hammer-head, bone-bending version. We're in a war, remember?"

"Exactly my point," Yithtra said. "We were told we would only be given our full capabilities once the training was over. I respectfully request that you give them to us now, so that we may learn all the more quickly how to use them."

Lorne suppressed a grimace. Fadil had warned them during the screening process that the Yithtra family had far more arrogance and self-confidence than was probably good for them, and that first-son Gama was definitely a product of that attitude.

But the Yithtras were also one of the strongest families in the village, and moreover had a long history of rivalry with the Sammon family as the two of them jockeyed for power and influence. Fadil had warned that cutting them out of the Cobra project would probably lead to dangerous accusations and turmoil that no one on Qasama could afford right now, least of all a small village like Milika.

In Lorne's opinion, that wasn't much of a reason to accept someone into a program that was already charged with psychological and physical land mines. But Jin had insisted that Fadil have final say on which of his fellow villagers were fit to become Cobras, and Fadil had recommended Yithtra, and so here he was.

But Fadil only had final say on entry to the program. It would be up to Lorne and his fellow Cobras as to which of the candidates ultimately passed the course.

Which was, after all, the true reason why wraparound computer collars were used to control their equipment during training. The Qasamans' nanocomputers were already in place beneath their brains, but for now they were dormant, awaiting the final induction-field signal that would activate them. Whether that activation gave the trainees full access to their implanted weapons and strength-enhancing servos, or whether they got the only the stripped-down version of the programming that would turn them into merely extra-strong civilians, was a decision that still lay down the road.

A road that started right now. "The collars stay," Lorne told him shortly. "Let me introduce you to your trainers." He gestured to his left. "This is Cobra Everette Beach; beside him is Cobra Wendell McCollom. Both have experience in training Cobras, and both have survived many years on the intensely dangerous world of Caelian. If anyone can teach you to handle the pressures of war, they're the ones who can do it."

He paused and tried to watch all twenty faces at once. "Next to Cobra McCollom is Jennifer McCollom," he continued. "As Cobras Beach and McCollom are only marginally familiar with the Qasaman language, she'll be translating all of their instructions and orders to you."

The facial twitches were small, and for the most part were hastily covered up. But they were there, once again exactly as Fadil had predicted.

Fully half of the Cobra trainees were not at all happy at the prospect of taking orders from a woman.

Fadil had warned about this. So had Jin. But there was nothing either of them could do about it. The unforgiving realities of life on Caelian left little time for leisure, and few on that world chose to squander that precious time on something as theoretical as foreign language studies. Particularly foreign languages no one ever expected to need.

Jennifer McCollom was a rare exception, a woman who loved

the challenge of new languages and had mastered at least four of them over the years, including Qasaman and Troft cattertalk. She'd been a great help to Lorne's parents over the past two weeks as they tried to give Wendell and Beach at least a working knowledge of the language.

But while the two men could now probably navigate their way through the Milika marketplace, neither had the fluency and vocabulary necessary for a military training regimen.

Hence, the need for a translator. And with everyone else who spoke both Anglic and Qasaman already tied up with other duties, Jennifer was going to be it.

Still, as Jin had pointed out, the slightly awkward situation might have a silver lining. Watching how the recruits accepted being ordered around by a woman might give an indication as to how they would accept being ordered around in combat situations by the Qasaman military hierarchy, most of whom were city dwellers.

It might also give Lorne some idea of how determined they really were to become Cobras. "Anyone have a problem with that?" he invited.

"Our only problem is the invaders occupying our world," Yithtra said shortly. "We waste time, Cobra Broom. Train us, and let us fight."

Lorne looked at McCollom and Beach, caught their microscopic nods. "Very well," he said. "Cobra Beach?"

"We're going to begin by teaching you how to run," Beach announced. He waited for Jennifer to translate, then continued, "Not normal running, of course, but the techniques of letting your new servos take all the strain and do most of the work. Once you've mastered the method, you'll be able to run for fifty kilometers without even working up a sweat. The first thing to remember—"

"Hold it," McCollom cut him off, holding up his hand as he frowned somewhere past Lorne's shoulder. "Someone's coming."

Frowning, Lorne keyed up his own audios.

And stiffened. It wasn't just some*one* jogging through the forest toward them. It was an entire group of someones, ten or fifteen at least, all of them marking the same brisk, almost mechanical pace.

He hadn't heard any reports of Trofts traveling through the forest on foot. But there was a first time for everything. "Cobras, spread out," he murmured to McCollom and Beach. "The rest of you, stay put." He took a few quiet steps to his right, peripherally aware that McCollom and Beach were drifting the other direction toward possible cover. The jogging footsteps were getting closer, and Lorne estimated the unknowns would pass a little to the east. He took another step, wincing as a particularly brittle dead branch snapped beneath his foot.

And within the space of two seconds, the footsteps suddenly came to a halt.

Lorne held his breath, notching up his audios again. There were new sounds coming from that direction now, murmured voices speaking words his enhancements couldn't quite make out. The voices appeared human, but he remembered that the Caelian invaders' translators had also sounded reasonably human.

The voices stopped. A moment later, he heard the faint sound of stealthy footsteps coming toward him.

Despite the tension, he had to smile at that one. Sneaking up on a Cobra was generally a pretty futile endeavor. Lorne glanced back, caught Beach's eye and gestured him to move further out of range of a quick one-two shot. The newcomers were splitting up, Lorne could hear now, moving to try to flank him.

It was actually a decent tracking challenge, it occurred to him, and if the recruits had been farther along in their training he might have been tempted to take advantage of the unexpected opportunity. As it was, though, they really didn't have time for this. "Come on out," he called. "Don't worry—we won't hurt you."

The whole group of footsteps again stopped, and there was a moment of silence. Then, the first set Lorne had heard resumed, this time with no attempt at stealth. Lorne adjusted his position slightly, making sure he was facing the figure that emerged from the forest cover.

It was, indeed, a Qasaman. A male, about Lorne's age, wrapped in badly rumpled clothing. "I greet you," Lorne said, making the sign of respect. "What brings you and your companions out into the middle of nowhere?"

"I could ask the same question of you," the other said, flashing a suspicious look at the silent crowd of trainees.

"We're hunters from Milika," Lorne told him. "We came out to practice our strategy for attacking the invaders' hunting parties."

"I see," the man said. "Your name?"

"This is our home territory," Lorne pointed out. "I believe it's customary for the stranger to first introduce himself."

The other smiled thinly. "It is indeed," he said. "And were you a genuine Qasaman, you would have had no hesitation about stating the custom as such." He drew himself up. "But no matter. I am Kaml Ghushtre, Ifrit of Qasama. And you, from your family likeness, I guess are the brother of Cobra Merrick Moreau."

"Correct," Lorne said, quickly covering his surprise. This man knew Merrick? "Cobra Lorne Moreau Broom. Are those with you more Djinn?"

"They are." Ghushtre gave a set of trilling whistles, and with a rustling of grass and branches a wide spread of silent men emerged into view on either side of him.

"We're pleased to see you," Lorne said, doing a quick count. Twenty in all, unless Ghushtre had decided to keep a few back in reserve. "Your help will be greatly appreciated."

"Yes," Ghushtre said, his voice studiously noncommittal. "We first have an errand in Milika. Can you direct us to the village?"

"I would be honored to escort you there personally," Lorne offered. "May I ask the nature of this errand?"

"No." Ghushtre took a second look at him, and something in his face subtly changed. "But I can tell you that it concerns Fadil Sammon, son of Daulo Sammon."

Lorne felt his stomach tighten. "I'm afraid Fadil Sammon is unwell."

"His condition is known to us," Ghushtre said. "Please take us to him."

"If you know his condition, you also know that he can be of only limited assistance to you," Lorne persisted. "Perhaps I can serve in his place."

"We will speak to Fadil Sammon, and no other," Ghushtre said, his voice darkening. "If you no longer feel able to take us to him, then give us a direction and we'll find the village ourselves."

"No, of course I can take you," Lorne said. And he'd thought villagers could be pushy and condescending. "Beach, McCollom—continue with the exercise. I'll be back as soon as I can."

He gestured. "If you'll follow me, Ifrit Ghushtre?"

"Rook to knight's seventh," Paul announced, moving one of his pieces on the chessboard set out in front of him. "Check."

"Interesting," Fadil murmured, gazing up at the implanted

star-like gemstones in the ceiling above his medical bed. "I was certain you would move your bishop. I'll have to think a moment."

"Take your time," Paul said. "Would you like me to move the board to where you can see it?"

"No, thank you," Fadil said, a bit of sadness edging into his tone. "I have little else to occupy my mind these days. I appreciate the challenge of having to keep track of the board."

"As you wish." Paul looked across the room at Jin and smiled. "You're beating me soundly enough as it is."

Jin smiled back, trying to keep her face as unconcerned as possible as she lounged casually on the comfortable cushions in Fadil's meditation nook, watching her crippled husband and the paralyzed Qasaman as they tried to fill the long, increasingly tiresome hours.

And as she herself waited for her head, and the room around her, to stop spinning.

It was getting worse. All of it—the dizzy spells, the lapses of logic and reasoning, the disconcerting derailing of her train of thought. The tumor in her brain, which the Qasaman doctors had temporarily shrunk before she and Siraj Akim's team had headed out for Aventine, was starting to come back. And it was coming back with a vengeance.

How long did she have? She had no idea. At her last treatment the doctors had guessed that without surgery she still had three months to live. But that had been only three weeks ago, and it was clear that things were progressing far quicker than anyone had thought. Even if she made it the full three months, she suspected she would be incapacitated long before her actual death. If she was going to survive this, she needed to get to a properly equipped Qasaman hospital, with properly trained Qasaman surgeons, and soon.

The problem was that every such hospital was either occupied or besieged by the Troft invaders.

She clenched her teeth, fighting against a sudden wave of nausea as she continued smiling at her husband. They didn't need the hospital just for her, either. The skin and muscle that had been burned away from Paul's leg could also be fixed, but Dr. Krites had warned her that the window of opportunity on that was rapidly closing as well. If he didn't start the treatments within another week or two the nerves would never properly reconnect. Even if they were later successful in regrowing the leg, he would end up with no feeling in the new sections of the limb.

"Are you expecting company?" Paul asked. "I hear someone coming."

Shaking away her morose thoughts, Jin keyed her audio enhancements. He was right. There were footsteps in the corridor, lots of them, all coming this way.

"I have nothing scheduled," Fadil said. "Perhaps Lorne Moreau is bringing the new Cobra trainees to visit."

Jin frowned. There was something about the footsteps that brought up the image of determined, resolute men. "They don't sound like villagers," she said, climbing awkwardly out of the pile of cushions and taking up position between the door and Fadil. The footsteps reached the door—

The door swung open, and Jin found herself facing her son. "Lorne," she said, her eyes flicking across the hard-faced young men lined up behind him. The face just over his shoulder seemed to jump out at her—it was a face she'd seen somewhere before—

And then the semi-familiar man pushed past Lorne through the doorway and into the room. "I greet you, Fadil Sammon," he said formally. "I am Kaml Ghushtre, Ifrit of Qasama."

Jin felt her lungs freeze. *That* was where she'd seen him before: in the Sollas subcity, when she and Merrick had first arrived and been hauled before Miron Akim under suspicion of collusion with the Trofts who had just landed on Qasama. Merrick had offered to show the Cobras' power as a way of proving their goodwill toward the Qasamans, and had instantly earned Ghushtre's ill will by not playing according to the young Djinni's expectations of how the demonstrations should go.

And given the icy temperature of Ghushtre's single glance at Jin as he came into Fadil's room, it was clear he hadn't forgotten the incident, either.

"I greet you, Ifrit Ghushtre," Fadil answered the other calmly. "How may I serve you?"

"We would speak with you." Ghushtre looked again at Jin. "Alone."

"May I ask what this is about?" Jin asked, making no effort to move out of his way.

"No, you may not," Ghushtre said. "The matter is a private one, between Qasamans only."

"Fadil Sammon's condition requires extra care," Paul pointed out. "One of us should remain in case he needs assistance."

"He will not need assistance during the brief period of our conversation," Ghushtre countered. "We are at war, Cobra Jin Moreau. We have no time to spare for foolish chatter. You and your family will leave this room. Now."

Jin focused on the other Djinn, still standing in orderly lines in the corridor behind Lorne. If she could signal her son, and if he could spin around and hit them with his sonic before they could react . . .

"It's all right, Jin Moreau," Fadil said quietly. "You may leave. I'll be all right."

Jin turned to look at him. His face was calm, but the tranquility had tension lurking beneath it. "Do you know what this is about?" she asked.

He looked away from her gaze. "For the most part, yes," he said, and she had the impression that he was choosing his words carefully. "Please go now. Ifrit Ghushtre and I must speak."

Jin took a deep breath. "We'll be outside if you need us," she said. "Paul? Do you need a hand?"

"I've got it," Paul said. Standing up on his one good leg, he got the crutches Dr. Krites had given him into position under his arms and made his awkward way across the room to the door. Jin joined him, and with Lorne bringing up the rear they stepped out into the corridor. At a terse command from Ghushtre the rest of the Djinn filed silently past them into the room, the last one closing the door behind him.

"Are you okay?" Jin asked, eyeing her husband. "You looked like a decrepit ninety-year-old in there."

"You mean with these?" Paul asked, twirling one of his crutches. "No, I'm fine. Just part of my on-going philosophy of looking as harmless as possible in front of potential enemies."

"The Djinn aren't potential enemies," Jin said firmly, wishing she completely believed that. Most of them, like Siraj Akim and Carsh Zoshak, had come around quickly enough. But there were a few like Ghushtre who were still question marks.

"If you say so," Paul said. "Lorne? Don't."

"Don't what?" Lorne asked.

"You know perfectly well," Paul said with mild reproof. "You were about to casually lean your ear against the door. But don't.

They asked for privacy—both of them did—and we need to honor that request."

"Even if Fadil's in trouble?" Lorne countered. "There's something about that Ghushtre guy that sets my teeth on edge."

"Probably because he doesn't like us," Jin told him. "Or at least he doesn't like me. Doesn't mean he won't be perfectly civil to Fadil."

"Yeah, right," Lorne growled. "How does he know us well enough not to like us?"

"He came in for a bit of embarrassment in front of his peers when Merrick and I first arrived," Jin said. "Not much—on a heat scale, no more than a light singeing."

"Though of course he might remember it differently," Paul pointed out. "How did you happen across them, Lorne? I thought you were out in the forest with the new recruits."

"I was," Lorne said. "They were heading through on a quick-march and ran into us in one of the clearings northeast of town."

"They were heading *through* the forest?" Paul asked, frowning. "And from the northeast?"

"Yes, and I don't blame them," Lorne said. "The latest scout reports say all the main roads are under constant Troft surveillance, with everything from drones flying overhead to those armored trucks parked outside the towns and at all the major intersections."

"It's the northeast part that interests me," Paul said. "That implies they didn't come from Azras or one of the other southerly cities. Sollas, perhaps?"

Lorne made a face. "There wasn't much left of Sollas when we flew in last week. There's probably even less now."

"Which would make it a good place to be running from," Paul said thoughtfully. "The question is, why come *here*? What in the Worlds would make Fadil so important that anyone would send twenty Djinn to talk to him?"

"Unless they're not just talking," Lorne said, moving toward the door again. "Dad, for Fadil's sake we need to find out what's going on in there."

"Lorne—"

"Hold it—they're coming," Jin interrupted. "Lorne?"

He nodded and took a long step back.

Just in time. A second later the door was flung open and a glowering Ghushtre strode out of the room. He stopped short, as if surprised to find the three Brooms still there, and for a moment he looked back and forth between Jin and Paul. Then, he drew himself up. "I've decided that my Djinn and I will avail ourselves of the alien equipment that now resides in the Sammon family mine," he said.

"What equipment is that?" Paul asked cautiously.

"Foolish games do not become you, Cobra Paul Broom," Ghushtre growled. "I refer to the Isis equipment which you and your countrymen brought from the Cobra World called Caelian." He turned to Jin and seemed to brace himself. "You'll take us there at once, that I and my Djinn may become Cobras."

"Well, *that's* new," Lorne murmured.

Jin felt her mouth go suddenly dry. If Ghushtre decided to take that as an insult, or worse, as a challenge...

But the Djinni didn't even twitch. "You will take us to Isis, Jasmine Moreau," he said.

"My mother's not well," Lorne said, stepping forward. "I can take you."

"You have duties elsewhere, Lorne Moreau," Ghushtre said. "You have Cobra soldiers of your own to train. Go."

Lorne's eyes narrowed— "It's all right, Lorne," Jin said quickly. "I can take them to Isis. Go back and assist Beach and McCollom."

She could see the objections flicker across his face: how there were still unpleasant levels of dust in the parts of the mine they had to pass through to reach the Isis setup, how her dizzy spells could lead to serious injury if she stumbled against a stone wall, how suddenly fainting in the partially open lift could be even more disastrous.

But while Lorne was her son, he was also a Cobra. He knew how to take orders, whether he liked those orders or not. "Fine," he said. "I'll see you later." With a last lingering look at Ghushtre, he turned and strode down the corridor.

"And you, I believe," Ghushtre added, turning to Paul, "have a position of assistance to return to."

"That's all right," Paul said. "As you said, Fadil Sammon can do without assistance for a short time. I'll come with you."

Ghushtre's eyes lowered pointedly to his injured leg. "He may need you," he said. "You will return to him." He looked at Jin. "At your convenience, Jasmine Moreau."

"Let me first make sure Fadil Sammon's comfortable," she told him. Without waiting for an answer, she slipped past him and Paul and hurried back into the room. The other Djinn, lined up as before behind their leader, moved out of her way without comment or complaint.

Fadil watched her as she crossed over to him. "Are you all right, Jin Moreau?" he asked as she stopped beside his bed.

"I was going to ask *you* that," Jin said, studying his face. The tension she'd noticed when Ghushtre first arrived had abated somewhat, but lingering bits of it were still present. "What's happened? What do they want?"

He smiled, his expression touched with sudden sadness. "What we all want," he said. "Victory."

Jin glanced over her shoulder. "On whose terms?"

"That's always the question," Fadil agreed. "For now, certain things must remain a mystery to you, Jin Moreau." He looked past her shoulder toward Ghushtre. "And now you must go."

Jin sighed. "All right," she said. "But you should know that I really hate mysteries. I'll probably be worrying about it the entire rest of the day."

"My apologies." Fadil smiled again, a more genuine one this time, then sobered. "In that case, perhaps you'll allow me to offer a more interesting puzzle. You told me earlier that the invaders had also invaded your home world of Aventine, where they released razorarms taken from Qasama into the cities. Tell me, have the forests of Aventine been emptied of similar predators?"

"Hardly," Jin said grimly. "Those razorarms are probably the only thing that's kept the government from cancelling the Cobra project entirely."

"Then tell me," Fadil said. "If there are razorarms available for the taking on Aventine, *why are the invaders still hunting them here in the Qasaman forest*?"

Jin stared down at him. Somehow, that thought hadn't even occurred to her.

But he was right. Why would anyone bother transporting dangerous animals all the way from Qasama to the Cobra Worlds when they had all they could ever want right there in Aventine's own expansion regions? "I don't know," she said.

"Nor do I," Fadil said. "But I very much fear that there is more to this invasion than meets the eye. And until we know the invaders' secrets—*all* of their secrets—we may never fully defeat them."

"Then I guess we'd better get busy and learn those secrets," Jin said. "Because I have no intention of letting any of the sons of chickens just walk away."

She reached down and squeezed his hand. "Take care, and I'll see you later."

"I'll look forward to it," Fadil said. "In the meantime, please ask Paul Broom to come in." He smiled. "We still have a chess game to finish."

Carsh Zoshak was lounging casually in an open-air café near the mine entrance when Lorne tracked him down. "Ah—Lorne Moreau," Zoshak said, waving in greeting as Lorne came up to him. "I thought you were out in the forest."

"I was, and I have to get back," Lorne said, pulling up a chair and sitting down. "But first I wanted to give you a heads-up. You know a Djinni named Kaml Ghushtre?"

"He was one of the Sollas contingent," Zoshak said, nodding. "Why do you ask?"

"Because he's here," Lorne told him. "He and a squad of twenty blew into Milika about an hour ago, had a short chat with Fadil Sammon, and are now on their way to meet Isis."

Zoshak's eyes widened. "They're coming *here*?"

"And apparently planning to undergo the treatment," Lorne said. "My question is, are they sincere, or could this be this a plan to destroy Isis and rid Qasama of alien influences, or some such insanity?"

"Wait, wait, I'm losing the line of your logic," Zoshak protested. "There's no possibility that Djinni Ghushtre would make such a decision on his own. Isis is part of the treaty between Qasama and the Cobra Worlds. Only the Shahni have the power to repudiate any aspect of the treaty, including Isis."

"That assumes there are members of the Shahni still around," Lorne pointed out. "What if there aren't?"

"Then rule would fall to the military commanders," Zoshak said, frowning in thought. "But your question raises a second, more interesting one. If Djinni Ghushtre wouldn't dare interfere with Isis without orders, so also wouldn't he dare undergo the procedure without orders."

"Unless, as you said, the military has taken over," Lorne pointed out grimly. "In that case, team and unit officers might have been given more autonomy than they used to have."

"Except that Djinni Ghushtre isn't an officer," Zoshak said. "He would need to be an Ifrit to even have unit command."

Lorne frowned. "He *is* an Ifrit. At least, that's how he introduced himself."

"Really," Zoshak said, an odd tone to his voice. "Djinni *Ghushtre* has been made an Ifrit?"

"That he has," Lorne confirmed. "Unless you think the rank might have been self-awarded."

"No," Zoshak said firmly. "The other Djinn in the unit would never stand for that. He must have been granted the rank, and only Marid Miron Akim or one of the Shahni could do that. Tell me, did he know about Isis before he arrived here?"

"I don't know," Lorne said. "But he didn't say anything about it before his chat with Fadil. *And* he definitely came out of the meeting looking annoyed."

"Still, my guess is that he already knew," Zoshak said slowly. "Which would imply in turn that Siraj Akim and Ghofl Khatir did indeed make it safely to Azras."

Lorne grimaced. Siraj and Khatir had disappeared the minute all the Isis crates were safely inside Milika, taking a small car and heading for Azras, the nearest large city, to try and make contact with whatever was left of the Qasaman government.

But that had been eight days ago, and neither man had been heard from since. Given the scout reports of the Troft activity in and around Azras, Lorne considered their silence to be ominous in the extreme.

Still, maybe Zoshak was right. Maybe the two Djinn had made it to Azras and were able to touch base with the Shahni remnant on the Qasamans' fancy underground communications system.

He hoped so, anyway. The idea of Qasaman rule dispersing to individual unit commanders sounded like the quick path to complete chaos. And Zoshak was right—even a freshly-minted Ifrit like Ghushtre was surely smart enough not to make critical decisions on things like Isis without some serious thought.

So then why had he looked so angry when he came out of his meeting with Fadil?

"Here they come."

Lorne looked furtively behind him. In the distance he saw his mother come into view around a vendor's stall with Ghushtre and the rest of the Djinn striding along behind her. "I'd better go before he spots me," he told Zoshak, getting up from his chair. "Keep an extra close eye on the mine from now on, will you?"

"I always take my duty seriously." Zoshak stood up, too. "In fact, I believe it's nearly time for me to do my prescribed check of the mine itself. I think perhaps I'll join your mother in escorting Ifrit Ghushtre and his men in to Isis."

"Do that," Lorne said. "And watch him, Carsh Zoshak. Watch him closely. He's up to something. We need to find out what that something is."

CHAPTER ELEVEN

When Harli had said that the group would be leaving Stronghold at first light, Jody had naturally assumed that he meant there would actually be light in the sky.

He hadn't. She was still waiting for her alarm to go off when Kemp's pounding at her door jolted her awake. By the time she settled herself groggily onto the spooker saddle behind him there was still not a single hint of glow in the eastern sky that she could detect. Apparently, first light was something that related only to Cobra optical enhancements.

Spooker travel, she'd learned the first time she experienced it, was simultaneously one of the fastest and yet one of the slowest methods of transportation ever invented. Fastest, because the sheer speed of the spike-covered grav-lift cycles chewed up the fifty kilometers to the wrecked freighter in less than an hour. Slowest, because the sheer terror of watching the Qasaman landscape shoot toward and past them at that speed stretched every millisecond of the ride into its own sizeable fraction of eternity.

Only once during the trip did she find herself wondering how Rashida was taking it. After that, she focused her full attention on getting through it herself.

By the time they reached the crash site there was enough of a glow in the eastern sky for her to see both the wrecked freighter and the long gouge through the forest it had created when it plowed its way to a stop. As was typical of Caelian, of course, while the demolished trees remained demolished, the rest of the undergrowth had already started retaking the scarred ground.

And where there was Caelian undergrowth, she knew, there were also Caelian predators. It was just as well, she reflected as Kemp and Smitty let the spookers coast to a halt beside the entry ramp, that she hadn't insisted that she and Rashida come alone.

"Well, there it is," Kemp said as he hopped off the spooker and offered a helping hand to Jody. "Not exactly in prime working condition."

"Looks better than the wrecked warship back at Stronghold," Jody said, taking his hand for balance as she climbed out of the saddle. She didn't really need the help, but it seemed impolite to refuse the offer.

"It also looks worse on the inside," Rashida warned as she took Jody's cue and accepted Smitty's help to the ground. "I don't think Ghofl Khatir locked the hatch when we left, so we should be able to get in easily enough."

"Whoa, there—not so fast," Kemp said, putting out a hand as she started up the ramp. "You and Jody are staying out here while I check for predators. Smitty, keep an eye on them."

They'd been waiting for over twenty minutes, and Smitty had killed two giggers and a screech tiger, when the freighter's hatch finally opened again. "Clear," Kemp called. "Sorry it took so long. On the plus side, it looks like we aren't going to have to go hunt for lunch."

"Gigger?" Jody hazarded as she and the others headed up the ramp.

"Hooded cloven, actually," Kemp said. "A small one—I'm still not sure how he managed to get in. Plus ribbon vine salad on the side, of course. Afraid the blue treacle's a bit overdone—I had to burn it off to get the command room door open."

"It all sounds delicious," Jody murmured. "I can hardly wait."

"Trust me," Kemp said with a sly smile. "Come on—I've got the power going."

Rashida had been right, Jody noted soberly as she followed Kemp through the narrow corridors toward the bow. The beating the freighter had taken, first from the invaders' brief attack and then from the crash landing, had seriously messed up the interior. Walls and bulkheads were buckled, floors were canted, and there was broken equipment everywhere. The vines and other plants already starting to fill the open areas merely added a bizarre aspect to the ship instead of hiding any of the damage.

"So now what?" Kemp asked when they were finally standing in the command room.

"Rashida and I need to do some reconstruction of the course," Jody said, a shiver running through her as she stared at the lumpy gray hull sealant running in a jagged line across the wall. Her mother had nearly died right here...

"What can we do to help?"

"Nothing, really," Jody said. "It's pretty much a job for us cattertalk-readers."

"There's a lounge just aft of the hatch, if you'd like to rest," Rashida offered.

"And if you get bored with that, you can poke around and see if there's anything aboard worth taking back to Stronghold," Jody added.

"Yeah, keeping busy sounds good," Kemp said. "Smitty, you stay here and keep an eye on them. I'll go start opening cabinets."

Jody looked at Rashida's suddenly tense face. If Smitty figured out what they were doing, they were going to be in big trouble with Harli. "It would be safer if you stuck together," she told Kemp. "Remember, you still don't know how that hooded cloven got in. The command room looks pretty secure—we'll be fine here on our own."

"Besides, we have these," Rashida added, holding up her arms to show the glove lasers on their combat suits.

For a moment Kemp eyed her thoughtfully. Then he shifted his gaze to the walls and floor, his eyes moving methodically across every centimeter of the command room's surfaces. "Okay," he said at last, pulling out a field radio and handing it to her. "We'll seal up behind us—call me immediately if you see anything that even looks like it might be trouble. And *don't* open the door until we get back, for any reason. Got it?"

"Got it," Jody said, clipping the radio to her belt. "Happy hunting."

Kemp gave the room a final sweep, then strode out. Smitty gave a last look at Rashida and then followed, sealing the door behind him.

Jody took a deep breath and pulled her recorder from her inside pocket. "Okay," she said, gesturing Rashida toward the helm. "Let's see what we've got."

After the way Rashida had talked, Jody had fully expected the script on the helm controls to be faded or scratched or otherwise difficult to read.

She hadn't expected for it to be completely incomprehensible.

Steady, girl, she told herself firmly as she studied the flowing characters. *These are Trofts. They speak cattertalk, and they* write *cattertalk. This has to be understandable.*

But the characters refused to resolve themselves into anything she was familiar with.

"You can't read it either?" Rashida asked anxiously as the silence lengthened. "What do we do?"

"We start by not panicking," Jody told her. "The Troft Assemblage is made up of hundreds of small demesnes, with probably dozens of different dialects and tonal shadings among them. This has got to be one of those differences. We just have to figure out how it . . . wait a minute."

"You have something?"

Jody smiled lopsidedly. Of course. "Got it," she said. "It's normal script, except with a bunch of extra twiggings and some really strange angles. Sort of like—let's see; what did they call it?—like Earth Gothic script. Something like that."

"Yes," Rashida said slowly, peering closely at the script. "Yes, I think I see it now. But don't these differences make communication difficult?"

"Apparently not to the Trofts," Jody said. "I've heard that groups who normally speak even extremely different dialects usually don't have any trouble understanding each other's cattertalk. I guess reading each other's script works the same way."

She took a deep breath and let it out in a relieved *whoof.* Now, with that realization, the whole board made sense again. Deciphering it would be slow and tricky, but at least it would be possible. "So okay," she continued briskly. "How do you want to work this?"

"I thought we could go down the same list of situations and responses that the interrogator used back on Qasama," Rashida said, sitting down in the main helm seat and flexing her fingers. "You can record both, and hopefully we can then adapt all the movements to the warship's controls after we return to Stronghold."

"Sounds reasonable," Jody said. "You think you can remember all the questions?"

Rashida frowned up at her. "Of course."

"Right," Jody murmured. Settling herself at Rashida's side, she aimed the recorder's lens over the board. "Whenever you're ready."

[The main drive engines, they are to be activated,] Rashida said, slipping into cattertalk as her hands traced out a sequence of eight different controls. [The grav lifts, they are to be activated . . .]

They'd been at it for four hours straight when Kemp and Smitty finally returned to the command room. "How's it going?" Smitty asked as the two Cobras again made sure to seal the door behind them.

"We're making progress," Jody confirmed. "You?"

"The same," Smitty said, pulling over one of the chairs and sitting down. "There's a lot more stuff back there than we realized."

"A little too much, in fact," Kemp said, passing Smitty and coming up beside the two women. "Rashida, how long did it take you to fly from Qasama to Aventine in this thing?"

"About five days," Rashida said. "That was the freighter's highest speed."

"Why, were you thinking they should have gotten there faster?" Jody asked.

"No, just the opposite," Kemp said, frowning down at the control board. "It looks like there was space for twelve spine leopards in the main hold. That sound about right?"

"Yes, I believe so," Rashida said. "I know Miron Akim removed ten, and there was room for one or two more."

"So ten to twelve of the beasts," Kemp said. "But the amount of food they had stored up for them—some kind of frozen carcasses, I think—looks like enough for a good three-week trip."

"'Course, we don't know how much Qasaman spinies usually eat," Smitty warned. "Could be they chow down more than their Aventinian cousins."

"No, they should be pretty much the same," Jody said, frowning. "I think Governor Telek made sure they did food compatibility tests before they released the first of them onto the planet." Rashida stirred, but didn't speak. "They were probably just planning a slower trip, that's all."

"Yeah, we thought of that," Kemp said. "Problem is, it brings up an even thornier question. Your mother and brother both told us that the Trofts had already invaded Aventine when your mother and the Qasamans arrived. That means that if the original Troft crew had still been in charge, they'd have been barely in time to offload their load of spinies before the first invasion wave finished consolidating their gains. If they'd been running at fuel-saver speeds, there's no way they would have arrived until the party was pretty much over."

"Maybe they were supposed to be part of the second wave," Jody suggested. "They were to bring in the next batch of spinies to replace the ones the Aventine Cobras would have killed."

"And they wanted to bring them all the way from Qasama?" Kemp asked. "Think about it—once the Trofts have Aventine, they can zip out to the expansion regions whenever they want and pick up as many spinies as they want."

"*And* they can get the things without having Qasamans shooting at them the whole time," Smitty added.

Jody frowned. They had a point. An extremely good point. "Okay," she said slowly. "So maybe the carcasses were also for the crew to eat?"

Kemp snorted. "You see a butcher shop or carving station on your way in?" he asked. "Come on—a simple freighter crew's not going to load a bunch of whole carcasses aboard a ship when pre-packaged meals are a hell of a lot easier to deal with."

"No, I suppose not." Jody looked at Rashida. "Feel free to jump in with any ideas," she invited.

"I have one thought," Rashida said slowly. "But I'm not sure it makes sense."

"Well, the one we came up with doesn't make sense, either," Smitty said. "How bad can yours be?"

"Go ahead, Rashida," Jody said encouragingly.

Rashida hunched her shoulders. "Perhaps the presence of extra supplies means the invaders never intended to bring these particular razorarms to your worlds. Perhaps the plan was to take them somewhere else."

"Congratulations," Kemp said sourly. "Looks like we're all going crazy together, because that's the same conclusion *we* came to. Problem is, we can't figure out where or why anyone would want to do that."

"I don't suppose the pilot your people interrogated might still be alive," Smitty said. "If he is, we might be able to ask him when this is all over."

"I don't know what happened to him," Rashida said, frowning into the distance. "That would have been Senior Advisor Omnathi's decision. But there may be another way."

She swiveled back to the board. "There should be a history of previous travel in the ship's log," she continued, keying the navigational section. "If we can find out where the ship has been, we may find a clue to where it was going."

"Good idea," Smitty said approvingly, getting up and stepping to her side. "Do we have some kind of—? Oh, you've got a recorder, Jody. Great. Does it have a Troft jack?"

"It has a standard one," Jody said, looking around. "But I didn't bring a cable for it."

"I'll look in here," Kemp offered, heading toward a cabinet fastened to the side wall. "Smitty, see if you can find any drawers under the control boards."

"There's another spare-parts cabinet in the anteroom," Rashida said.

"I'll check it," Jody said, turning toward the door.

"*I'll* check it," Kemp said firmly, changing direction. "You can look in this one."

They'd collected a total of five data cables by the time Rashida found the freighter's course history. Three of the cables were of an odd and non-standard configuration, which Jody suspected went along with the script variant used by the ship's owners. Fortunately, the control board had several different jacks, one of which was the kind Jody was used to and that her recorder could take. Even more fortunately, the other two cables were of that same type.

Three minutes later, she had a full recording of everywhere the wrecked freighter had been in the past eight Troft standard months.

"For all the good it'll do us," Kemp said with a grunt as Jody disconnected the cable. "If it's been flying someplace off our charts, we won't know where any of those planets is anyway."

"There are more extensive maps back on Aventine," Jody said, double-checking the download. It would be embarrassing to get back to Stronghold and only then discover that her recorder hadn't encoded the data properly. But everything seemed to be there. "And the Tlossies should be able to pull up data on everything any group of Trofts have ever put their status curlies on. When Warrior's people get here we can have him take a look."

"Let's hope *they're* not running at fuel-saver speeds," Kemp said. "So what now?"

"We still have some work to do in here," Jody said, looking at Rashida and getting a small nod of confirmation in return. "You said something earlier about lunch?"

"That we did," Kemp agreed. "Come on, Smitty, let's go outside and get a fire going. Might as well give our guests the full Wonderland experience."

"Sure," Smitty said. "Rashida, how do you like your hooded cloven steaks?"

For a moment Rashida looked uncertainly at him, as if trying to figure out if he was making fun of her. She must have seen something in his face, though, because Jody saw her tense muscles relax. "Not too deeply cooked," she told him. "The very center part should remain the color of the original meat."

"We'll call that a rare," Smitty said, looking at Jody. "Jody?"

"Medium rare," Jody told him. "And char the outside, if you don't think it'll make the meat too tough."

"It won't," Smitty promised. "You two get back to work. One of us will come get you when it's ready."

By the time Smitty came to get them, Rashida and Jody were nearly finished with the read-through on the piloting instructions Rashida and Khatir had received back on Qasama. Long before that point was reached Jody found herself utterly astonished by the sheer amount of information the Qasaman treatments had enabled Rashida to retain.

And not just information, either, but also the detailed muscle memory that had allowed her to pilot an alien ship across the stars to Aventine and then to Caelian.

Khatir and Siraj had assured Governor Uy that the Qasamans would be able to learn how to be Cobras in days rather than weeks. At the time, Jody had assumed that was fifty percent boasting and fifty percent finger-crossed hope. Now, she wasn't so sure it wasn't a hundred percent truth.

The lunch the two Cobras had prepared was excellent, far better than Jody had expected untreated and unseasoned meat cooked on an open fire could ever be. Kemp hadn't been kidding about including a ribbon-vine salad, either, which was also delicious.

The fact that they had to eat everything with their field knives only added a dash of adventure to the whole experience.

The rest of the piloting read-through took less than an hour. By the time Jody announced they were ready to leave, Kemp and Smitty had finished searching the ship and had assembled a small collection of electronics and other small items they thought might be useable and that could be carried on the spookers.

By the time the sun had reached the tops of the tallest western trees, they were back in Stronghold.

Jody's plan had been to head immediately to her house and see how Freylan and Geoff were doing with the spore-repellant cloth. But Rashida insisted on first going to the Troft warship to look over the helm board again and run a quick comparison with the records Jody had made of the freighter's controls. Reluctantly, Jody agreed.

It was just as well that she had.

"The good news is that we should be able to translate everything you did in the freighter to here," she told Rashida after a quick but careful study of the boards. "The bad news is that you're not going to be able to do it alone."

"What?" Rashida asked, looking stunned. "But you said the pilot should be able to fly the ship alone."

"Under normal circumstances, he probably could," Jody said grimly. "But that didn't count on Captain Eubujak having five last minutes in here before the Cobras broke in."

Rashida's eyes widened some more. "Sabotage?"

"Yes, of a very clever sort," Jody said. "See here, how the power section and sensor monitor sections of the helm board are dark? Looks like he had just enough time to cut the cables that echoed those control systems from those particular boards over to here."

Rashida looked at the areas Jody had pointed out. "I don't understand," she said. "If he wished to completely disable the ship, why didn't he just destroy the entire board? I was told he and those with him were armed with lasers when they surrendered."

"Because he *didn't* want to completely disable the ship," Jody said. "A wrecked board would have meant no one would ever get the thing off the ground, at least not without a lot of work. What he did was make sure it took three people who knew what they were doing to fly the thing."

"His thought being that there wouldn't be that many humans on Caelian with such knowledge?"

"Exactly," Jody said. "Besides which, I don't think he'd given up hope of pulling a last-minute run for it. I'm guessing they had the grav lifts coming up to power when the Cobras came charging through that door."

Rashida let out a long, thoughtful breath. "All right," she said, still staring at the board. "You say three people can fly it. What about two?"

"Like who?" Jody countered. "Eubujak was right, you know. No one else on Caelian has even a clue how to run systems like this."

Rashida turned her gaze on Jody. "Except you."

"*Including* me," Jody retorted. "I've never flown anything more complicated than an aircar in my life. I've never even *watched* anyone fly something this big."

"But you understand the language," Rashida reminded her, gesturing at the cattertalk script. "You watched while I ran through the procedures for flying the freighter, and you've already promised to help me adapt the procedures here. How much more complicated can it be for you to learn while you also teach me?"

"Rashida—" Jody held out her hands, palms upward. "I can't do this. I'm sorry. It's not that I *won't* do it. It's that I *can't*."

"You're wrong," Rashida said quietly. "I've seen your family in action, Jody Moreau Broom. I've seen what your parents and brothers can do. You're part of a remarkable family, more remarkable even than the rest of your people. Whatever you choose to do, you *can* do it. I know you can."

Jody shook her head. "My family is Cobras, Rashida," she said. "The parents and brothers you so admire—they're all Cobras. That's the reason they're special, not some historical or mystical family name." She sighed. "But that being said, if we don't get this thing off the ground, it's going to sit here until the invaders' reinforcements arrive, at which point it probably gets turned back around against us."

"Yes, it does," Rashida said. "Which leaves us only two choices: fly it, or destroy it."

"And we can't destroy it this close to Stronghold without risking the city," Jody concluded reluctantly. "Which means that either way we have to learn how to fly the damn thing." She sighed again. "Sometimes I hate logic. Okay, fine. I'm in."

"Thank you," Rashida said. "You said the power and sensor functions have been detached?"

"Yes," Jody said. "And since power is probably more important than sensors, I'll have to handle that board."

"But won't we need the sensors, too?"

"Given that Eubujak made a point of disconnecting them, I'd say we probably will," Jody conceded. "We'll just have to hope we can find a way to preset them."

"Or," a voice said calmly from the doorway behind them, "you get a third person to run them."

Jody spun around, nearly wrenching her back in the process, a taste of bile welling suddenly into her throat. Kemp and Smitty stood just inside the doorway, their faces expressionless.

A brittle silence filled the room. "I don't suppose," Jody said, just to try to spark some reaction from those stone faces, "that we can convince you we were just goofing around."

"No," Kemp said with a simple, cold flatness that made her wince. "What the *hell* were you thinking, Broom?"

"She's not to blame," Rashida cut in before Jody could find an answer to that. "I insisted she not tell anyone."

"You can insist all you want," Kemp growled back, glowering openly at her now. "She's under no obligation to baby-sit your feelings or your honor or anything else." He shifted the glower to Jody. "She *is* under obligation to keep the people in charge up to date on everything that in any way impinges on our plans for the defense of Caelian."

"I'm sorry," Jody said between stiff lips, her stomach knotted painfully. It was one thing, she realized dimly, to talk with casual unconcern about her family's name when that name wasn't on the line. Only now, with it in danger of being dragged into public shame, did she realize how much it truly meant to her.

And yet, paradoxically, in that same instant she realized how little a name meant. Not when it was weighed against such things as life and freedom and victory. "I'm sorry," she said again. "But assuming you've been listening the whole time, you know that we're right. We have to move this ship, and Rashida's the only one who can do that. You want to lock me away, or whatever you do to prisoners, fine. I'll take whatever punishment you or Harli want to throw at me."

Bracing herself, she sent as stern a look as she could manage upstream against Kemp's glare. "But Rashida has to stay free and able to work."

Kemp's eyebrows rose slightly on his forehead. "Are you bargaining with me, Broom?" he demanded. "*You*, of all people?"

Jody took a deep breath—

"*Especially* you, who needs a third person to help you fly this bird?" he added in the same gruff tone.

Jody blinked, feeling the sudden discomfiting sensation of having been leaning against a wind that had suddenly stopped blowing. "Excuse me?" she asked cautiously. "Are you saying . . . ?"

"That we're going to join the crazy offworlders who can't seem to understand basic simple orders?" Smitty suggested. "Yeah, I guess we are."

"Don't misunderstand," Kemp warned. "I'm still mad as hell that you didn't go to Harli the minute you realized there was a problem. But that's water long under the bridge. You're right, we have to move this damn chunk of alien hardware."

He looked at Rashida. "And *she's* right that you're going to need a third person. Smitty?"

"I'll do it," Smitty said without hesitation. "You've got enough on your own plate already. Besides, I can make myself scarce easier than you can. Just switch me to Babool's roving-patrol shift, and I'll have an excuse to be in here while Rashida and Jody are working."

"Safer to just assign you to guard and assist them," Kemp said, eyeing Jody thoughtfully. "A more critical question is whether they can spare Jody from work on that fancy curtain they're putting together."

"Easily," Jody assured him. "My degrees are in animal physiology and management—Geoff and Freylan only brought me in on this job to deal with the fauna we were going to capture and study. All the electrical and mechanical stuff was their department. Once they figure out how to build the curtain, all they'll need is extra hands for the grunt work. Anyone in Stronghold can do that as well as I can. Probably better."

"Well, we'll see," Kemp said. "And for the record, they've already started work on the curtain, along with about thirty of Stronghold's finest. If no one starts screaming in panic for your help, I guess we'll be okay with leaving you here."

He took a step closer to Jody. "But let me make one thing *very* clear. From now on everything you do gets reported. Every success, every failure, every strange thought or idea—*everything*. Understood?"

"Understood," Jody said. "Do we report to you, or to Harli?"

Kemp looked sideways at Smitty. "What do you think?"

"Harli's way too busy with everything else he has to do," Smitty said. "And since I'll already be here, you can just report to me."

"Yeah, let's keep the chain of command simple," Kemp agreed with a hint of sarcasm. "Wouldn't want you to get all confused again."

"We appreciate that," Jody said, finally starting to breathe again. "Thank you."

"Thank me after you get this bird off the ground," Kemp growled. "*And* you've put it down again where Harli's told you to."

He took a deep breath, let it out in a huff. "Okay. Logistics. Your house is going to be the center of a round-the-clock sewing and soldering marathon for a while, so you might as well move into the governor's spare room with Rashida. Smitty will pick you both up there at oh-five-thirty tomorrow, and the three of you will get to work. Any questions?"

"Just one," Rashida said, a bit timidly. "We had a late and very filling lunch, and I'm not yet tired."

"Neither am I," Jody agreed.

"I could stick around another hour or two myself," Smitty offered. "In case they find something for me to do."

Kemp hesitated, then gave a reluctant nod. "Fine," he said. "But no more than a couple of hours. The next guard shift starts about then, and I'd just as soon avoid any awkward questions as long as possible." He turned and headed across the room. "Just be careful," he called over his shoulder, "and try not to fire any thrusters or whatever else this thing's got."

He reached the door and turned back. "And no matter what you do tonight," he added, "tomorrow will *still* start at oh-five thirty."

CHAPTER TWELVE

The first night with Anya in his cell was rough on Merrick. Every time she rolled over, it seemed, or made any kind of unexpected noise or strange movement he snapped awake, his brain and reflexes on hair trigger, his body in full fight-or-flight mode. By the time the guard delivered the breakfast tray through the slot at the bottom of the door, he felt almost as tired as when he'd gone to bed.

Fortunately, the day itself turned out to be uneventful. The Troft doctor came by once with another injection, but aside from that Merrick didn't see any of the aliens. Every half hour or so Anya asked if there was anything she could do for him, subsiding without comment or complaint when he told her there wasn't. He tried faking a nap after lunch, just to see if she or the Trofts would try to pull something when he was wasn't watching. Nothing had happened by the time he did accidentally fall asleep, nor did anything seem changed when he woke up.

At bedtime Anya again offered him a dose from her medicine vial. Again, he turned her down.

And life settled into an odd but not unpleasant routine.

Merrick had told himself firmly that he wasn't going to get emotionally involved with Anya, no matter what she did to encourage such a relationship. To his mild surprise, she did absolutely nothing in that direction. She never spoke to him unless she was asking if he had any orders, or was answering one of his infrequent questions. She was always first at the door when meals arrived, retrieving the tray and bringing it to Merrick, then retreating to her bed to sit silently and patiently until he turned over her half of the food to her. When it was time to sleep, she asked one final time what she could do for him, offered him some of her medicine, then retreated again to her bed. She never joined Merrick in his daily workout regimen, but he often noticed her doing quiet isometric exercises of her own. Once, when he woke up in the middle of the night, he spotted her doing some stretching and limbering and something that looked like a combination of tai chi chuan and ballet.

Once, out of a sudden sheer desperation for human companionship, he invited her to eat with him. As she had with his offer of the room's bed that first night, she reminded him that he was the master and she was the slave, and that she would eat only what he didn't want, and only after he'd decided what that portion was. The strangest part of the conversation was the sense Merrick had afterward that Anya had made the same decision he had about not becoming emotionally entangled with her unasked-for roommate.

All of which, to Merrick's mind, made her a most unlikely Troft spy. So who was she? And why had they put her in his cell?

By the fourth day of their captivity together, he'd still come up with only one answer.

She really was, in fact, nothing more or less than a slave.

And it was frightening how easy it was to get used to having such a person around.

It was on the sixth day, an hour after Anya had sent the empty lunch tray out through the door slot, when the routine changed.

It began with the usual double click of the lock. But this time, instead of the Troft doctor, a pair of armored soldiers stepped through the doorway. [The Games, you are ordered to accompany us to them,] one of them announced.

"Am I, now," Merrick murmured, eyeing the aliens. Both carried small lasers, but the weapons were belted at their sides, with the security straps still attached. Apparently, they weren't expecting trouble from the prisoner.

What they *were* clearly expecting was an uneventful trip to wherever they were going. Each of the aliens was carrying a set of shackles, thick metal cuffs connected by thirty centimeters of heavy-looking chain. One set was probably for Merrick's wrists, those cuffs including fan-shaped palm pieces he assumed were designed to limit the use of his fingertip lasers. The other set was probably ankle cuffs, a bit larger than the wrist versions but just as sturdy-looking.

Merrick suppressed a cynical smile. If they thought that was all they needed to immobilize a Cobra, they were in for a rude awakening. [The Games, of what do they consist?] he asked in cattertalk.

[The truth about them, you will learn it soon,] the guard said. [The shackles, you will submit to them.]

Merrick flicked a glance over their shoulders at the corridor beyond. Once again, whoever was in charge had set up the pop-in/pop-out arrangement of gunners in the various doorways near Merrick's cell. Even if he barreled through the two guards standing in front of him, he wouldn't get very far.

But if he went along with the shackles another opportunity might present itself along the way. Even alert people sometimes got sloppy when they thought they were holding all the cards. [The shackles, I will submit to them,] he agreed, hopping off the bed and offering his wrists. [The shackles, you may attach them.]

The two Trofts stepped warily forward, one of them fastening the wrist cuffs around Merrick's arms, the other squatting down and doing the same with the ankle cuffs. All four of the cuffs, Merrick noticed as they were locked in place, had thick round rings welded to their sides, too sturdy to be simple hanging rings. Perhaps they were planning to transport him by vehicle and the rings would be attached to more chains to anchor him to the floor or walls.

The guards finished and stepped back. [To the arena, you will follow us,] the first guard said. He turned and gestured to Anya. [Merrick Moreau, you will also accompany him.]

[Obedience, I give it,] Anya said, standing up and coming to Merrick's side.

[Behind him, you will walk there,] the guard said, gesturing again.

Silently, Anya took two steps back, stopping a meter behind Merrick. The guard took up position behind her, the other guard settled in two meters in front of Merrick, and at a curt order the whole procession trooped off together out of the cell and down the corridor in parade-style single file.

With the prisoner now theoretically helpless, Merrick had assumed the randomized guard rotation would end after they passed the first group of doorways. But the Troft commander was smarter or warier than that. As they continued on, more doorways ahead began sprouting soldiers, running the same target-lock-defeating pattern as the first group.

Still, sooner or later the Trofts were bound to make a mistake.

And then, twenty meters dead ahead, there it was. In the center of a cross-corridor a large, heavy-looking metal ring had been set up in front of their procession. The structure was about a meter and a half in diameter, standing vertically on a wide, flat stand, with the look of a security metal detector about it. Power cables snaked away to the left, while a small control board on the right glowed with blue and green status lights.

Mentally, Merrick shook his head. What in the Worlds they thought a metal detector would teach them at this stage he couldn't imagine.

What it *was* going to teach them, though, was that powered electrical equipment and Cobras were a very bad mix.

It would have to be quick, he knew. But he could do it. He would wait until the first three of their group had passed through the detector, and as the Troft bringing up the rear stepped into the ring Merrick would turn and trigger his arcthrower, flash-vaporizing the electronics and electrical components inside the ring and blowing the whole device, hopefully with enough force to take out the guard. At the same instant, he would stun the Troft in front of him with a blast from his sonic. A fingertip laser burst at his ankle chain to free his legs, a pretzel-twisted leg and antiarmor blast into his wrist chain, and he and Anya would be clear to make a run for it.

If Anya was interested in escape, that is. If she wasn't...

Merrick set his jaw. If she wasn't, he told himself firmly, he wouldn't waste precious seconds trying to argue or reason with her. She came with him the instant he was free, or he would have no choice but to leave her to her own devices.

The lead Troft reached the ring and passed through it. Merrick frowned, flicking a glance at the status board. As far as he could tell, none of the lights had changed. Yet the Troft was obviously loaded with metal, electronics, power supplies, and everything else that a security detector might be programmed to search for. Could the ring be something else instead? He stepped into it, momentarily dismissing the question as he readied his arcthrower.

And in a violent fraction of a second he was yanked to a halt, his arms snapping to either side to slam into the ring, the chain between his wrists breaking with barely even a sound or a tug. Simultaneously, his legs were pulled forcibly together, that chain not breaking but simply bunching together between his ankles with links digging painfully into his skin.

The ring wasn't a security detector at all. It was a giant, electromagnetic trap.

And Merrick had literally walked right into it.

He flexed his chest and arm muscles with all his strength, adding full servo power to the effort. But with his arms spread-eagled to the sides his leverage was effectively zero. He looked up at his right hand, peripherally noticing the breakaway link that had been coyly nestled in amidst the real ones in his wrist chain, wondering if he could still fire his arcthrower. But with the cuff pinned to the ring, his little finger was now pointed along the side of the metal arc instead of directly at it. Triggering the arcthrower would just send the bulk of the current away from the mechanism instead of directly into it.

And even if enough of the charge got into the ring to do some damage, with his cuff pinned to the metal there was a good chance that much of the jolt would flow into his own arm. There were, he reflected bitterly, few more humiliating ways to die than by the careless use of his own weapons.

From behind him came the sound of hurrying feet. He tried twisting his torso against his wrists, hoping he could at least turn the edge of his sonic toward whatever was about to happen back there. But again, his lack of leverage defeated the attempt.

A pair of Troft hands appeared at his right and deftly slid a sturdy-looking rod into the small ring he'd noticed earlier welded onto his right wrist cuff. A quick turn of his head to the left showed the other end of the rod now being attached to that cuff. A second rod was fastened to the horizontal bar near his left wrist, and he glanced down to see the other end sliding into the ring on his left ankle cuff. A third rod mirrored the second's by linking his right wrist and ankle.

And with that the activity ceased. A hum Merrick hadn't noticed faded, and the pull on his wrists and ankles vanished as the electromagnets were powered down.

For all the good it did him. With a yoke-style bar across his shoulders keeping his arms rigidly apart, and with his legs able to move only forward and backward, and then only a few centimeters at time, he was as thoroughly trapped as if he was still pinned to the ring.

But if his lasers and arcthrower were now useless, he still had his sonics. He focused on the Troft guard in front of him, who had stopped and turned to face the operation. It would be a useless and fairly juvenile gesture to flatten the soldier, Merrick knew. But at the moment he was in the insanely frustrated mood to do it anyway.

And then, even that small token act of defiance was taken away from him. With a Troft hand gripping her wrist, Anya stumbled under Merrick's pinioned right arm and was hauled to a stop directly in front of him, right exactly where she would take the brunt of his sonic.

Merrick took a deep breath. [My cooperation, you could have simply asked for it,] he called.

[Your forgiveness, I ask it,] the same disembodied Troft voice he'd heard that first day replied. [Your pledge of cooperation, you only gave it until the Games. The risk, I could not take it.]

[A drug, you could have used it instead,] Merrick pointed out. [Unless such elaborate schemes as this, you enjoy them.]

[A drug, it might dangerously slow your reactions in the Games,] the Troft said. [A point, it was also necessary to make. This demonstration, it is intended to teach you truth.]

Merrick grimaced. [The truth, that my mind and intentions can be read in advance?]

[The truth, you recognize it,] the Troft confirmed. [A transport dolly, it will now be brought to take you to the Games.]

Merrick squared his shoulders as best as he could with a pole digging into his back. [Your offer, I acknowledge it,] he said. [The Games, I will travel there under my own strength.]

There was a pause, and then something that sounded like a rasping chuckle. [Your spirit of rebellion, I approve of it,] the disembodied voice said. [Your destination, the soldiers will lead you to it.]

Traveling in his current situation, Merrick quickly discovered, was easier said than done. The rods allowed him less than half his usual stride, and even those small steps transmitted an awkward and unpleasant torsion to the shoulder rod with each movement.

But there was no way he was going to change his mind and ask the Trofts for a ride. Not now. Especially not when he had a sneaking suspicion that the alien commander was hoping that he would do so.

Besides, the leisurely pace forced by his restraints gave him a better opportunity to study the layout of the maze of corridors as they passed through it.

And for the first time since his capture, he finally knew beyond the shadow of a doubt where he was.

The Trofts had indeed locked him in the Sollas subcity. And not only in the subcity, but in the southwest area, the part of the labyrinth he was most familiar with.

Like Merrick himself, though, the place was no longer in pristine shape. The walls and ceilings showed signs of stress or battering, as if the Trofts had been at them with giant sledgehammers. Or, more likely, that someone had been busy at ground level with explosives and bulldozers, pummeling the subcity with random shock waves and toppling buildings across areas that hadn't been properly prepared to take that kind of weight.

Finally, after fifteen minutes of plodding through increasingly familiar territory, they arrived at their destination: the very arena where Merrick and the Djinn had planned and trained for that final attack on the invaders' warships.

The battle in which Merrick had nearly been killed.

He looked around the room, the memories of those long hours of practice mixing with the remembered stress and agony of the battle itself. The arena was good-sized, fifty meters by thirty, with an eight-meter-high ceiling. The walls were lined with doors of various sizes, six of them exits, the others leading to storage for the equipment, ramps, and prefab structures that could be used to turn the empty room into a duplicate of whatever the Djinn would be facing on their next mission. Near the ceiling were a set of catwalks and projectors that could handle lighting and other optical and audio effects. Lower down were display screens that could add further visual details and cues that the team might need to know.

The arena hadn't escaped the general subcity damage. One of the catwalks had lost its supports at one end and was hanging at an angle, its lower end suspended in midair about three meters above the floor. Two of the exit doors had been shattered, with the pieces still lying nearby, and the walls near all the other exits were pitted with laser marks. Behind the broken doors he could see stacks of rubble that blocked any chance of movement in those directions. In the center of the room the entire ceiling had been bowed downward, with several square meters of the concrete broken away and the exposed rebar hanging open like a strange abstract sculpture.

More ominous were the dark stains of dried blood scattered across the floor. Whatever had happened here, the Qasamans hadn't given up without a fight.

[Ten more steps, you will take them,] the unseen Troft ordered, his voice coming now from one of the speakers in the arena's upper walls.

Merrick grimaced. Another ten steps with this stupid rig he was wearing? [The Games, what do they consist of?] he called as he obediently set off toward the center of the arena.

[The Games, they are from Anya Winghunter's culture,] the Troft said. [Their purpose, she will explain it.]

Merrick focused on the woman still walking in front of him. The Games were *her* idea? "Anya?" he prompted.

"Commander Ukuthi speaks truth," Anya said over her shoulder. "The Games are the way my people test our young ones."

"I thought you said you were slaves," Merrick said. At least now he had a name for the Troft who'd been running him in rings ever since he was brought here. The question was, how did Anya know him? "What do you test them for?"

Anya stopped and turned around, her eyes cool and measuring as she looked at him. "For skills of combat," she said, as if it was obvious. "Our masters enjoy watching us fight."

Merrick was still trying to find a response to that when there was a multiple *snick* from his wrists and ankles. The cuffs popped free and dropped clattering to the floor, the three connecting rods dropping with them.

He turned around, flexing his arms and fingers, just in time to see the last of their two Troft escorts hurriedly disappear through the doorway they'd entered by. The door swung shut with a thud, and he heard a double click as it was locked.

Locked; but not for long. Merrick's cell door had been specifically designed to keep people from getting through it. The arena's doors hadn't. Flicking a target lock onto the bolted side, he shifted his weight onto his right leg—

[The exits from the room, explosives have been attached to them,] Commander Ukuthi's voice drifted down from the ceiling. [A devastating blast, it will occur if you attempt to escape.]

Merrick hesitated, still balanced on one foot. The Troft might be bluffing, though from what Merrick had seen of him so far that didn't seem likely. But even if he wasn't, Merrick and Anya were a good five meters back from the door. There would have to be a hell of a lot of explosives back there to reach them at this distance. The gamble was probably worth taking.

He looked up at the cracked ceiling. On the other hand, he had no idea how much damage this part of the subcity had taken. It was conceivable that an explosion of any size would bring the whole arena down on top of them.

His programmed Cobra reflexes might still get him safely through a catastrophe like that. But they wouldn't help Anya.

He'd promised himself that he wouldn't get in any way emotionally attached to this mysterious woman. But whether he liked it or not, she was a fellow human being, and he couldn't risk her life so casually. Certainly not on a plan that had such a limited chance of ultimate success anyway.

"Fine," he muttered. "Whatever." He raised his voice. [The Games, begin them.]

There was a short pause. Then, across the arena, one of the storage room doors opened, and a razorarm strode into the room. It caught sight of the two humans and broke into a loping run toward them.

Merrick frowned. Was Ukuthi kidding? Razorarms had decentralized nervous systems that made them tricky to kill, but Aventine's Cobras had long since learned the necessary tricks. Targeting three of the easiest kill points, he waited for the predator to get closer.

And as it closed to within ten meters and threw itself into an attack sprint, he swiveled his left leg up and fired his antiarmor laser. There were three brilliant bursts of light, and the spine leopard slammed into the floor and skidded to a halt at Merrick's feet.

Merrick gave it a few seconds, just to make sure, then looked up at the speaker. "Is that it?" he called. "Can we go home now?"

"There will be more," Anya murmured into the silence, her voice odd. "They will not stop with just one."

Merrick looked at her, frowning. The oddness of her voice, he saw now, was matched by the oddness in her face. In place of the wooden, distant expression he'd become accustomed to was a mixture of surprise, disbelief, and a touch of fear.

Only then did it occur to Merrick that she'd probably never seen what a Cobra could do.

"Don't worry about it," he said as soothingly as he could. There was something disconcerting about being looked at in that way. "Whatever they throw at me, I can handle it."

[The next predator, it will not be the same,] Commander Ukuthi's voice came over the speaker. [Concussion charges, they will be attached to its hide. Detonation of the charges, your lasers will cause. Understanding, do you have it?]

Merrick looked at Anya again. This one seemed new to her, too. [Understanding, I have it,] he called. [Danger to us, do the charges possess it?]

[Danger, they certainly possess it,] Ukuthi assured him. [The charges, they are shaped to spread their force outward. The predator, it will not be harmed.]

[Understanding, I have it,] Merrick repeated sourly. In other words, if the concussion charges were close enough when they detonated, they would stun or otherwise disable Merrick and Anya but not the razorarm, leaving the predator free to maul them at its leisure.

But that shouldn't be a problem. He knew at least four different ways to kill a razorarm, and if this was Ukuthi's way of learning the full range of Merrick's Cobra weaponry he was going to be disappointed. All four ways involved his lasers, which the Trofts had already seen.

To Merrick's left another of the storage room doors swung open and a second razorarm bounded out. This one, he saw, was noticeably more agitated than the first had been.

Small wonder. Attached to its head, looking like some sort of strange lily pads floating on a misshapen pond, were three cup-like devices about ten centimeters across.

And they were positioned precisely over the three spots where Merrick had shot the first razorarm.

This time Merrick didn't bother to let the predator find and identify its potential prey and launch itself into a charge. With three more rapid-fire laser shots, he dropped it where it stood.

"Amazing," Anya murmured from his side.

"It's all in the wrist," Merrick told her, glancing around the room. The rest of the arena's doors were still closed. "Stay here," he ordered. Warily, he crossed to the dead razorarm and squatted down beside it.

The devices fastened to the animal's hide weren't anything he was familiar with. But the trigger mechanism did indeed look like a temperature fuse, which meant Ukuthi hadn't been lying about the risk if Merrick's aim went awry.

What was interesting was that a temperature fuse would also be triggered by Merrick's arcthrower or possibly even the lower-intensity current of his stunner. Yet Ukuthi had only warned him against laser misfires. Did that mean Ukuthi didn't know about those weapons? Or had that been a test to see if Merrick was smart enough to extrapolate to such conclusions on his own?

He was pondering that question, and trying to figure out what he might be able to do to the concussion charges without setting them off, when a third door swung open across the room. This time, the razorarm sported six of the concussion-charge lily pads, the collection covering both sets of Merrick's earlier kill points.

Merrick sighed as he got back to his feet. Now it was just getting ridiculous.

He killed the razorarm, and the one after that, and the one after that. Each time, the next predator emerged with more and more of the concussion charges in place, until the last one came out looking like some high-fashion satire.

But there was nothing amusing about the fact that all the predator's best target zones were now off-limits. Merrick wound up lasering its legs to bring it to a halt, then moving right up beside it and carefully lasering three shots into its head beneath the charges. Once again he confirmed that the predator was dead, then returned to Anya's side to wait for whatever Ukuthi and the Games had planned for him next. Another door opened, much earlier than Merrick had expected, and he turned to face it.

And felt his mouth drop open. It wasn't a razorarm this time, but a creature like nothing he'd ever seen before.

Its basic shape was that of a tapered cylinder, five meters long and half a meter in diameter at its largest, heavily scaled, with no legs and a barely discernable head with tiny eyes and a wide slit of a mouth. It rippled its way out of the storage room onto the arena floor in a fluid, snake-like motion, its movement accompanied by the muted crackle of hard scales against concrete floor. Its front segment swayed back and forth a few times, as if the creature was surveying its new territory. Then, with almost arrogant leisure, it turned to face Merrick and Anya.

"What the *hell* is that?" Merrick muttered, taking Anya's arm and backing them slowly away from the creature.

"It is called a jormungand," she said, her voice trembling. Merrick spared her a quick glance, his stomach tightening at the sight of her wide eyes and suddenly pale face. Whatever this thing was, she was very unhappy to see it. "How did he find—?"

"Save it," Merrick cut her off. The armored snake was on the move, rippling toward them with deceptive speed.

There was no time for finesse. Swiveling on his right leg, Merrick brought up his left and fired his antiarmor laser into the creature's head. The shot sent a burst of thick green smoke from the impact point, momentarily hiding the jormungand from sight.

The smoke cleared away to reveal the creature still slithering toward them as if nothing had happened.

"You have to kill it!" Anya said frantically. "Please."

"I'm trying, I'm trying," Merrick snarled, wrinkling his nose as the fetid odor from the smoke reached him. He fired again, still targeting the head, then again, and again. The results were the same: clouds of smoke, some charring of the scales where the shots hit, but no serious damage and no obvious effect on the jormungand's ability to function. The scales were ablative, Merrick realized with a sinking feeling, the first microsecond of the laser's heat vaporizing a thin layer, with the resulting smoke then diffusing the rest of the shot and probably also carrying away most of the energy. If the scales were thick enough, he could probably pump fifty shots into the damn thing and still not kill it.

He didn't have time for fifty shots. And he definitely didn't have time to experiment. Angered or stung by Merrick's useless attacks, the jormungand had picked up speed and was now coming at them at the pace of a brisk jog. "Go," Merrick told Anya, giving her a push back behind him. "Go. Run!"

"Run where?" she asked, taking a few steps and then stopping.

Merrick glanced around. Aside from the dead razorarms the arena was bare, with no cover anywhere. The catwalks would be safe enough from something that couldn't jump, but they were all too high to reach.

Except for the broken one hanging precariously from one end.

It would be dangerous, Merrick knew—the supports might be in bad enough shape that any extra weight would bring the whole thing crashing down. But it was all they had. "Over by the catwalk's lower end," he ordered, jabbing a finger toward it. "Go there and wait for me."

"Be careful," Anya said, and took off running.

Merrick turned back to the jormungand slithering toward him and tried to think. Distance shots weren't working. Maybe something a little closer would be more effective.

The problem was that closer also meant more dangerous. He hadn't seen what kind of teeth the thing had, but he had no doubt they were as formidable as the rest of it. But he had to risk it. Bending his knees, he stretched out his right hand toward the creature and braced himself.

And as the jormungand got to within two meters he fired his arcthrower, sending a bolt of high-voltage current into the creature's head. As the thunderclap echoed across the arena he shoved off the floor, leaping up and over the armored snake.

He nearly died right there. The entire lower half of the jormungand's body whipped upward like a thick, scaled whip as he jumped, barely missing him as he soared past overhead. He hit the floor and spun around.

To find that the arcthrower hadn't done any better than the laser.

Or maybe it had, just a little. The jormungand seemed fractionally more sluggish as it turned around toward him again. Fifty shots with the arcthrower, maybe, would do as well as fifty with the antiarmor laser.

Across the room, Anya had reached the hanging catwalk and turned back to watch the drama. Merrick gave the jormungand a wide berth and sprinted over to join her.

"Are we going up there?" she asked, pointing at the catwalk as he braked to a halt.

"*You* are," Merrick said, crouching down in front of her and holding his hand, palm-upward, beside her foot. "Step on my hand. Come on—do it."

Hesitantly, she did as ordered. Merrick straightened, hearing the faint whine as his servos took the woman's weight, and lifted her up to the catwalk. "Grab the rail and pull yourself up," he instructed. "If it feels safe, try climbing another meter or so—we don't want the snake thinking you're close enough to be worth making a snatch for."

"What about you?" Anya asked as she eased herself onto the catwalk. The structure swayed ominously, but the anchors at the upper end seemed to be holding.

"I'll be back soon," Merrick said, giving the catwalk one last look and then turning back around.

And leaping instantly to the side as his nanocomputer took over, the jormungand's snapping jaws nearly catching his leg as he flew away out of its reach. It had teeth, all right, lots of big, sharp ones. Merrick hit the floor, rolled, and came back up onto his feet.

His first fear was that the jormungand might decide to try for the low-hanging catwalk and the stationary prey clinging to it. But apparently it was smart enough to recognize that Merrick posed the more immediate threat. It had already turned again and was slithering toward him, its beady eyes barely visible beneath the scaled brow ridges. Briefly, Merrick considered trying to blind it, decided his better option right now would be to get the hell out of there, and took off running.

He reached the far wall and again turned around. The jormungand was still charging toward him, but his sprint had opened up a wide enough gap to give him some breathing space. Time to breathe, and time to think.

The snake could be killed. Everything could. He just had to find the right way to do it.

Glancing up at the ceiling, wondering if Ukuthi was enjoying the show, he keyed his infrareds.

The facial-mapping system his generation of Cobras had been fitted with had been designed mainly to study human faces, with the goal of detecting stress, fatigue, and possible bald-faced lies. But it should work equally well on large armored snakes. Warm spots, Merrick knew, would indicate places where the scaling was thinner, or where the jormungand's blood vessels were closer to the surface, which might give him a clue as to where his weapons would be most effective.

Only there weren't any such warm spots, not anywhere on the creature's head, back, or sides. There was heat there, certainly, but it seemed to be radiating pretty uniformly across the whole of the jormungand's hide.

But there had to be *someplace* that was less protected. At the very least, the snake had to have an opening for dumping its wastes. Probably somewhere in the tail area, either underneath the animal or otherwise blocked from Merrick's current vantage point. He waited for it to slither closer, then leaped over it, making sure this time that he went high enough to avoid its lunge.

And as he reached the top of his arc and started back to the floor, he finally spotted it. The whole tip of the jormungand's tail was blazing with infrared. Thinner, possibly newer scales, and the place where he was going to have to nail it.

He hit the floor and spun around, readying his laser. But it was too late. The jormungand had already twisted around and was heading for him again. Clearly, the first challenge was going to be getting the damn thing to hold still.

He glanced around the room, looking for inspiration. Could he get Anya to somehow hold the jormungand's attention long enough for him to get behind it? But the snake had already shown it was more interested in Merrick than it was in her.

Could he lure it close to one of the dead razorarms and then laser some of the concussion charges? But fine-tuning the snake's positioning that way would require Merrick to be dangerously close himself, and there was a fair chance the concussion would affect him more than it did the jormungand.

But there was one other option.

He set off across the room again, keeping an eye over his shoulder and adjusting his pace to let the jormungand slowly gain on him. This was going to require careful timing, and be horrendously risky even if he nailed it precisely. He checked the distance in front of him, slowed down a bit, then looked back again. The jormungand, perhaps concluding its prey was starting to tire, had put on an impressive burst of speed, closing to within a meter of his heels as Merrick neared the wall. Again, he adjusted his pace to maintain his lead. He reached his jump-off point, two meters from the wall, and leaped up and forward, throwing out his hands to catch the wall that was now rushing toward him.

And as he soared above the exit door directly beneath him, the door Commander Ukuthi had warned had been wired with explosives, he sent an antiarmor shot straight through the panel.

The explosion was every bit as powerful as Merrick had expected, the blast hammering into his ears as the shock wave buffeted him. He slammed palms-first into the wall, his arm servos absorbing the impact, his hooked fingers finding a tenuous grip in cracks in the masonry.

But Ukuthi's explosives experts had done their job right. As hard as Merrick had been hit by the edge of the blast, the main force had been straight outward, disintegrating the door and hurling the pieces across the room like multiple champagne corks as a gigantic fireball burst out behind them. Merrick peered down through the swirling dust and superheated air to see a wide section of blackened and newly cracked floor.

And in the center of the destruction, the charred and motionless form of the jormungand.

The best-case scenario had been that the explosion would kill the thing outright. Incredibly, though, it was still alive, its tail making small twitching movements, its whole body shaking with the shock of the damage. Merrick had no idea how extensive the creature's injuries were or if, left to itself, it might survive and recover.

He also had no intention of finding out.

It took five long antiarmor blasts to finally burn a small hole through the scales in the very tip of the jormungand's tail. But once that was done, the rest was straightforward. Sitting down behind the snake, he lined up his left leg with the opening and opened fire.

The snake could have all the armor it wanted on the outside. But its insides should cook just as well as those of any other living being.

The flexible laser conduit across Merrick's ankle was starting to become uncomfortably hot when the jormungand's twitching and shaking finally stopped.

Taking a shaking breath, Merrick got back to his feet, wincing as the assorted aches and pains he'd collected started making themselves felt through the fading adrenaline in his system. He looked across the room, wondering if the shock of the blast had knocked the dangling catwalk the rest of the way off the wall. But it was still hanging on.

So, to his quiet relief, was Anya. "You okay?" he called.

She nodded, a jerky movement. "Hang on," he said, starting toward her. "I'm coming."

He'd taken three steps when he heard a scurrying sound behind him. Instantly, he spun around, snapping his hands up into firing position.

But it wasn't another razorarm or jormungand. It was just a few Troft soldiers, scrambling madly to guard the corridor that now lay wide open in front of him.

An hour ago, Merrick might have been tempted. But not now.

[The effort, don't bother with it,] he called. Turning around again, he continued walking toward the catwalk.

A minute later, he had Anya safely down. [The Games, do they now continue?] he called toward the ceiling.

[The Games, they are over,] Ukuthi said. [Your abilities, they are beyond even my expectations.]

[My satisfaction, it swells with your enjoyment,] Merrick said sarcastically. [Your associates, did they also enjoy the show?]

There was no answer. But across the room, one of the large display panels came to life.

And Merrick saw a row of silent Trofts seated in a small room. All were in uniforms, and most were wearing what the Qasaman military had tentatively identified as senior officer insignia. The one in the center was also wearing the distinctive red sash of a demesne-heir.

Merrick had just enough time to wonder what that was all about when the image winked off. [The demonstration, my associates did indeed enjoy it,] Ukuthi confirmed calmly. [Rest and food, you may now have them.]

Merrick grimaced. [The shackles, must I submit to them?]

[The shackles, there will be no need for them.] Behind Anya, a door swung open to reveal another of the arena's storage rooms, this one furnished like Merrick's old cell. [The doctor, I will also send him to you,] Ukuthi added.

[A doctor, I do not need one,] Merrick said.

[The doctor, I will send him,] Ukuthi said, his tone making it clear that it was an order. [A conversation, we will have one soon.]

"Sure," Merrick said under his breath. [The woman, her services I also no longer need.]

[The woman, she will remain with you.]

Merrick snorted. With Ukuthi no doubt hoping the two captive humans would bond even more closely.

But it was already too late, and Merrick knew it. He'd put his life on the line to get Anya to safety. Despite his best efforts to keep his distance, he was already emotionally entangled with her.

What Ukuthi was planning to do with that connection he didn't know. But he knew it wouldn't be good.

Anya was standing quietly, watching Merrick. Waiting for orders. "Come on," he said, trudging toward his new cell. "Let's get some rest."

CHAPTER THIRTEEN

It had been five days since Jody, Rashida, and Smitty had started poring over the Troft warship's control boards. They had translated everything, relabeled most of the controls, especially the ones Smitty would need to use, and painstakingly applied Rashida's freighter techniques to the larger ship. As far as Jody could tell, they had everything down cold.

But ultimately, the only way to know whether they did or not was to actually try it.

Kemp had strongly urged that they finally tell Harli the whole truth about what they'd been doing before the test. But Rashida was still terrified of the consequences of admitting her earlier evasions, and Jody had backed her up. Both women readily agreed, though, that they should warn Harli to move the Caelians still working on the downed ship to a safe distance.

And with that now done, it was finally the moment of truth.

"Grav-lift power levels?" Rashida called across the control room.

"Ready," Jody reported, eyeing the proper displays and then checking the main drive registers. "Drive's still coming up. Probably two more minutes."

"Everything outside looks good," Smitty added from the sensor station. "Everyone's back far enough. Temp and oscillation-resonance readings on the engines are holding."

Standing out of the way by the door, Kemp keyed his field

radio. "We're about ready," he reported. "Grav lifts are at power; Jody says two more minutes on the drive."

"Acknowledged," Harli's voice came back. "Remind them to take it easy. We've got plenty of time, and the last thing we need is *two* Troft warships lying on their sides."

"Right," Kemp said. "You get that, Rashida?"

"Yes," Rashida said. Her voice seemed steady enough, but Jody could sense the tension beneath it. "Let me know when the drive power—"

"I've got movement," Smitty said suddenly, leaning toward one of his displays. "A Troft—make that *two* Trofts—running toward the downed ship."

"Harli, you've got runners," Kemp snapped into the radio. "Vector ninety, heading for the downed ship."

"We're on them," Harli said tightly. "We've got three—oh, *hell*."

"What is it?" Jody demanded, craning her neck and trying to see Smitty's monitors. But from her angle she could barely even tell which ones were active and which ones weren't. "Smitty? What's going on?"

"I can't tell," Smitty said tautly. "Got some smoke—where the *hell* did they get smoke bombs?—laser flashes—okay; one of them's down. The other's still running—wait a minute, there are two more now. Still going all-out for the downed ship—"

"Get that ship out of there," Harli's voice barked suddenly from the radio. "Kemp? You copy?"

"We copy," Kemp said. "Where do you want them to put it?"

"Anywhere!" Harli snarled. "Just *get it out of there*!"

"You heard him, Rashida," Jody put in. "Do it."

For a second nothing happened. Then, with a sudden lurch, the warship lifted into the sky. "You did it!" Jody called. "Rashida—"

She broke off, grabbing for the edge of her control board as the ship tilted forward. "Straighten up!" she snapped. "Rashida—we're falling! You have to straighten up."

"No, no, she's right," Smitty said. "She's leaning us forward so the grav lifts can buy us some distance."

Distance from what? Jody clamped down hard on the question. Whatever was going on, at least Rashida and Smitty seemed to be on the same page about it.

"Drive power?" Rashida called.

With an effort, Jody focused on the display. "Low but functional."

"Smitty?" Rashida asked.

"Right," Smitty said. "Tip 'er back three degrees and give it a try."

"Wait a second," Jody protested, grabbing for her board again as the ship leveled itself. "What are we—?"

"Now!" Smitty barked.

And with another, even more violent lurch the ship shot forward.

"Good," Smitty said, raising his voice over the laboring rumble of the engines. "Ease 'er back—straighten up—that's good. A little more . . ."

"Kemp?" Harli called.

"We're here," Kemp said. "Situation?"

"Resolved," Harli bit out. "Mostly. How's the ship doing?"

"Seems fine," Kemp said. "Rashida and the others are running it like pros. You want us to bring it back?"

"Yes," Harli said. "No, wait. Can you maneuver it over to the landing field?"

"Rashida?" Kemp asked.

For a moment nothing happened. Then, the ship began to turn, slowly and gently enough that only Jody's inner ear was aware of the motion. "Yes, I think so," Rashida said.

"She says yes," Kemp relayed. "As close to the wall as possible, I assume?"

"Without actually hitting it, yes," Harli said sourly. "Actually, give it a few meters farther than she thinks she can do without hitting it. I've had enough disasters and near-disasters for one day."

"What happened?" Jody called. "Harli?"

"You just concentrate on landing the damn warship," Harli called back. "There'll be time for talk later. I'll send an aircar to meet you."

"We can walk it if you'd rather," Kemp offered.

"I wouldn't," Harli said flatly. "Not with the shape the field's in. When you're down, just wait inside until the aircar gets there." There was a click and the radio went dead.

"Okay," Kemp said. "Nice and easy, now. Like he said, we've got time."

The ship began to turn again. "What did he mean by the shape the field's in?" Rashida asked.

"It's like the clear zone around Stronghold, only more so," Smitty said. "As in, seriously on the overgrown side."

Jody grimaced. *Overgrown* was putting it mildly. Three weeks of neglect had allowed Caelian's aggressive plant life a head start on reclaiming the fifty-meter zone around the city that was normally kept clear of such intrusions. The rectangular landing field south of the city, without even the continual human and Troft trampling that was currently taking place in the area around the two warships, would be even worse. "He means knee-deep in hookgrass and razor fern," she told Rashida.

"And all the other delightful things that live there," Smitty said. "Waiting for an aircar will be a lot simpler."

"Not to mention that it'll get us back across town faster," Kemp said grimly. "I for one want to find out what the hell just happened back there."

"And whether it's going to complicate our lives?" Smitty asked.

Kemp snorted. "Oh, well, that's pretty much a given. The only question is how badly."

"This," Harli said, holding up a double-fist-sized piece of smashed electronics, "is what the ship techs call a grav-lift cascade regulator. Or at least, that's what it used to be. Now, it's a desktop junk sculpture."

"Any chance of fixing it?" Kemp asked, taking the device and turning it over in his hands.

"Anything can be fixed if you have spare parts and know how to put them together," Harli growled. "Which means, no, we can't. Not a chance." He gestured toward the downed ship. "We're just damned lucky you got the other ship out of there in time."

Jody gazed at the downed warship, a shiver running through her. "So it really would have flipped all the way over if they'd gotten to the generators and started up the grav lifts?"

"We don't know for sure," Harli said. "But the techs say there's a good chance that it would have. Straight up, straight over, and a nice little domino effect when it slammed into yours." He gestured to Jody. "That was fast thinking, by the way, using a drive pulse to blow away the smoke once you were clear. Made it a lot easier to spot and laser them."

"Actually, it was Rashida's idea," Jody told him. "She and Smitty coordinated it together."

"In that case, good job, Rashida and Smitty," Harli said, a little testily. "As long as you two are brimming with ideas, you got one for making sure the Trofts don't pull another stunt like this?"

"You know my views," Smitty muttered. "Shoot them all and be done with it."

"We've been through this," Jody said firmly. "Moral high ground, remember?"

"Yeah, I know," Smitty said. "It just feels good to say it every so often, that's all."

"Harli's right, though," Kemp said. "A homemade smoke bomb's reasonably harmless, and even with that Eubujak nearly caused a catastrophe. The next gadget he comes up with will be a lot nastier."

"Bet on it," Harli said grimly. He hissed out a sigh. "And that about wraps things up for your fancy curtain, too, Jody. I'm sorry, but we're going to have to leave the downed ship right where it is. There's no way we can risk trying to lift it now."

"Why not?" Smitty asked, frowning. "If the lifts flip it over, so what? In fact, that'll put it even more out of the way of the wall gap."

"The *so what* is that we don't know what a second impact might do to the internal workings," Harli said. "Especially the fuel and other fluids that we'd just as soon keep inside. We were lucky the first time—warships are built tough, and the impact with the wall may have cushioned the fall a little. But we can't count on being that lucky twice."

Jody looked away from the ship, focusing on the partially trampled hookgrass and other plants outside the wall. "So we're not going to use the curtain at all?" she asked, an idea starting to take shape in the back of her mind.

"I don't think we can risk it," Harli said. "I know your friends put a lot of work into it, but—"

"Hold it," Kemp said, lifting a hand. "I don't think that's where she was going. You have something, Jody?"

"Maybe," Jody said slowly. "We can't just drive the Trofts into the forest, because that would be the same as shooting them. But what if we could put them out there and at the same time keep most of the wildlife away?"

"You mean like a bunker?" Smitty asked.

"She means like a spore-repellent curtain," Kemp said. "Right?"

"Right," Jody said. "We were planning on, what, seventy or eighty meters to cover the gap in the wall?"

"I told them we needed seventy-five," Harli said, eyeing her closely. "And three meters high."

"Okay," Jody said, running a quick mental calculation. "So if we lay the curtain out in a ring seventy-five meters in circumference, that makes the area inside something like four hundred thirty square meters. Right?"

"Closer to four-forty, I think," Harli said.

"Either way, with a hundred ninety prisoners that comes to over two square meters each," Jody said. "Not comfortable, but feasible. They'll be mostly safe, *and* they'll be out of our hair."

"What about the big predators?" Smitty asked. "The curtain's not going to keep them out."

"But most of them won't bother to investigate," Harli said thoughtfully. "For those who do, I guess the Trofts are on their own."

"Or we could give them a couple of shotguns with ten rounds each," Kemp suggested.

"If they've got weapons, Eubujak might order them to come back here," Smitty warned.

"Only if he knows where we are," Jody said. "We could burn away a path half a kilometer or so into the forest, burn out a clearing, and march them there under the curtain to keep them from seeing where they're going."

"Couldn't they just follow the burned path back?" Smitty asked.

"We could burn two or three of them," Jody said.

"Probably not necessary," Kemp said. "They head through any part of the forest and the giggers'll get them before they get fifty meters. We just nail the generator to a tree so they can't take the curtain with them, and they'll be stuck there."

"That's a lot of burning," Harli pointed out. "Don't know if we have time for that." He looked at Jody, his lips twisting in a slightly evil smile as he pulled out his radio. "But I think we can come up with something simpler, *and* maybe even a bit more elegant." He keyed the radio. "Nissa? You there?"

"I'm here," the woman's cool voice came back.

"Any update on the curtain timeline?"

"Just a minute." There was a brief pause filled with muffled and distant voices. "They say it'll be ready by tomorrow morning," Nissa reported. "Possibly tonight, if they hurry."

"Then tell them to hurry," Harli told her. "I want to know the minute it's ready."

"You will," Nissa said.

"Good. Get back to work." Harli keyed off the radio and put it away. "We'll need to rig some stands to hold the thing up," he said, almost as if talking to himself. "But we were going to have to do that anyway. I figure we should be ready to march them out by mid-morning at the latest."

"We're never going to burn them a clearing by then," Kemp warned.

"No clearing needed," Harli assured him. "We're going to put them at the far end of the landing field."

"That close to Stronghold?" Kemp asked, frowning. "How do you expect to keep them there?"

"You'll see." Harli smiled tightly, then sobered. "I'm glad you've got the ship running. We need to start the evacuation this afternoon, and this'll make it a lot easier than running a line of overloaded aircars back and forth across the forest."

"Be easier on the wounded, too," Kemp said. "At least they'll get to stretch out for the trip. You and the Governor still going to put everyone in Aerie?"

"No, we thought about it and decided that an influx of nine hundred new citizens would strain even their traditional hospitality," Harli said. "We're now figuring three hundred each to Aerie, Essbend, and Rockhouse."

"Even that's going to be pushing it," Kemp warned. "Especially for Rockhouse."

"I know," Harli conceded. "But I don't see any other way. When those Troft reinforcements come, they'll be coming to Stronghold first. We have to get the citizens out of harm's way, and dividing them up is the best way to do that."

"Unless you moved everyone into the Octagon Caves," Smitty said suddenly. "I didn't think about that earlier, but there's plenty of room in there for a mass camp-out. Or they could split up into smaller rooms—Danny and Kirstin and I found dozens of them back when we used to poke around in there."

"Actually, I'm thinking we might use the caves for something else," Harli said. "I'll want to talk to you about that later."

"Perhaps Smitty's right about hiding away in caverns," Rashida spoke up hesitantly. "Even if the invaders come here first, they'll surely travel afterward to the other towns you spoke of."

"Yes, that'll probably be their plan," Harli agreed. "Our job is to make sure that doesn't happen." He gestured to her. "Your job is to get better at flying that thing. The Trofts could arrive in anywhere from two to three days. In six hours I'm going to start moving people out of Stronghold. Think you'll be ready to start taking passengers by then?"

Rashida looked at Jody and Smitty, then back at Harli. "We'll be ready in three," she promised.

"Good," Harli said. "Kemp, go grab Popescu and Brady and get them working on support frames for that curtain. I'll go tell Dad to alert the first evacuee list."

He looked up at the sun. "We're burning daylight. Let's get to work."

Nine weeks.

The words swirled through Jin's mind, disturbing and mocking, as the car bounced along the wide road leading toward Azras. *Nine weeks.*

That was how long it took on Aventine to turn a new recruit into a full Cobra. That was always how long it had taken, ever since Jin could remember. The exact regimen had been adjusted over the years, as the instructors experimented with new techniques or as the implanted equipment itself was tweaked. But the total length of the training period never wavered. *Nine weeks.*

Yithtra and the Milika villagers had had six days.

Ghushtre and his fellow Djinn had had one.

She focused on the back of the Yithtra's head as he steered the car along the winding forest road, smelling the very Qasaman scent of the two others in the front seat and the one on Paul's other side here in the back. Beach and McCollom thought the group was ready, though both of them had expressed varying degrees of astonishment at that fact. Certainly the villagers and Djinn themselves thought they were ready.

But were they? That was the question that had been nagging at Jin since the convoy left Milika two hours ago. Were they really ready for war?

But then, was anyone ever really ready for war? Or did everyone just do what they could with what they had, struggling along and hoping for the best?

"There," Gama Yithtra said, taking one hand from the wheel and pointing ahead. "That's Azras."

Jin leaned across Paul's chest to look past Yithtra's head. Ahead and to the right, she could see the top edge of a city wall above the rolling hills a couple of kilometers beyond the edge of the forest.

On the other side of the road, a kilometer from the city itself, she could see the top of another of the tall, narrow Troft warships.

"I see they've learned from their Sollas drubbing," Paul murmured. "Sitting way out there, they can shoot down any SkyJos the Qasamans launch from Azras before they get into their own attack range."

"Their cunning goes far deeper than that," Yithtra said. "They have the entire city under siege, with eight of their armored troop trucks roaming the streets at all times. They also have drones overhead, watching every gathering of citizens and tracking where they come from and where they go."

"Trying to find a way into the subcity," Jin said, nodding. "Still, if they're waiting for someone to get sloppy, they're going to have a long wait."

"Ah, but they *aren't* merely hoping for carelessness," Yithtra said grimly. "They hope also to elicit treason."

Jin snorted. "Good luck with that one."

"Perhaps," Yithtra said. "But as you'll see, we and the food we bring to the blockaded citizens will be readily allowed in. But we'll find that we're then forbidden to leave."

Jin frowned; and then she got it. "Thereby increasing the number of mouths that need to be fed, which adds more strain on the city's resources."

"And adds more to the usual tension existing between city dwellers and villagers," Yithtra said. "Especially as the villagers now trapped by their errand of mercy will be increasingly frantic to return to their homes and families."

"Let me guess," Paul murmured. "Point out an entrance to the subcity and you can go home."

"Exactly," Yithtra said. "Or deliver a military weapon to them, or identify a Djinn or soldier to the invaders, and likewise buy your escape." Yithtra made a spitting sound. "A futile hope, of course, that any villager would betray our world. We aren't city dwellers, who might—"

"Enough of that," Jin interrupted firmly. "You're not a villager anymore, Gama Yithtra, any more than the Djinn riding behind us and the people you'll meet in Azras are city dwellers. You're Qasamans. Nothing more, nothing less."

"Of course," Yithtra said. But he didn't say it like he really believed it. Or meant it.

Jin looked sideways at Paul. He grimaced, but merely gave a small shrug.

Even under the pressures of war, the old rivalries remained.

There were four of the Troft armored trucks arrayed around the main gate into Azras: two of them flanking the road, facing opposite directions with their roof-mounted swivel guns guarding both approaches to the city. The other two trucks flanked the short access spur that led from the main road to the gate, their swivel guns both pointed into the city.

There were also Troft soldiers on duty, at least twenty of them, standing guard at the gate, perched on top of the trucks, or manning the checkpoint barrier that had been set up along the road. All were dressed in the enemy's familiar armored leotards and full-face helmets, all carried big hand-and-a-half lasers, and all had their full attention on the eight-car convoy now rolling toward the checkpoint.

As a no doubt unintentional touch of irony, the Azras gate itself stood wide open.

One of the Trofts strode toward their car as Yithtra brought the vehicle to a halt. "State your name, point of origin, and business," the translator pin on the alien's left shoulder said in a flat voice.

"Gama Yithtra, son of Bejran Yithtra of Milika," Yithtra identified himself. "We bring aid and food for the besieged citizens of Azras."

The Troft looked back at the other seven cars now stopped in a line behind them. "You will leave your vehicles," he ordered, stepping back and leveling his laser at Yithtra. "All will remove their tunics and upper robes."

"Our group includes two women," Yithtra objected. "Such public exposure is shameful and cannot be allowed."

For a moment the Troft regarded him silently, his mouth moving behind his faceplate as he either discussed it with his fellow guards or else checked in with higher authority. Jin watched him closely, mentally crossing her fingers. Stripping to their underwear, she knew, wouldn't bother either her or Jennifer nearly as much as it would a typical Qasaman woman. But that was the point:

they were supposed to *be* Qasaman women, with typical Qasaman sensibilities. If the Trofts refused to grant them an exemption, they would have to leave the men here and hope they could figure out another way into the city.

Fortunately, it wasn't going to come to that. "The females will pull back their sleeves and show their arms to be bare," the Troft ordered. "The males will remove their tunics and upper robes."

Jin gave a silent sigh of relief. Still, the concession to modesty wasn't all that unexpected. The Trofts were clearly looking for Djinni combat suits, and the Qasamans were even worse at permitting women into the ranks of their elite soldiers as Aventine was at accepting female Cobras.

"Understood," Yithtra said. He opened the door and started to get out of the car.

"And after you have done that," the Troft continued, "you will leave your vehicles and carry your supplies by hand through the gate."

Jin had never done any acting herself, and didn't know the first thing about the art or science of that craft. But she knew a good performance when she saw it, and Yithtra's was definitely it. He froze in mid-step, his eyes widening as he looked sharply at the Troft. "What?" he asked, his tone more bewildered than anything else.

"You will carry your supplies in through the gate," the Troft repeated. "Your vehicles will remain here."

Yithtra shot a disbelieving look back down the line of cars, then turned back to the guard. "Why?" he asked. "What's wrong with the cars?"

"You will carry your supplies—"

"Yes, I heard you the first two times," Yithtra cut him off, outrage starting to replace bewilderment in his voice. "That makes no sense. You have any idea how *heavy* those parcels are? And one of our doctors is on crutches—you expect him to *walk* the whole way to the aid center?"

The Troft lifted his laser warningly. "You will go into the city now," he said, the flat translator voice somehow managing to carry an edge of menace. "If you leave the supplies, they will be confiscated along with the vehicles."

Yithtra glared at him. But there was no power behind the defiance, only frustration and anger. He looked through the window at Jin, looked back along the cars again, and muttered a long, feeling curse. "Everybody out!" he shouted, waving his arm over his head. "And—" He grimaced. "Take off your tunics."

Five minutes later, with their tunics now tied around their waists and stacks of food and medical supplies in their arms, they all marched silently between the sentries and through the open city gate. There was another sentry line of Trofts inside, apparently positioned to keep the city dwellers back.

After all, Jin thought cynically, the invaders wouldn't want anyone shouting a warning to all those well-meaning visitors about the trap they were walking into.

Given what newcomers meant to the supply situation within the city, Jin had wondered if the citizens would greet the newcomers with disdain or even hostility. But as they passed the inner sentry line and approached the line of onlookers who'd gathered to watch this latest version of the oft-repeated drama, she saw nothing but resolve and solidarity in their faces. In fact, as she and the others approached, many of the citizens broke ranks and stepped forward, probably risking Troft laser fire, quietly greeting the villagers and gently but firmly relieving them of their burdens. Two of them, spotting Paul lurching along on his crutches, found a wheelchair somewhere and had it ready by the time he reached the edge of the crowd. Another of the citizens, this one a well-dressed man in his sixties, gestured toward a store a block away, which from the stacks of boxes around it had apparently been set up as a distribution center, and led the way toward it.

They had covered half the distance, and the Trofts at the gate were no longer visible through the crowd, when a slightly scruffy-looking man sidled up beside Jin and took her last remaining package. "Welcome to Azras, Jin Moreau," he murmured. "We're pleased you arrived safely."

Jin smiled. "Thank you, Siraj Akim," she greeted him in turn. "I'm pleased to find you also safe and well. I was told you and Ghofl Khatir had come here, but I never heard what happened after that."

"Like everyone else on Qasama, we've been busy," he said with a touch of dry humor. "As you clearly have also been." He threw a glance behind them at the rest of the group. "The recruits seem eager for combat."

"They are," Jin agreed heavily. "And their instructors also seem to think they're ready. But whether they actually are . . ." She shook her head. "I'm hoping we'll have a few days before we leave here so that Beach and McCollom can run them through a few more drills."

"You weren't told?" Siraj asked, an odd tone to his voice.

"Told what?"

Siraj moved a little closer and lowered his voice. "We won't be going to Purma or elsewhere," he said. "The attack will be here. And it'll be launched tomorrow."

Jin felt her eyes widen. "*Tomorrow*? But—" she broke off. "I thought we'd want to run at least a few more groups through Isis first."

"Such was indeed the original plan," Siraj said grimly. "But it's not to be. Five days ago a Drim courier ship arrived at the invaders' Sollas encampment, carrying what our spotters described as a highly agitated commander and crew. They were taken into one of their demesne's warships, where they stayed for two hours. Four hours after that, two other Drim warships lifted from the encampment and left Qasama."

Jin's stomach tightened. "They found out about Caelian."

"So we believe," Siraj agreed. "We feared our new ally was about to come under renewed attack."

Jin nodded, feeling suddenly ill. And when that happened, the Caelians wouldn't have a chance. Not a second time. Not with the Trofts knowing what they were flying into.

And Jody was there with them.

"There was nothing we could do directly to help them," Siraj continued. "But what we *could* attempt to do was create the conditions that would hopefully end the entire war, our part as well as Caelian's."

Jin nodded again as she understood. "By handing the invaders a massive defeat," she said. "Thereby giving the Tlossies and the other local demesnes the leverage they need to step in and force the Drims and their allies to back off."

"Exactly," Siraj agreed. "Even at that we may have waited too long—our estimate is that the Drim ships are now only a day removed from Caelian. But we needed all the new warriors we could get, and it was decided to wait until Ifrit Ghushtre and his Djinn had completed the Isis transformation."

"So that's why they were so adamant about leaving Milika with us," Jin said, the past few days' worth of puzzling conversations suddenly coming clear. "And why they insisted they didn't need any further training."

"Which may in fact be the truth," Siraj said. "Their combat suit capabilities in many ways parallel their new internal ones. That expertise combined with the learning drugs makes it quite possible that a few hours of practice with the attack plan will be all the further training they need. We'll find out shortly."

"I hope we're not all going to the subcity together," Jin warned. "I'm told the Trofts are watching for that kind of parade."

Siraj chuckled. "Never fear, Jin Moreau. After we deliver the supplies to the distribution center, your group will be broken up into three-man teams and escorted by different routes to the subcity and the designated practice arena."

"Good," Jin said, forcing her mind away from Jody and Caelian. "I trust that Paul will instead be taken directly to the hospital?"

"He and you both," Siraj said, nodding. "The doctors have been briefed about his leg and your tumor, and are already prepared to begin their work."

"Thank you." Jin glanced behind her. Paul was far enough back to be safely out of earshot. "But they'll only be working on Paul. I'll be coming with you to the briefing."

"We appreciate your courage and your commitment to Qasama," Siraj said gravely. "More than you can imagine. But your part of the war is over."

"No," Jin said firmly. "My husband's may be, but mine isn't. Not as long as Lorne is still fighting. Certainly not as long as Merrick is a prisoner of the invaders and Jody is in their crosshairs."

"Jin Moreau—"

"And whether you like it or not, you need me," Jin said. "You said it yourself: you need all of us that you can get."

"We'll have enough," Siraj assured her.

"Will you?" Jin countered. "By my count, you have exactly four—Lorne, Beach, McCollom, and me—who've fought as Cobras, plus ten who've only fought as Djinn, plus ten who've never fought at all. So tell me again how you've got all the warriors you need."

Siraj was silent a few more steps. "If I were braver, I'd stand up to you and simply tell you no," he said. "If I were more like my father, I'd find a clever way to make you think you were getting what you want while also achieving my own goals. But I'm neither. Besides, I suspect far too many of those marching with you would come to your support, and I have no interest in fighting all of them."

"Thank you," Jin said quietly.

"Just promise you'll come to *my* defense when your husband learns of your decision." Siraj gave a gentle snort. "Do you recall, back when you and your son were first brought into the Sollas subcity, Kaml Ghushtre questioned my father on the place of honor and pride in warfare?"

"Very well," Jin assured him, wincing at the memory. She and Merrick had come very close to dying that day. "Your father told him that victory was more important even than honor."

"Yes," Siraj said. "I find it supremely ironic that the choice he presented Djinn Ghushtre has not, in fact, been made. Nor has it been required to be made. Whatever happens tomorrow, whether we succeed or fall, honor nevertheless remains ours."

He half turned; and to Jin's surprise he made the sign of respect to her. "Ours," he added, "and yours."

Jin swallowed hard as she returned the sign. "Thank you, Siraj Akim. Whatever happens tomorrow, it's been a privilege to serve with you. And with all of Qasama."

"As it has been for us to serve with you." Siraj smiled tightly. "But I also have no doubt that honor in victory is better than honor in defeat. Let us go and prepare ourselves as best we can for the challenges we will soon face."

"Absolutely," Jin agreed. "Lead the way."

CHAPTER FOURTEEN

From the very beginning of his incarceration in the Djinn command post, Daulo had tried to keep to himself as much as possible.

It had turned out to be surprisingly easy. Much easier than he'd expected given the post's compact size. But with Miron Akim having sent twenty of the Djinn to Milika, and with at least six of the remaining fourteen on patrol in the forest at any given time, the post sometimes felt almost like the Sammon family mine on a workers' holiday.

Most days the only person he saw was the doctor, and he usually only stayed long enough to check the progress of Daulo's recovery and occasionally adjust the level of his medications. As long as Daulo took his meals from the self-service galley at non-standard hours, his chances of avoiding everyone else were really quite high.

Fortunately, the one person he most urgently wanted to avoid seemed to also be trying to keep to himself. Daulo only saw Shahni Haafiz twice during those first few days, both of them chance encounters as Daulo was entering the galley and Haafiz was leaving.

The first of those times, Haafiz had demanded to know why Daulo wasn't under direct guard, and had warned he would be asking Ifrit Narayan the same question. The second time, he simply glared at Daulo and passed by without a word. Apparently, whatever answer he'd gotten from Narayan hadn't been the one he wanted.

As to Omnathi and Akim, Daulo didn't see either of them at all. He asked the doctor about it once, concerned that they might have taken ill, and was assured that both men were simply busy elsewhere on the post. That was all the doctor would say, and Daulo hadn't asked since.

The disadvantage of Daulo's self-imposed isolation was that the silence gave him that much more time to brood about the false charges against him and his son, and to worry about Fadil's safety as the Djinn transported him through the forest.

But he knew down deep that surrounding himself with company wouldn't have distracted his mind from those issues, either. Better not to have to gaze into other people's faces and wonder if they believed Akim's charges against him.

It was on the tenth day after his arrival when it all suddenly came apart.

He was alone in the galley, finishing up the late breakfast/early lunch meal he'd become accustomed to, when Haafiz entered. "There you are," the Shahni said, his voice cold and stiff. "I've been looking all over for you."

Which was probably a lie, Daulo knew, or at least an overly dramatic overstatement. There were only three places he ever went: his quarters, the galley, and the shower room. If Haafiz hadn't figured that out by now, he had no business being a Shahni.

But it wasn't Daulo's place to make such points, at least not out loud. "Can I help you, Shahni Haafiz?" he asked instead, making the sign of respect.

And caught his breath. Nestled in the Shahni's hand was a small but nasty-looking handgun.

"I don't know, Daulo Sammon," Haafiz said darkly as he strode across the galley. "Can you tell me why you, accused of treason, still walk free and unhindered around a secret base of the Djinn? Can you tell me why there's been no movement on any trial or interrogation, which is supposedly why I'm still here instead of at Purma?"

He stopped two meters from Daulo and lifted the gun to point squarely at Daulo's face. "And why," he added, his voice suddenly deadly, "your son is still not here?"

Daulo's whole body suddenly felt cold. "It's only been ten days," he managed, trying not to stare at the gun. "Ifrit Akim said it would take a week in both directions."

"Miron Akim lied," Haafiz said flatly. "I've calculated the numbers. A Djinni with combat suit assistance should be able to cover the distance to Milika in no more than five days. Four, if they chose to push themselves." He lifted the gun slightly. "So I ask you again, Daulo Sammon: where is your son?"

"You don't really expect him to know that, do you?" a voice called from the doorway.

Daulo tore his gaze from the gun and looked over Haafiz's shoulder. It was Narayan, walking casually across the galley toward them.

But there was nothing casual about the tight expression on his face. Nor was there anything casual about the way his gloved hands, still swinging at his sides, were already curled into laser-firing positions.

Only Haafiz, with his glare on Daulo, couldn't see that. "Why not?" Haafiz bit out over his shoulder. "Everyone else claims to know nothing. Perhaps only Daulo Sammon knows the truth. Shall we not ask him?"

"How could he possibly know things that are happening hundreds of kilometers away?" Narayan asked reasonably. "He's been locked up in here ever since he arrived."

"One radio has already been found in his possession," Haafiz reminded him. "Perhaps he had two."

Abruptly, the Shahni spun around, his gun now leveled at Narayan's chest. "Or perhaps," Haafiz said softly, "he's not the only traitor here."

Narayan stopped. "Perhaps he's not," he said, his voice as soft as Haafiz's.

Haafiz seemed taken aback by the other's response. "Then you agree," he said, lowering his gun barrel a few degrees. "Using the excuse of Daulo Sammon to keep me trapped here can only be attributed to cowardice, incompetence, or treason. And I know neither Moffren Omnathi nor Miron Akim is incompetent or a coward."

"Is *that* what you referred to?" Narayan said, his forehead wrinkling as if in confusion. "Your pardon, Shahni Haafiz. I misunderstood what you meant by treason."

"What did you *think* I meant?" Haafiz countered.

Narayan shrugged. "I assumed you were speaking of attempted murder," he said.

And suddenly his hands came up, the lasers in his gloves pointing at Haafiz's chest. "The attempted murders," he continued quietly, "of Senior Advisor Moffren Omnathi and Marid Siraj Akim."

Daulo felt his jaw drop. Haafiz had been planning to *murder* Omnathi and Akim? He opened his mouth to demand an explanation.

And closed it again. This was nothing he wanted to get in the middle of.

But if Haafiz was thrown by the accusation, he didn't show it. "Moffren Omnathi is a traitor," the Shahni spat. "With utter contempt for the rule of the Shahni he sent an emissary to make a devil's bargain with our enemies."

"He *had* approval from the Shahni," Narayan said.

"Not *all* the Shahni," Haafiz retorted.

"All the Shahni who were present."

"Yes, and how very convenient that was for him," Haafiz bit out. "I was available. I should have been called. And his treason was then compounded by Siraj Akim, who went so far as to send his own son on the mission. All of them are traitors. All of them deserve to die."

"If you believed that you should have brought formal charges against them," Narayan countered. "Instead, like a coward, you ordered them on a mission which would leave them dead." He took a step closer to the Shahni. "And then ordered six good and loyal men to die alongside them."

Daulo caught his breath, that confrontation in the Sollas subcity suddenly coming clear. Haafiz hadn't cared about slowing the invaders' penetration into the city's last remaining stronghold. The sole purpose of his proposed ambush had been to put Omnathi and Akim in front of enemy lasers where they would die.

"And how useful do you think it would have been to bring charges?" Haafiz asked scornfully. "You know what happened—those good and loyal men, as you call them, defied my direct orders. What use is it to follow the rule of law when the Djinn have chosen to put themselves above both the law and the Shahni?"

"We're at war," Narayan said. "Sometimes rules must be broken if we're to throw the invaders off our soil."

"The rule of law and the Shahni cannot and will not be broken,"

Haafiz insisted. "*We* are the leaders of the Qasaman people, Ifrit Narayan. *We* are the ones who make the decisions for our world."

He lifted his gun higher, ignoring the lasers pointed at him and leveling the weapon at Narayan's chest. "And if I make the decision to dispense justice here and now," he said, "you *will* stand aside and permit it."

Narayan drew himself up. "No, I will not," he said flatly. "You have no evidence, and without evidence there cannot be justice."

"The evidence is that I'm still here, which proves a conspiracy to keep me here," Haafiz said. "For the good of Qasama, I must return at once to the business of saving my world."

Narayan spat a curse under his breath. "Do you think you're the only one who hates this place?" he bit out. "You think that none of the rest of us teeter at the edge of insanity at being forced to remain idle while—?" He broke off abruptly.

But too late. "While what?" Haafiz demanded. "What's going on out there that I should know about?"

"The war is going on," Narayan said. "You already know that."

But the words were an evasion. Daulo knew it, and so did Haafiz. "I'm leaving now, Ifrit Narayan," the Shahni said, his voice quiet but as unyielding as granite. "Assign your Djinn to escort me, or let me go alone. But I will not spend another day here. I *will* know what is going on across my world."

Narayan's eyes flicked down to the gun pointed at his chest. "I have my orders, Shahni Haafiz," he said. "I can't allow you to leave. Not yet."

"Move aside," Haafiz ordered in the same stony voice. "Or I kill you where you stand."

Slowly, Narayan shook his head. "I can't."

Daulo curled his hands into helpless fists. And with that, he knew, Narayan was dead. Haafiz wouldn't back away from his order and his threat. Not Haafiz. Narayan would stand there until the Shahni pulled the trigger. Then Haafiz would walk over the body, leave the outpost and head out into the forest, and start the long journey toward Purma.

And alone in a swirl of dangerous predators and even more dangerous Troft invaders, he too would almost certainly die.

Daulo had to stop this. Somehow, he had to break the impasse.

And there was only one way to do that. "Then let the trial begin," he said. "Right now."

"Be quiet, Daulo Sammon," Narayan said, his eyes still on Haafiz's face. "This isn't your fight."

"It's every bit my fight," Daulo retorted. "Shahni Haafiz is right—I'm the reason he's been stuck here all this time. Very well, then. Try me, acquit or convict me, and allow Shahni Haafiz to travel to Purma."

For the first time Narayan's eyes shifted to Daulo's face. "You have no idea what you're saying," he said. "You have no evidence of your innocence, only your word against Marid Akim's. We need to wait until your son arrives to speak on your behalf."

"My son has apparently been delayed," Daulo said, his heart tearing yet again at the thought of what might have happened to Fadil. "Enough time has been wasted. One way or the other, it ends now."

"Not now," a new voice said quietly from across the galley. "But it ends tomorrow."

Daulo leaned to the side to see around Haafiz and Narayan. Miron Akim was standing calmly in the doorway. "What did you say?" he asked.

"I said you will have your wish, Daulo Sammon," Akim said. "And you will have yours, Shahni Haafiz. Daulo Sammon's trial for treason will begin tomorrow."

His eyes seemed to glitter. "And it will end tomorrow."

"And I'll finally be permitted to leave this place?" Haafiz demanded suspiciously.

Akim nodded. "With a full Djinn escort, if you wish."

Haafiz hesitated, then lowered his gun. "Very well," he said. "But I warn you: I'll stand for no further delays."

"There will be none," Akim promised. "Have you finished your meal, Daulo Sammon?"

Daulo nodded. "I have."

"Then return to your quarters," Akim ordered. "The computer will have the necessary legal guides for preparing your defense. I suggest you study them."

Daulo swallowed. "I will, Miron Akim."

"Good," Akim said. "Then go."

Gingerly, Daulo eased past Haafiz and Narayan and headed across the galley. Narayan, he noted in passing, had also lowered his arms and lasers.

The confrontation had been defused. For the moment, at least, both men were safe.

Leaving Daulo alone facing the risk of death.

He started to walk past Akim, stopped as the other caught his arm. "And don't give up hope," Akim murmured. "It may still be that your son will come to your rescue."

Daulo took a deep breath. "I fear that my son can no longer come to anyone's rescue," he said.

"Perhaps," Akim said. "We shall see."

Three days earlier, at the close of the cat-and-rat survival contest that Anya and Commander Ukuthi had euphemistically called the Games, Ukuthi had said that he and Merrick would be having a conversation soon. Now, three days later, the Troft had yet to summon Merrick to that promised conference. Perhaps, Merrick thought sourly, he was spending his time trying to dig up a few more jormungands to amuse his guests with.

Personally, Merrick was in no hurry for either talk or combat. The physical exertion in the arena hadn't reopened any of his old injuries, but he'd collected a fresh assortment of scrapes, bruises, and small cuts along the way. Nothing that the Troft doctor seemed concerned about, at least not according to Anya's translation of his still indecipherable dialect. But then, the doctor could afford to be unconcerned. It wasn't his skin that had taken all the abuse.

It was an hour after lunch on that third day when the lock clicked and the door swung open to reveal a middle-aged Troft wearing a non-armored leotard, a senior officer's insignia, and—most surprising of all—a red heir sash. [Merrick Moreau, I greet him,] he said.

[Merrick Moreau, he greets you in return,] Merrick said, slipping off the bed and standing up. He'd been given only a glimpse of his audience back in the arena, but he was pretty sure this was the same Troft he'd seen in the center of the group of observers. [A demesne-heir, to which am I honored to speak?]

[Commander Ukuthi, I am he,] the Troft said. His radiator membranes fluttered and his beak cracked slightly open. [Surprise, you have it.]

[Surprise, I have it,] Merrick conceded with a flush of embarrassment. It was double surprise, actually: first that a demesne-heir would risk facing a dangerous prisoner with his guards standing uselessly outside the door behind him, and second that the heir in question could actually read human expressions well enough to have picked up on Merrick's emotion. [Your forgiveness, I ask it.]

[My forgiveness, it is unnecessary,] Ukuthi assured him. He lifted a hand and made a gesture.

And to Merrick's even greater surprise, the cell door closed behind him, leaving the guards outside. [Privacy, we now have it,] Ukuthi said calmly.

[Surprises, you are filled with them,] Merrick said, glancing at Anya. She was sitting cross-legged on her bed, her face expressionless. Either she wasn't surprised by Ukuthi's actions or she hid it very well. [Serious risks, you take them.]

[Surprises, I have even more of them,] Ukuthi said, his beak cracking open again. Was that supposed to be an attempt at a human-type smile? He ruffled his shoulders and seemed to clear his throat— "As for risks," he said, in an accent that closely mimicked Anya's own inflections, "I do not believe I am taking one."

It took Merrick three tries to get his own voice working again. In all his years of dealing with Troft merchants and diplomats, he'd never, ever had one speak to him in Anglic. He wasn't even sure anyone in the Cobra Worlds knew they *could* speak Anglic. "You're—yes, very surprising," he managed. "I've never heard a Troft speak our language before."

"It is not easy for us to do," Ukuthi conceded. "Much easier for your vocal apparatus to speak cattertalk."

"We can return to that if you'd like," Merrick offered.

"This is better." Ukuthi's beak cracked open again. "The practice, it is useful. Tell me, what are your feelings toward Anya Winghunter?"

The intellectual curiosity Merrick had been feeling at this new revelation vanished. "I have no feelings toward her," he said, letting his voice go dark and rigid.

"Yet she is human like yourself," Ukuthi pointed out. "Have you no consideration at all for her?"

Merrick looked over at Anya. She was looking back at him, her face still expressionless.

Expressionless, but perhaps not emotionless? On sudden impulse, Merrick activated his infrareds.

To discover that the woman was anything but emotionless. Her face was a swirl of heat, a pattern that seemed to indicate both fear and hope. "We call this beating around the bush," Merrick said, keying off the infrareds and turning back to Ukuthi. "Get to the point, and tell me what you want."

"I am unfamiliar with that turn of phrase," Ukuthi said. "You must tell me its origin someday. What do you know about this war?"

"I know we didn't start it," Merrick said. "I also think we're going to win it. Aside from that, not much."

"You may be correct on the second point," Ukuthi said. "But you are not correct on the first. The war *was* begun by humans. Specifically, the humans of the Dominion of Man."

Merrick felt his stomach tighten. He and his mother had speculated that the invasion of their worlds might have been a response to something happening on the far side of the Troft Assemblage. "The Dominion of Man is a hundred thirty light-years away, and we haven't had contact with them in seven decades," he said. "Why are we being punished for their actions?"

"That I cannot say," Ukuthi admitted. "All I know is that the demesnes fighting that war have contracted with the Tua'lanek'zia demesne to conquer and subdue the human worlds at this side of the Trof'te Assemblage. The Tua'lanek'zia contracted further with the Drim'hco'plai, the Gla'lupt'flae, and my own Balin'ekha'spmi for our assistance."

"I see," Merrick said sourly. Four entire Troft demesnes, plus the implied threat of whoever had organized this military dogpile in the first place. No wonder the Tlossies and the Cobra Worlds' other trading parties hadn't lifted a finger to stop them. "I hope you're at least making a decent profit."

"Our profit is not to be made in currency," Ukuthi assured him. "My demesne-lord has other objectives in sight." He gestured to Anya. "Anya Winghunter, tell Merrick Moreau of your people."

Anya hesitated. Then, she got to her feet, bowed once to Ukuthi, and turned to Merrick. "We are slaves," she said. "We create sculptures, which our masters take for their enjoyment. We hunt rare animals and find rare plants, which our masters take for their tables." She lowered her gaze to the floor, then looked back up at Merrick. "But mostly we fight in the Games."

"What do you fight?" Merrick asked. "Animals like that jormungand?"

"Sometimes," Anya said. "Most times, we fight each other."

Merrick looked at Ukuthi, his hands dropping into laser-firing position. "For you?"

Ukuthi's radiator membranes fluttered. "Not us," he said. "The Drim'hco'plai are their masters."

Merrick pointed to Anya. "Yet she's here. With you."

"She is," Ukuthi acknowledged. "Some years ago the Drim'hco'plai began selling human slaves to other demesne-lords for their amusement. My demesne-lord was intrigued, so he bought several to study." He cocked his head. "Yet now, within the past two months, the Drim'hco'plai demesne-lord has suddenly and urgently requested that all slaves be returned to him."

Merrick frowned. "Why?"

"We do not know," Ukuthi said. "I also note two other curious happenstances. First, the invasion of the Cobra Worlds is well advanced, yet the Drim'hco'plai continue to take razorarms from Qasama. Where do they take them? Second, their demesne-lord insisted that the Drim'hco'plai be solely responsible for the subjugation of the Cobra World of Caelian."

Where there were dozens of predators every bit as dangerous as razorarms. "Sounds like they're looking for new animals to throw at Anya's people on Game night," he said.

"That was also my thought," Ukuthi said. "But why keep that goal secret from the other demesne-lords? All four demesnes involved in this war have bought Drim'hco'plai slaves. Why not simply state that refreshed games are the purpose? And again, why does the demesne-lord spend the money necessary to buy back all his slaves?"

Merrick scratched his cheek. "Maybe they're worried that the Tua demesne won't like the Drim playing animal hunting games when they're supposed to be concentrating on fighting a war," he said slowly. "But that doesn't explain the slave recall."

"It does not," Ukuthi agreed. "It is a puzzle, one which my demesne-lord wishes to solve."

"Okay," Merrick said. "So why are you telling me this?"

Ukuthi cocked his head to the side. "I wish you to travel to Anya's world with her and seek truth for my demesne-lord."

Merrick felt his eyes bulge. "You *what*?"

"But we do not send you merely for information." Ukuthi gestured to Anya. "Anya Winghunter?"

"We need your help, Merrick Moreau," Anya said quietly. "My people do not wish to be slaves anymore."

"I sympathize," Merrick said. "But you're asking me—I don't even know *what* you're asking me."

"You are a *koubrah*-soldier," Ukuthi said. "I have seen you do remarkable feats."

"I'm *one* Cobra soldier," Merrick said tartly. "What you need is a battalion of us. Better yet, you need a battalion of armored troops and a Dominion of Man war fleet." He waved a hand. "Why are we even discussing this? The Drim will know what all their slaves look like. How do you expect to slip me into that group?"

"You are wrong," Ukuthi said. "They will not know each slave's appearance. Nor will they care. To them, one human slave is no different than any other."

"Well, then, the other slaves will know I'm not one of them."

"You will have nothing to fear from the other slaves," Ukuthi said. "They will listen to Anya, and will keep their silence concerning your true identity."

"The doctor might not," Merrick persisted. "The one who's been treating me. He comes from Anya's world, doesn't he?"

"No," Ukuthi said. "He is my personal physician. He spoke in the dialect of those of Anya's world because I wished to know if you understood that dialog, or could learn to understand it. Can you?"

"I don't know," Merrick said. "Probably. But that's not the point. The point is that there's no way I can fight a whole planetful of slave-owning Trofts alone."

"You will not be fighting alone," Anya said. "We too are fighters, and we yearn for freedom. We will fight at your side."

"With what, sticks and rocks?" Merrick demanded. "Swords and spears? No offense, Anya, but whatever you've got isn't going to be much good against Troft lasers and body armor." He shook his head. "I'm sorry, but it can't be done."

"It can be done," Ukuthi said firmly. "History has shown how successful revolutions are often started by a single spark. Anya's people are strong, but they require a leader who can fight. A leader with vision and the knowledge of strategy and tactics. You can be that leader."

"You don't know that," Merrick insisted. "You don't know that I have any of those skills."

"I am confident that you do," Ukuthi said.

"But you ran me through the Games to make sure anyway?"

"You misunderstand," Ukuthi said. "The test was not for my benefit, but for Anya's. It was she who needed to see your skills."

"Really." Merrick glared at the woman. "Are you satisfied?"

"I am," she said quietly.

"But more important than combat skill is an honorable character," Ukuthi continued. "That too is a quality I know you possess."

Merrick snorted. "Why? Because I haven't killed you yet?"

"Because you risked yourself to protect Anya in the arena," the Troft said. "And because you targeted the weapons and not the soldiers when you attacked them in the forest near Milika."

Merrick frowned. He'd forgotten all about that incident. He'd also forgotten Fadil Sammon's intriguing questions about it. "It seemed only fair, given that their missile launcher was aimed over our heads."

"Did you know they were on mercy setting before you chose to attack only the weapons?"

Merrick thought back. "No, I guess not," he admitted, frowning suddenly. "Wait a minute. I thought you said that was a Drim ship out there hunting for razorarms."

"The ship was Drim'hco'plai," Ukuthi confirmed. "But the tactics and weapons settings were mine." His beak cracked open. "After our coalition was temporarily thrown off Qasama, the Tua'lanek'zia ordered that tactical leadership on this world would henceforth be provided by the Balin'ekha'spmi."

"In other words, by you," Merrick said, nodding. He'd thought he'd sensed a new skill and subtlety in the invaders' techniques since their return to Qasama. Now he knew why. "So the Tua just handed their command over to you? Risky of them."

"The Tua'lanek'zia decision had little effect on their forces," Ukuthi said. "Their main strength is on the Cobra Worlds capital of Aventine, with only an observer force on Qasama. It is the Drim'hco'plai who have the strongest presence here, and it was they who spoke the strongest objections against the Tua'lanek'zia decision."

Merrick's mind flicked back to some of the conflicts he and his mother had had early in the campaign with Miron Akim and the rest of the Qasaman military. "I'm not surprised," he said. "No one likes to have someone else telling him what to do."

"Indeed," Ukuthi said. "Unfortunately, that is the situation a slave faces every day of his life."

Merrick sighed. "Look, it's not that I don't feel for them. I do. It's just that—"

"Will you at least think on my offer," Ukuthi asked.

"Like I've got anything else to do," Merrick growled. "Fine, I'll think. How long do I have?"

"You have one day."

Merrick stared at him. "One *day*?"

"I am convinced that the decisive battle will take place tomorrow in the city of Azras," Ukuthi said. "Whether the Qasamans succeed or fail, the Trof'te forces will be thrown into disarray. That confusion will give us the opportunity to collect whatever equipment from Qasaman stores that you wish to take with you when my demesne-lord returns you and the rest of his slaves to the Drim'hco'plai."

Merrick snorted. "Right. You're expecting the Drim to let their slaves just march back home lugging satchels full of weapons and explosives?"

"Grant the Drim'hco'plai a higher intelligence," Ukuthi said, and for the first time there was a hint of annoyance in his tone. "But also grant us the same. Our weapons smiths and technicians will naturally camouflage them first."

"You think there'll be time for that?"

"The Drim'hco'plai request specified all slaves would be returned within the next six weeks," Ukuthi said. "That will permit us adequate time."

"Probably," Merrick said, a sudden strange thought drifting up through the utter insanity of this whole thing. If Ukuthi was willing to collect weapons and supplies from Qasama . . . "What about more people?" he asked. "More soldiers, I mean. If you can slip one non-slave ringer into the Drim shipment, why not five or six or twenty?"

"That may be possible," Ukuthi said, eyeing Merrick thoughtfully. "Are there Qasamans here who you trust with such a mission?"

Merrick looked at Anya again. At her wooden, hopeful face. "There are a few," he said. "The question is whether you could camouflage their combat suits well enough to get them past the Drim."

"I am confident that can be done," Ukuthi said. "Do you then accept the mission?"

"Not so fast," Merrick warned. "So far all I'm accepting is the job of thinking about it. *And* my answer will probably also depend on the outcome of tomorrow's activity. If the particular Qasamans

I'm thinking about inviting are killed, that'll change things. You'll want to keep that in mind when you're preparing your strategy."

"My strategy will be the same whether you accept or not," Ukuthi said. "The soldiers and warships of the Balin'ekha'spmi will remain at their current stations at Sollas and Purma. The Drim'hco'plai at Azras will be left to succeed or fail on their own strength."

"Or you could help the Qasamans more actively," Merrick suggested, feeling his heart beating harder. If he could actually create a rift in the Troft coalition and bring the Balins onto the human side, the Azras battle Ukuthi was anticipating might not even have to be fought.

But the Troft shook his head. "I cannot," he said in a voice that left no room for argument. "The Drim'hco'plai are still our contractual allies. Furthermore, they outnumber us greatly. I cannot and will not actively fight them. I can only deny them my skills and the resources of the Balin'ekha'spmi."

Merrick nodded. Not as good as he'd hoped, but better than he could have expected. "I have your pledge of that?" he asked.

"My pledge, I give it," Ukuthi said without hesitation. "And I will do more. If you wish, you may watch the battle unfold at my side in my warship's command center. You will see for yourself that I and the Balin'ekha'spmi are not aiding the Drim'hco'plai."

"You'd let me aboard your ship?" Merrick asked carefully, trying to keep his voice casual. To be inside a Troft warship's command center, with its weaponry right there at his fingertips...

"You will be required to pledge that you will attempt neither escape nor sabotage," Ukuthi added.

"Of course," Merrick said, suppressing a sigh. Once again, the temptation to lie tugged at him. Once again, he knew he couldn't. "Very well. I so pledge."

"Then I shall see you again tomorrow," Ukuthi said, taking a step back toward the door. "Together we shall watch the Qasamans make their final bid for victory."

Merrick grimaced. "Yes," he murmured.

Ukuthi paused with his hand raised to the door. "You fear for their lives," he said, almost gently. "And so you should, for warfare is too often a random destroyer. But I do not think you need worry about the final outcome. You humans are an inventive and determined and resilient species, superior in many ways even to the Trof'te."

"Maybe," Merrick said. "But we also play politics among ourselves at least as well as you do. Our internal conflicts and power games often weaken us and destroy that determination and resilience. Sometimes they even bring about our defeat without the actions of an external enemy."

"Let us both hope that will not be the case here," Ukuthi said. "For I feel in the deepest core of my being that whatever the Drim'hco'plai are planning will be of great evil, for human and Trof'te alike."

He rapped sharply, three times, on the door. [That danger, think on it as well,] he added in cattertalk as the door swung open. [Your presence, I will request it at the proper time tomorrow.]

[My presence, you will have it,] Merrick promised.

His last view of Ukuthi as the door swung closed was the commander standing firm and tall, with only a small flutter in his radiator membranes showing the stresses of his position and command.

And, perhaps, the looming betrayal that he was planning of his fellow Trofts.

"You will think on this?" Anya asked hopefully.

Merrick nodded. "As I promised."

He expected her to say more, either to continue Ukuthi's pleading of her people's case or else to launch into a showering of thanks they both knew was as yet underserved. But she merely nodded and sat down again on her bed.

With a sigh, Merrick climbed back onto his own bed and stretched out, staring at the plain concrete ceiling above him. Ukuthi wanted an answer by tomorrow. Merrick would give him that answer.

He just wished he had some idea what the hell that answer would be.

"Fadil Sammon?"

With an effort, Fadil forced his way out of the tortured dream and clawed his way toward consciousness. It was the same dream, the one he'd had so many times since the mind-enhancing drug had robbed him of the use of his body. He opened his eyes and turned his head, the only part of him he could still move.

Carsh Zoshak stood beside his medical bed, gazing at him

with an odd expression. A few paces behind him was Dr. Krites. "Yes?" Fadil asked. "What do you want?"

Zoshak's forehead furrowed, and he looked back at Krites. "You don't already know?" Krites asked.

Fadil frowned in turn . . . and slowly—far too slowly—the truth dawned on him. "It's gone, isn't it?" he said.

Krites shrugged. "You've been all but reading everyone's expressions ever since your return to this house," he reminded Fadil. "If those powers of observation and analysis have left you, the rest probably has also."

Fadil swallowed hard. And so the glory passed. Fadil Sammon, super-genius, was no more. Only Fadil Sammon, cripple, remained.

In his mind, he closed his hands into fists. Laying motionless beside his body, his hands didn't even twitch. "Why have you awakened me?"

"Forgive me," Zoshak said. "I just wanted to tell you that they've arrived at Azras."

Fadil stared at him in disbelief, then shifted his eyes to the clock on the wall. He'd had no idea that he'd slept that long. "And Paul Broom has been taken to the hospital?"

"He has," Zoshak confirmed. "The regrowth treatments for his leg will begin shortly."

Fadil felt a cheek muscle twitch. And in two or three weeks, Paul Broom would have a brand-new, fully functional leg. For a moment, he felt a spark of envy.

But envy was a trap, and a sin, and an utter waste of energy. Ruthlessly, Fadil pushed it aside. "Jin Moreau is there with him?"

"The report didn't say, but I assume so," Zoshak said. "That *was* the arrangement you made with Ifrit Ghushtre, was it not?"

Despite the seriousness of the situation, Fadil had to smile. Zoshak was working hard at looking all solemn and professional now, but Fadil remembered the staggered expression on his face two days ago when Ghushtre first told him what Fadil had done. That look alone had almost made it worth what it had cost him.

But all that was in the past. This was the present. Miron Akim had done as he promised, sending Jin Moreau and Paul Broom to Azras with the new Cobras so that they could begin their healing. Now, it was time for Fadil to fulfill his part of the bargain.

And despite Zoshak's emotionless expression it was clear he was ready, even eager, to carry it out.

"And Gama Yithtra played his part adequately?" Fadil asked.

"Again, the report didn't say," Zoshak said. "But since the passage at the Azras gate went smoothly, I think we can assume he did."

"Good," Fadil said, his final twinge of uncertainty fading away. "That's why I chose him to be one of the recruits, you know."

"Not because his father is an important village leader?"

"Partially," Fadil conceded. "But mainly because I knew what an accomplished liar he is. I knew he could manage any deception that was required of him."

"Apparently so," Zoshak said. "And now, it's time to go."

Fadil sighed. He'd argued against this path, argued and pleaded both. It was wrong to waste Qasaman resources like this, especially in the midst of war. But Miron Akim had refused to listen to reason.

And as Fadil had already noted, the Marid had fulfilled his part of the bargain.

"Could I wait one more day?" Fadil asked Zoshak, trying one last time. "I'd like to see the outcome of tomorrow's battle."

"No," Krites said firmly before Zoshak could answer. "I sympathize, Fadil Sammon. But we have our orders."

"And those orders state that the time is now," Zoshak said. "Is there anything you'd like before we go?"

Fadil turned his head back and gazed up at the ceiling. He'd seen that ceiling thousands of times growing up. Yet it was only now, in the three and a half weeks since his return from Sollas, that he'd actually *looked* at it.

And only at this moment did he suddenly realize that, in the midst of war and the lurking threat of despair, things of beauty were somehow made even more beautiful.

He took a deep breath. "No, thank you," he said.

He gave the ceiling one final lingering look, then turned back to Zoshak. "I'm ready."

CHAPTER FIFTEEN

"There," Siraj said, nodding along the crowded street as he and Lorne pretended to examine the sparse wares at a vegetable stand. "That one's ours."

Lorne half turned to bring the tomato he was holding more fully into the mid-morning sunlight streaming down across the Azras buildings. Half a block away, parked squarely in the middle of the road, was one of the Troft armored trucks he'd had way too much experience with lately. Its swivel gun was pointed more or less in their direction, but the five armored soldiers sitting on the roof were arrayed in a tight circle, all facing outward, where they could watch all approaches. On both sides of the vehicle, citizens streamed sullenly or nervously past as they went about their daily lives. "Any idea how many more are inside?" he asked, replacing the tomato in its tray and selecting another one.

"Typically, each truck carries ten of the invaders," Siraj said. "That would indicate a driver, gunner, and three more soldiers inside."

"Not too bad," Lorne said, trying to sound casual. He'd tackled the things twice, but neither time had been exactly easy. "The open-sesame is . . . ?"

"Is ready," Siraj said with a touch of amusement. "Don't concern yourself with the opening, Lorne Moreau. Concern yourself with the task once the opening has occurred."

"I know," Lorne said with a touch of offended dignity. "I'm just a bit concerned about what happens if the opening *doesn't* occur. Like, for example, if the rotating password pattern got reset this morning."

"The rotation is unchanged," Siraj assured him. "We've monitored two to three openings for each truck since dawn, and all are still running the same system they were when they first came into Azras."

"Okay," Lorne said, still unable to shake his nervousness about this whole scheme. "And you're sure about these radios?"

"Very sure," Siraj said. "My father himself has vouched for their safety and security."

Lorne took a deep breath and returned the tomato to the tray. "Okay, then," he said, doing a quick check of his nanocomputer's clock circuit. "Three minutes ten to go."

"There," Siraj said, putting down the vegetable he'd been examining and nodding toward the sky. Lorne looked up, to see three hovering Troft drones suddenly begin moving toward the eastern part of the city. "The Brigane Street road work has caught their attention."

"Looks like it," Lorne agreed, watching the drones as they disappeared from sight behind the buildings. "Let's hope they can hold their audience for the next six minutes. *And* that we can get in fast enough to keep any of their friends from calling them back here."

"We will," Siraj assured him. "We should begin walking now."

Lorne checked his clock circuit again. "Right," he confirmed.

"And remember to keep your sleeves pushed up," Siraj added as they joined the stream of pedestrians walking down the street. "The invaders insist on seeing bare arms, and we don't want to give them any reason for concern."

Lorne nodded and pushed his sleeves up, tucking them into large, ungainly knots on his shoulders. It still felt awkward, but after all the practice yesterday afternoon and evening at least he knew how to function with them that way. "Okay," he said, taking a deep breath and letting it out slowly. "Ready or not, here we come."

"We are gathered here," Shahni Haafiz intoned from his place at the center of the briefing room table, "for the trial of Daulo Sammon, son of Kruin Sammon, of the village of Milika. The charge is treason in the highest degree."

Treason. The word echoed through Daulo's mind as he stood stiffly before the three men at the table, sending weakness into his knees and a trembling blackness into his soul. His life was on the line here, and his family holdings, and his sacred honor.

But at least Fadil wasn't going to have to brave the dangers of the forest in order to stand trial alongside him. Miron Akim had come to him privately yesterday and assured him that his son was still in Milika, and that he would be permitted to remain there.

"The charge has two points," Haafiz continued in the same solemn voice. "First, that Daulo Sammon was in possession of a radio, as forbidden by the Shahni since the invasion of our world." He waved a hand over the cylindrical device sitting on the table in front of Akim, his fingers stopping short of actually touching it. "Second, that Daulo Sammon used this same radio to contact the invaders and make an as-yet unknown bargain of betrayal against the Shahni and the people of Qasama."

Daulo caught his breath, his eyes sudden frozen on the radio. The radio Akim claimed to have found in his wheelchair carrier bag. The radio that had been the reason he'd been locked underground in the command post for the past thirteen days.

Akim had told him yesterday that Fadil was still in Milika. *How could he possibly have known that*?

Had the Djinn he'd sent to the village returned with that news? But Daulo had heard nothing about new arrivals, nor had he seen Ghushtre or any of the others since their departure. Had some other messenger or courier arrived? But why would a courier waste time traveling around the outlying villages when the cities of Qasama were under siege?

There was only one answer. One horrible, terrifying answer.

Slowly, Daulo raised his eyes to Akim. The other was watching him, a faint smile at the corners of his lips.

"—is the procedure we will follow," Haafiz was saying. "The first statement—"

"Forgive me," Daulo interrupted, his knees suddenly shaking so hard he could barely stand. "Forgive me, Your Excellency, but it's urgent that I speak."

"You dare make a mockery of these proceedings?" Haafiz bit out. "You will remain silent—"

"No," Moffren Omnathi interrupted mildly from his seat at Haafiz's other side. "Let the accused speak."

Daulo stared into Omnathi's calm, unconcerned face. Was he in this along with Akim?

His mouth went dry. Of course he was. It had been both men, working together, who had kept Daulo trapped here, unable to communicate with the outside world. It had to be both of them.

But why?

And then, his eyes shifted back to Haafiz. The Shahni's expression, in sharp contrast with Omnathi's, was brimming with anger, frustration, and impatience.

And with that, it was suddenly obvious.

"As I told you before, Your Excellency, the radio isn't mine," Daulo said, the words stumbling over themselves as he hurried to get them out before one or the other of the traitors could stop him. "It's Miron Akim's, and always was. Miron Akim is the one who accused me of treason, using that excuse to force us all to remain here."

"To what end?" Akim asked, his voice perfectly calm.

"To keep His Excellency Shahni Haafiz away from Purma," Daulo said, glancing to both sides of the room where Narayan and the other Djinn stood ceremonial guard. Could he convince them of the truth before Akim ordered him and Haafiz both murdered? "To keep him from all communication with the remaining Shahni."

"But to what end?" Akim persisted. "Why would I wish that His Excellency not communicate with Purma?"

"I don't know," Daulo said, looking desperately at Narayan. But the Djinni was just standing there. "Perhaps he knows something you didn't want becoming known. Perhaps—" He broke off, looking sharply back at Akim. "Because he tried to have you and Moffren Omnathi condemned as traitors," he breathed. "You knew that if he went to Purma he would tell the rest of the Shahni what had happened and might persuade them to confirm his charges against you."

Akim shook his head. But to Daulo's dismay, it was more a gesture of admiration than one of denial. "You're amazing, Daulo Sammon," he said. "I see where your son Fadil got his intellect and perception."

"Are you saying he's *right*?" Haafiz asked, sending an uncertain glare toward Akim.

"Only partially," Akim said. "But he deduced all the parts that he reasonably could have."

Haafiz shot a look at Daulo. "Which parts? What are you talking about?"

"The parts about my accusation being nothing more than an excuse for keeping you here, Your Excellency." Akim inclined his head. "But thankfully, it wasn't for the purpose he supposes."

"Whatever the purpose," Haafiz bit out, "restraining a Shahni against his will is still treason."

"Perhaps," Akim said. "But it was for a higher good."

Haafiz snorted. "What higher good can treason possibly serve?"

"The higher good," Akim said quietly, "of protecting our world. Of preventing you, Your Excellency, from destroying it."

Two of the five Trofts sitting on top of the armored truck turned their faceplates toward Lorne and Siraj as they walked toward the vehicle. But they apparently looked no more dangerous than the rest of the citizens passing by. By the time the two men came alongside the vehicle the aliens had shifted their attention elsewhere in the milling crowd.

They were passing the truck, and Lorne had just finished putting target locks on the five soldiers, when the short, sharp warning whistle came from one of the buildings above them.

Out of the corner of his eye he saw the Trofts look up, probably trying to locate the sound. In three seconds, Lorne's mother would be calling the password into a radio transmitter in hopes of getting the soldiers inside the truck to open the rear door. If they did, this should be a straightforward exercise in combat timing.

If they didn't, he and Siraj were going to have to do this the hard way.

Fortunately, they did. Lorne had just reached the rear of the truck when there was a thunk from the lock mechanism and the door swung open.

And as Siraj lobbed a concussion grenade past the shocked Troft and in through the opening, Lorne spun around and leaped for the top of the truck, his stunner spitting bursts of current into the soldiers scrambling madly to bring their weapons around.

Like the soldiers inside the truck, they were far too late. Even as Lorne landed in a crouch in the middle of the sprawled bodies the truck shuddered beneath him with the muffled thud of the grenade's detonation. A quick check to make sure all five Trofts were well and truly unconscious, and he hopped back down to the street.

Siraj was holding the rear door open a crack and peering cautiously inside. "Looks clear," he said.

"I'll check," Lorne told him, keying his infrareds and looking inside. It was impossible to read the three soldiers through their armor and helmets, but the unhelmeted driver and swivel gunner were definitely unconscious. "Clear," he told Siraj. "Get the welders started and get into your combat suit. We've got exactly two minutes and thirty-five seconds to get moving."

"How *dare* you?" Haafiz demanded, his face darkening with barely-controlled fury. "You overstep your bounds for the final time, Miron Akim." He stabbed a finger at Narayan. "Ifrit Narayan, you are ordered to place Miron Akim under immediate arrest."

Daulo tensed. But to his astonishment, neither Narayan nor any of the rest of the Djinn stirred from their places. "Ifrit Narayan!" Haafiz snapped. "That's a direct order."

"They won't obey you," Akim said quietly. "As of this morning, they know the truth. They know what you would have done if you'd been permitted to travel to Purma."

"And what would I have done?" Haafiz retorted. "Destroyed Qasama with my own hand?"

"Yes," Akim said. "Because you would have ordered the Djinn to turn against our allies."

"Our—?" Haafiz broke off. "So it was done," he said, his voice turning even colder. "Ghofl Khatir brought demon warriors from the worlds of our enemies."

"From the worlds of our allies," Akim corrected. "We now have a treaty with them."

Haafiz spat. "Treason."

"They've brought resources for our war against the invaders," Akim said.

"Treason."

"Even now, they fight alongside our forces in Azras."

Haafiz slammed his fist on the table. "*Treason*!" he snarled. "Treason and madness. They'll turn on us, Miron Akim—if not today, then the moment the other invaders have been thrown off our world. They must be stopped *now*, before they know all our secrets. We don't need their so-called help, and we don't *want* it."

"You're wrong, Your Excellency, on both counts," Akim said.

"Besides, it's too late. The battle for our world has already begun." He picked up the radio from the table in front of him. "I received the word from the military commander of Azras fifteen minutes ago."

Haafiz's eyes dropped to the radio, his glare slipping a bit. "So it's true," he said bitterly. "The radio was yours. *You're* the traitor communicating with the invaders."

"The radio is mine," Akim acknowledged. "But I'm not in communication with the invaders. In fact, the invaders don't even know these exist. They operate in a special and undetectable way, piggybacking their signal onto the invaders' own radio communications. They can thus send messages back and forth without the invaders ever noticing a transmission or being able to search and lock onto it."

And then, to Daulo's amazement, Akim looked at Daulo and smiled. "The technique, and the radios themselves," he added, "were created in large part by Fadil Sammon, son of Daulo Sammon."

Daulo felt his mouth drop open. Fadil had done *that*? "But you said..."

"I said you and your son were traitors," Akim said, "and for that I beg your forgiveness. But it was necessary that we prevent Shahni Haafiz from traveling to Purma, and you were the only excuse I could think of to give him."

"But how could he have stopped Jin Moreau and the Cobras from aiding us?" Daulo asked in bewilderment. There was something here he still wasn't getting. "He's only one voice of many, and you said the Shahni had already approved the treaty. Wouldn't it require all the Shahni together to abrogate it?"

"It would," Omnathi said quietly. "If there were any Shahni left."

"God above," Haafiz said, his voice sounding shaken, his anger gone for the first time since the meeting began. "They're dead? *All* of them?"

"All of them," Omnathi said. "Killed during the defense of our world."

"And even you escaped Sollas only by the barest of margins," Akim added. "Either the soldiers who confronted us didn't recognize you, or else they deliberately let you leave in hopes that you would travel to Purma and unwittingly identify the military leaders to their drones." He waved a hand around them. "Yet another reason Moffren Omnathi and I felt it vital to hide you here."

Haafiz looked at him, then at Daulo, and finally at Narayan. "Then Qasama is gone," he said. "We have enemies on all sides, and you've deliberately prevented the one remaining leader from resuming command of our defense."

"There are other leaders, Your Excellency," Omnathi assured him. "Military leaders, who can see past old memories to what must be done for our world."

"If you believe that, then you're a fool," Haafiz said bluntly. "The Cobra Worlds care nothing for us beyond our destruction."

"I think not," Akim said. "They have, in fact, already given us a great gift."

Haafiz snorted. "The *gift* of demon warriors who will soon stab us in the back?"

"You may not like this, Your Excellency," Akim warned. "In fact, I'm quite certain you won't. But it's now time for you to know the rest of it."

He gestured. "So if Ifrit Narayan will take his Djinn and Daulo Sammon out of the room, Moffren Omnathi and I will tell you about a project called *Isis*."

Merrick's usual morning routine involved sleeping or at least dozing until the breakfast tray arrived at his cell, then doing some exercises and plotting escape until lunch. But not this morning. He and Anya were awakened an hour after dawn by a pair of soldiers whose armor bore the curlies, highlighted in red, of the Balin'ekha'spmi demesne. Ukuthi's personal guard, Merrick tentatively concluded. The soldiers brought new clothing for both humans—simple, unadorned gray jumpsuits—and an order from Ukuthi to dress quickly and accompany the soldiers to his warship.

Merrick also noted with some dark amusement that the soldiers seemed a bit jumpier than the other soldiers he'd encountered so far in this war. Ukuthi had probably alerted them as to exactly who and what they were dealing with.

They needn't have worried. Merrick had already given his word.

More than that, he'd done some serious thinking since yesterday's conversation. And while he wasn't yet ready to commit to Ukuthi's insane mission he had some definite ideas of how it might be done.

He would need help, of course. Five to ten Qasamans, or an

equal number of Cobras if he could get his hands on them. His father hadn't specified in that hurried Dida conversation back at Milika how many Cobras he and Jin had brought from Caelian, but surely they'd brought at least that many. Assuming they could spare a few, and assuming Ukuthi had been right about being able to disguise any equipment they wanted to smuggle onto Anya's world, this whole thing might actually be possible.

The soldiers had a ground vehicle waiting at the subcity exit when they emerged into the sunlight. Merrick winced as they rode across the battered landscape, both at the horrible wasteland Sollas had become and also at the sheer number of Troft warships gathered on the plains north of where the city had once stood. Whatever the Qasamans were planning at Azras, it had better be good.

The Balin ships, as best as Merrick could read the curlies, were gathered together at the eastern end of the group. The driver steered the car to the base of one of them and tapped a signaling button on the control board.

And to Merrick's surprise, one of the warship's bow doors opened and Ubujak stepped out. [The vehicle, remain in it,] he called to Merrick as he strode up to the car. [The Drim'hco'plai command ship, I am ordered to report to it.]

An unpleasant tingle ran up Merrick's back. [The battle, it has begun?] he asked as he slid hastily across the seat to give Ukuthi room to get in.

[The battle, I have yet seen no signs of it,] the other said. [Commander Inxeba, I believe he merely wishes to consult with his colleagues.]

Merrick grabbed for a handrail as the car lurched forward again. [Slaves, are they also invited to this meeting?] he asked pointedly.

[A problem, it will not be one.] Ukuthi paused. [My proposal, have you given more thought to it?]

[The proposal, I have given a great deal of thought to it,] Merrick assured him. [The details, I will wish to discuss them further.]

[Further discussion, I will look forward to it.] Ukuthi gestured to Anya. [A slave, you must now behave as one. Anya Winghunter's behavior and manner, you must imitate them.]

Merrick grimaced. He hadn't thought about that aspect of this masquerade. If the other Trofts tumbled to the fact that he wasn't, in fact, one of Ukuthi's slaves, there would be serious hell to pay.

Still, if he wanted to monitor Ukuthi's behavior during the upcoming action and confirm he wasn't helping the Drim against the Qasamans, this was where he needed to be. [My best, I will do it,] he told the other.

There were four soldiers waiting at the base of the Drim command ship when the Balin car arrived. Merrick thought he saw some surprise in their faces when Ukuthi strode toward them with a pair of human slaves in tow, but it might have been his imagination. Certainly neither of them said anything. Two of the soldiers ushered the visitors through the bow door into what seemed to be a guard room, then led the way up a switchback stairway to the ship's top deck. There, they were shown into a conference room where four Trofts wearing senior officers' insignia and identical sets of curlies were already seated on upholstered couches.

The couches, Merrick noted, came equipped with small control boards and tables to hold the Trofts' drinks. A fifth couch, currently unoccupied, had a drink poured and waiting.

The soldiers had been too polite or too discreet to mention Ukuthi's slave entourage. But one of the officers had no such compunctions. [The meaning, what is this?] he demanded, glaring at Merrick and Anya. [Commander Ukuthi, does he now bring slaves to military conferences?]

[Commander Ukuthi, he is training them to military capabilities,] Ukuthi said calmly. [Constant service, I require them to learn it.]

[Unseemly, it is,] the other Troft growled. [Commander Inxeba's slaves, he has not brought them.] He gestured to the other Drim officers. [My officers, their slaves they have also left elsewhere.]

[Commander Inxeba's forgiveness, I ask it,] Ukuthi said. [My departure, do you wish it?]

Inxeba sent Merrick another glare, but pointed to the empty couch. [Your presence, I request it,] he said tartly. [The slaves, they will stand silently.]

Ukuthi looked at Merrick as he settled onto his couch. [Silence, you will maintain it,] he ordered.

Anya bowed. Merrick caught the beginning of the gesture in time to follow suit. [The order, we obey it,] she said. She looked sideways at Merrick and gave a small warning shake of her head.

Merrick nodded back and remained silent. Apparently, all the members of a group of slaves were to bow, but it was sufficient for only one of them to acknowledge a general order.

[The purpose of this meeting, what is it?] Ukuthi asked as he sampled his drink.

[Activity in Purma, it has suddenly increased,] Inxeba said, pointing to one of a bank of sixty small monitors arrayed across two of the room's walls. That particular display showed an aerial view of a city intersection, with twenty Qasamans moving purposefully around the area. At the bottom of the image were the words *Purma/Five* in cattertalk script. [A SkyJo lair, it is,] Inxeba identified the view. [The Qasamans' attack helicopters, they are about to deploy them.]

Merrick frowned. Ukuthi had predicted an attack, but in Azras, not Purma. Had he been wrong? Or was Purma just a diversion?

Ukuthi was apparently wondering along the same lines. [The SkyJos, have you yet seen one?] he asked.

[The SkyJos, I have not seen them,] Inxeba admitted. [A SkyJo lair, I am still convinced it is.]

[The truth, perhaps you speak it,] Ukuthi said. [Azras, is there activity there?]

[Activity, it is also occurring in Azras,] Inxeba said, a note of impatience in his voice. [But the activity, it is less urgent. Purma, the center of enemy government it is. Purma, from there will the enemy's next attack arise.]

[Purma, the attack will perhaps arise from there,] Ukuthi said noncommittally. [The truth, you appear to have it. My presence, why have you requested it?]

[Strategic command, the Drim'hco'plai have given you,] Inxeba said, and there was no mistaking the resentment in his tone. [Commander Goqana, he requests your approval for my action.]

[Your action, what form does it take?] Ukuthi asked.

The Drim commander launched into a convoluted explanation, much of it involving military terms that Merrick didn't know. As he listened with half an ear, he looked across the rest of the monitor bank until he found the set of eight images that were marked with the identifying word *Azras*. Like the Purma cityscape, all the Azras images were coming from hovering drones. All eight showed the same sort of street activity that the Purma drones were watching, though as Inxeba had said the Azras version didn't seem nearly as intense or surreptitious.

He frowned as something odd caught his eye. The eight Azras monitors showed street activity; but it was the *same* street activity. Whoever was directing operations had apparently been intrigued enough by what was happening on that particular street to gather all the drones together to monitor it.

Leaving the rest of the city completely unwatched.

Merrick's guess had been right. Purma was a diversion.

He stole a look at Inxeba. The Drim commander was still gazing intently at the wrong displays, his radiator membranes fluttering slowly with anticipation of the coup he was fully expecting to achieve today.

[Slave.]

Startled, Merrick looked at Ukuthi. The Balin commander was pointing at his empty glass.

[Your wish, we obey it,] Anya said. Nudging Merrick, she nodded across the room to a sideboard where a large, half-full pitcher sat on a cooling plate.

Merrick nodded back and crossed to the pitcher. It was heavier than it looked, but his arm servos were more than up to the task. Returning to Ukuthi's couch, he carefully refilled the glass. [The others, you will serve them,] Ukuthi said when he'd finished.

[The order, I obey it,] Merrick said, wincing. Here he was, trying to hold still and remain invisible; and here Ukuthi was, thrusting him squarely into the center of attention.

But for all he didn't know about proper slave protocol, he *did* know that he wasn't supposed to argue with his master. Steeling himself, he set off around the room, stopping at each of the occupied couches and topping off the other Trofts' drinks.

To his mild surprise, none of them looked at him. Certainly none of them thanked him. It was entirely possible, in fact, that they didn't even notice him. Perhaps that was the point Ukuthi had intended to make.

Still, Merrick didn't breathe easy again until he'd finished his task, returned the pitcher to the sideboard, and resumed his place at Anya's side.

[My thought, I will give it to your proposal,] Ukuthi continued, gesturing to the Purma displays. [My attention, I will now give it to the situation.]

His eyes flicked to Merrick. [Useful knowledge, I will hope to gain it.]

Merrick swallowed hard, his eyes on the Azras displays. There was useful knowledge out there, all right. Ukuthi seemed to have already spotted it.

The question was whether Inxeba would also pick up on it in time. Merrick would bet heavily that he wouldn't.

The Qasamans of Azras were betting, too. Only they were betting their lives.

CHAPTER SIXTEEN

The first task, once the eight armored trucks had been captured and their crews neutralized, was to get the vehicles out of Azras.

That part was more or less easy. Lorne had driven one of the trucks back on Aventine and had spent an hour the previous night coaching the Djinn who would be in charge of that part of the operation. The relative simplicity of the task, combined with the learning-enhancement drugs the Qasamans had been given during the session, pretty much guaranteed they'd do a decent job.

And they did. Lorne watched with only mild trepidation as their driver maneuvered his truck through the city streets with a minimum of hesitation and only a single badly-taken corner. Along the way the other captured trucks swung out of other streets to join them, and by the time they came in sight of the main city gate the full eight-truck convoy was running together in a tight battle-phalanx array.

The second task was to get past the Trofts guarding the gate. That one was slightly less easy. The individual soldiers weren't a problem—most of them goggled at the armored column bearing down on them, made frantic radio calls back to the warship for help or fired a useless shot or two before diving out of the way to the sides of the road. The four armored trucks, though their occupants were obviously as startled as the soldiers, stood their ground, their swivel guns turning toward the attackers and opening fire.

They got off perhaps two shots each before the missiles the Djinn had set up in concealed launch tubes on top of the wall blasted down on them, destroying all four trucks and sending mushroom clouds of fire and debris curling high into the air.

But with that, the real job began . . . because while the truck crews and the gate guards had been taken more or less by surprise, the warship a kilometer away was now on full alert. As the trucks set off toward it across the empty field, their swivel guns firing madly, the heavy lasers on the pylons beneath the warship's stubby wings began returning fire.

And suddenly the landscape around the trucks became a blazing hell of fire and smoke.

Beside Lorne, Siraj was quietly cursing through clenched teeth, anger and fear mixing together in his voice. Not fear for himself, Lorne knew. Hanging underneath the truck on the hand- and footholds that had been quick-welded into place before they drove out of the city, and with the entire bulk of the truck between them and the warship's lasers, he and the rest of the strike team were as safe as it was possible to be.

But the drivers and gunners inside the trucks didn't have nearly as much protection. They were heading straight into the deadly fire, fully aware of the danger, fully aware that most or all of them would probably die in the next ninety seconds, but fully committed to getting the strike team as close to the warship as they possibly could.

A fresh wave of smoke billowed across the ground beneath the truck as a near-miss ignited a patch of low bushes. Lorne squeezed his eyes closed against the sting, relying on his implanted opticals to see what was happening. They'd made it across the first small ridge, he could tell, and he could hear the *crack* of the relays through the thick metal above him that meant their swivel gun was still sending laser fire back at the warship's weapons clusters. The assumption had been that the warship would target the swivel guns first, trying to knock them out before they could do serious damage to the ship's own lasers, missiles, and point-defense systems, and only then concentrate on disabling the trucks themselves.

The truck lurched and seemed briefly to float in midair before crashing heavily to the ground again. Second ridge passed. Two more to go, then a shallow dip twenty meters wide that led right up to the warship's base and the two bow doors that were the strike team's hoped-for way in. Third ridge should be coming up...

And then, with a final sputtering *snap* from the capacitors, the swivel gun above them went silent. "Siraj Akim?" Lorne called.

"Our gun's been silenced," Siraj confirmed, his head tilted sideways as he listened to the small radio attached to his right shoulder. "Three of the others have also lost their guns. The others are still firing."

Lorne grimaced. The assumption that the warship would take out the trucks' guns first was a reasonable one. But it *was* only an assumption. If the Troft commander decided he'd rather keep the stolen vehicles at arm's length than disarm them, the strike team could find themselves hanging under broken vehicles too far away from the warship to have any chance of breaching it.

And then, to Lorne's dismay, a new sound joined the snapping of displaced air and the louder crackling of stressed metal and burning vegetation: the sizzle-roar of missiles. Had the Trofts decided it was time to escalate from lasers to missiles? "Siraj Akim?"

"It's all right," Siraj said, his lips pulling back into an evil-looking smile. "Ghofl Khatir has ordered more missiles to be launched from the Azras wall."

Lorne felt his own lips curl back. And now the Trofts were being forced to deal with the more immediate threat of a missile attack before they could return to the task of disabling or destroying the approaching trucks. Khatir had just bought them a few more precious seconds.

His smile turned into a grimace... because the strike team's extra seconds were being bought with Qasaman lives. Back in Sollas, during the first invasion, he'd seen how the Trofts dealt with incoming fire: blanket the area with laser and missile fire, taking out the enemy positions as well as much of the architecture around them. If they kept to that pattern, many of the men manning the Azras missile launchers would be killed, along with probably dozens of civilians.

The truck shot up and lofted itself down from another ridge. Lorne held on grimly, trying to figure out which of the five ridges that had been. To his embarrassed chagrin, he realized that in the confusion of the moment he'd lost count.

But his nanocomputer clock circuit showed a minute twenty

had passed since they'd blown out of Azras. It should only be another ten seconds to the ship.

And then, with an ear-hammering blast and a jolt that nearly wrenched Lorne's hands from the bars, the truck ground to a halt.

"Are we there?" the Djinni on Siraj's far side asked.

"Either there or as close as we're going to get," Lorne told him. He lowered himself onto the ground, wincing at the heat from the burned grass against his back, and made his way to the front of the truck.

The gamble had worked. The Troft warship was right in front of them, the nearest of the bow doors no more than five meters away.

And now came the *really* hard part.

"We're here," he confirmed, looking both directions. "We're five meters out—the rest are no farther than seven or eight. If we all hurry, we should be able to make it before they notice us and open fire from the wing clusters."

"Assuming the invaders are foolish enough to open the doors," Siraj warned, crawling up beside him.

Lorne nodded silently. Again, the assumption was sound: the Trofts would want to quickly deal with whoever might still be alive inside the trucks, but deal with them in a way that wouldn't require them to expend energy or missiles and also wouldn't end up with the utter destruction of their trucks. But again, it was only an assumption. "They will," he assured Siraj. "Anyone still alive in here will by definition be military, and the Trofts will want to question any survivors about Azras's SkyJo contingent."

"Or if not question him, at least identify his face," Siraj said. "If they've been recording their drone observations, they may try to backtrack their prisoners and see which buildings they've been using."

Lorne looked at Siraj in mild surprise. That one hadn't even occurred to him. "That *would* be clever, wouldn't it?"

"One of my father's thoughts," Siraj explained with a tight smile. "He *is* the Marid of Djinn, after all. One should expect him to have an occasional good idea or flash of wisdom."

"One should," Lorne agreed, looking back at the still sealed bow door. "Come on," he muttered. "Come *on*."

"Give them a moment," Gama Yithtra advised as he crawled up beside Siraj. "They were taken by surprise. They may still be rushing madly to don their armor."

Lorne nodded, looking down at the device clutched in Yithtra's hand. Its cross shape and flat sides, he'd been told, harkened back to an ancient hunting weapon called a *chalip*, which had long ago been relegated to the status of children's toy.

But this version, consisting of four metal crossarms thirty centimeters across, was considerably more sophisticated. "Just stay alert," Lorne cautioned. "There won't be much time once they charge out."

"Don't worry, Lorne Moreau," Yithtra said, wiggling the *chalip* for emphasis. "You may be an expert on hunting Troft invaders, but *I'm* the expert with this."

And then, abruptly, the warship door swung open and a double line of armored Troft soldiers charged out, lasers held ready. The first four broke to their left, heading for the farthest of the stalled and battered trucks, while the next four split into pairs and headed toward Lorne's vehicle.

Lorne froze, pressing himself against the ground. But the soldiers' eyes were on the truck's partially blackened windshield and side windows, clearly expecting any further attack to come from one of those directions. Quickly, Lorne flicked a target lock onto the two on his side of the truck as they strode around the front and headed warily toward the rear. Behind them, more Trofts filed from the warship, breaking into more foursomes and heading for the other trucks. The flow stopped, and Lorne got a glimpse of two more Trofts inside the ship, keying the control that started the bow door swinging swing shut.

Lurching his torso up off the ground, Yithtra hurled the *chalip* low over the ground toward the closing door, sailing it like a horizontal pinwheel firespitter through the smoky air. It reached the gap just as the door closed on it, getting caught between door and jamb and blocking the door open a few centimeters. There was a flash of bright yellow where the crossarms touched the door and the jamb—

"Attack!" Ghushtre shouted.

Grabbing the wide bar at the front of the truck, Lorne pulled hard, flinging himself out into the open like a missile from its launch tube. He flipped over onto his back, catching a glimpse of the Trofts who'd been heading toward the rear, now trying desperately to bring their weapons around to face this unexpected threat that had appeared behind them.

They were still trying when Lorne's antiarmor laser flashed twice, sending both soldiers sprawling to the smoldering ground.

Lorne kicked his legs over his head, flipping himself back to his feet as more flashes of laser fire lit up the area between the trucks. He glanced around, confirmed that the Cobras and Djinn of the strike force were all emerging from beneath their vehicles, then turned back to the warship.

The two Trofts he'd seen inside hadn't been caught as thoroughly by surprise as their late comrades outside had been. Both aliens were at the jammed door, struggling with the *chalip* as they tried to pry it loose so that they could seal the door against this unexpected attack.

But the exothermic fast-setting adhesive pellets spaced along the crossarms had fastened it in place as effectively as if it had been welded there. The Trofts were still trying to get it free when Siraj reached the door and took them out with two quick shots from his glove lasers.

Yithtra was already on his knees by the *chalip*, working the hidden catch that broke the weapon apart, finally freeing the door. Grabbing the door edge with one hand and the jamb with the other, he started trying to force the door open again. Standing braced above him, Siraj and his combat suit servos were pushing at it as well.

Braking to a halt beside them, Lorne grabbed the edge of the door below Siraj's hands, adding his own servos to the task. It was surprisingly difficult, more difficult than he'd expected. "Motor's still trying to close it," Siraj grunted. "You have hold? Good—keep pulling."

Resettling his grip on the edge of the door, the Qasaman flipped himself up above Lorne's head into a horizontal position, his hands shifting to a hold on the top of the door with his feet braced against the side of the ship. "Now," he grunted.

For a moment all three of them continued to strain. Then, abruptly, there was the soft *snap* of a burned-out motor, and the door swung free, nearly sending Siraj tumbling to the ground before he could catch himself. "Clear!" Lorne shouted. "Everyone in!"

Siraj was already inside, Yithtra right behind him. Ghushtre ran up at the head of the next group, gesturing Lorne through the door. "Inside," he ordered. "Wait in the guard room until the stairway's clear."

Lorne made a face, but nodded and ducked inside. Part of him wanted to be at the forefront of the attack, an even larger part of him knowing that he *should* be at the forefront. He was, after all, one of only four people in the strike force who'd ever been inside one of these ships.

Which was, of course, the exact reason why the mission's planners had insisted that he stay out of the assault's main spearhead. Not only was he one of the few who knew the ship's layout, but he was the only one who'd had experience controlling the drones.

Lorne understood the logic, and he agreed with it. But he didn't have to like it.

The sounds of combat were starting to come from the stairwell by the time the last of the strike force slipped in through the door. A *lot* of combat, too, Lorne realized uneasily as he notched up his audio enhancements. There was the hiss and small thuds of laser fire and the heavier thuds of falling bodies, all mixed with grunts and moans and stifled screams, both human and Troft.

And none of that was supposed to be happening. Not yet.

The rest of the strike force knew it, too. The Djinn and Cobras still waiting in the guard room were standing tensely in their individual groups, their eyes on the door or else raised to the ceiling, their hands or mouths twitching with suppressed nervousness as they listened to the sounds coming from the stairway.

A few meters away, Siraj was standing with Wendell and Jennifer McCollom, his lips compressed into a tight line as he pressed his radio to his ear. Lorne worked his way over to him and touched his arm. "What's going on?" he asked quietly.

"They've learned from their experience in Sollas," Siraj said tautly. "Their helmets are now equipped with air filters. The spearhead's gas grenades aren't affecting them."

Lorne chewed at his lip, feeling a small throbbing in his still-tender nose from the nostril filters the doctors had implanted yesterday. The quick-acting sleep gas was one of the Qasamans' most effective weapons, and had figured heavily in the mission's planning.

Worse, the mission had banked on the Qasamans keeping the initiative all the way to the command deck. With the attack bogged down in the stairway, that momentum was gone. "How far up are they?" he asked.

"They've pushed back the invaders to Deck Four," Siraj said. "One more deck, and it should be safe to breach the door and try to get you to the drone control room."

Unless the Trofts had already set up their defenses in the corridor. If Lorne had been in charge, that was certainly what he would have done.

But there might be another way. Maybe. "Never mind Deck Four," he said. "Let's see if we can breach Deck Six."

"The vehicle bay?" Siraj asked, frowning. "What do you expect to find in there?"

"I don't know yet," Lorne said. "Let's grab a squad and go look for inspiration."

The stairway battle was even louder as Lorne, Siraj, and the six other Djinn Siraj had commandeered slipped through the door and headed up. But it was also clearly winding down, and as they reached the Deck Six doorway Lorne heard the final Troft body tumble down one of the upper flights of stairs as the laser fire finally ceased. "Stairway's secured," one of the other Djinn said. "We're needed at Deck One."

"We'll do this first," Siraj told him as Lorne pressed his ear against the door. "As soon as the bay's secured, you can join the rest of the spearhead."

"Our orders are to—"

"Your orders have been changed," Siraj cut him off. "Now be quiet. Lorne Moreau?"

Lorne held his breath, keying his audios all the way up. There was plenty of noise being conducted through the metal walls and floors, but it didn't sound like there was anything coming from the bay itself. "It's either clear, or else they're set up and ready for us."

"I suspect the former," Siraj said, pointing to the edge of the door. "The door's been welded shut."

Lorne nodded as he saw the rippling and faint discoloration. "I can fix that. Everyone get back."

The welding had apparently been part of a general order. As Lorne began cutting at the metal, he could see more reflected laser light from the Cobras and Djinn on the landings above him. Whoever was calling the shots for the Trofts these days, he at least knew how to generate delaying tactics.

Unfortunately, he also knew what to do with the time those tactics bought him. As Lorne turned his antiarmor laser on the last section of weld he suddenly noticed that the warship was rumbling with a deep, almost subsonic vibration. The warship's engines were in startup mode, working their slow but steady way toward full power.

And if there was one thing no one in the strike team wanted, it was to fight the rest of this battle while the ship was flying over the Qasaman landscape toward the bulk of the invaders' forces at Sollas.

The last bit of weld sputtered and disintegrated in a shower of liquid metal droplets. "Done," Lorne announced. "Stay back, and let me—"

He broke off as Siraj brushed past him, shoved the door open, and leaped inside, his combat suit's low-power sonic blasting across the bay. The other six Djinn were right behind him. Swearing under his breath, Lorne lunged through the opening after them.

To find the bay deserted.

"Incredible," Siraj murmured as they spread out across the open space. "They haven't even bothered to defend this place?"

"What's there to defend?" one of the Djinn growled, looking around.

He had a point, Lorne had to admit. There were no vehicles, all apparently having been deployed into and around Azras. There were tools and spare parts racked neatly along the walls on either side of the wide vehicle ramp, but nothing that looked like it might be a heavy laser or other weapon.

Outside in the stairway, the laser fire was suddenly joined by the sounds of explosives and rapid-fire projectile weapons. "They're through the doors," the Djinni said urgently. "We're needed up there, Ifrit."

"Go," Siraj ordered, still looking around.

The Djinni gestured, and he and the others took off toward the stairwell. "On your way," Lorne called after him, "give a shout to the guard room and have Wendell and Jennifer McCollom join us."

There was no response, but a second later Lorne heard the Djinni's booming voice as he delivered the message.

"What do you want them for?" Siraj asked.

"Jennifer's the only other one in the team who can read catter-talk script," Lorne told him. "She's going to help me look through all this stuff and see if there's something we can use."

"And if there isn't?"

Lorne felt his stomach tighten. "There will be," he said. "There has to be."

✧ ✧ ✧

[My ship, the enemy has penetrated it!] a taut voice came from the speaker in Commander Inxeba's conference room. [New weapons, the enemy has them.]

Inxeba spat a phrase that had never shown up in Merrick's cattertalk classes. [The enemy, you must destroy them,] he snarled. [Our ridicule, it must not be seen.]

Merrick frowned. Seen by whom? The Qasamans?

No. Not by the Qasamans, but by the rest of the Trofts. The force that the Azras Djinn had attacked were, like Inxeba, members of the Drim demesne. Inxeba desperately wanted to keep his allies from finding out that enemy soldiers had basically just strolled aboard one of his warships.

And that shyness might work to the Qasamans' advantage. Keeping the other Troft demesnes in the dark meant Inxeba wouldn't be able to call on their ships and soldiers to support his.

Unfortunately, it might also mean that Inxeba would decide to cover his embarrassment by eliminating all witnesses to the fiasco. Even if it meant ignoring the normal Troft military policy against mass slaughter of civilians.

Merrick's hands curled almost unconsciously into fingertip laser firing position. He could stop that from happening, he knew. There were only two guards at the door, with danger probably the last thing on either of their minds. A set of targeting locks on them, Inxeba, and Inxeba's officers, and with six quick shots Merrick would effectively cut the head off the Qasaman invasion force.

Then he would die, of course, because there was no way he could get out of a ship full of enemy soldiers alive. But his death might buy a chance for the Azras team to pull out a victory.

Only it wouldn't be just *his* death, he realized with a sinking feeling. Anya would die, too, whether Merrick tried to take her with him or left her here. The Drim would certainly take revenge for their commander's death, and she was after all only a human and a slave. Commander Ukuthi would die, too. He was the one who'd brought the assassin aboard.

He was also the one to whom Merrick had given his pledge.

Slowly, he straightened his hands again, the flash of uncertainty and courage fading away into quiet frustration. What could he do? What *should* he do?

He had no idea.

[Your courage, I am impressed by it,] Ukuthi said quietly.

Merrick shifted his eyes to the Troft. Ukuthi was gazing at him, ignoring the sound and fury going on between Inxeba and the Azras ship commander, a knowing look on his face. [My courage, I have none,] Merrick said bitterly.

[Courage, you do have it,] Ukuthi insisted. [Inaction, the hardest task it always is. Yet inaction, the proper course it often is.]

[Commander Ukuthi, his attention I would have it,] Inxeba called angrily.

[Commander Ukuthi, his attention you have it,] Ukuthi said, turning away from Merrick.

[Balin'ekha'spmi warships, I request them,] Inxeba said. [A new force, I would send it to Azras.]

It seemed to Merrick that Ukuthi sent a small glance over his shoulder at the two humans. [Balin'ekha'spmi warships, I will not send them,] he said.

Inxeba's radiator membranes snapped rigid with surprise. [Your statement, repeat it,] he demanded.

[Balin'ekha'spmi warships, I will not send them,] Ukuthi repeated. [A trap, I believe this is one. Balin'ekha'spmi warships, I will not send them into ambush.]

Slowly, deliberately, Inxeba rose from his couch. [Balin'ekha'spmi warships, I demand them,] he said, his voice dark, his radiator membranes stretched to their limit. [Balin'ekha'spmi warships, I demand them *now*.]

[My answer, you already have it,] Ukuthi said calmly. [Drim'hco'plai warships, you may send them if you wish.]

For a long moment the room was silent except for the muffled sounds of battle coming from the speaker. Even the Azras commander had stopped talking. Keeping his head and body motionless, Merrick put target locks on both guards and on the small pistol holstered at Inxeba's side. His pledge to Ukuthi hadn't included defending the Balin commander from his own people.

Slowly, Inxeba's membranes folded back against his upper arms. [Glory, this operation will yet bring it,] he said, stepping back to his couch. [Glory, it will belong wholly to the Drim'hco'plai.]

He dropped onto the couch and gestured to one of his officers. [Two warships from Purma, they will travel to Azras,] he ordered. [Arrival, what is the time until it?]

[Floatator activation, there will be seventeen minutes until it,] the officer said. [Travel to Azras, eleven minutes will be required for it.]

[The order, give it,] Inxeba said. [Captain Vuma, his courage and determination are required. Assistance, in twenty-eight minutes it will arrive.]

[Captain Vuma, his strength and determination will be sufficient,] the voice from the speaker promised. [The attackers, we will hold them.]

[Commander Inxeba, he is pleased.] Inxeba's membranes fluttered. [Death, the enemy shall have it.] He looked balefully at Ukuthi. [And then glory, *we* shall have it.]

They'd been searching the vehicle bay for five solid minutes, and Lorne was sifting rapidly and uselessly through a collection of laser actuators and cooling modules when he heard a short, sharp whistle from the small machine shop at the rear of the bay. "Broom? Akim?" McCollom called. "Got something."

They found McCollom and Jennifer leaning over a workbench tucked away between two stacks of meter-square metal plates that were strapped securely to the wall. The bench and the storage shelf behind it held a bewildering collection of tools and equipment. "What did you find?" Siraj asked as he and Lorne came up to the bench.

"For starters, these," Jennifer said, pointing to the plates. "They look to me like replacement hull plates."

"Yes, that makes sense," Lorne said, eyeing the plates. "And?"

She gave him an odd look. "*And* whatever weapons the Trofts are using against the Qasamans probably aren't designed to handle hullmetal," she said with exaggerated patience.

"She's right," Siraj said, keying his radio. "Ifrit Ghushtre? Send three men to the vehicle bay immediately, and then pull back to harassment positions. We've found something the spearheads can use as shields."

He got an acknowledgment and started unfastening the straps securing the plates to the wall. "I'll get these," he said. "McCollom?"

"On it," McCollom said, starting on the other set of plates.

"Hang on, I'm not done," Jennifer said. "If they want to put in replacement plates, they first have to take out the damaged ones, right? So I figure—"

"They must have a cutting torch somewhere," Lorne interrupted, stepping to her side and scanning the equipment at the back of the bench.

"And I figure something designed for hull plates should cut through deck plates like a laser through blue treacle," Jennifer continued. "You might be able to cut through the ceiling and climb up behind the Trofts while they're concentrating on the Djinn coming in the stairway."

"Can't do it from down here," McCollom told her, glancing up at the bay's high ceiling. "That's too far for a cutting torch to reach."

Lorne felt his breath catch as an idea suddenly popped into his mind. "Not *up*," he said. "*Down*. We get on top of the ship, cut through the hatch up there, and *then* come in behind them."

"Nice," McCollom complimented him. "Problem: we're on Deck Six, the top of the ship is above Deck One. How exactly do you plan to get up there?"

"You'll see," Lorne said. "Siraj Akim, what happened to Gama Yithtra's *chalip*?"

"Still glued to the entry door," Siraj said, his eyes hard on Lorne's face. "You're not serious."

"Why not?" Lorne countered. "There were four adhesive pellets on each of the *chalip*'s cross-arms, and only two of the arms got triggered. That leaves eight pellets still available."

"That's not enough," Siraj said. "Wendell McCollom is right—it's a climb of nearly twenty meters. You can't do it in eight steps."

"Wait a minute," Jennifer said, frowning back and forth between them. "*Climb*? Climb where?"

"Along the outside of the ship," McCollom told her. "He's right, Broom. And you're not going to be able to jump from one and attach the next one in midair. The glue can't possibly set *that* fast."

"Trust me," Lorne said with a tight smile. "The trick is that once we get going, it'll be *ten* meters, not twenty."

McCollom huffed out a breath. "Okay, *this* one I have to see."

"Three minutes," Lorne promised. "Siraj, get someone to bring that *chalip* up here. McCollom, you and Jennifer find and assemble the torch. You know how to use one?"

"Probably better than you do," McCollom assured him.

"No argument there," Lorne agreed. "I'll go find something we can use as hand- and foot-holds."

There was a rattling sound from the main bay. Lorne tensed,

then relaxed as he saw it was just the three Djinn Siraj had sent for. "And let's get it done before the grav lifts come on line. I don't want to do this from a thousand meters in the air."

Three minutes later, right on schedule, they were standing at the bow end of the bay, watching as Lorne lowered the wide vehicle ramp.

But not all the way to the ground. In fact, he hardly lowered it at all, but only opened it enough to leave a meter-wide gap at the top.

A gap big enough for them to crawl through.

"I'll go first," Lorne said, sliding the makeshift pouch bouncing against his left to ride farther around his back. "Then Siraj, then McCollom. Jennifer, you stay here and watch the ramp. If it starts to drift—open *or* closed—give us a shout and try to get it back to where it is right now. Everyone ready? Let's go."

Lorne's initial worry was that the ramp would prove unclimbable. Fortunately, that turned out not to be the case. Not only did it have low ridges to aid with traction, but it had also collected a number of pits and cracks over the years that provided plenty of fingerholds. His second worry was that Siraj, who lacked both Cobra climbing training and lockable fingers, would have to be hauled up by one of the others. But apparently his Djinn instructors had recognized the possible need for scaling nearly sheer walls, and Siraj made it up the ramp with nearly as much ease as Lorne and McCollom. Within half a minute, all three of them were perched on the end of the ramp, gazing up the smooth hullmetal of the warship's bow.

"Nice view," McCollom grunted as Lorne pulled out the first of the wide, long armored-truck door hinges that he'd taken from the vehicle bay's collection of spare parts. "Especially the part of the view where we can't see the weapons pylons."

"If we can't see them, they can't shoot us," Lorne agreed. Getting to his feet on the end of the ramp, balancing himself cautiously, he reached as far up as he could and slammed the edge of the hinge firmly against the hull.

There was a yellow flash, and Lorne felt a brief wave of heat on his hand as the highly exothermic adhesive inside the pellet was exposed to the air. He held the hinge in place a few seconds, then cautiously gave it a pull.

The hinge didn't budge. He pulled harder, and harder, until he was hanging free with his full weight being supported. "We're in business," he told the others. "I'm heading up. Follow as you can."

Pulling himself up, he worked his way into a crouching position on the hinge, stood upright, and reached up to glue his second hinge to the hull.

Four minutes later, he'd made it to the crest of the ship.

He was at the stern, using his antiarmor laser to burn away the radar-absorption coating from around the dorsal hatch, when the others caught up to him. "Okay, the rest should be just standard hullmetal," he said as McCollom laid the torch's fuel tank on the crest. "Anything we can do to help?"

"Just stand clear," McCollom said, lowering a set of slightly-too-small goggles over his eyes and igniting the torch.

Lorne stepped back, wincing as a glimpse of the cutting jet tried to burn its way into his retinas before he could look away. Blinking against the afterimage, he peered out toward Azras.

And felt his stomach tighten. The city had paid heavily for those diversionary missiles Ghushtre had launched earlier. A huge section of the outer wall had been disintegrated, turned by the warship's lasers and missiles into a sixty-meter-long ridge of broken steel and masonry. Beyond it, nearly all of the first row of buildings had likewise been turned to rubble.

Lorne and his mother had urged that the Qasamans move the civilians out of that part of the city before the attack. Ghushtre and Siraj had argued in turn that suddenly underpopulated streets could tip off the invaders that something was about to happen.

As usual, the Qasamans had won the argument. Their sole concession had been to agree to put volunteers in the most dangerous zones, and to move them out as quickly as possible once the strike force and their commandeered trucks were on the move.

Distantly, Lorne wondered how many of those volunteers had made it out before the warship's lasers began collapsing the city around them.

Behind him, the acrid blaze of the torch winked out. "We're in," McCollom announced. "Who's going first?"

Lorne turned back, pushing the image of dead civilians out of his mind as best he could. McCollom had carved a groove in the hull around the hatch, burning through all three of its locks, and was carefully levering it open. "Definitely not you," he told the big Cobra, leaning over the open hatchway and listening closely. There were the sounds of laser and projectile fire down there, but it was all reasonably distant. Probably in the command section's main corridor. "You're way too easy a target."

"Besides which, Lorne Moreau and I are the only ones who've already fought inside one of these ships," Siraj added, handing McCollom the radio and starting down the ladder. "We'll be first and second. You'll be backup."

"Typical," McCollom grumbled. "Pick on the big guy, why don't you?"

"If it'll make you feel better, you can have first crack at getting the command room door open after we clear out the corridor," Lorne offered as he headed down behind Siraj. "Give Ifrit Ghushtre a call and warn him we're coming in."

The sounds of battle were much louder down here. As Lorne moved along the short corridor leading to the command area, he was able to pick out individual weapons as well as the sounds of grunted cattertalk, and tried to form a mental map of the enemy's deployment. All of the sound and fury was coming from the left, the direction to the stairwell the Qasamans had secured. He reached the corridor, motioned Siraj to stay back, and eased an eye around the corner.

The Trofts' defense was set up pretty much the way he'd envisioned it: a double row of armored aliens set up a few meters back from the stairway, one standing, the other crouching, all with lasers blazing toward the open door and the shadowy figures visible beyond. In the front-center of the group was a much larger wheel-mounted laser with a wide shield attached to protect its gunner. The Qasamans in the stairway were keeping up what Ghushtre had described during their practice sessions as a random-edge system: Djinn popping out at various places around the door edge, firing their glove lasers, and immediately withdrawing. A half dozen Trofts were lying motionless on the deck among the defenders, some of them surrounded by the scorch marks left by the handful of grenades the Qasamans had brought along. In the stairwell behind the Qasamans, he could see a pair of the hull plates Jennifer had found in the vehicle bay being readied for use as shields.

The right end of the corridor, in contrast, was silent. Lorne gave a quick look in that direction, expecting to find the area empty of both attackers and defenders. To his surprise, he found a mirror-image of the force currently engaging the Qasamans, this second force facing the other stairway with their backs to Lorne. Clearly, the Troft commander was expecting the attackers to eventually make a sortie through that door, and had laid out his forces in anticipation of that second front.

Lorne smiled humorlessly as he drew back again. Right idea. Wrong direction. Motioning Siraj forward, he gestured him to the right. Siraj glanced out, nodded acceptance of his part of the counterattack, and stepped fully out into the corridor, raising his glove lasers to the right. Lorne stepped out behind him, turning to the left, and flicked targeting locks onto the heavy laser's power pack and as many of the Troft hand weapons as he could see from his position.

And as Siraj's glove lasers began spitting fire behind him, he swiveled up on his right leg and fired his antiarmor laser.

The power pack went first, exploding in a burst of shrapnel that staggered the four aliens closest to it. A chopped second later Lorne's next group of shots took out the smaller weapons, their smaller blasts also sending their owners reeling. He heard grunts and screams of pain from behind him as he charged forward, targeting the rest of the aliens' weapons as he ran and firing his fingertip lasers to neutralize them.

And then he was in the middle of the rear line, jabbing at chests and throats with servo-powered fists and forearms, scattering the soldiers like sticks in a gale as they fell to the deck or first bounced off the walls before collapsing into individual heaps. There was a shout from in front of him, and he saw the Djinn from the stairwell rushing to his aid.

Bravely, but unnecessarily. By the time they reached him, it was all over.

"Very courageous," Ghushtre growled as he stepped over the stunned or unconscious Trofts. "Also very foolish. You have your lasers—why didn't you just kill them?"

"Because I'm hoping to talk the captain into surrendering," Lorne told him, breathing hard. His servos had done most of the actual work during the fight, but the adrenaline rush was still tingling through him. "Easier to do if we've demonstrated some restraint." There was the sizzle of a laser behind him, and he turned around.

Just in time to see McCollom vaporize the last of the hinges and throw himself shoulder-first against the command room door. With a teeth-aching sound of tearing metal the door collapsed inward and crashed to the deck.

And from the opening came a flurry of laser fire that once again lit up the corridor.

Cursing under his breath, Lorne sprinted for the door. He reached the open doorway, wincing at the laser shots flashing around him. Inside the room McCollom was on his back, his knees and torso curled inward toward his belly as he spun around in a circle, his antiarmor laser spitting fire across the command room.

Lorne glanced up, targeted the ceiling, and jumped.

The ceiling jump was one of a Cobra's pre-programmed reflexes, and as usual Lorne's nanocomputer performed the stunt flawlessly. Before his feet even left the floor the computer had taken control of his servos, tucking his head inward and spinning him a hundred eighty degrees around just in time for his feet to be uppermost as he reached the ceiling. His knees bent, absorbing the impact, then straightened again, shoving him off at a new angle with enough spin to turn him upright again as he hit the deck between two banks of monitor displays. As his knees bent again with the impact, he glanced around the room, putting quick targeting locks on the weapons trying to track toward him. His fingertip lasers fired their scattered shots, and once again broken weapons went flying. [Your firing, cease it!] he shouted into the chaos.

For a moment the Trofts froze, their lasers still held ready, their radiator fins fluttering with stress. Lorne took advantage of the pause to target the rest of the weapons in sight, knowing that McCollom would be doing the same. [Your captain, I would speak with him,] he said into the frozen silence. [His surrender, I demand it.]

One of the Trofts stepped forward, senior officer insignia on his leotard, his radiator membranes stretched fully out. [Captain Vuma, his surrender you will not have it,] he bit out. [The Drim'hco'plai, they do not surrender to aliens.]

[Then the Drim'hco'plai, they will die at the hand of aliens,] Lorne said flatly.

Vuma looked at the line of Qasamans now standing just inside the door, their own weapons aimed and ready. [The disgrace of surrender, I will not accept it,] he insisted.

Defiant words . . . and yet he was still talking. If he'd really been insistent on going out in a blaze of glory, he should have already done so. [Useless deaths, they also bring disgrace,] Lorne pointed out. [Courage, a good warrior must have it. Wisdom, a warrior must also have it.]

Vuma looked at the Qasamans again. [Our lives, do you guarantee them?] he asked.

[Your lives, I guarantee them,] Lorne promised. [Your weapons, your soldiers will lay them down. The nearest quarters, they will go immediately to them.]

[The exits, we will instead leave by them,] Vuma offered. [The ship, we will give it to you.]

[The nearest quarters, your soldiers will go immediately to them,] Lorne said firmly. [Three minutes, they have only them.]

Vuma's membranes fluttered. But he bowed his head and gestured to a Troft standing beside one of the consoles. [My words, broadcast them,] he ordered. [Soldiers of the Drim'hco'plai demesne, my surrender, I have given it. Your weapons, you must lay them down. Your quarters, you will return immediately to them.]

He gestured again. Silently, the Trofts in the command room laid their weapons on the deck. [Three minutes, you have only them,] Lorne reminded him. [Death, a Troft outside the quarters will receive it.]

[Your orders, we will obey them.] Turning, Vuma strode past the Qasamans and out into the corridor, the other Trofts following.

Lorne waited until they were all gone. Then, circling the console, he walked over to McCollom, who was still on his back on the floor. "I think that was the definition of damn fool," he commented, offering the big Cobra a hand.

"Hey, you *said* I could take out the door," McCollom reminded him, not taking the hand or getting up on his own. "Why should I let you and Akim have all the fun?"

"As long as you had a good reason," Lorne said, frowning down at him. "You all right?"

"Mostly," McCollom said. "A few small burns. Nothing serious."

"Except that you can't get up?"

"I'm sure I could," McCollom said in a dignified tone. "I just think it would probably hurt, and I don't want you to hear me swear."

Lorne looked over at Ghushtre. "Ifrit?"

"The medical area has been alerted," Ghushtre confirmed as he stepped to Lorne's side. "I'll have him carried there as soon as the invaders are clear of the corridors."

"Thank you," Lorne said, wincing as some of the pain from his own collection of laser burns started to throb their way through the fading adrenaline. "What do you think?"

Ghushtre looked down at McCollom, then back up at Lorne. "Too easy," he said darkly. "Far too easy."

"Agreed," Lorne said, nodding. "I'm guessing that he expects reinforcements any time now, and figures there's no point getting himself killed for nothing. Probably why he wanted to get out of the ship—he wanted the reinforcements to be able to come aboard with lasers blazing and not have to worry about hitting friendlies."

"Yes," Ghushtre said. "But as yet no other warships have left their positions."

"Probably still warming up," Lorne said. "If we hurry, we should still have time. I'll get downstairs and deal with the drones. You'd better call Azras and tell them phase two is on."

"Already done," Ghushtre said. "The explosives will be ready when you are."

"Good," Lorne said. "And have someone get Jennifer McCollom up here. I want someone who reads cattertalk script to look over the weapon firing systems."

"I'll send for her," Ghushtre said, frowning. "You *do* remember that we can't use those weapons, don't you?"

"Of course," Lorne assured him. "But we may be able to at least get the lasers and missile tubes to swivel a little." He shrugged. "With a plan like this, it's all in the perception."

"Perhaps," Ghushtre said. "Just don't forget that once the warships leave Purma you'll have no more than ten or twelve minutes until their arrival."

"Don't worry," Lorne said grimly. "We'll be ready."

CHAPTER SEVENTEEN

It had taken a full day to get the new spore-repellent curtain set up at the south end of Stronghold's landing area, and Jody Broom's friends Geoff and Freylan had insisted on giving it another two hours of testing to make sure that the transportation and setup hadn't knocked anything loose. Harli had had a chance to examine it as he oversaw the operation, and had quickly concluded that the curtain was the ugliest stretch of cloth he'd ever seen in his life.

It was even uglier on the inside, where the Trofts were now gathered. But it worked, and that was all that mattered.

Not that he was expecting Captain Eubujak to comment on either the aesthetics or the practicality. He was expecting Eubujak to be sputtering mad about the prisoners' new accommodations, and he was right.

"This is unacceptable," Eubujak said, the emotionless tone of his translator pin in sharp contrast to the violent fluttering of his radiator membranes. "It is barbaric. There is no space, there are no sanitary facilities, there is no proper bedding—"

"There are two square meters of space each," Harli interrupted the tirade. He really didn't have time for this. "Sanitary facilities are right outside the curtain if you want them. As for the rest of it, there should be Tlossie ships arriving any time now to take you to a proper prisoner-of-war camp."

Eubujak glared at him a moment, probably waiting for the running translation to finish. "There will be consequences," he warned, gesturing toward the crazy-quilt patchwork rising over the Caelian greenery behind him. "The Drim'hco'plai demesne will not accept such treatment of its citizens."

"The Drim'hco'plai demesne should have thought of that before they decided to invade other people's worlds," Harli said bluntly.

Eubujak continued to glare. But as his eyes shifted from Harli to the Stronghold wall, half a kilometer to the north, his radiator membranes settled lower against his upper arms.

Harli smiled cynically. The Troft had certainly noticed their warship ferrying the civilians out of the city over the past few hours. The final group, in fact, had left just as the prisoners were being marched across the overgrown field to their new open-air quarters. Apparently, Eubujak had just put the pieces together and realized that once the last few Cobras had also left he could simply march his troops back to the deserted city and settle into the far more comfortable homes of its residents.

It was almost a shame to have to burst his bubble. Almost.

"Oh, and there's one other thing," Harli said, keying on his field radio. "Popescu? You ready?"

"We're ready," Popescu's voice came, sounding every bit as pleased as Harli was feeling. "Got a really nice load, too."

"Great," Harli said. "Go ahead and drop 'em."

From one of the clearings east of the city, one of Caelian's two air-transport vans lifted into view. It flew across the forest to the field of knee-high hookgrass and razor fern that the Trofts had just slogged through to their new quarters. As it reached the area between the curtain and Stronghold, the rear doors opened and one of the Cobras started tossing out objects that sent ripples through the grasses as they thudded to the ground.

Out of the corner of his eye, Harli saw Eubujak's radiator membranes starting to stretch out again. "What is this?" the Troft asked. "What do they throw from the vehicle?"

"Carcasses," Harli told him. "Dead animals. Hooded clovens, orctangs, giggers, maybe a saberclaw or two. Basically, everything they were able to hunt down and kill over the past couple of hours."

Eubujak looked at the transport, then at the ground, then back at Harli. "Explain," he demanded.

"Give it a minute," Harli said, keying his audios. Over the hum of the transport's grav lifts, he could hear the quiet whispering of small creatures moving through the flora around them.

And then, one of the bodies twenty meters away suddenly began writhing violently.

Eubujak's membranes snapped all the way out. "You said they were dead!"

"They are," Harli said as two of the other carcasses also began twitching. "Those are some of Caelian's scavenger animals—ratteeth and scrimmers, mostly, with probably some picklenose and a *lot* of different insects thrown in. We've just laid out the best buffet they've ever seen in their short, violent, miserable little lives."

He pointed to the edge of the forest, where his infrareds now spotted the tell-tale profile of a screech tiger. "And speaking of buffets . . ."

Right on cue, the screech tiger bounded from cover, driving a rippling shock wave through the grasses as it raced toward one of the twitching carcasses. From the other side of the forest, a pair of smaller wakes marked the arrival of giggers or saberclaws.

"It's kind of like those museum dioramas I used to see pictures of when I was a kid," Harli said as a flock of split-tails appeared and made a diving run over one of the shaking carcasses. Two of them shot back out of the grass a second later with mouse-whiskers clutched in their talons. "Pretty much the whole Caelian ecosystem is about to settle in right here in front of you. It'll be great fun—and *very* educational—for you to watch. Though I strongly recommend you do so from *inside* the curtain."

He looked significantly at Eubujak. "Out here, it's not going to be very healthy." He tapped the greenish patina of spores already collecting on the Troft's leotard sleeve. "Especially since you're starting to look a lot like lunch."

Eubujak looked down at his sleeve, then at the increasingly active kill zone between him and the city wall. "There will be consequences," he warned again, and stepped back toward the curtain.

"Only if you try to come out," Harli said. "But don't take my word for it. Feel free to—"

"Harli!" Popescu's voice came urgently from the radio. "Harli, you there?"

Frowning, Harli keyed the transmitter. "I'm here," he said. "What's up?"

"Whistler just picked up visual on two bogies coming in from the east," Popescu said tautly. "Still too far away for a positive ID, but they sure as hell look like Drim warships."

Harli felt his throat tighten. "You sure?"

"Whistler is," Popescu said. "He said he tried hailing, but there was no answer."

Harli looked toward the east, cursing under his breath. The ships that the Tlossie demesne-heir Warrior had promised to send for the prisoners would be transports, not warships. And they definitely wouldn't ignore a hail.

The Drim reinforcements had arrived.

Only they'd arrived a whole damn day too early.

"Get inside," he ordered Eubujak, hooking a thumb toward the curtain. "Get *inside*. Now."

Eubujak flicked a look of his own toward the east. Then, without a word, he stepped back, pulled up the lower edge of the curtain and ducked down, and disappeared into the enclosure.

"What do you want us to do?" Popescu asked.

For a pair of heartbeats Harli gazed into the eastern sky, trying to think. Rashida and their one functional Troft warship should have dropped off the last load of civilians by now and be heading back to Stronghold to collect the rest of the Cobras. Probably no way they could make it before the new ships arrived.

Or maybe they could. Warrior had said that Drim warships couldn't fire on each other. If he was right about that, Rashida might just barely be able to bring the warship in, grab the remaining twenty Cobras, and hightail it out of here.

But hightail it to where? One of the other settlements, where the invaders would be sure to follow? Somewhere out into Wonderland, where the Cobras would have the lethal Caelian ecology to help take them out?

He glanced over his shoulder at the curtain. Whatever he decided, he realized suddenly, he first needed to move out of Troft earshot. He'd already seen how inventive Eubujak was at getting messages to his fellow Drims.

Unless Harli could come up with something he *wanted* the incoming warships to know about...

"Here's what you do," he told Popescu. Actually, now that he thought about it, the warships were probably monitoring their radio transmissions anyway. Still, better to double down on this one and stay close to the curtain. "First, get a message to Smitty and have him divert Rashida to the Octagon Caves. Tell him to forget the booby-trap. He's to get the missiles and the rest of the gear out of the chimney, load 'em aboard, and get 'em back here. Got it?"

"Whoa, whoa," Popescu protested, sounding thoroughly confused. "What—?"

"Shut up and listen, you stupid spelunker," Harli snarled. "Don't worry—between the construction crew and the ordnance team he'll have at least fifty Cobras to help him with the loading. While he does that, we're going to fire up the weapons on the downed ship. Our new guests should be flying pretty much straight over us, so we should be able to take out at least one of them before they know what's up. Got all that?"

"Yeah, I got it," Popescu growled. "And lay off calling me a spelunker. Do it again and I'll come over there and pop your wings off."

Harli smiled grimly. Popescu had gotten the message, all right. "I'd like to see you try it," he growled back. "Go on, get moving."

The predators were still churning up the hookgrass. Harli ran as close as he dared to the frenzy, then did a full-servo flying leap that took him safely over the feeding melee. He hit the ground running and headed for Stronghold.

Popescu was waiting for him at the broken section of wall, along with the last of the Cobras still in the city. "I hope that was an act," he said as Harli came up to them. "If it wasn't, I have no idea what you're up to."

"You got it just fine," Harli assured him. "You relay all that to Smitty?"

"Word for word," Popescu said. "So what's our part of the plan?"

Harli pointed at the Troft ship lying on its side. "Basically, we get inside the ship and wait," he said. "I'm figuring that between Eubujak and the newcomers' own eavesdropping they'll get the word that we're going to try to ambush him."

"I thought we couldn't do that," Popescu said. "Didn't Warrior tell you there was an IFF setup on the lasers that would keep us from shooting at other Drim warships?"

"Right, but Eubujak doesn't know we haven't found a way around that," Harli said, gesturing the others to follow and heading at a fast jog toward the downed ship. "I'm hoping one or both of the Drims will land and try to get to us before we can get the weapons activated."

"And when they come charging in we ambush them?" Popescu asked doubtfully.

"I know it's not much of a plan," Harli said, "but with something like seven to one odds against, making them come at us in mostly single file is the best we're going to get."

"Especially since they're not going to have any more experience than we do fighting inside a sideways spaceship." Popescu lifted his radio. "Torrance? We're making our stand in there. Kick everything off standby and run it to full power. Might as well make a good show of it for them."

"Got it," Torrance's voice came back. "I'll start making a list of good places to set up traps."

"Thanks." Popescu lowered the radio and pointed east. "Whistler estimated another ten minutes before they get here. That's not much time."

"We'll make it," Harli assured him. "I just hope Smitty and his crew can figure out what it was I was trying to tell them."

"And can pull it off?"

Harli grimaced. "Yeah. And can pull it off."

"Got it," Smitty said into the radio. "Going silent now. Good luck."

"You too," Popescu said.

Smitty keyed off the radio and busied himself at the control board. "Well," he said. "Nothing brightens up a dull day like an alien invasion. You two doing all right?"

"Sure," Jody said, trying to keep her voice from shaking as her heart thudded in her throat and her stomach tried to do polespins around her esophagus. The Drim reinforcements were a day early. A whole day early.

And she wasn't prepared yet. None of them were.

"I'm fine," Rashida said, and Jody felt a flash of envy at how much calmer the other woman sounded than she did. "But I'm confused by Harli Uy's message. I'm also not familiar with the word *verbatim*."

"That means Popescu gave us Harli's exact words," Smitty told her, tapping one final key. "Okay, I think I've sent you the course heading for the Octagon Caves. Did it come through?"

"Yes, I have it," Rashida confirmed, and Jody's inner ear registered the change as the ship angled onto a new vector. "We'll be there in approximately eight minutes. But I still don't understand the message. When did Harli Uy send fifty Cobras to the cave?"

"He didn't," Smitty said. "He and Popescu must have figured the

Trofts were listening in on the conversation and had to make up a code on the fly. We just have to connect the dots to translate from what he *said* to what he *meant*."

Jody winced. And they probably had to do it in the next eight minutes, before they reached the caves.

"For instance," Smitty continued, holding up a finger. "Popescu's not a spelunker, which is a person who likes exploring caves. But I am. That says Harli's counting on my knowledge of the caves, and my skill at moving around in them."

"Right," Jody said, her brain starting to work again "He talked about a chimney, too. That's some kind of cave formation, isn't it?"

"A rock formation in general, yes," Smitty confirmed. "I know of at least three in the caves that can be climbed, the best one right off the rear of the main chamber."

"But there are no missiles there, correct?" Rashida asked, still sounding bemused.

"No missiles, and no fifty Cobras," Smitty confirmed. "I'm guessing both of those were Harli's attempt to dangle enough bait in front of the Drims so that at least one of the ships ignores Stronghold and the other towns and comes after us instead."

Jody winced. "Wonderful," she murmured.

"Hey, that's our job, Jody," Smitty reminded her soberly. "Well, maybe not *your* job, or Rashida's—"

"It's our job now," Rashida said firmly. "What about the rest of the message?"

"Right," Jody seconded, ashamed of her momentary twinge of self-pity. They had a job to do. Besides, her parents and brothers were undoubtedly in far worse danger on Qasama than she was here. "Harli talked about booby-traps. Was anything set up?"

"Not yet," Smitty said, and Jody thought she could hear a new note of respect in his voice. Probably for Rashida—she was certainly behaving more like a Cobra than Jody was. "That work was supposed to start tonight, after Stronghold was evacuated and the prisoners had been settled in their new home and we had a little breathing space."

"He also talked about the weapons in the downed ship," Rashida said. "But he can't actually use those, can he?"

"Not unless he's got a miracle up his sleeve," Smitty said. "That must be the same window-dressing as the missiles in the chimney—he's giving the invaders another target to go after."

"So if they're smart, they'll assign one ship to each of us," Rashida concluded. "And with the implied threat of immediate attack, we may hope they'll come after us quickly, without careful tactical thought."

"Exactly," Smitty said, nodding. "Your best chance when you're outnumbered this badly is to get the other side moving faster than they can think."

"Hopefully, that means he already has a plan for Stronghold," Jody said.

"Or else he's making it up as he goes," Smitty said. "Of course, he's also got twenty Cobras to work with. We've just got you two and me."

"*And* these," Rashida reminded him, lifting her arm to show the sleeve of her Djinni combat suit.

"For whatever that's worth," Jody said.

"Oh, it's worth a lot," Smitty said. "More than that—" He tapped the edge of his control board. "We've got this."

Jody frowned. "The sensors?"

"The ship," Smitty said. "You're forgetting Popescu's threat to pop Harli's wings off."

Jody felt her back stiffen. "*And* Harli saying he'd like to see Popescu do it."

"Exactly," Smitty said as he got to his feet. "I'll be right back. Jody, you'll have to keep an eye on the sensors."

"Where are you going?" Rashida asked.

"We've got everything we need to make one hell of a booby-trap," Smitty told her as he headed for the door. "Namely, a bunch of high-explosive missiles tucked under our wings."

He threw her a tight smile. "We just have to figure out a way to set them off."

[The images, what has become of them?] Inxeba demanded, gesturing angrily at the dark displays where the views from Azras had been up until thirty seconds ago. [Their return, I demand it.]

[The images, they cannot be returned,] one of the Drim officers reported, peering at his couch's board. [The images, they have been shut off at the source.]

Inxeba swore viciously. [Captain Vuma, I would speak with him.]

[Captain Vuma, he is not responding,] the officer told him. [Captain Vuma, I fear he has been taken prisoner.]

[Captain Vuma, you believe he has been taken prisoner?] Ukuthi asked. [Captain Vuma, you do not believe he has been killed?]

[Officer Cebed, he has misspoken,] Inxeba bit out, sending a glare at the Troft who'd just spoken. [Captain Vuma, he has most likely been killed.]

[The enemy war pattern, perhaps you know more of it than I do?] Ukuthi suggested politely. [News from Caelian, the courier ship brought it?]

Deliberately, Inxeba turned to look at him. [News from Caelian, what would you know of it?] he demanded in a low voice.

[News from Caelian, I know nothing of it,] Ukuthi assured him. [Captain Vuma, I merely observe Officer Cebed assumed his capture. The enemy war pattern, I therefore conclude it to favor capture over death.]

[Captain Vuma's fate, it will ultimately reveal the enemy war pattern,] Inxeba said stiffly.

[The choice of capture, it reveals an enemy's confidence,] Ukuthi continued, as if talking to himself. [Such restraint, it has a strong appeal to the ethos of other Trof'te demesnes.]

[Your silence, I will have it,] Inxeba snarled off. He spun half around on his couch and glared again at Cebed. [The two Purma warships, what is their status?]

[The two Purma warships, they are ready to lift,] Cebed reported, sounding like he wished he was somewhere else.

[The delay, what then is its purpose?] Inxeba demanded. [The ships, send them at once.]

[The order, I obey it.] Hurriedly, Cebed keyed his board. [The ships, they are sent. Their arrival at Azras, eleven minutes there will be until it.]

[The time, perhaps it can be put to use,] Ukuthi suggested. [The situation at Caelian, I would like to learn of it.]

[The situation at Caelian, it is not your concern,] Inxeba said tartly. [The control of Caelian, the Drim'hco'plai were assigned it.]

[The truth, you speak it,] Ukuthi acknowledged. [Yet the enemy's war patterns, they would be useful to know.]

[The war patterns, those of the two human demesnes are different,] Inxeba said. [Your supremacy, only on Qasama have the Tua'lanek'zia granted it to the Balin'ekha'spmi.]

[The Tua'lanek'zia, perhaps they would believe it otherwise,] Ukuthi suggested.

[The Tua'lanek'zia, do you wish to ask it of them?] Inxeba countered.

For a dozen seconds the two Trofts stared at each other, their radiator membranes half extended. It was clearly some kind of confrontation, but like nothing Merrick had ever seen before.

It was also clear that there were high stakes being played for. He kept himself as motionless and unobtrusive as possible, wondering if Ukuthi was going to get caught up in the moment and forget his larger plan.

To Merrick's relief, he didn't. [The Tua'lanek'zia, I do not wish to ask it of them,] Ukuthi said, lowering his head in an abbreviated bow as his membranes folded themselves back onto his upper arms.

[The subject, it is then closed.] Inxeba shut his beak with an audible click, then turned back to the displays.

The minutes crept past. Merrick spent the time looking back and forth across the various city views, trying to guess what the Qasamans might be up to. But aside from the blank screens and the still suspicious-looking street work in Purma everything looked normal.

There were still two minutes to go until the Purma warships' arrival at Azras when the eight blank displays suddenly came to life again. [The enemy, their ignorance is now revealed,] Inxeba said with malicious satisfaction. [The drone sensors, that they can be activated by other Drim'hco'plai warships was unknown to them.]

Merrick studied the displays. They seemed to be in the same positions they'd been in when the cameras were cut off, hovering about fifty meters above the Azras cityscape. In contrast with the earlier shots, though, six of the eight monitors now showed streets that were largely deserted, with only a few people still visible. Only on the two that gave a view of the main gate—or rather, where the main gate had once been—was there any human activity.

And surrounding that activity was utter devastation.

Merrick felt his stomach churn. He'd gotten a glimpse of the destruction earlier, but the probes' cameras hadn't really been focused on that area before. Now, they were showing the Trofts' handiwork in all its terrible glory. A long section of the wall had been leveled, along with an entire row of the buildings just behind it. Dozens of people lay unmoving among the rubble, most of them men but a few of them women. All were battered and bloody, and all still had the bare arms and shoulders that had been mandated by the occupying forces in their effort to thwart attacks by combat-suited Djinn.

[The pavement, to the right look at it!] one of the officers said abruptly, jabbing a finger at the edge of the monitor.

Merrick felt his stomach tighten. Barely visible amid the broken stone and twisted metal was a crack in the street, perhaps half a meter wide.

But it wasn't like the other cracks he could see, the ones presumably created by the falling buildings. This one was straight and smooth, cutting across the pavement at perfect right angles. And the men he could see working feverishly at its edges weren't digging out bodies, but seemed to be trying to remove a pair of long girders, probably pieces of the wall, that had wedged themselves into the opening.

Somehow, the attack by the warship had popped open one of the entrances to the Azras subcity. Not only opened it, but jammed it open.

With a pair of Troft warships only a minute away.

An unpleasant tingle ran through Merrick's skin. It was still possible that the ships hadn't noticed the security breach. If Merrick acted right now, if he killed Inxeba and the officers in this room before they could sound the alert, the Qasamans might have a chance to get the gap sealed in time.

Once again, Merrick felt his hands curl into laser firing positions. Once again, hesitation at the thought of betraying his pledge to Ukuthi slowed his resolve.

And then it was too late. [An opening, in the pavement there is one!] the officer continued excitedly. [The subcity, it lies open before us!]

[The opening, we see it,] someone on the warship acknowledged. [The soldiers, I am preparing them. A landing site, I have located one.]

One of the display images scrolled sideways as the drone shifted position, its sensors zeroing in on a spot of pavement twenty meters back from the subcity entrance that had somehow managed to stay clear of rubble. The camera zoomed in on the site, touching momentarily on yet another group of bedraggled, bloodstained bodies lying amid the chunks of concrete as it panned across the area.

And Merrick felt his blood suddenly turn to ice. For a fraction of a second the camera had touched the casualties' faces...

Anya must have sensed Merrick's reaction. "What is it?" she murmured, leaning closer to him. "Merrick?"

Merrick took a deep breath, the air freezing in his lungs, his mind swirling with horror and helplessness, with unbearable pain and murderous rage. "One of the bodies," he murmured back, his voice shaking. "In the group there by all the rubble.

"It was my mother."

The dark spot was clearly visible in the cliffs rising in front of them when Smitty returned. "We there yet?" he asked as he crossed to the sensor station.

"I think so," Jody said, stepping away from his chair with a twinge of relief. Keeping tabs on his station and her own had been harder than she'd expected. More than ever she was glad he'd talked her and Rashida into letting him join their little piloting group. "As far as I can tell, it's the only cave around."

"Yep, that's it," Smitty confirmed as he resumed his seat. "The Octagon Cave complex. Thirty kilometers of the most beautiful caverns on Caelian."

"Never mind how they look," Jody said as she sat down and strapped in, giving the power displays a quick check. "My question is whether this thing will actually fit inside. That opening looks pretty small."

"Don't worry, it's big enough," Smitty assured her. "If not, I'm sure we can make it big enough."

"Oh, *that's* encouraging," Jody said. "I don't suppose you've actually measured it?"

"Not officially," Smitty conceded. "But I've walked in there a hundred times." He waved at his board. "Besides, I'm pretty sure the sensor readings are on my side."

"I guess we'll find out," Jody said. "Rashida, if you turn out having to shave off something, shave off the topside. The bottom—"

Without warning the whole ship jerked hard, twisting and shuddering violently. Jody grabbed at her straps with one hand and the edge of her board with the other, clamping her mouth tightly to keep from accidentally biting down on her tongue. For a second the ship straightened out, only to start rocking again.

And suddenly, it lurched forward and to the right and then came to a halt at a forty-five-degree angle.

For a moment all three of them just sat there. Then, Jody exhaled a breath she'd somewhere along the line decided to hold. "I was about to say, the bottom is where most of the grav lifts are," she said into the sudden silence. "But never mind—I don't think we're flying this thing any farther today anyway."

"It would seem not," Rashida agreed. For once, even her usually calm demeanor sounded a little shaken. "I don't believe the opening was quite as large as you thought, Smitty."

"Well, it is now," Smitty said calmly. "Good flying, Rashida. You two sit tight while I get what's left of our cameras online and see what we've got to work with."

"Do we have any idea what's happening with the incoming ships?" Jody asked as she unstrapped and eased herself gingerly out of her canted chair and onto the canted deck. Everything seemed more or less steady, but she couldn't shake the feeling that the whole ship was teetering on a precipice, that it might suddenly break loose from wherever it was pinned and topple into some dark chasm looming beneath them. "I didn't want to mess with your settings while you were on your scavenger hunt."

"Yeah, I checked just before we hit the cave," Smitty said. "It looks like one of them landed at Stronghold, and the other one's heading our direction. I guess the chance to deal with some missiles and fifty Cobras was too tempting to pass up."

Jody looked at Rashida. The Qasaman had her calm expression on again, but her face looked a little pale. "Sounds like fun," Jody murmured.

"Don't worry, we can take them," Smitty assured her. "Remember, I know these caves and they don't. Okay, here's the deal. The whole lower part of the ship is jammed into the floor, so the bow exits are out. The good news is that I was planning to use the dorsal hatch anyway. The even *better* news is that we're not going to have to jump or find ourselves a thirty-meter rope, because there's a big snake trail no more than three meters from the forward wing that'll take us the direction we want to go."

"What's a snake trail?" Rashida asked.

"A partially-open rock tube that runs along a cave's wall or ceiling," Smitty explained, getting to his feet. "I've never traveled this particular one, but it looks sturdy enough to hold our weight, and it's even big enough to stand up in."

"Where does it go?" Jody asked.

"Don't know yet," Smitty said. "Rashida, give me that other radio."

Rashida nodded and unclipped it from her belt. Smitty took it, turned it off, and fastened it beside his own radio. "Let's go."

He led the way down the corridor to the stairway leading to the dorsal hatch. Lying at the foot of the stairway was a large silliweave bag. "I found an arc welder down in the vehicle bay that someone missed," Smitty said, picking up the bag. "You two might want to stay here while I go rig it up to the missiles on the wing."

"We'll come with you," Rashida said firmly. "You may need a hand."

Smitty eyed her for a second, then nodded. "Okay," he said, starting up the stairs. "Watch your footing."

He reached the top, unfastened the hatch, and climbed out. Rashida was right behind him. Taking a deep breath, Jody followed.

It wasn't as bad as she'd expected. The hull crest was as badly tilted as the rest of the ship, but with the cavern roof pressing down to within a meter or two of the ship it was more like being in a sloping tunnel than being thirty meters above an unyielding stone floor. She eased over to one of the lower ceiling sections, got a reassuringly firm grip on a section of pockmarked rock, and looked around.

There wasn't a lot of sunlight seeping through the opening they'd just battered their way into. But there was enough for her to see that the chamber included a wide variety of different formations: curtains, stalactites, hourglass-shaped columns, and some hanging vine-shaped things she didn't have a name for. Most of the rock was dark, possibly some kind of basalt, but she could see a few layers of lighter stone, plus a generous sprinkling of glittering gem-like objects that added an eerie night-sky effect.

"Ready," Smitty called, and Jody looked over to see him walking carefully back from the aft wing onto the hull crest, Rashida beside him clutching his arm, the now empty bag tucked into her belt. One of Smitty's two radios, Jody noted, was gone. "Snake trail's over here."

The snake trail was just as Smitty had described it: a two-meter-diameter horizontal tube running along the ceiling near the ship's bow, with a section of its side wall open to the air. "You two feel comfortable enough with those suits' servos to jump on your own?" Smitty asked as they eased their way out onto the slanting forward wing. "If not, I can throw you over to it."

"No, we can do it," Rashida assured him.

"Okay," Smitty said. "I'll go first. Just watch me and do what I do."

He bent his knees slightly and jumped, ducking his head and drawing his knees up toward his chest as he arced through the air toward the tube. He slipped through the gap with a good half meter to spare and straightened out his knees again just in time to land upright. "Your turn," he said, turning and holding out his hand. "Nice and easy."

The jump was one of the most nerve-wracking things Jody had ever had to do. But she made it, and a minute later Smitty was leading them down the snake trail toward the rear of the chamber.

They were nearly to the back wall, and Jody had just noticed that their conduit abruptly narrowed a few meters ahead, when she heard the faint sound of approaching grav lifts. "Smitty?" she murmured.

"Yeah, I hear them," Smitty murmured back. "Okay, snake trail's ending. Looks like we're going to have to jump."

Gingerly, Jody eased her head out through the gap in the wall and looked down. The cavern floor had gradually risen as they'd neared the back wall, but there was still a good five meters of empty space beneath them. "You mean down, right?"

"Don't worry, your servos can handle the landing," Smitty assured her. "We drop, cross that ridge ahead, and the entrance to the chimney is just past that soda-straw formation to the left."

Abruptly, the edges of the cavern lit up with reflected light. Jody twisted her head around and saw a hint of crackling flame in the distance behind the wrecked warship. "Looks like they're laser-burning the foliage around the edge of the entrance," Smitty said. "Making sure we don't launch an ambush from out there."

He touched Jody's arm. "Come on. I'll go first."

CHAPTER EIGHTEEN

The two Troft warships had raced up toward Azras with almost frightening speed, fast enough that Lorne thought for a very bad few seconds that he'd cut his margins too close and that he wouldn't have enough time to pull this off. But then, to his surprise and relief, they coasted to a halt, one settling into position twenty meters above the broken section of wall, the other a hundred meters higher and fifty meters back.

And for the past minute and a half, they'd held those exact same positions.

"They're not going for it," he murmured to Ghushtre, standing behind him in the drone control/monitor room. "They smell a trap."

"Not necessarily," Ghushtre said, leaning over Lorne's seat and studying the displays. "Remember, they were coming to give battle to us in this warship. Now, they've suddenly been presented with a new goal. This may simply be the delay necessary for them to dress their soldiers in their armor."

"I hope so," Lorne said. "If whoever's in charge has come up with something clever, we could be in trouble."

"Whatever they hand us, we'll send it back down their throats," Ghushtre said with a deadliness in his voice that sent a tingle across the back of Lorne's neck. "What's the situation with the drones?"

"They're on their way," Lorne assured him, turning to the drone displays. The incoming ships had taken command of the drones long enough to turn their cameras back on, just as the Qasaman analysis of the invaders' radio operations in Sollas had guessed they could do. But the minute the Trofts had spotted the open SkyJo lair they'd apparently lost all interest in the drones.

Now, with the eight drones again under Lorne's control, the six that had been watching the deserted parts of Azras—the areas the invaders had presumably glanced at and dismissed—were drifting toward their new positions. Two of them were heading toward the warship still hovering low over the gate, moving as if to support the two drones currently feeding the invaders their view of the SkyJo lair. The other four drones were moving back and up, rising into the air above the second, higher warship.

"Movement," Ghushtre said.

Lorne turned back to the other bank of monitors. The lower of the two warships had stopped hovering and was sinking down into the clear spot the Qasamans had carefully prepared for it between the stacks of wall and building rubble. "Okay," he said, part of him relaxing a bit even as, paradoxically, another part of him felt the tension ratcheting up. The Trofts were back on track, which meant that the phase two strike team was that much closer to risking their lives in battle.

But there was nothing Lorne could do except make sure he gave them the best possible chance of living through the next hour. He watched the warship settle to the ground, then turned back to the drone controls, making sure the drones were on schedule—

"Game change!" an urgent voice came from the radio on the board in front of him. "The invaders are lowering the ramp. Repeat, the invaders are lowering the ramp."

Lorne spun back around, his breath catching in his throat. Lowering the vehicle ramp meant the Trofts had decided to roll out their armored trucks instead of coming out on foot through the bow doors.

Only that wasn't what the strike team was prepared for. And unless they came up with a new plan, and fast, they were going to be slaughtered right there in the Azras streets.

And Lorne's mother was right in the middle of it.

"Game change!" a barely audible voice came from the radio lying half hidden beneath a thin piece of stone at Jin's head. "The invaders are lowering the ramp. Repeat, the invaders are lowering the ramp."

"God in heaven," one of the Qasaman Cobras murmured from the pile of stone behind her. "Jin Moreau? What do we do?"

Keeping her eyes closed, knowing that the cameras in the warships' weapons wings would be watching everything, Jin slowly turned her head just far enough for her opticals to see up along the ship's bow. Sure enough, the ramp had been unfastened and was starting to swing ponderously down toward the ground.

Only that wasn't what she and the strike team had planned for. The Trofts were supposed to have seen all the rubble in the area around the SkyJo lair, correctly concluded that their armored trucks wouldn't make it five meters without getting hung up, and sent the soldiers out on foot instead through the bow doors three meters from her and the rest of the team. This was supposed to be a variation of the operation Lorne's strike team had already pulled off: a fast-break incursion and neutralization, only this one with the added advantages that Lorne and the others in the captured ship could provide.

"We can't let them get those trucks out," a new voice murmured from the radio.

Jin shifted her attention to the other side of the warship's bow. Beach was lying there with his half of the strike team, his face grim behind the fake blood staining his forehead. "Agreed," she said. "I'm reading five meters to the top of the ramp. How many do we want to take with us?"

"I don't think anyone," Beach said. "Not until the portside wings are down. Too big a chance they'll get blasted on their way in."

Jin grimaced. But it made sense. Just the two of them, her and Beach, leaping suddenly to the top of the ramp before the gunners inside the warship could react, might make it inside. A whole squad trying it would be mass suicide. "We move just before the ramp hits ground and try to knock out the first truck in line," she said. "That'll block in all the others."

"Sounds good," Beach agreed. "Lorne, you said a few arcthrower shots up beneath the engine compartment would do it?"

"I said that that trick worked *once*," Lorne's tight voice cut into the conversation. "There's no guarantee I didn't just get lucky."

"It's still our best shot," Beach said.

"There's another solution," the Qasaman behind Jin said. "You two stay here and Domo Pareka and I will go in."

"No," Beach said. "I mean, you can take Jin's place if you want—that would be fine—but I have to go along. Arcthrowers are notoriously tricky, and none of you has had nearly enough practice with them."

"Which is why it has to be Beach and me," Jin agreed reluctantly. "Okay. Here it comes..."

"Wait a second," Lorne said suddenly. "How about if I put one of the drones in there instead? Neat and clean, and no one has to get shot at."

For a second Jin was sorely tempted. Going up against a whole vehicle bay's worth of Trofts and armored vehicles, just her and Beach, wasn't a plan with a huge margin for error.

But it wouldn't work, and she and Lorne both knew it. "No good," she said. "If you don't take out both portside wings the SkyJos won't be able to launch. If they can't disable the ship before it lifts and heads for the hills, we won't get the drones we need for phase three."

"So we don't get the drones," Lorne said doggedly. "Maybe if we—"

"No maybes," Jin said firmly. "There's no time for a whole new plan. We have to go, and we have to go now."

"But feel free to blow the wings as soon as we're clear of the blast zone," Beach added. "Jin?"

"Ready," Jin said. "On three?"

"On three," Beach confirmed. "One, two, *three*."

Jin surged to her feet, trying not to think of the heavy lasers looming over her and sprinted the half dozen steps to the edge of the ramp. Bending her knees, she leaped straight up, caught the edge of the sloping metal right where it joined the hull and swung herself up onto her side. The first armored truck in line was waiting at the edge of the ramp, and a quick roll took her past the massive front wheel and underneath the vehicle.

Beach was already there, running his fingers along the smooth metal overhead as he looked for a likely target. "Watch your eyes," he warned, and triggered his arcthrower.

The brilliant lightning bolt lashed out from his little finger, lighting up the underside of the truck. Jin squeezed her eyes shut, again shifting her vision to her opticals. Picking a spot half a meter from where Beach was sending his fire, she added her arcthrower's high-voltage current to his.

For a second nothing happened. The truck didn't move, its driver possibly frozen with astonishment at having seen two dead bodies suddenly appear five meters off the ground and disappear under his vehicle. But she could hear the low rumble that meant the engine was still functioning. Clenching her teeth, she shifted her aim to a different spot and again fired the arcthrower.

"Keep at it!" Beach called over the roar. "I'm going to try something else." Before Jin could reply he swiveled around on his back, lined up his left leg on the inside of the front right wheel, and triggered his antiarmor laser. Trying to wreck or fuse the wheel mechanism? There was a flicker of movement to her left, and she turned her head to look.

Just in time to see an armored Troft crouch down and poke the muzzle of his laser under the truck.

Instantly, Jin flicked a target lock on the weapon and triggered her antiarmor laser. Her nanocomputer responded to the order by rolling her up onto her right hip and twisting her left leg around to line up the laser, then sending a flash of blue fire into the alien's weapon. It shattered in his hand, staggering him back. Jin fired again, this time into his torso, and he fell backward onto the deck and didn't move.

She grimaced. One down. Dozens, maybe hundreds to go.

And until she and Beach managed to immobilize the truck, they were going to be trapped under here, with a limited firing range and near zero maneuverability. All the Trofts had to do was line up along the sides and start shooting, and it would be all over.

"Blast it, Lorne," she snarled under her breath. "Where *are* you?"

"They're in!" the radio announced. "In, and under."

Ghushtre slapped Lorne on the shoulder. "Go."

"Already going," Lorne snapped, his tension crackling all the way to his fingertips as he keyed the controls. Like he needed Ghushtre or anyone else to tell him.

The four drones that had been hovering innocently above the backup ship, out of view of its mostly downward-looking cameras, were dropping now toward the weapons wings. At the same time, the two drones that had been flanking the grounded ship were drifting more subtly toward its portside wings, the ones that pointed into the city and had the best angle on the half-open SkyJo lair.

A sudden, odd thought flicked across the back of Lorne's mind: whether in the urgency of the moment it had ever occurred to the Troft commanders in Sollas to wonder what the Qasamans might have done to the drones during the minutes when Lorne had been blacking out their transmissions. With a sudden, final surge all six drones rounded their designated wings and came up beneath them, nestling in close to the weapons clusters— "Now," Lorne said. Behind him, he heard the click as Ghushtre triggered the radio transmitter.

And with a multiple, stuttering roar, the bombs the Qasamans had packed aboard the drones exploded.

"*Yes*," Lorne hissed under his breath, curling his hands into tight fists. The brilliant yellow-white of the blasts quickly turned to reddish black as the fireballs faded and mixed with bits of shattered warship. The last bits of fire vanished into the expanding cloud of debris, and Lorne tightened his fists even harder as he waited anxiously to see if the Qasamans' gamble had paid off.

It had. The upper backup ship was reeling violently, wobbling like a drunken politician as it fought to maintain altitude after the multiple shocks to its hydraulic, control, and power systems. As it twisted around, Lorne got a clear view of both sides, enough to see that all four of its weapons wings had been disintegrated.

"Misfire!" the radio barked suddenly. "Forward-portside-beta has not triggered. Repeat, forward-portside-beta has not triggered."

Lorne's heart seemed to freeze. The forward portside weapons cluster on the lower ship covered the side of the ramp that Lorne's mother had just jumped up onto. That was also the side any Qasaman reinforcements would have to use to follow her and Beach inside. If that cluster was still active— "Ghushtre!" he snapped.

"Trying," Ghushtre said tightly, toggling the firing switch again and again. "It's not working. A connection must have been lost."

"We have to do something," Lorne insisted, his stomach churning as he stared at the ship squatting at the edge of the city a kilometer away.

But there wasn't anything that could be done. With both forward weapons clusters still intact, the warship had the ramp completely covered, blocking any chance for Jin or Beach to escape or for any Qasamans to reinforce them. Even worse, the fire zone of the undamaged portside cluster covered the two closest SkyJo lairs, the ones that should even now be disgorging a stream of attack helicopters that could quickly batter the alien warships to rubble.

And unless the commanders in Azras could make that happen, and fast, Lorne's mother would die. This final gamble would be lost, and Qasama and the Cobra Worlds would remain under Troft domination. Maybe forever.

"Don't underestimate them, Lorne Moreau," Ghushtre said quietly. "You and I may be out of the fight in here. But they aren't. They *will* find a way."

"They who?" Lorne asked, his frozen mind barely even registering Ghushtre's words. "My mom and Beach?"

Ghushtre rested his hand reassuringly on Lorne's shoulder. "Your mother and Everette Beach . . . and the Qasamans."

[The three Purma warships, they will proceed immediately to Azras,] Inxeba snarled, his radiator membranes fluttering with consternation or surprise or rage. Probably, Merrick thought, mostly rage. [Captain Geceg, he will be in command of them. Captain Zimise and Captain Dinga, they will withdraw immediately to rendezvous with him.]

[Captain Zimise, his floatators are malfunctioning,] Officer Cebed reported, his membranes showing even more agitation than his commander's. [Captain Zimise, he warns his warship may need to be grounded for safety.]

[Safety, there is none of it in war,] Inxeba retorted. [Captain Zimise, he *will* withdraw toward Purma. The order, you will send it.]

[The order, I obey it,] Cebed said reluctantly. [Captain Dinga, his floatators are also malfunctioning. The floatators, they must be restarted.]

[The floatators, they will *not* be restarted,] Inxeba snarled. [Captain Dinga, he *will* seal his ramp and lift his ship. Captain Dinga, he will then kill the enemies in his vehicle bay.]

He turned challenging eyes to Ukuthi. [Commander Ukuthi, has he objections to this path?] he demanded.

[Commander Ukuthi, he is content to allow you to choose the path,] Ukuthi said calmly. [The results, I will be interested in seeing them.]

Merrick swallowed hard. If the warship lifted with his mother and Beach still inside, all hope for them would be lost. Did Ukuthi realize that? Or did he simply not care?

Or could it be that he had some inkling of what the Qasamans were planning, and had no intention of sharing that insight with Inxeba?

[The results, you will see them soon,] Inxeba promised, turning back to the displays. [The order, give it. The victory, it will soon be ours.]

Beach's antiarmor laser stopped firing, and Jin glanced over to see a reddish glow coming from the wheel mechanism he'd been firing at. If he hadn't slagged the mechanism into uselessness, she guessed, it wasn't ever going to happen.

Still, it wouldn't hurt to be sure. She fired another arcthrower burst into the engine, and then another.

And with a violent shudder, the engine finally went silent.

Jin took a deep breath. They'd done it. The truck was disabled, and the other four vehicles lined up behind it were now well and truly trapped.

Only as she paused to evaluate the situation, she realized with a sinking sensation that the risk she and Beach had taken had been rendered moot. Outside the bay, she could see the flashes of laser fire coming from above—not the fire of SkyJos, with their distinctive rotor sound, but fire from one of the warship's weapons clusters. Somehow, the Qasamans' drone attack had failed.

And with that failure, she and Beach were dead.

She looked at Beach, found him looking back at her. "I think," he said, "we'd better find a way out of here."

"Agreed," Jin said, shifting her eyes again to scan what she could of the rest of the bay.

Only there wasn't anywhere to go. Armored Troft feet were hitting the deck all across the bay as the soldiers who'd been inside the trucks scrambled out to deal with this new threat to their ship. Even if Jin and Beach had time to get out into the open before the Trofts began firing, there was only so much their nanocomputers and programmed reflexes could do. In an enclosed space, even this large an enclosed space, the kind of firepower about to be brought to bear would kill them within seconds.

Outside, the flashes of laser fire seemed to intensify, and Jin felt a new vibration against her back as the ramp started rising again from the ground. With all hope of an armored sortie now thwarted, the Trofts were sealing the ship, probably in preparation for getting the hell out of Azras.

And once the ramp was closed, there would literally be nowhere for Jin and Beach to go.

A pair of Trofts moved suddenly into view alongside the truck. Jin rolled partially over and gave them each a shot from her anti-armor laser. Not that the ramp had ever offered any real chance anyway. With one weapons clusters on each side of the ship still intact, the whole ramp area would be open to Troft attack.

Or rather, most of it would be. Abruptly, Jin's mind flashed back to Lorne's own daring climb up the outside of the other warship during the phase one attack. He and McCollom had shown that there was a blind spot at the very end of the ramp just as it rose into its closed position.

Of course, here there would be no chance of stopping it partially open the way Lorne and McCollom had. There would certainly be no time to climb it like they had.

But if she and Beach could get out from under the truck without getting themselves killed, there should be enough time for Jin to throw Beach up the ramp to the far end before it sealed itself shut. From there he might be able to jump all the way to the top of the ship, or possibly to one of the nearby Qasaman buildings.

Or maybe he could get onto the wing and destroy the remaining portside weapons cluster.

A rush of painful memory flooded back in on her as she thought back to Caelian and her own attempt to pull that stunt. She'd succeeded, but had nearly died in the process.

But if she could survive, there was a chance Beach could, too. And even the small odds out there were better than the nonexistent ones in here. "Beach—"

"Ramp's closing," he cut her off. "Roll over here, will you?"

"There's no time—"

"When I give the word, we're going to get out from under here, and I'm going to throw you up onto the end of the ramp," Beach continued. "Got it?"

Jin felt her mouth drop open. "That was *my* idea."

"It's mine now," Beach said. "No time to argue. Get over here—" He broke off, spinning to the side and sending a Troft sprawling to the deck with an arcthrower jolt. "Get over here and let's do it."

There was a movement beside Jin, and she again turned up onto her side as a trio of Trofts sprinted toward her. "All right," she called to Beach, targeting the attackers. "I'll be right—"

She jerked violently back as, without warning, a huge slab of concrete dropped out of nowhere, slamming into the Trofts she'd been about to shoot and throwing them to the deck amid a cloud of white dust and an impact that seemed to shake the whole ship. Jin had just enough time to blink at the slab in disbelief when, all around her, she heard and felt the heavy thuds of a dozen more impacts. Somewhere behind her a Troft shouted in rage or agony—

And from the direction of the still-rising ramp came a firestorm of laser bolts, crackling the air and throwing a flickering blue glow across the walls and deck.

Against all odds, against the awesome firepower of the warship's heavy lasers, the Qasamans had arrived.

And as the firestorm continued against the screams and panicked footsteps of the Troft soldiers, Jin finally focused her full attention on the slab of concrete lying on the deck beside her. On the heat-stress cracks all through it, on its burned and blistered upper side . . .

"Jin Moreau?" a Qasaman voice called anxiously.

"We're here, Domo Pareka," Jin called back. "Under the truck."

"Stay there," Pareka ordered, and as Jin lifted her gaze from the half-melted concrete she could see from the reflected laser light that the Cobras' attack was moving back through the bay. "Give us a moment to clear them out."

"Nice to have someone else take point for a change," Beach murmured from his side of the truck. "I just hope they didn't lose too many getting in here."

"I don't think so," Jin said. "It looks like they grabbed chunks of the broken buildings and wall and used them as shields while they ran up the ramp."

"Nicely done," Beach said approvingly. "Also amazingly done. Those slabs are heavy as hell."

"You'd be amazed at how far sheer stubbornness will take someone," Jin said, listening with half an ear to the battle. It was all the way in the back now, and was definitely winding down. "But all the stubbornness in the world won't help the SkyJos," she added. "We still have to knock out that weapon cluster."

"Yeah, well, I've got an idea on that one," Beach said.

Jin's stomach tightened. "Just bear in mind that I'm the only one who's ever actually pulled it off," she warned him. "If anyone's going to do it, I am."

"Actually, I've got something a little safer in mind," Beach said. "Come on—sounds like the fighting's about over."

They crawled out from under the truck to find that the fighting was indeed over. A few of the Qasaman Cobras were at each of the two stairwell doors, listening closely or else firing at the door jambs with their fingertip lasers. The rest were going methodically through the trucks and other vehicles, checking to make sure no one was still hiding inside. "Are you all right?" Pareka asked, hurrying toward them. "There's no time to lose—we have to find a way to get you out and to safety."

"What happened out there?" Jin asked. "It sounded like only one of the drones exploded."

"Yes, the one planned for the forward cluster failed," Pareka said. "And with weapons still on both sides of the warship, the SkyJos can't lift from their lairs without risking destruction. The warship is preparing to lift, and we find that the retreating invaders have welded the stairway doors against us."

"Not a problem," Beach assured him. "We have—"

"You don't understand," Pareka said sharply, changing direction toward the ramp controls and waving Jin and Beach to join him. "Once you're safely outside—we'll detach two of the truck doors for you to use as shields—we'll need to force the stairway doors and try to reach the control room before the ship escapes."

"And you think we're just going to run off and leave you?" Jin asked.

"You of the Cobra Worlds have done your share, Jasmine Moreau," Pareka said firmly. "In truth, you've done far more than your share. The rest of the fighting—and the dying—will be ours."

"Or we could do it without any dying at all," Beach suggested, extending a finger to point at the nearest truck. "You see those trucks, Cobra Pareka? You see those swivel guns on their roofs?"

"Of course," Pareka said impatiently. "How else do you think we plan to breach the stairwell doors?"

"And do you see *that*?" Beach continued, turning his finger to point at the machine shop at the far end of the bay. "Behind that bulkhead—behind, above and below—is the ship's engineering section. Where all the generators are. Including the ones that power the grav lifts and the weapons clusters."

For a second Pareka just stared at him. Then, his lips twisted in a tight smile. "And you think the swivel guns can penetrate the bulkheads?"

"All I know is that even warships have to save weight somewhere," Beach said, setting off at a fast stride toward the rear of the bay. "I see eight trucks and eight swivel guns," he added over his shoulder. "I've got dibs on the one at the rear. Get your people inside the others, and let's give it a try. Sooner or later, if we keep at it, we're bound to hit something vital."

Three and a half minutes later, they did.

[Captain Dinga, he urgently requests assistance,] Officer Cebed reported tightly. [Emergency battery power, his ship relies now upon it. His weapons, they are no longer functional.]

[Captain Dinga, do his soldiers do battle with the enemy?] Inxeba demanded.

[The enemy, they are barricaded inside the vehicle bay,] Cebed said. [The enemy, they have contented themselves with crippling his ship.] His membranes twitched abruptly as he leaned closer to his board. [The drones, the enemy has remote-accessed them,] he said, sounding bewildered. [The drones, the enemy has flown all twelve from Captain Dinga's ship.]

[Captain Zimise, he reports the Azras SkyJos have risen from their lairs,] one of the other officers spoke up. [Six SkyJos, they are flying toward Purma.]

[Captain Dinga, he confirms the report,] Cebed said, still sounding confused by the drones' mass exodus. [Two drones, they are now being flown in point before each of the SkyJos.]

Inxeba gave a rasping snort. [Foolishness, the enemy has it,] he said contemptuously. [Their plan, I see it. The ally-identification system, they believe the drones to be connected with it. The drones, the enemy expects them to prevent the warships from firing upon the SkyJos.]

[Captain Geceg, he reports his warships are in visual range of

Azras and the approaching SkyJos,] the third officer spoke up. [The SkyJos, do you wish them destroyed?]

[Their destruction, it will not be yet,] Inxeba said. [The SkyJos, they will be allowed to fly closer. The enemy's hopes, I will allow them to remain a few minutes longer. The enemy's confidence, I will then shatter it in a single thrust.]

He turned to Ukuthi, seated quietly on his couch. [And the honor of the Drim'hco'plai, it *will* be restored.]

CHAPTER NINETEEN

"There they go," Popescu announced, craning his neck and looking up at the display hanging in midair over them in the sideways control room. "Rather, here they come. I guess they're done talking to Eubujak."

"They stayed in the air the whole time?" Kemp asked.

"Yeah," Popescu said. "Too bad, too. I was hoping they'd put down in the middle of our Wonderland buffet and try to walk over to the cage. Or better yet, land right on top of the curtain and let Wonderland in."

"You couldn't have seen anything anyway," Harli pointed out, resting his hand on the edge of the command room's power-control console and trying not to let the weirdness of the sideways room get to him. He hadn't spent much time inside the downed ship, and he'd never gotten used to walking on bulkheads while decks and ceilings pretended to be walls. Or looking up at consoles and control panels jutting out from those walls, or maneuvering through doors that were now wide slits halfway up the walls. "The wing would have blocked your view."

"I know," Popescu said. "But it would have been nice to think about."

"Dream on," Kemp said, stepping around a circuit-test setup that someone had left behind and crossing over to Harli. "Everyone ready?" he asked quietly.

"As ready as we can be," Harli said. Which, he admitted silently, wasn't very much. "There's really only one door they can come at us through, assuming they don't want to launch their assault from hovering aircars or long ladders. I've got a layered defense down there, and Whistler's doing what he can to put a few barriers in place. I've also got some small booby-traps on the other two doors, just in case they decide they like aircar assaults."

"Sounds good," Kemp said. "Though of course you realize that with their numerical advantage we could take out the first four waves and still end up on the short end."

"Yes, I used to get medals in simple math," Harli said dryly. "Not to mention that even if by some miracle we were able to clean out this one there's another whole ship over at the Octagon Caves. Unless Smitty pulls off his own class-A miracle, we'll eventually have that bunch to deal with, too."

"Maybe," Kemp said. "But don't sell Smitty short. Between him, Jody, Rashida, and the caves, he could pull it off."

"Here they come," Popescu reported. "Making a long circle back over Stronghold. Maybe they bought your bluff about being able to shoot them down."

"We'll find out soon enough," Harli said, mentally running through the traps and blocks he'd put around the dorsal hatch. That was the only way in that didn't involve coming in under the downed warship's weapons.

Of course, that entrance was also seven meters above the ground, with all the tricky aircar or ladder logistics.

Unless the newcomer put his ship right up against the downed ship's upper side and rigged some kind of ramp from somewhere to the dorsal hatch. Harli hadn't thought about that possibility.

But that would require the ship to land inside Stronghold, and there wasn't a lot of room to spare inside the wall. They would probably have to level a few buildings first, which would give the Cobras plenty of time to shift more of their defenses to that end of their refuge.

"Whoa—there they are," Popescu said suddenly. "Coming across straight overhead."

And without warning the ship suddenly bucked like a stung horse, sending equipment flying as a muffled double explosion rocked the room.

Harli grabbed for the console beside him, shaking his head

sharply against the ringing sensation echoing through his ears. He swallowed once, swallowed again—

"—completely gone," Popescu's distant voice faded in through the aftershock. "Say again: both wings are blown to hell."

A hand grabbed at Harli's arm, and he looked down to see Kemp struggling to his feet, a trickle of blood running down the side of his head. Beside him, a circuit multitester with a freshly cracked display and torn wire connecters had a spot of the same bright red on one corner. "You okay?" Harli called as he helped Kemp back to his feet.

"Sure—fine," Kemp called back, wincing as he wiped away the blood. "I guess you *can* fire on another Troft ship."

"Yeah, but you probably need a special passkey to do it," Harli said. There was another, smaller thud, a vibration mostly felt through the bulkhead they were standing on. "Sounds like he's down," he said. "Any idea where he landed?"

"Nope—the cameras went when he blew up the wings," Popescu said. "You want me to call down to Whistler and have him send someone outside to look?"

"No, don't bother," Harli told him. "It doesn't really matter—"

He broke off, a sudden surge of adrenaline flooding into him.

He was wrong. It *did* matter where the invaders had put down. It mattered a hell of a lot. "Kemp, take command," he said, heading for the horizontal door. "Make sure Whistler's ready to receive company."

"Where are you going?" Kemp called after him as Harli grabbed the door jamb and pulled himself through.

"Out," Harli called back through the door. "Back in five."

The traps he'd set up at the dorsal hatch were simple ones, and it took him only a minute to deactivate them. For a moment he held his ear against the hatch itself, his audios at full power as he listened for any sound of activity.

Nothing. Unfastening the hatch, he pushed it open, and eased his head through the opening.

The broken and battle-scarred city lay stretched out before him in the afternoon sun. Fortunately, the scene wasn't further blighted by the presence of armed Trofts, either on the ground or patrolling the sky. Getting a grip on the upper edge of the hatchway, he ducked through the opening, standing precariously on the lower edge. Above him, the starboard side of the hull crest rose another seven meters into the sky, tall enough to block his view of the newly arrived ship.

He focused on the hull. It was fairly smooth, certainly comfortable enough to walk on in the ship's usual upright position, but hardly designed for climbing. But at the very top of his view was a monstrous tangle of broken and twisted metal where the aft weapons wing had been before the incoming Trofts blew it to shrapnel. If he could jump up there and get a handhold on one of those pieces, he should be able to see exactly where the other ship had put down.

Assuming, of course, that he didn't slice his fingers off on the torn metal. But it was the only way. Putting a targeting lock on the sturdiest-looking ribbon to give his nanocomputer the range, he carefully bent his knees—

"So when you said *out*," Kemp's voice came from the direction of his shins, "you really meant it."

Harli jerked, nearly losing his grip, and peered into the hatchway. Kemp was standing there, looking out at him. "What the hell are you doing here?" he demanded. "I gave you an order."

"I wrote myself a medical excuse," Kemp said, pointing at the blood still trickling down his head. "Popescu and I thought someone should see what you were up to and find out if you needed a hand."

"I had an idea, that's all," Harli said, gesturing up the side of the hull crest. "It suddenly occurred to me that Eubujak probably told the other Troft captain that we'd been setting up booby-traps."

"Which we hadn't gotten around to yet."

"Which Eubujak doesn't know," Harli reminded him. "More importantly, he doesn't know whether these supposed traps are in the ship, in Stronghold, or out in Wonderland. Given all that uncertainty, where's the absolute safest spot for a clever and cautious captain to land his ship?"

Kemp shook his head. "No idea."

"Come on, it's obvious," Harli said, hoping desperately that it really *was* obvious, that his mind wasn't playing some macabre trick on him. "The one place where he can actually see the ground, and not a waving field of hookgrass that could be hiding a collection of pressure mines—"

"Is right where the other ship was before Rashida flew off with it," Kemp interrupted, his eyes going wide. "You're right. Hell in a handbasket. You got confirmation?"

"I'm about to," Harli told him, stepping out of the opening and up onto the edge of the hatch. "As long as you're here anyway, make yourself useful. Lean out here and catch me if I don't stick the landing on my way back."

He looked up at the broken metal, took a deep breath, and jumped.

Survival on Caelian, his Cobra instructors had often told him, was less a matter of courage or brute strength than it was a matter of timing and precision. Over the years Harli had taken that advice to heart, and he reached the top of his leap with his outstretched hands precisely at the torn metal ribbon he'd been aiming for. He hooked his fingers gingerly around it and held on as he let his residual momentum and swaying dampen out. Then, slowly and carefully, he pulled himself up until he could see the top of the alien ship.

And for the first time in days, he smiled.

Kemp was holding the hatch steady as Harli slid back down the hull crest and landed on its edge. "Well?" he asked, holding his other hand where Harli could grab it for balance if necessary.

"He is indeed clever and cautious," Harli confirmed. "I think we're in."

"Terrific," Kemp said. "Assuming it's still set up."

"It is." Harli turned and looked at the work station a hundred meters away beside the broken wall, a sobering thought suddenly occurring to him. "Of course, we *will* be visible to the other ship's wing cameras over there."

"You're right," Kemp muttered. "Ouch. Any thoughts?"

Harli looked down at the hatch cover he was balancing on. Too small to be a useful shield, even if they could get it off quickly enough. There were other, heftier slabs of metal inside the ship, but it would take equal amounts of time to get them free and most wouldn't pass through the hatch opening anyway.

He shifted his focus to the ground below them. The matted hookgrass was a good sixty centimeters tall and completely filled the space between them and the work station. It could theoretically be crawled through if they didn't mind running into a few unpleasant animals and insect nests along the way.

Unfortunately, sixty centimeters wasn't nearly tall enough to hide them, especially from cameras that would be looking more or less straight down.

On the other hand, it wasn't *just* hookgrass down there. "You've been tramping back and forth through that stuff more than I have," he said, keying in his telescopics for a closer look at the tangled plants. "How much blue lettros did you spot mixed in?"

"Enough," Kemp said thoughtfully. "It'll be risky, though. The stuff burns like hell once you get it going, and the razor fern is even worse. It's also growing right through where the wall used to be, which means there's a fair chance we could burn down the whole town."

"Noted," Harli said. "But it's still our best shot. You'd better get back and warn Popescu and the others."

"Popescu and the others will figure it out for themselves," Kemp said firmly, swiveling around to dangle his legs out the hatchway. "Ready?"

"Ready," Harli said. "You take north; I'll take south."

Their antiarmor lasers flashed in unison, blazing across the landscape as they traced out patterns through the mix of grasses below. Harli keyed in his infrareds, spotted the hot spots he'd created, and sent another blast into each of those areas. A few seconds later the smoldering blue lettros popped out small yellow flames that began to grow and spread. He shifted his attention to the edges of the fires, located the telltale trail of sub-flashpoint ribbon vine and fired another laser blast into it. More flames popped up, and tendrils of oily black smoke began to rise into the air. Harli kept firing, nurturing the growing flames, watching out of the corner of his eye as Kemp similarly worked his end of the field.

And then, all at once, the whole expanse ignited, the flames leaping up almost instantly obscured by the billowing clouds of smoke.

Harli set his teeth, wincing as the first blast of hot air blew up across his face. This was *not* going to be fun. "Last chance to go warn Popescu," he shouted to Kemp.

"We're wasting time," Kemp shouted back. "Last one to the work station's a cooked egg."

Lurching forward, he dropped off the edge of the hatchway and disappeared into the smoke and flame. Taking a final deep breath, squeezing his eyes shut and keying in his opticals, Harli jumped after him.

He hit the ground hard, the landing sending up a double splash of bright sparks and flaming vegetation as he bent his knees to absorb the impact. The smoke and flames were all around him now, tingling his nostrils and washing waves of heat against his clothes and skin. Through the blaze of infrared he could just barely see Kemp already charging through the inferno.

Belatedly, it occurred to him that if the fire made it to the work station before he or Kemp did, this whole thing would be for nothing. Clenching his teeth against the heat and rapidly increasing pain, he set off at a dead run.

He didn't remember much of the trip afterward. The only thing he was ever able to fully recall was the terrible agony as the fire burned across his skin and hair, the acrid smell of the smoke eating away at his throat and lungs, and the quietly horrifying fear that his eyes would be destroyed despite the forearms he had pressed across his face. His feet pounded against the ground, his servos pushing him along faster than his own muscles could ever manage, the cooling wind that would have normally accompanied such a race turned by the fire into a furnace blast. He struggled on, knowing it was their only chance, knowing that Kemp wasn't going to give up and that he damn well wasn't going to either—

And then, suddenly, he was in clear, cool air again. Five meters ahead, he saw Kemp stumble and collapse to his knees beside the work station, small flames still burning on the half-melted silliweave fabric on his shoulders and upper thighs. Harli staggered toward him, blinking his eyes open, wincing at the new wave of pain that effort cost him.

According to his nanocomputer, the entire run had lasted just seven point two seconds.

"Kemp?" he croaked. Two meters past the station was an empty food table with a half-full hundred-liter jug of water in a dispenser beside it. Limping past Kemp, he headed toward it.

"Got it," Kemp croaked back. "System coming up—activating—God, don't let the power and control cables have been burned through—"

"Step back," Harli ordered, pulling the jug from the dispenser and sloshing a little of the water out onto the ground as he turned it upright. "Come on, step back."

"It's done," Kemp said, breathing shallowly as he pulled himself to his feet and staggered back from the control board. "But if it doesn't work—"

"It'll work," Harli said, directing splashes of water onto the remaining flames and then, for good measure, pouring some over Kemp's head. "Trust me. It'll work."

The words were barely out of his mouth when, through the roar of the fire, he heard the creaking of moving metal.

He looked over at the downed ship. Through the billowing smoke he could see that it was on the move, rising ponderously up from the ground as the grav lifts the Troft prisoners had moved to the sides and broken lower wings ran to full power. The ship continued to rise, moving faster now as it approached the top of its arc. It reached it, and for a brief moment it stood proudly upright again for the first time since Harli and the other Cobras had knocked it over.

But it didn't stay vertical for more than that brief second. The grav lifts were still pushing, the wrecked cascade regulator was no longer there to ease back their power, and the huge mass of metal had built up way too much momentum. The ship kept moving and toppled over in the other direction, slamming into the newly-arrived ship with an ear-splitting grinding of metal against metal.

For a moment the two ships seemed to pause, teetering and shaking. Then, with an even louder shriek of grinding metal, they fell over together in a violent crash that shook the ground so hard it nearly knocked Harli off his feet.

For a long moment the only sound was the crackling roar of the frames. Finally, Kemp stirred. "Popescu," he said in a hoarse voice, "is going to be furious."

Harli drew a careful breath into his aching lungs. "I *said* you should go back and warn him."

"He'll get over it." Taking the jug from Harli's blackened hands, he sprayed some of the water onto a smoldering fire on Harli's shoulder that he hadn't even noticed was there. "But we should probably let him know that the Trofts probably won't be up for a fight anytime soon," he added. "Might be a good time for him to call on the captain to surrender."

"Sorry, I didn't think to grab a radio," Harli apologized. He waved wearily at the fire. "And I don't think I'm up to delivering the message in person."

"Me, neither," Kemp conceded. "Well, if Popescu wants us, he'll find us."

"Sure," Harli said. "Come on, let's see if they left any burn salve or painkillers in the hospital when they moved everyone out."

"Sounds like a plan." Kemp peered at his blistered hands. "You really think the Qasamans were able to grow Paul Broom's leg back?"

"They said they could," Harli said. "Don't know how they'll do with burns, but it's worth checking out. When this is over, we'll talk to Rashida about setting us up."

"Assuming she survives," Kemp said quietly.

Harli winced. "Yes," he said. "Assuming she survives."

Jody's original concern had been that the Trofts would come charging into the caves the minute their ship landed, catching her and the others out in the open. But the captain's decision to first burn away any nearby ambush positions had given their prey the time they needed to cross the chamber and get to Smitty's chosen rock chimney.

Getting there, unfortunately, turned out to be only half the battle. Smitty was an expert at that kind of climbing, and Rashida had the method down after her first try. But for some reason it took Jody a dozen attempts and ten minutes of intensive coaching before she finally figured out the necessary technique: back and feet braced on opposite sides of the chimney, hands pushing down to move her back upward, feet simultaneously walking up the other side. She still felt a lot more awkward than either of the others looked, but at least she was able to do it.

And with that, they finally started up.

Smitty, who knew the route and the tricky parts of the chimney, took the lead. Jody came next, a meter behind him, still struggling. Rashida, moving much more gracefully, brought up the rear. Smitty hadn't been able to find any rope aboard the ship during their race to the caves, but Rashida had used Jody's prolonged tutoring time to carefully tear the silliweave bag into strips and then braid them the sturdy-looking lines that now tied the three climbers to each other.

Though *sturdy-looking*, Jody knew, didn't necessarily mean *sturdy*. As they worked their way up the rock tube she found herself staring at the rope hanging loosely between her belt and Smitty's, wondering how much weight the thing could actually take. Hoping fervently that they never had to find out.

They were nearly to the top of the chimney, and Jody could see the glow of diffuse sunlight seeping between Smitty's torso and arms, when she heard the clink of metal on rock beneath her.

She froze, wondering fleetingly if she dared speak up to warn Smitty and Rashida. Fortunately, they'd apparently also heard the noise, and stopped as quickly as she had.

For a moment there was nothing more. Jody peered down over her shoulder, trying to see past Rashida to the bottom. But all she could see was the dark rock of the chimney and the even darker rock far below.

But other sounds were now starting to drift up: the sound of feet shuffling across pebble-strewn rock, an occasional distant and muffled Troft voice, a few more random clinks and thuds. Jody strained her ears, trying to figure out if all of it was getting closer to them, but the natural echo of the huge chamber thwarted her efforts.

And then, without warning, a Troft stepped into view beneath them.

Jody held her breath. He seemed to be looking around, his helmet and laser turning slowly as he surveyed the area.

There was a breath of movement above Jody, and she looked up to see Smitty ease his left leg out of its bracing position against the rock wall and stretch it out along the side of the chimney, aiming his antiarmor laser downward. Clenching her teeth, trying not to dislodge any loose stone from the wall, Jody eased herself as far out of his line of fire as she could. She looked down, hoping Rashida had also spotted Smitty's maneuver and was likewise giving him room to shoot.

She wasn't. Her eyes were still on the Troft, her left hand pointed downward, the glove laser along the little finger lined up on the alien's helmet. Either she hadn't seen what Smitty was doing, or else had decided for some other reason to take this one on herself.

Only she'd apparently forgotten that her laser didn't have enough power to cut through that helmet. In fact, at this range, it might not be able to penetrate even his much more vulnerable faceplate.

Jody reached down, trying to touch Rashida's shoulder, trying to get her attention. But the shoulder was out of her reach. "Rashida, no," she whispered as loudly as she dared.

Rashida didn't respond. The Troft looked around once more and started to step away from the chimney.

And then, almost as if it was an afterthought, he tilted his head back and looked up. His radiator membranes snapped out from his upper arms, and he swung his laser up.

Rashida fired first, her laser sending a bolt squarely into the Troft's faceplate. An instant later, the Troft's much more powerful shot flashed up the chimney, shattering a section of wall near Rashida's feet and sending out a stinging spray of jagged rock chips.

And with that part of Rashida's support suddenly cut out from under her feet, she lost her hold and tumbled down the chimney.

In that first frozen half second the only thing that saved her was the makeshift rope tying her belt to Jody's. The rope jerked taut as she fell, spinning her upright and bouncing her shoulders and back against the chimney wall. The sudden additional weight yanked at Jody, dragging her a few centimeters downward before she and her suit's servos could increase the pressure against the rock and bring her to a halt. Her upper arms were pressed hard against the stone at her back, adding their pressure to help hold her in place. Risking the loss of some of that pressure, she reached down and managed to grab Rashida's arm as the other woman flailed for balance.

Her fingers had barely closed around Rashida's wrist when the silliweave rope snapped.

Jody braced herself. But this latest jolt was too much. With a surge of helpless horror she felt her back being pulled inexorably downward, the rough stone digging grooves into her skin beneath the power suit material. Clenching her teeth, she pressed her feet even harder against the other side, trying to halt her slide.

But she was already too far out of balance. Desperately, she dropped her right foot to a lower section of wall, hoping to reestablish a brace. But even as she tried to get it wedged a second laser blast sizzled up from below, this one shattering a section of wall above her and raining stone fragments into her face. She winced away, reflexively raising her other arm to protect her eyes.

With a wrenching twist, she lost her fight for balance and started to tumble down the chimney, jerking to a halt an instant later as the rope tying her to Smitty snapped taut. Blinking the swirling rock dust from her eyes, she looked up to see Smitty's hand reaching down and grabbed it just as the rope broke. She slammed back-first against the wall, her legs bouncing off Rashida's torso.

And then, even as she tried to catch her breath, a brilliant flash of blue lanced through the air in front of her face.

With Jody and Rashida finally out of his way, Smitty had fired his antiarmor laser.

Jody never actually heard the sound of the Troft hitting the stone. But as she peered down the chimney, trying to look around the afterimage Smitty's shot had burned into her retinas, she could see the alien's smoldering body sprawled on the cavern floor.

"Don't just hang there," Smitty grunted from above her. "Get your feet back up, and let's move it. Jody, you have to go first—Rashida can't move with you in her way."

"Right." Carefully, remembering to let her suit's servos do most of the work, Jody lifted her legs and planted them again on the opposite side of the chimney. "Okay," she said. "Rashida?"

"No," Rashida said quietly.

Jody looked down in surprise. Rashida was still hanging from Jody's grip, making no attempt to get back into climbing position. "What?"

"We can't do it," Rashida said, her voice dark but determined. "Not all of us. The other invaders will surely have seen the battle and even now will be coming."

"So stop jabbering and get moving," Smitty snapped. "Come *on*."

"There's no time," Rashida said. "We can't reach the top this way. Not before they arrive. Our only chance is for me to stay here and hold them off while you try to reach safety."

Jody felt her stomach tighten. "No," she said firmly.

"Absolutely not," Smitty seconded. "We leave together, or we don't leave at all."

"So three die instead of one?" Rashida demanded. "Where's the honor in that?"

"Where's the honor in leaving one of your own behind?" Smitty countered.

"I can't answer for your honor," Rashida said. "I can only answer for my own. Farewell." She reached up her other hand toward where Jody was gripping her wrist—

"Hold it," Smitty said hastily. "Okay—here's what we do. We'll all go back down, but just long enough to change positions. You'll take point, Rashida, with Jody next and me bringing up the rear. That way we'll have my antiarmor laser and target-locks where they can actually do us some good. Okay?"

Rashida hesitated, then nodded. "All right," she said.

"Here's the plan," Smitty said. "Rashida drops first, obviously—your leg servos should be able to handle the landing, but watch your footing. As soon as you're down, move out of the way so Jody can join you. Jody, ditto. Once I'm down, I'll throw you one at a time as high up the chimney as I can—if I do it right, you should be able to just push out with back and legs at the top of your arc and get back to climbing. Got it?"

"Got it," Jody said, frowning. There was something in his tone that was sending warning sirens screaming through her brain.

"Yes," Rashida said.

"Okay, then," Smitty said. "Rashida, bend your knees a little. Jody, let go of her."

And even as Jody started to open her hand the horrible truth flooded in on her. "No!" she snapped, tightening her grip again. "Rashida, it's a trick. He's not planning to come back with us. He's going to stay down there and fight the Trofts so we can get away."

"Oh, for—" Smitty choked off a curse. "*Damn* it, Broom."

"We leave together, or we don't leave at all," Jody reminded him tightly.

He took a deep breath. "Listen to me, Jody," he said. "We have only two choices. One, you let me stay behind and keep the Trofts off your backs. Two, we keep climbing and they blow all three of us out of here in pieces."

"Or three," Rashida put in, "we let *me* go down and do the fighting."

"No," Smitty said flatly. "I can't let a civilian make that kind of sacrifice. Not while I'm still alive and able to fight."

"I'm not a civilian," Rashida said, and Jody shivered at the sudden darkness in her voice. "No Qasaman is. Not anymore. When our world was invaded, we all became soldiers."

"I don't care if you all became cybernetic screech tigers," Smitty retorted. "I'm not leaving you—"

"Wait a second," Jody interrupted as a sudden, crazy, possibly lethal idea struck her. "There may be one more option." She braced herself. "We blow your booby-trap."

"Sorry, but that won't help," Smitty told her. "Not enough, anyway. It'll flatten everyone already in the chamber, but they'll have plenty of soldiers still in reserve on the ship. And there's no way we can make all the way to the top before the reinforcements arrive—" He broke off. "I'll be damned," he said his voice suddenly thoughtful. "You're right—it's worth a shot. Rashida, get your feet up. *Now*."

"I don't understand," Rashida said. But she nevertheless pulled her legs up and set them against the far wall. "What are we doing?"

"We're taking the express," Smitty said, and Jody glanced up to see him pull out his radio. "Heads tucked to your chests, eyes closed, and everyone hold tight to each other. Here we go."

Jody pressed her chin against her chest and squeezed her eyes shut. Rashida's arm rotated slightly in her grasp, and she felt the other woman's fingers close around her wrist. Taking the cue, Jody shifted her wrist in Smitty's grip and locked her fingers around his arm. Below them, she could hear the multiple scurrying of feet as the other Trofts in the cavern converged on their refuge. In the near distance there was a violent thundercrack as Smitty's booby-trapped missiles exploded—

And an instant later a blast of hot air slammed into her from below, breaking her friction grip on the chimney wall and throwing her violently upward.

She kept her chin tucked, her hands gripping Rashida's and Smitty's, her teeth clenched against the pain as she was bounced back and forth off the chimney walls. An old memory flashed unexpectedly to mind: the first time she'd ever climbed up on a chair as a toddler and stuck her face over a pan where her mother was boiling water. The buffeting slowed, the heat that had been flowing up around her back and legs fading away. She felt herself slowing—

And with a wrenching of her arm she came to a sudden halt.

She looked up. Smitty was still gripping her arm, but he was no longer twisted like half a pretzel and braced against the sides of the chimney. Instead, he was standing vertically, his legs stretched to either side of her.

For a second it didn't register. Then her mind cleared, and she realized Smitty was vertical because he was no longer inside the chimney. Instead, he was standing in a larger chamber, straddling the chimney opening from above.

The shock wave from the explosion hadn't just sent them flying higher up the chimney. It had thrown them all the way up to the top.

"You all right?" Smitty asked as he pulled her up. "Rashida?"

"I think so," Jody said, frowning. Somewhere along the way on that turbulent ride, Rashida's grip around her arm had loosened.

And now, as she looked down, she saw that the other woman's head was hanging limply against her chest. "Smitty!" Jody said.

"I'm on it," Smitty said grimly, pulling her the rest of the way out of the chimney and setting her down on solid rock. As he did so, he reached down with his other hand and took Rashida's arm. "Rashida?" he called, peering anxiously into the woman's face as he set her feet down on the opposite side. "Come on, girl, wake up."

There was no response. He shifted his grip on her, putting his other arm around her shoulders as Jody circled the chimney opening and got a grip on Rashida's head and belt. Together, they eased her into a half-sitting, half-lying position on a slanted rock ledge at the side of the chamber. "Rashida?" Smitty called again, kneeling down beside her, his fingertips gently tapping her cheek. "Rashida?"

And then, to Jody's relief, Rashida's eyes blinked open. She looked at Smitty, then at Jody, then back at Smitty. A frown creased her face, as if she was sifting through jumbled memories trying to figure out what had happened. Then, the creases in her forehead smoothed and the faintest hint of a tentative smile touched her lips. "Ouch," she said.

Smitty chuckled, sounding relieved, amused, and slightly embarrassed at the same time. "That's for sure," he agreed. "And naturally you got the worst of it. I'm sorry."

"I'm not," Rashida said, wincing as she reached a hand down to her ribs. "Whatever injuries I may have received, they were a small price to pay for our survival."

Abruptly, Smitty seemed to realize that his fingertips were still resting against Rashida's cheek, and he dropped his hand to his side. "Okay, then," he said briskly, getting back to his feet. "There's an exit onto the top of the cliff nearby. Jody, why don't you wait here with Rashida while I check it out."

"Wouldn't it be safer for us to stay together?" Rashida asked, putting her hand on the rock wall beside her, her fingers searching for a grip. "I can travel."

"You sure?" Smitty asked, taking her hand and helping her to her feet.

"Yes," Rashida said firmly. "Besides, I want to see with my own eyes what the explosion did to the invaders' other warship."

"Fair enough," Smitty conceded. "Okay. Follow me."

Ten minutes later, they emerged through a ragged opening onto a jumble of small rocks overgrown with ribbon vine and green treacle and dotted with bushy solotropes. Holding both women by the hand, Smitty cautiously led the way to the crumbling edge of the cliff.

Jody had hoped the explosion had been strong enough to tip the newly arrived warship over onto its side. To her mild disappointment, the ship was still upright, squatting on the relatively flat area below the cave with its bow weapons clusters pointed into the entrance. It was hard for Jody to tell through the drifting smoke from the burned-off areas, but it didn't look like the ship had taken any damage at all. "Well, at least we probably took out a few of their soldiers," she said philosophically. "What now?"

"We wait," Smitty said, moving them back from the cliff edge to more secure footing. "Sooner or later someone will come looking for us—that smoke will be visible for dozens of kilometers, and Harli and the others know where we went. Either they'll come, or the Tlossies will whenever they finally get here."

"Or the invaders will," Rashida murmured.

"Let 'em try," Smitty said. "There are places in the upper caves where we could hold out for weeks where even a missile would have a hard time getting to us."

He gestured around them. "In the meantime, this is probably the best place in Wonderland we could have picked to hang out for a while. We've got edible plants, plenty of food animals, and only the smaller predators."

He let go of Jody's hand, holding Rashida's another moment before also releasing it. "Come on. I'll get you back inside, then go hunt us up some dinner."

CHAPTER TWENTY

"Ten seconds," Ghushtre announced from behind Lorne.

"Acknowledged," one of the two Djinn at the weapons board replied. "All missiles armed and ready to go."

Lorne felt a shiver run up his back. Here it was: the final make-or-break moment. The moment when the Qasamans either won their freedom from the Trofts who had invaded their world, or the moment when they settled into a long, bitter war of attrition that might never be won.

"Lorne Moreau?"

Lorne shook away the thoughts. "The drones have closed to within a kilometer of the incoming warships," he reported. "SkyJos holding close formation behind them."

"Two seconds," the Djinni warned.

Lorne closed his hand on the edge of his seat. A moment later, the warship gave a gentle lurch, far gentler than he'd expected. "Missiles away," the Djinni announced. "Two targeted on each SkyJo."

"And yet the invaders hold their fire," Ghushtre murmured, sounding vaguely bemused.

"As Moffren Omnathi predicted they would," Lorne reminded him. "The Troft commanders got to see the SkyJos' capabilities when you chased them out of Sollas, and they know the three incoming warships are still out of their optimal weapons range.

They want to make sure there's no chance any of the SkyJos has time or room to maneuver when they finally do open fire."

"And perhaps they think we still believe the drones will protect the SkyJos until they've closed to that range?"

Lorne shrugged uncomfortably. That one had been his parents' prediction, and it was clear Ghushtre didn't have nearly as much confidence in it as he did in Omnathi's own drug-enhanced pronouncements. "Warrior told us the drones carry IFF transponders," he reminded Ghushtre. "It's obvious that something with such a small cross-section won't be able to shield the SkyJos once they're close enough. But again, the invaders don't know we know that."

"Perhaps," Ghushtre said. "We shall know soon enough."

[Missiles, Captain Vuma has launched them,] Officer Cebed said, his radiator membranes fluttering with confusion. [The SkyJos, the missiles are targeting them.]

[Captain Vuma, *he* has launched missiles?] Inxeba demanded, frowning at Cebed. [Captain Vuma, was he not captured by the enemy?]

[The missiles, they have been launched,] Cebed repeated. [Captain Vuma, perhaps he has retaken control of his ship.]

[Captain Vuma, no communication has he made,] one of the other officers objected suspiciously.

[The SkyJos, they have increased speed,] one of the other Trofts spoke up urgently.

[The SkyJos, they seek to escape the missiles,] Inxeba said, his own suspicions fading into anticipation. [The SkyJos, what is their combat status?]

[Their weapons, they will be in optimal firing range in ten seconds,] Cebed said. [Captain Geceg, he reports all of his point defenses are functional.]

[A race, it shall then be,] Inxeba said. [Captain Vuma, his missiles; Captain Geceg, his point defenses. The SkyJos, we shall see which destroys them first.]

And it was at that moment, as he frowned at the drone monitors and the views from Geceg's three-ship task force, that Merrick suddenly understood.

Surreptitiously, he looked at Ukuthi. The Balin commander was looking back at him, and from his expression Merrick knew he'd also figured it out.

For a pair of heartbeats he held Merrick's gaze. Then, calmly and deliberately, he turned back to the displays. Reaching for his drink, he took a sip and then set it back on its table.

Merrick smiled tightly. Ukuthi had figured it out, all right. But Inxeba had demanded the glory of this operation go to his demesne, and Ukuthi had graciously conceded it to him. Only it wouldn't be glory. It would be disaster.

And Inxeba would never even see it coming.

The missiles closed to within two seconds of the SkyJos . . . and with that, Lorne knew, they had won.

And yet, he still marveled at the Trofts' arrogant blindness. They'd recognized quickly enough the overt part of Omnathi's plan, that the drones' IFF systems would shield the SkyJos from the warships' weapons.

What they still apparently hadn't realized was that such shielding worked both ways.

The missiles from the Qasamans' captured warship couldn't target the three incoming ships. But they *could* target the Qasamans' attack helicopters.

And if those SkyJos happened to be directly between the missiles and the Troft warships when the missiles locked on . . .

He was gazing at the displays, wondering at the fortunes of war, when the SkyJo pilots ejected. Half a second later, the helicopters' self-destructs went off, shattering them along preset stress lines as the blasts disintegrated them into clouds of dust.

Half a second after that, the incoming missiles, already armed and with no time for a course readjustment, swept through the debris and detonated against the bows and wings of the oncoming warships.

And as the entire bank of displays flared and then blanked, the conference room erupted in pandemonium.

Merrick listened to the shouts of rage and disbelief, the demand for information and the demands that someone do something. And as he listened, he felt a warm glow of triumph and relief flow through him.

The Qasamans had pulled it off. Against all odds, they'd pulled it off.

And Inxeba knew it. The fury in his voice was tinged with fear, his shouted demands edged with near panic. In a single day, he'd lost at least three and maybe as many as six of his warships.

And with them, he'd also lost the war.

[Captain Geceg, he reports,] Cebed called out, his voice managing to penetrate Inxeba's ranting and the other officers' scrambling orders. [One warship, it is crippled and has fallen. Two warships, they are still functional.]

[Captain Geceg, he is to retreat immediately to Sollas,] Inxeba ordered, clearly fighting hard to try to calm himself.

[Captain Geceg, he will not arrive,] Ukuthi said, gesturing toward the blank displays. [Blind, his two remaining warships have become.]

[Sensors, Captain Geceg does not require them to locate Sollas,] Inxeba retorted acidly.

[Sollas, Captain Geceg will not reach it,] Ukuthi repeated. He shifted his finger to point at the drone images still coming from Purma. [SkyJos from Purma, they are being launched as we speak. Captain Geceg, they will easily destroy his remaining ships.]

Inxeba stared at the displays, his radiator membranes shaking. [More ships, I will send them from Sollas,] he said. [Commander Ukuthi, the Balin'ekha'spmi ships, you will send them as well.]

[The Balin'ekha'spmi ships, I will not send them,] Ukuthi said quietly. [The war, it can no longer be won.]

Inxeba turned toward him, his hand fumbling for his pistol. [Treason, you speak it,] he snarled. [Warships, the Drim'hco'plai have more than enough to destroy this world.]

[The Drim'hco'plai warships, they will not be permitted to destroy this world,] Ukuthi said flatly. [Warships of the Tlos'khin'fahi and Chrii'pra'pfwoi demesnes, they wait in the outer system. Your defeat today, they will soon have reports of it.]

Inxeba's hand tightened on his weapon's grip. [Reports, they will *not* receive them,] he warned coldly.

[Reports, they will not be sent by the Balin'ekha'spmi,] Ukuthi said, his voice chilling to match Inxeba's. [Reports, from the Qasaman Shahni they will obtain them.]

Inxeba spat. [The Qasaman Shahni, there are no more of them. Their deaths, they have been achieved.]

[The Qasaman Shahni, there remains one,] Inxeba corrected. [His departure from Sollas, fifteen days ago, I permitted it.]

Inxeba stared at him. [My direct order, you have violated it. The reason, you will explain it at once.]

[An official leader, one must always be left,] Ukuthi said, facing Inxeba's glare without flinching. [The leader, a conquered people may be more easily be controlled through him.]

He gestured again to the images of Purma and the SkyJos rising into the sky like a cloud of angry wasplings. [The leader, a truce may also be requested through him.]

[A truce, I will *not* request it,] Inxeba snarled.

[The Drim'hco'plai warships, more of them will then be lost.] Deliberately, Ukuthi stood up. [But the Drim'hco'plai warships, they will be lost alone. The Balin'ekha'spmi warships, I am removing them from Qasama.]

[Treason, you speak it,] Inxeba said again.

But even Merrick could see that the words had no power behind them. Ukuthi had been given tactical command of the Qasaman forces by the overall commander of the invasion forces. If he chose to withdraw, there was nothing Inxeba could do to stop him. Not without declaring war on the whole Balin'ekha'spmi demesne.

Everyone else in the room knew it, too. [Your warship, I now leave it,] Ukuthi said into the silence. Turning, he gestured to the two guards at the door. Without a word, they stepped aside.

[Your departure, I cannot stop it,] Inxeba said bitterly. [Your slaves, you will leave them here.]

Ukuthi turned back to him, and for the first time since Merrick had met him the commander seemed genuinely to have been caught off-balance. [My slaves, they will leave with me,] he said cautiously.

[Your slaves, they are the property of the Drim'hco'plai demesne-lord,] Inxeba countered. [All slaves, my demesne-lord has ordered their return. That request, have you not heard it?]

[The request, I have heard it,] Ukuthi said. [These slaves, my demesne-lord will return them with the others.]

[These slaves, they will stay,] Inxeba insisted.

And they would, too, Merrick realized as a hollow feeling settled into his stomach. Inxeba had lost the war and been humiliated in front of his officers. This small and meaningless act of revenge was all he had left to slap Ukuthi with.

For a long moment the two commanders stood facing each

other. Merrick once again found his hands curling into firing positions, a hundred plans racing through his mind, each one more impossible and insane than the last.

And in the end, as that long, tense moment drew to a close, he knew he really had only one option. [Anya and I, to her world we will go,] he murmured, low enough for only Ukuthi to hear. So much for leading a team of Cobras equipped with Qasaman weapons to help free Anya's people. So much even for saying good-bye to his family.

Unless, perhaps, Ukuthi was as observant as he was clever. [The drogfowl cacciatore of home, I will look forward to tasting it again soon,] he added. [My family, they will welcome my return.]

For a brief moment Ukuthi continued to stare at Inxeba. Then, he gave a little snort and waved in a gesture of dismissal. [The slaves, you may keep them,] he said contemptuously as he headed for the door. [The slaves, they are of no concern.] Passing between the guards, he disappeared through the door.

For another moment the room was silent. [Commander Inxeba, what are his orders?] Cebed asked carefully.

Inxeba turned and looked back at the displays. [Commander Inxeba, what are his orders?] Cebed repeated.

Inxeba's membranes flared out with a final surge of emotion. Then, almost delicately, they settled back against his arms. [A signal, send it to Captain Geceg,] he said quietly. [Sollas, he will not return to it. High orbit, he will instead rise to it.] He lowered his head. [A signal, you will then send it to all Drim'hco'plai,] he said. [Their immediate departure from this world, I order it.]

The officers looked at each other. [The order, I obey it,] Cebed said.

Inxeba rose from his couch, and as he did so his eyes flicked to Merrick and Anya. [The slaves, you will then put them with the others,] he said.

Turning his back on the other officers, he started for the door. [Clarification, I seek it,] Cebed called hesitantly after him. [The Drim'hco'plai departure, to high orbit is it?]

[Our departure, to the Drim'hco'plai demesne it is,] Inxeba said without turning around. [The war, the Tua'lanek'zia demesne may continue it alone if they choose.]

[Our departure, the Tua'lanek'zia demesne-lord will be angry with it,] Cebed warned.

[The Tua'lanek'zia's demesne-lord, his anger is meaningless,] Inxeba countered. [The anger of his master, it only is to be feared.]

He sent a measuring look at Merrick and Anya. [But his anger, it will soon be soothed,] he added, his voice thoughtful. [Commander Inxeba, he will then be rewarded.]

It had been a long and bitter struggle, full of half-felt pain and strange disorientation, surrounded by hunger and thirst and freakish dreams. But finally, finally, it had come to an end.

The first thing Fadil saw when he opened his eyes was the ceiling of his room, the gem-glittered replica of the night sky that he'd stared at for so many hours from his medical bed, soaked in meaningless perspiration and the helplessness and despair of his broken body. Now he was back, and the thought fleetingly touched his mind that it was as if the past few days had been merely a long nightmare.

But they had indeed been real . . . because the second thing he saw, looming over him from beside his bed, was his father's face.

For a moment Fadil just stared into those dark eyes, his mind flashing back to all the nightmares, wondering if this was just one last bit of mockery from the depths of a feverish mind.

But then his father smiled; and with that, the fears and misgivings vanished like morning mist. "Hello, Father," Fadil said. His voice sounded strange, cracking with thirst or disuse or perhaps simple emotion. "You're looking well."

"Hello, my son," Daulo said; and his voice, too, had the same strange tone as Fadil's own. "How do you feel?"

Fadil took a deep breath. "I feel well," he said. "I feel . . . alive. As I thought I'd never feel again." He felt his throat tighten with shame. "As I never should have been allowed to feel."

"It's all right," Daulo soothed as he reached across the bed and took Fadil's hands. "Truly it is. You have no cause for regret or shame."

"Don't I?" Fadil asked, lowering his eyes from his father's gaze. "I've taken resources that Qasama desperately needs for my own selfish ends."

"The decision wasn't yours," Daulo reminded him. "It was Moffren Omnathi's, and was made in honor and thanks for your service to Qasama."

"How can I accept such thanks in the midst of war?" Fadil bit out, more angrily than he'd intended. "How can I let them do this to me when others even now die for our world?"

Daulo shook his head. "You misunderstand, Fadil. No one is dying for Qasama. Not anymore. The war is over."

Fadil stared at him, disbelief and hope churning together in his heart. "Impossible," he said. "It's been only—" He broke off, trying to count. Had it really been only five days?

"Only five days," Daulo confirmed. "But it's the truth. The invaders and their warships are gone. Warships of the Tlos'khin'fahi demesne, allies of the Cobra Worlds, now patrol the skies above Qasama. Even as we speak, their cargo ships bring in food and pre-built structures for those city dwellers who still huddle in tents. Shahni Haafiz and Senior Advisor Moffren Omnathi have had personal discussions with the demesne-heir known as Warrior, with the promise of more assistance to come."

Fadil grimaced. "So despite it all, we still have no choice but to deal with the Trofts?"

Daulo shrugged. "Perhaps that's the way of our future. Perhaps not. Only time will tell." He let go of Fadil's hands and stood up. "I was told you would be extremely hungry when you awoke. Dinner awaits downstairs in the dining hall. Will you come share it with me?"

Fadil took a deep breath. He lowered his eyes to his left hand, and as he had every day since his return from Sollas he silently ordered it to rise.

Only this time, it obeyed him.

He let his breath out in a sound that was half gasp and half laugh. The fingers worked too, he saw as he moved the hand to the bed rail and closed the fingers around it. Still holding onto the rail, he willed his right arm to also move, to the bed beside his torso so that he could lever himself upright.

And his right arm, too, obeyed him.

Carefully, he sat up. Just as carefully, he shifted his legs sideways across the bed, then over the edge, and finally planted his feet on the floor.

And for the first time in nearly a month, he stood upright.

His father stepped forward and gripped his arm, and Fadil could see tears glistening in his eyes. "Welcome back, my son," he said quietly. "Welcome back, Cobra Fadil Sammon."

CHAPTER TWENTY-ONE

It had been a quiet dinner, uncharacteristically quiet for a Moreau family gathering.

Not that any of the six gathered around the table had expected anything like the loud and boisterous celebrations taking place elsewhere across Aventine and the other Cobra Worlds. Not considering the multiple dark clouds hanging over all of them.

Especially not since the six should have been seven.

The meal was over and Jody and Paul had cleared the table—at Paul's insistence and over Jody's and Jin's objections—when the unexpected guest Jin had been expecting all evening finally arrived.

"I'm sorry to crash your family time this way," Governor-General Chintawa apologized as Thena Moreau escorted him into the conversation room. "But I thought someone should unofficially welcome you all back to Aventine." He grimaced. "Especially considering how the official welcome went."

"That's all right," Corwin Moreau said, ever the gracious host, as he waved Chintawa to an empty seat. "So she's actually going through with it?"

Chintawa sighed as he lowered himself into the chair. "I'm sorry, Corwin. All of you. I tried to talk her out of it—I really did. But as you may have discovered, Nissa Gendreves is an extremely stubborn person."

"With, I dare say, more than her share of political ambition?" Paul suggested.

"You don't hang around the Dome putting in long hours for low pay without some of that," Chintawa conceded. "But I don't think she's out to get you simply to make a name for herself. She genuinely believes that all of you—well, you four Brooms, anyway—committed high treason by giving Isis to the Qasamans." He hesitated. "And unfortunately, according to the law, she's right."

"So has she also brought charges against Governor Uy?" Lorne asked. "She was just as mad at him as she was at us."

"I'm sure she'd like to," Chintawa said. "No, that's not fair. She was very clear about his part of the decision in her closed Council testimony, and I know she intends to make those additional charges official as soon as she's been given clearance to do so."

"Only she hasn't," Lorne suggested acidly, "because Uy's one of the Council's own, and you don't throw the big fish to the sharks?"

Jody stirred. "Governor Uy did a lot to help win the war, Governor Chintawa. Everyone on Caelian did."

"As did everyone in this room," Lorne said. "I don't see the Council throwing us parades or hushing up *our* collection of ridiculous charges."

"Easy, Lorne," Corwin murmured. "Governor-General Chintawa's not the enemy here."

"He's right, Cobra Broom," Chintawa agreed. "Believe me, I'd like nothing better than to give you full pardons right now and sweep this whole thing out the door. But the fact is that Governor Treakness *did* give Ms. Gendreves full diplomatic authority, and she *did* order you not to give Isis to the Qasamans. Even you admit that, and we have Dr. Croi's testimony as well."

"And we're sure Governor Treakness never said anything to clarify his authorization?" Thena asked.

Chintawa shook his head. "I doubt the Trofts ever bothered to ask him. I'm not even sure how much of those last few hours he was conscious. The point is that charges have been made and corroborated. Unless the Council reaches deep within itself for understanding and charity—and you know the chances of *that* happening—you're going to have to be arrested and stand trial."

"So much for the Cobra-haters suddenly seeing the light," Paul murmured.

"Not likely," Chintawa said with a sigh. "You can force-read them the reports from Caelian and Qasama all day long, but what they *saw* was our Aventinian Cobras sitting around not doing a damn thing."

"At *their* specific orders," Corwin reminded him.

"Of course," Chintawa said. "You want logic and consistency, get out of politics." His lip twitched in a smile. "As, of course, you did. Sometimes I have to admit I envy you that decision."

Jin looked at Paul, and she could tell he was thinking the same thing she was: that her Uncle Corwin hadn't left politics so much as he'd been booted out. But of course Chintawa knew that.

"And now with Isis in Qasaman hands they've got an even bigger Cobra bugaboo to worry about," Lorne pointed out.

"With more than a little justification," Chintawa said, an edge of annoyance in his tone. "I know how warm and trusting you all are when it comes to the Qasamans, but there's no guarantee that your decision won't someday turn sour on us. And if the Qasamans ever decide they want vengeance for whatever real or imagined wrongs the Worlds have inflicted on them, what we've just gone through with the Trofts will seem like a stroll down the river."

"It won't happen," Lorne said firmly.

"I hope to God it doesn't." Chintawa hesitated, then looked at Jin. "I understand there was a letter," he said, the annoyance gone. "May I see it?"

Jin hesitated. But he probably had a right to see the actual note. Reaching into her tunic, she slipped the envelope out of the inner pocket, the one closest to her heart. She pulled out the single slip of paper, unfolded it, and for the hundred thousandth time in the past three days her eyes traced across the confusing, bleak, hopeful words.

The drogfowl cacciatore of home, I will look forward to tasting it again soon. My family, they will welcome my return. Courage.

Jody was standing quietly beside her when Jin looked up. Blinking back sudden tears, she handed her daughter the note. Holding it like she would a piece of fine crystal, Jody crossed the room and offered it to Chintawa.

For a long moment he gazed down at it. Then, he looked up again. "What do you make of it?"

"We're not sure," Paul admitted. "The words are Anglic, but the grammar form is Troft. The handwriting isn't Merrick's, and

I doubt very much it's even human. It was delivered to Jin by the Tlossies, but they claim it didn't originate with them. We've made at least a hundred inquiries, but every one of them has either been ignored or run straight into a steel-core wall."

"*Someone* knows what happened to Merrick," Lorne put in. "But whoever that is, he isn't talking."

"Hmm," Chintawa said, looking at the letter again. "And you're sure the message is from him?"

"We had drogfowl cacciatore the night we got the first letter," Paul said. "The one that took Jin and Merrick to Qasama in the first place. More than that, I used those words as an identifier when I communicated with him just before his capture. No, Merrick's the only one who could have sent this message."

"I see," Chintawa murmured. "*Courage.* That's probably good advice right now. For all of us."

Corwin cleared his throat. "And speaking of drogfowl cacciatore and conspiracies," he said, "I'd like to point out that Thena and I were also at that meeting. If you're going to charge my niece and her family with treason, you'd best put us in the docket along with them."

Chintawa snorted. "If you think I'm going to put any more necks into Ms. Gendreves's noose than I have to, you can forget it." Carefully, reverently, he handed the letter back to Jody and stood up. "At any rate, I should be getting back to the Dome. I just wanted to let you all know that I, personally, am very glad to see you all safe and sound."

Jin's throat tightened. All of them except Merrick.

"I also wanted to let you know that I'm not the only one on the Council who appreciates what you've done," the governor-general added. "Let's all just hope and pray that the Qasamans are as friendly as you believe."

"We don't need them to be our friends," Corwin said mildly. "All we need is for them to *not* be our enemies."

"Right now, I'd be happy with either," Chintawa said. "Well . . . good night, all. Don't get up, Thena—I'll let myself out."

He walked out of the room. Jin keyed in her audio enhancers, following his footsteps as he continued down the hallway and then opened and closed the door. "Any thoughts?" she asked, keying the audios back down. "Uncle Corwin?"

Corwin shrugged. "I think he's sincere, for whatever that's worth."

"Probably not much," Jody said, an edge of bitterness in her voice as she returned the precious letter to her mother. "All we went through on Caelian—and she *saw* all of it—and she *still* turns around and stabs us in the back."

"Don't be too hard on her," Corwin advised. "The first thing a politician learns is not to make threats he isn't willing or able to carry out. Having accused you of treason in front of a room full of witnesses, she really had no choice but to follow through on it."

"Besides, from her point of view she's entirely correct," Paul pointed out. "If we're wrong about the Qasamans, our giving Isis to them is going to get *all* of us stabbed in the back."

"And on that cheery note," Jin said, giving Merrick's note one final lingering look before returning it to its envelope, "we should probably get going. It's been a long day, and tomorrow's likely to be even longer."

"And you two are still recovering from surgery," Lorne added, standing up and stepping to Jin's side. "Let me give you a hand."

"Can I ask one last question?" Jody spoke up suddenly. "It's funny how when you think you're going to die the weirdest questions pop into your head." She turned to Corwin. "Uncle Corwin: why do you call this house the Island?"

Jin looked at her daughter in surprise. But Corwin merely chuckled. "You know, I've been waiting twenty years for one of you to give up on all your private and group speculation and just come out and ask. Well done, Jody. Direct questions are a sign of maturity, you know."

"Hey, I've asked you before," Jin protested. "You would never tell me."

"You hinted broadly, but you never actually asked," Corwin corrected. "Any of you ever hear the old saying *a mind is like a parachute—it only works when it's open*?"

"You've got to be kidding," Lorne said with a snort. "I think that one goes all the way back to DaVinci."

"Granted," Corwin said. "What's often forgotten is that the purpose of a parachute isn't to *stay* open, but to guide you safely to the ground."

"Interesting point," Paul murmured. "You're right; most people don't think it all the way through."

"I always had to keep an open mind in politics, you see," Corwin continued. "Not open in the sense of listening to different ideas and positions, but open in the sense of too often having to compromise my deepest moral and ethical convictions in the name of unity or other high-sounding but usually meaningless concepts."

He reached across to Thena's chair and took his wife's hand. "But then I retired," he said. "Now, I can hold those convictions as tightly as I want. As tightly as I always promised myself I would."

Jin caught her breath. Finally, after all these years, she got it. "Island," she murmured. "I *land*."

"Exactly," Corwin said. "I'm sorry if the solution isn't nearly as intriguing or interesting as the mystery. But I'm old, you know, and I was never very clever to begin with."

"There's nothing wrong with the solution," Jin assured him. "It's both elegant and clever—"

"Just a moment," Corwin said, lifting a finger as he pulled out his phone. He frowned at the display, then keyed it on and held it to his ear. "Yes?"

For a few seconds he listened in silence, his expression tightening. "We'll be right there," he said at last. "Yes, just as soon as we can."

He keyed off. "That was Chintawa," he told the others. "He just got a call from the Dome, and he wants all of us to join him there right away. Front entrance, he said, and just leave your car at the curb."

"We're going to the Dome *now*?" Lorne echoed, frowning. "What, have they got treason trials on the night shift?"

"Maybe they decided to skip the trial and go straight to the execution," Jody suggested.

"You can write out your impassioned appeal on the way," Corwin said, gesturing toward the front door. "For now, just drive. Thena and I will get our car and meet you there."

To Jin, the Dome looked its usual nighttime self as they drove up to the front entrance—dark, quiet, and peopled mainly by overworked clerks and aides.

But that first look was deceiving. Even as they got out of the car, she could see a dozen other vehicles converging on different parts of the building, plus multiple flashes of headlights from the parking structure across they street. Whatever was happening, she and her family weren't the only ones who'd been called in.

Even more ominously, there were *six* Cobra guards flanking the door instead of the usual two.

An aide was waiting for them just inside the building. He waited in silence with them until Corwin and Thena arrived, then led the whole group to the small communications routing room near the center of the Dome.

Chintawa was already there, his face tight as he gazed at the status display above the two techs seated at the board. "Thank you for coming," he said as the aide ushered the six of them into the room. "I think we may have just gotten an answer to the question of why the Trofts picked this particular moment to try to conquer us and the Qasamans." He gestured to one of the techs. "Put it up."

The tech nodded and touched a switch, and the display became a telescopic view of the sky over Capitalia.

A sky with three huge ships floating against the stars.

Jin gasped. "Are those—?"

"Trofts?" Chintawa shook his head. "Fortunately, no. Or maybe not so fortunately." He took a deep breath. "I asked you here because—well, listen for yourselves."

Stepping to the board, he picked up a mike and keyed the switch. "Commodore Santores, this is Governor-General Michaelo Chintawa," he said. "My apologies for not being here when you first made contact."

"Quite understandable, Governor Chintawa," a booming, cheerful voice came from the speaker. "It *is* night there, after all. Permit me, if you will, to formally introduce myself to you: Commodore Rubo Santores of the Dominion of Man, commanding the Star Cruisers *Megalith*, *Algonquin*, and *Dorian*. After nearly three-quarters of a century of wondering what happened to their grand Cobra Worlds experiment, the Dome finally decided it was time to send someone to see for themselves. That someone would be us."

"We're honored by your presence," Chintawa said cautiously. "As you can see, we're alive and well."

"And from the looks of things, even thriving," Santores agreed. "We're pleased and relieved to find you so."

"Thank you," Chintawa said. "I understand there was also something in your mission profile about bringing us back into the Dominion fold?"

"Oh, I wouldn't worry about that," Santores said off-handedly.

"Everything Dome does has some kind of political subtext, you know. Well, no, of course you don't know that. But we can discuss all that later, perhaps when I come down to formally present my credentials."

"Yes, of course," Chintawa said. "I trust morning will be soon enough? It may take a while to assemble the Council."

"Take whatever time you need," Santores said. "My task force and I are entirely at your disposal."

"Thank you." Chintawa looked over at Jin and the others and visibly braced himself. "I understand there was one other matter one of your officers expressed some interest in?"

"Oh, yes," Santores said. "Though this one's purely unofficial, of course. The commander of the *Dorian*, Captain Barrington Jame Moreau, was hoping that some descendents of his grandfather, the First Cobra Jonny Moreau, might still be with you. If so, he'd be most interested in meeting them."

"I think we'll be able to find a few family members for him to talk to," Chintawa said. "With your permission, Commodore, we'll continue this conversation tomorrow morning."

"At your convenience, Governor," Santores said. "*Megalith* out."

The radio went silent. For a long moment, the room remained likewise. "You see," Chintawa said at last, "why I asked you all to come here."

"Indeed," Corwin said. "Am I to assume that my retirement from politics has just ended?"

"Yes," Chintawa said soberly. "I'm very much afraid that it has."